WHEN *the*

Heart

BRINGS *you*

Home

WHEN *the* *Heart*

BRINGS *you* *Home*

A CONNOR FALLS CHRISTMAS
COLLECTION

Robin Maderich

POTTER STREET BOOKS
ZIONSVILLE PA
2022

ISBN: 978-1-7345419-7-7

© 2022 Robin Maderich
All rights reserved.

Printed in the U.S.A.

Cover design by Robin Maderich

Potter Street Books/Robin Maderich Publishing
www.potterstreetbooks.com

This book is also available in digital format.

DEDICATION

to the child in all of us

"Our hearts grow tender with childhood
memories and love of kindred, and we are better
throughout the year for having, in spirit, become a
child again at Christmastime."
— **Laura Ingalls Wilder**

AUTHOR'S NOTE

Every year, all year, I look forward to Christmas. I used to blame it on the kid in me, but I think my anticipation has more to do with hope and the special joy that comes with the season. I know the sentiment doesn't only have to reside in those few weeks, so I do endeavor like Charles Dickens' most memorable character to honor Christmas in my heart and keep it all the year.

This is why I love writing the Connor Falls Christmas series, because when I was a child the town I was growing up in was still at that time a close-knit community with a smalltown feel, despite being the capitol of the state. I like hearkening back to the remembered atmosphere, especially what it was during Christmas. I don't think my memories are falsely colored by nostalgic sentiment and the passing years. I mean, we sang carols in class, for goodness' sake. Try that nowadays.

In *When The Heart Brings You Home* I have attempted to recapture not only the smalltown feel, but the ofttimes messy, always heartfelt interaction in family life—the pain, the joy, the love, the forgiveness—and the promise of the season.

I do so hope you enjoy these three novellas. Merry Christmas, everyone. And happy holiday, no matter what wonders you celebrate.

Winter
LIGHT

Chapter One

On her knees in the barren display window, Allie considered the challenge of vacant space. If nothing else, it could be a great topic for her next blog post. Her last had been on the most recent release in a young adult trilogy, the type of thing her customers had come to expect. They might not be so happy with a complaint about her inability to focus on this year's Christmas display. Thanksgiving had come and gone and the four by eight foot area contained nothing but twinkling white lights affixed with tape along three sides. Blue painter's tape. She couldn't even muster the gumption to go out and purchase red duct tape from a hardware store that was no more than a five minute walk from the front door. Thank goodness her parents were in Florida. Even though they'd turned Connor Falls Book Emporium over to what they termed, perhaps facetiously, her 'capable hands', she was still answerable to them for the holiday receipts. Seasonal sales accounted for more than half the year's income. A window that was not only undecorated for Christmas but without any content whatsoever might put a teensy bit of a damper on customer enthusiasm.

Sunlight through the two huge windows gilded the recently swept hardwood flooring, highlighting its sterile condition. Shadows came and went across the surface as people passed by, no doubt wondering when Allie was going to get her act together. One shadow stopped and stayed. Allie looked up from contemplating disaster. A child's face was pressed against the window, handprints outlining her sleek, dark head like a smudged wreath.

The little girl's fingers curled into a fist. She rapped three times on the glass, the effect in the empty, echoing space like a series of small cannon blasts. Allie flinched.

"Don't do that!"

Seeing the child prepared to knock again, Allie lurched onto all fours and scrambled over to the window, crouching to get her face level with the little girl's. "I said, don't do that. Haven't you ever had a fish?"

"A fish?" the girl shouted back at her.

"Yes. A goldfish? In a fish bowl? Never mind." Allie scanned the sidewalk. "Where are your parents?"

The girl jerked her still-fisted hand, thumb raised, toward the opposite side of the street. "My dad's at the bakery."

Allie frowned in the general direction of From the Hart bakery, the establishment owned by Gina Hart. People passed along the sidewalk, but none of them appeared to be searching for a small, dark-haired girl. Allie shook her head, wondering why a child who looked no older than six or seven had been permitted to wander across the main street and to the bookstore unaccompanied.

"My mom's in California. She lives there now."

"Entirely too much information to be shouting out to the world," Allie said.

"What?"

"Wait there. I'll be right out." Allie slid to the edge of the display space and hopped off, grabbing her coat from the stepstool. She headed to the front door with a shout over her shoulder to whichever employee might be within earshot that she'd be back in a few minutes. Outside, she found the little girl leaning with her back against the window, arms folded across her puffy, pink coat, fine dark hair blowing into her eyes. A backpack hanging off her shoulder pressed against the glass, revealing a doll sticking out the top and what looked like a potato chip bag clipped shut with a clothespin. Allie pushed her arms into her own jacket sleeves and zipped up. Her breath frosted in the air.

"Aren't you cold?"

The girl shook her head.

"Let's go find your dad," Allie said.

"No."

"Excuse me?"

"He knows where I am."

Allie tipped her head to the side, eyes narrowing. "He let you cross the street by yourself?"

The child tightened her grip across her narrow

torso and glared at the sidewalk. Allie studied her defiant demeanor. She had a feeling the girl's father possessed no clue his daughter had wandered.

"What's your name?"

"Lydia," the girl said.

"Lydia. That's a nice name. Mine's Allie. And your dad's in Gina's bakery?"

Lydia glanced up from beneath frowning brows. "Who's Gina?"

"The woman who owns the bakery."

"Oh."

Allie looked again toward the bakery for a man in frantic search for a missing child. The people she saw striding from place to place appeared unconcerned, absorbed in their independent activities. Reaching down, Allie extracted Lydia's left hand from under her right arm and closed her fingers around the little girl's. "I can't be responsible for you outside my window and would feel guilty as all get out if you disappeared, so let's go find out what kind of goodies your dad's bought, shall we?"

Allie took three steps before Lydia pulled back on her hand, digging the heels of her pink rubber boots into the sidewalk. "I don't think I should go with you. You're a stranger. I think I should stay right here where my dad can find me."

Allie released Lydia's fingers. Lydia shoved her hand into her coat pocket as far as it would go.

"Well, you're right about that. I am a stranger. Your dad really knows you're here?" That seemed irresponsible, allowing a child Lydia's age to wander freely about the streets, no matter how safe everyone viewed Connor Falls to be. "Can I call him for you, then? Do you know his cell phone number?"

"He doesn't have one," Lydia mumbled.

"He doesn't have a cell phone?"

Lydia shook her head.

"In this day and age?"

"He doesn't like that stuff."

"That seems odd," Allie said, more to herself than the child standing beside her.

"I'm not lying!"

Allie glanced down in surprise at Lydia's vehemence. "I didn't think you were." She studied Lydia's heart-shaped face a moment longer, noticing how the child avoided her eye, how her blue gaze focused earnestly across the street, but not at the bakery. A deeper suspicion settled in. "Lydia. Lydia, look at me, okay?"

The girl turned her whole body to Allie, her attention glued to Allie's denim-covered legs. Allie dropped to her knees, gazing up into Lydia's face. "Lydia, is there something you're not telling me?"

"What do you mean?" The girl's chin trembled, eyes welling up with moisture.

Despite herself, Allie's heart went out to her. She touched Lydia's arm. "Did you sneak away from your father? He could be very worried, you know. I would be."

"I…" Lydia hesitated, her mouth working. "He…he doesn't know where I am. I ran away from home, Allie. Daddy doesn't know where I am at all."

Curling her fingers over Lydia's sleeve, Allie

drew her nearer. Huge, shining tears ran down the child's cheeks and dropped onto her coat. Allie inhaled, thinking hard. She'd run away herself a couple times in defiance of one restriction or another, but she'd never gotten very far before realizing her foolishness. She wondered how far Lydia had walked before coming to stop at the bookstore window.

"Where do you live?"

Lydia shook her head.

"You need to tell me. I'm sure your dad is scared."

"Scared?"

"Yes, scared. Because you're not there and he doesn't know where you've gone."

Lydia withdrew her hands from her pockets and wiped her face. Allie settled back on her heels to avoid the sidewalk chilling her knees through her jeans.

"Do you and your daddy live in one of the apartments above the stores?"

Lydia shook her head.

"A house on one of the side streets?"

Lips compressed, the child wagged her head again from side to side.

"Okay," said Allie, "I'll have to figure it out. Do you live in Paris, France?"

Lydia's chin jerked up. "What?"

"In a sunny little apartment on the Seine? Or perhaps in New York City? Just off Central Park?"

"Of course not." A reluctant giggle escaped Lydia's lips.

"Well, where then? Am I even close?"

Lydia shook her head so hard her hair circled out like a ballerina's tulle skirt. She gazed up at Allie, eyes wide. "Dad and I live in a place that used to be magic," she said, "but it isn't anymore."

Sadness pinched at Allie's chest. She remembered the days of magic, too. This child was way too young for enchantment to have left her life. "And where is that, sweetie? I really need to know."

Releasing a trembling breath, Lydia nodded. "Luke's Tree Farm. Do you know where that is?"

Of course Allie knew. Even if she had no other reason to know the farm, most everyone got their Christmas trees at Luke's, a huge place growing every type of evergreen imaginable.

Nearly two miles outside of town.

"How on earth did you get here, Lydia?"

Lydia burst into tears.

*   *   *

Luke hung up the phone. He pushed his palm across his head, fingers dragging through disheveled hair.

"Damn it."

Snatching his coat from the rack by the door, Luke swore again. He shoved his arms into the garment, the fabric still chilled from his recent trek among the douglas firs. Pulling the truck keys from his pocket, he headed back outside to his pickup.

"Where're you going, boss?"

"Into town," Luke muttered as he yanked opened the pickup's door. He slid behind the wheel, pausing to take a steadying breath before turning the key in the ignition. It wouldn't do any good to go tearing along the roads like a lunatic. Lydia was safe with the woman from the bookstore. But how the hell had she gotten there? Normally, when Lydia got it into her head to take off, she headed up into the trees and he'd always find her in short order. This time, he hadn't even known she was gone.

"Lydia Hollis, you're going to be the death of me," he said as he put the truck into reverse and backed from the space in front of the house. Pausing before heading for the long driveway, he rolled down the window. "Frank!"

The sandy-haired man ambled up to the truck. "Yeah, boss?"

"Is your wife still out of work?"

Frank's left brow twisted up toward his hairline. "Why are you asking?"

"Because I need some help with Lyddie. I can't keep an eye on her all the time. I thought I could, working around the farm, but apparently I'm an idiot."

"She take off again?"

Luke nodded.

"Sorry, Beth's back at work. Started last week at the hospital. That eight-year-old of yours is going to turn your hair gray. If she's this willful now, imagine what she'll be like as a teenager. My girls—"

"She wants her mother, Frank. And I don't know what to do about that."

As Luke drove the winding roads, he understood he could do nothing about Lydia wanting her mother. It was a frustrating, heartbreaking situation. Luke wasn't a fool. He'd consulted with professionals about what to do and basically received conflicting recommendations. Give her space; keep her close. Let her work through it in her own time; make her talk about the issue. The only thing consistent throughout was making certain Lydia knew he loved her. He thought he'd been doing that. Because he did. With his whole heart. Somehow, that wasn't enough.

Moving slowly through town, the main street decked out with wreaths and lights and bright flags for the holidays, he considered his own dark living room. Thanksgiving had come late this year. The business of selling Christmas trees was in full swing, giving him little time for anything else. Lydia loved Christmas. Once again, he'd let her down. After a brief and suitable punishment for her reckless behavior today, he'd make sure they broke out all the boxes filled with decorations and together they would do the house up right. The way it used to be.

Finding a parking space, Luke maneuvered the pickup into it and got out. He shut the door and took a deep breath, filling his lungs with crisp air, doing his best not to swear again as he thought of the distance he'd driven from the tree farm to Connor Falls. How had a little girl with legs the length of his arm managed to make it all that way without him noticing her absence? Safely, thank God, but even so.

Shoving his hands into his coat pockets, Luke marched toward Connor Falls Book Emporium. He hadn't been inside the bookstore in nearly two years. Lydia used to love to come here, especially at Christmastime.

Luke paused outside the large display window, surprised to find it empty at this late date. Obviously, it had been cleared in preparation for decorating, but shouldn't that have been done days ago? He was a fine one to talk, with a little girl who loved Christmas and a house as bland and uninviting as a cardboard box. Luke strode up to the bookstore door and yanked it open.

"Dad!"

Lydia barreled into his legs. With a grunt, Luke scooped his daughter into his embrace and held her close, breathing in the scent of her hair before holding her out again at arm's length, her legs dangling. "Lyddie! Why did you run away again?"

As he spoke, he spotted powdered sugar on his daughter's lips. She swiped at her mouth with her knuckles. Luke set her on the floor.

"Lydia, I'm serious. What you did was dangerous. How did you get here?" He still couldn't believe she'd walked all the way into town, and yet he prayed she'd done exactly that, because the idea she might have managed to find someone to give her a ride, somebody without the sense they were born with, or worse, made his blood run cold. Lydia stared up at him through shining, tear-filled eyes.

"I walked, Daddy. My legs hurt. And I'm sorry. I'm really sorry. Can we go home?"

Luke took a deep breath and slowly released the air through his nose. Maybe this was the problem. She always accepted immediate responsibility for her actions, and he couldn't bear her sadness. They'd developed a pattern that neither one could break.

"Lydia…"

"Daddy."

"You can't keep doing this. You could have been hurt, or gotten lost, or any number of things." Yes, things the town of Connor Falls, despite its reputation, couldn't guarantee wouldn't happen.

"But I didn't," Lydia said. "And I found a friend."

Luke frowned. "A friend?"

At the sound of a female clearing her throat, Luke glanced up from Lydia. Dressed in an oversized sweatshirt and jeans tucked into boots on slim legs, a woman stood behind his daughter. Her brown eyes gazed back at him from a small face framed by wispy, auburn curls. She looked vaguely familiar. He'd probably seen her around town, or picking up a tree. After giving him a quick onceover, she held out her hand.

"Hi. I'm Allie Roberts."

He grasped the hand in a brief shake. "Any relation to the Roberts who own the place?"

"They're my parents," she said. "They're semi-retired these days, so I'm running the bookstore now." She shrugged beneath the voluminous gray cotton of her shirt. "I bought Lydia a donut from the bakery. I hope you don't mind. I asked her first if she was allowed to eat sugar. You know, some parents are particular about that."

"It's not a problem," said Luke. "I appreciate you taking her in. I don't…I don't know what she's thinking, running off like this."

"Right here, Dad," said Lydia in a comical adult manner. Allie reached out and ruffled her hair. Luke's stomach flipped as if he'd dropped too fast in an elevator, the caress making him both sad and angry. Apparently, Lydia sensed his sudden mood shift, because she turned her head to gape up at Allie, blue eyes wide. Luke bent and grabbed Lydia's fingers in his own.

"Well, thank you again, Miss Roberts—"

"Allie. Please don't call me Miss Roberts."

"Yeah," said Lydia, "she likes Allie. Better

than Allison, she told me.”

Allie, better than Allison. The phrase struck him with a brief flash of déjà vu. He couldn't imagine why. “Okay. Got it.” He took a step backward toward the door. “And Lyddie, this is the final straw. I'm going to have to hire somebody to look after you. This is the busy season and I can't keep worrying that you're going to disappear. Do you understand me?”

Lydia hung her head, stealing a glance at Allie from beneath her bangs. “Allie said I could help her decorate the window.”

“That was if I did it today,” Allie explained. “As you can see, it's still empty. At this rate, Christmas will have come and gone and there'll be nothing in that window but dust.”

“What's the problem?” Luke asked.

“I don't know. Even before my parents decided to back away from the business, I always did the displays. This year I wanted to come up with something really incredible, and instead my mind's a blank. I'm lacking inspiration, I guess.”

“So's my dad,” said Lydia. “You should see our house. Not one single decoration.”

Luke bit the inside of his mouth. Yes, punishment, and then they would drag out the boxes and get to work.

“You could start with a tree,” Lydia suggested.

“Do you have yours?” Allie asked.

"Not yet," Luke said. "You know the story of the shoemaker's family? That's me. But tonight. I promise," he said to Lydia. "And you come by, too, Allie. I'll give you a tree for the window, as a thank you."

"That's not necessary. I really didn't do anything."

"Yes, you did," said Luke. "I'm just grateful Lydia ended up with someone who looked after her. Stop by after dinner. We'll take flashlights and you can have your pick. I'll cut it down for you."

Allie hesitated. He wondered why. A free tree should appeal to anyone this time of year, especially somebody with an empty window three and a half weeks before Christmas.

"If you insist," she finally said.

"I do. So does Lyddie, don't you?"

"Yep," said his daughter. "And maybe tomorrow Dad can bring me here to give you a hand? I won't talk as much as I did today. I'll let you concentrate."

Allie laughed. The sound was shockingly infectious and, again, familiar. Smiling, Luke considered Allie more closely.

"Well, if you put it that way…" Allie jerked her head in the direction of the counter. "Don't forget your coat, Lydia."

As Lydia skipped across the store to retrieve her garment, Luke hastened to nip the plans in the bud. He couldn't let Lydia inconvenience this stranger more than she had. "You don't have to do that. Really. I—"

"It's fine."

"But—"

"It's fine."

"It's just that she misses her mother so much."

"I know. She told me."

Luke's focus snapped from the antics his daughter was going through in putting on her coat back to Allie's face. His shoulders tensed. "What did she tell you, exactly?"

Allie tucked her hands into her pockets. "That her mother's in California. That she doesn't see her."

Luke compressed his lips, blowing a breath out his nose. His gaze strayed again to Lydia, still struggling into her coat beside the counter. He wondered if his daughter had said something more. He could tell by Allie's expression, though, that she hadn't.

"Okay," he said. "You come by tonight and pick a tree, and Lydia and I will deliver it tomorrow after you open."

"Deal," said Allie.

Lydia returned and Luke took her fingers. Striding to the door, he paused and looked back, the knob circled in his left hand and Lydia tugging on the other one. "I'm sorry. I didn't even introduce myself. I know we just spoke on the phone when you called, but I was a little agitated then. I feel like I've been rude. I'm Luke Hollis."

Allie met his gaze. "I remember exactly who you are," she said.

Chapter Two

Allie realized straightaway she should have just let him introduce himself and be done with it. Sometimes she didn't know when to leave well enough alone. She understood that, and yet she still managed to open her mouth and stick her foot in on a regular basis.

She watched his hand drop from the door knob. He bent and scooped his daughter up onto his hip, his expression caught between troubled and curious. Allie wanted to kick herself, or turn and walk away with a casual 'see you later', as if she hadn't said anything. Instead, she took a step closer.

"Have we met?" Luke asked.

"A long time ago."

"I...I don't remember."

"Yes," said Allie. "I can see that."

He stood silently in contemplation. Someone

attempted to enter, bumping him in the elbow with the door. He moved to the side, Lydia in his arms. The customer entered, easing past them both.

"When?"

"More than half a lifetime ago."

"So we were kids."

Allie nodded.

"It's no wonder I don't remember. I'm surprised you do."

"You kissed me." Damn it, why couldn't she just shut up?

Luke's eyes widened. He glanced down at Lydia, who looked both bewildered and amused. "Well, I—"

"It was no big deal."

"Obviously it was."

"No. It was a silly peck between two kids. It was what came after that made the incident significant."

His blue eyes narrowed. "What came after?"

She might as well get it over with, rip the bandage off with one quick pull, expose an old wound to the air. She'd forced the conversation and couldn't back down now. "I fell. On the ice on your father's pond. Broke my wrist."

"Broke your—oh."

"Yep," said Allie, as the skin on her cheeks heated up. He definitely remembered now. She could see memory blossom across his face. As a scrawny kid a couple of years ahead of her in school, he'd been awfully damned cute. As an adult, a father, a man grown into his own strength, he was handsome enough to make her stutter. Somehow, she'd been managing not to.

"I'm sorry," said Luke. "How could I have forgotten?"

"It wasn't quite as traumatic an experience for you," Allie said.

"Do you still skate?"

Allie faltered. "Oh. Sure. But I don't allow strange males to kiss me on the ice."

Luke threw back his head with a deep, rolling laugh. From the way Lydia looked at him, Allie figured he didn't do it often enough. He stopped, breathless from his amusement. "Did I know your name then?"

"I don't…I don't know."

"Wait. Sure I did. Allie, better than Allison. I knew that phrase sounded familiar."

The temperature in Allie's cheeks zoomed. "I really do have to get back to work, so…"

"I understand." He chuckled again. "We're leaving. Are you still stopping by later?"

"A free tree? I'd be crazy not to."

"Bye, Allie," called Lydia with a wave as the door closed behind them. Allie watched the two of them walk past the plate glass window, dark heads close together. Lydia twisted in her dad's arms, waving again like a participant in a parade. Allie lifted her hand in response, holding it aloft until they were out of sight.

"Why'd you tell him that?"

Allie jerked toward the sound of her employee's voice. "Don't you have work to do, Todd?"

"Yeah. And I was working right here. I heard

the whole thing.”

“He was bound to remember at some point,” Allie said. “Better a preemptive strike before he did recall and I had to admit I’d never forgotten the incident, or lie. Either action would have been distinctly creepy.”

Todd, eighteen years old and apparently blasé about matters creepy or otherwise, shrugged, lifting and placing the last book from the open cardboard box at his feet onto the display table. “So, once you get the tree, what are you going to do about the window? I don’t ever remember you leaving it empty this long. People are going to start to wonder.”

“Wonder what?”

“If we’re open or closed.”

“Good point,” Allie said.

“I know. That’s why I deserve a raise.”

“Oh, hush, I’m trying to think.”

“About what? That guy you kissed when you were fourteen?”

“How do you know how old I was?”

“Just a guess.”

Allie surveyed the window again, twinkling lights reflecting off glass. “Well, I’m not thinking about him. I’m trying to figure out what to do with that blasted window. If worse comes to worse, I suppose I could recycle last year’s idea.”

“I wouldn’t,” Todd mumbled. He bent and picked up the empty carton, tucking it under his arm. Tossing his shoulder-length, yellow hair away from his face, he set a tiny jingle bell dangling from the wire in his ear to tinkling.

"Why not?"

"Isn't that like wearing the same dress to a party two nights in a row? People tend to notice."

Allie laughed. "What would you know about that?"

"I have a sister."

Shaking her head vigorously, Allie left him and went to answer the ringing phone. On her way across the floor, she reflected on that long-ago kiss. Although it meant nothing to Luke, she'd been a fourteen-year-old with an awful crush on a boy who didn't even know her name. The kiss had caught her so off guard, she'd lost her balance and fallen on the ice, causing the night among her friends to go from something magical to an embarrassing—and painful—mess. Luke had managed to find her a few days later at school to ask how she was doing. After that, she avoided him and his circle of friends like the plague. He graduated later that year, solving her dilemma.

As she lifted the phone from the cradle, she thought perhaps Todd had been right. She really did need to keep her mouth shut. What point had there been in reminding Luke of the fool she'd made of herself? And now, she had to meet him in a few hours to pick out a tree, right near where the whole incident had taken place. It didn't matter how many years had passed since, because she'd been stupid enough to remind him. For crying out loud, she needed to carry a sock around to stuff in her mouth next time she opened it.

*　*　*

Lydia was unusually silent in the truck's passenger seat. Luke glanced at her several times, trying to gauge what she might be thinking. "Pumpkin—"

"Did you really kiss the bookstore lady?"

Crud. Was *that* what she was thinking about? "I did. We were very young."

"What about Mommy?"

"I hadn't even met your mommy yet."

"Oh."

Luke waited a few more minutes. "Does that bother you?"

"No…well, do you like her now? Allie, I mean."

"I know who you mean, Lyddie. And I don't know her now. I didn't really know her then."

"But you kissed her."

"Well, yeah. She was wearing this white fluffy hat and her cheeks were pink and she skated like a pro." Good Lord, he couldn't believe he was having this conversation with his daughter. He put on the turn signal, concentrating on steering into the driveway, remembering suddenly that Allie had worn her unruly cinnamon hair long back then, and it had been braided down her back, tied with a thin, blue ribbon. Lydia remained silent beside him. "Sometimes teenage boys can be stupid like that," he said. "When you're a teenager, I want you to promise me you won't let any boy kiss you, okay?"

"Yuk," said Lydia, shooting a glance at him before she turned her gaze out the window. "I like Allie."

"That's good," Luke responded, uncertain where his daughter was headed with that comment.

"She told me she ran away once when she was little."

"Did she?"

"She ran away with her brother, so she said it wasn't as scary as being alone. She said they got as far as the bridge over Morgan Creek—do you know where that is, Dad?"

"I think so," he said.

"And then something bad almost happened to them. She didn't say what it was, but she told me I must never, ever run away again."

Would that Lydia's behavior might actually cease on a word from a stranger. But he understood the issues behind it were too deeply entrenched to be rooted out by a simple story. Still, one could hope.

"She asked me where I thought I was going when I started out. I told her I didn't know. Why do I do that, Dad? I can't walk all the way to California. I know it's far away. And I don't want to. That would be stupid."

"Wanting to see your mother isn't stupid, honey," he said, reaching over to pat her hand. She let him for a moment and then pulled her fingers away, tucking them into her lap. She got like that, sometimes. Not wanting to be touched, as if she were afraid of being vulnerable.

"But she doesn't want to see me, does she?"

This was as close as Lyddie ever came to the pain she carried inside. Luke held his breath for a second. He knew he should be honest with his daughter, but he couldn't bear it. Besides, he didn't know the truth. Not really. Not enough to dash all hope. "Sure she does. Just give her time."

"What did I do?"

Anger colored Luke's vision for a moment as he steered through people carrying wrapped trees to their cars. He headed toward the house. "Nothing, Lyddie. You did nothing wrong. If you don't believe anything else, believe that."

In silence, Lydia picked at a ball of lint on her coat. Even after Luke parked the truck, she continued to pluck her garment hem. Despite the topic between them and his daughter's withdrawal, Luke's thoughts were stirred by a vague optimism. He'd always been told things happened for a reason. Although Lydia's running away again, managing to make it into town, was both disheartening and frightening, maybe her ending up at the bookstore had been a blessing in disguise. She'd listened to Allie. Really listened, and spoke in her turn. Perhaps the wound had at last been exposed to a little healing balm.

Chapter Three

As she zipped up her coat, Allie reminded Todd to pull the a-frame sign from the sidewalk before he locked up. The newest books in their stock were listed on the sign. She'd decorated the corners with holly leaves and berries depicted in green and red chalk which had been scuffed off in certain sections. She really needed to break out the chalk and fix them. The pieces were right behind the counter in a coffee can. What on earth was wrong with her?

"Off to see lover boy?" Todd asked from his position at the register.

Allie pointed at the sign, visible through the glass door. "Do me a favor and fix those holly leaves when you bring the sign in, will you?"

"Am I paid to be an artist or a clerk?"

Allie didn't answer. She yanked the door open and stepped outside, frowning at the lights framing the floor inside the window. They created a soft illumination of winter white, and if no one looked too carefully, they might believe something else existed inside the rectangle. Of course, if anyone came close to the window they would find only strings of bulbs taped along the boundaries of bare wood. Tomorrow, though, a live tree would be in the space. There'd better be a lot more than that before the morning was done. A complete display, in fact, or she'd be forced to give up and fall back on a bit of recycling.

Allie headed down the block in the direction of her car. Luke hadn't been too specific about the time she should come over, but she figured most normal people would have had dinner by now. With business picking up for the holidays, she ate her evening meal standing at the counter, usually just before closing. Fortunately, she had Todd and two others working tonight, allowing her the freedom to leave, but she hadn't eaten yet. As if reminded of the fact, her stomach gave a low growl. Eyeing the front of Gina's bakery covetously, Allie decided she would have something when she got home. No matter how delicious, a pastry did not constitute a solid meal.

Sliding behind the wheel of her car, Allie thought of Luke's brave but foolhardy daughter. Lydia was no doubt a handful for her father. He'd mentioned something when he'd come to pick her up about hiring help to look after her. Allie had no idea how long ago Lydia's mother had left, but it seemed Luke should have been seeking aid of some sort before now. Allie was in no position to offer any assistance herself, nor was she inclined to, since she barely knew the two of them, but she was looking forward to having Lydia in the store tomorrow. If nothing else, a pair of young eyes might be just the thing she needed for that stupid window.

Allie pulled the car from the parking space and headed out of town. She'd bought more than a few of her trees in the past from Luke's Tree Farm, but she'd always dealt with Luke, Sr. or one of his men. She'd heard in recent years that the younger Luke had taken over from his father. Maybe that was why she stopped going there and started buying pre-cut trees in the parking lot of the hardware store. She hadn't done it consciously, but now that she'd opened up to Luke about the incident on the pond, she realized she'd been avoiding him.

"Allie, you're an idiot," she said as she pushed her foot down on the accelerator, climbing the hill toward the sign in the distance. As she neared, she saw the driveway lined with lights leading to the red barn where the cut trees were brought to be wrapped for transport. A middle-aged man with sandy hair stepped out to pull a length of chain with a "closed" sign hanging from the center across the driveway. Allie stopped the car and rolled down the window. She leaned her head out. "Hi."

"Sorry, miss, we're closing for the evening. If you could come back tomorrow?"

Allie smiled, tipping her chin in the direction of a house on the hillside, windows glowing golden in the darkness. "I'm actually here to see Luke and his daughter. He told me to stop by. Is that his place up there?"

"Are you the one from the bookstore? Who found Lydia?"

"I didn't find Lydia. Lydia found me." She stuck her hand out the window. "Allie Roberts."

"Frank Mohr. Pleased to meet you. Yes, that's Luke's place up there. His dad still lives in the house further down, but Luke built that one when he got hitched. Nice little place. A bit lonely for Lydia, though."

With a nod, Frank backed away to let her car through. Allie thanked him and proceeded to the point where the smaller drive veered off to the left and up the incline. Her stomach fluttered as she made the turn, exactly like the butterflies she used to experience in high school. High school? She still got them with inordinate frequency for a variety of reasons. Right now, it was if a kaleidoscope of the lovely creatures had taken residence in her gut.

It couldn't be because of Luke. It *couldn't* be. Not after all this time.

Biting her lip, Allie pulled up next to a pickup truck and parked her car. She sat for a full minute behind the wheel in silent debate before climbing out and shutting the door as quietly as possible. Hands shoved deep into her pockets, Allie made her way up a series of concrete steps to the lit porch, where she saw evidence of decorating in progress. Fir roping lay across the porch floor surrounded by strings of lights in various stages of disentanglement. A wreath hung on the front door. Allie spotted a Luke's Tree Farm tag dangling from the greenery. She reached up and tucked the tag out of sight.

An oval of glass behind the wreath revealed an open, high-ceilinged room that combined living and eating, with the most beautiful kitchen at the far end. Seated at an island rather than the table, Lydia was engaged in consuming what appeared to be a grilled cheese sandwich. Luke stood beside her, the expression on his face a naked declaration of anxiety and awe and wrenching love as he turned to speak to his daughter. Allie took a hasty step back, not wanting to be an unwelcome witness to such honest emotion. As she did, she trod on a pair of pliers and sent them skittering against a metal table leg. She heard a shout from inside and looked up to see Lydia racing across the floor. The child yanked the door open.

"Allie!"

"Hi." Allie lifted her hand in greeting.

"Allie," said Luke, coming to stand behind his daughter, his fingers resting on her dark head.

"I'm sorry. I didn't realize you'd still be eating."

"We're running a little behind. I thought we'd get this porch done before dark, but..." He shrugged. "Come on in."

Allie stepped inside. Luke shut the door behind her.

"Lovely house," she said.

"Thanks. Lyddie, go finish your sandwich. I'll get my boots back on."

"I want to go, too." Lydia stopped mid-protest, mouth twisting. Allie figured she had to realize she was on thin ice. Making any demands after what had happened earlier in the day was not a good idea. "Please?" she said instead.

"Finish eating and we'll see."

Reluctantly, Lydia returned to the counter island, glancing back twice as she went. Defeated, she climbed up onto the stool and resumed eating.

Luke turned to Allie. He looked down. "What do you have on your feet?"

"I—what? I changed into my sneakers. I didn't want to muddy up my good boots."

"That won't do."

"Why?"

"Ground's way too wet out in the fields. Your feet will be soaked. Hold on, I'll be right back."

He walked toward the back of the house, leaving Allie standing in the living room. Allie did her best to act casual, studying the various photographs in simple black frames on the wall. They were quite good. She took a step closer to view the nearest group hanging to the right of the fireplace.

"My uncle Rory took all of those," Lydia said from the kitchen. "He's a photographer. He has a book. You should carry it in your store."

Allie smiled, returning her gaze to the photos. She knew Rory Hollis was Luke's brother. She'd seen his work before and should have recognized it. "I'll check into ordering the book. I'd be happy to carry it."

"That's me and Mommy and Dad," said Lydia, nearer now. Allie turned to find the little girl standing on the opposite side of the long, gray sofa, the last of her sandwich in one hand, her other hand lifted and pointing. Allie followed the direction of Lydia's outstretched finger to a photo of a beautifully unguarded moment with Luke, a much younger Lydia and a brunette woman, laughing over something during dinner at the table in this very house. The lighting, the clarity, the particulars of position, amazed Allie. But something about the photo saddened her, too. After a moment, she understood what it was. Luke and Lydia were clearly attuned to the humor of the moment, but Lydia's mother, though possessing a broad smile, watched them both with a certain melancholy visible in her eyes.

Quickly, Allie rejected her conclusions. In the next instant, unmarked by the camera, Luke's wife had probably been laughing as openly as Luke and Lydia.

Even so, the woman had left her family behind.

At the sound of footsteps, Allie turned her back on the wall of photos over the fireplace. Luke entered the room with a pair of old-fashioned galoshes in his hand. Allie forced her features into an innocent appearance, as if she hadn't been analyzing his life in the finite moment of a photograph.

"Lydia," he said, "if you're finished eating, put your plate in the dishwasher and go get your coat and boots."

As Lydia hastened to do as told, Luke continued across the room, coming to stand beside Allie. "My brother's an extremely talented man," he said, nodding toward the black and white photos. "That's my favorite. The big one in the middle."

Allie pivoted and moved to her left for a closer inspection. Rory had taken the photo from behind the two figures, the taller bending low, gloved hand hovering above his daughter's shoulder as they skated away from the lens across a frozen pond. Soft, diffuse illumination fell over them, around them, haunting in a way. Allie recognized the pond as the one outside Luke's dad's house, where she'd fallen. She refrained from comment.

"I can see why it's your favorite," she said. "The image speaks volumes. They all do, really, but this one seems to epitomize the father-daughter relationship. Trust, guardianship, love, shared adventure. I'd say, based on the way she's holding her arms, that was one of Lydia's first times out on the ice?"

"Yes."

Allie glanced at Luke and away. He couldn't possibly be conscious of the unguarded, raw emotion on his face right then. Allie nodded at the photo. "The light is…I don't know what it is, except perfect."

"Winter light," said Luke.

"What's that?"

"Winter light. That's what Rory calls it. He loves to shoot when the air is cold and snow is pending and the world is without shadow and time seems held in abeyance. That's what he says, anyway. I can see what he means."

Allie looked up at the picture again. She could see it, too.

"Dad? Are you guys ready?"

Luke collected himself with a visible movement of his head, like a dog shaking rain from its coat. "Yep. Allie just has to put these galoshes on. Allie, you can slip your feet in, sneakers and all. That's what they're made for."

Allie sat on the edge of the sofa, reaching for the boots. The metal clasps had already been unfastened and she stuck her foot into the right boot, tugging it on. Her sneaker slid straight to the bottom in a nearly perfect fit. Not a pair of Luke's boots, then, and far too large for his daughter. Allie bit her lip. The symbolism of stepping into another woman's shoes wasn't lost on her. Neither was the ridiculousness of the sentiment. She certainly had no intention of becoming a part of Luke and Lydia's life. Not in that way. Not in any way. She didn't know either of them. Luke had been a one-sided high school crush, and Lydia...Lydia was a sweet child who had ended up at her store after an improbable trek to run from feelings she couldn't really escape. And that was that.

But things happened for a reason. Her mother said so all the time. Many people did, and believed it.

With a grunt of dismissal disguised as effort, Allie pulled on the left boot and rose. "Okay," she said. "Let's go find us a tree."

*   *   *

33

Luke strode in front of Allie, leading the way. Lydia had dropped back to walk with her and he could hear them chattering away behind him. He didn't want to feel what he was feeling, hopeful and interested. He had Lydia to think of. Part of what he was feeling had a great deal to do with her. She liked Allie, responded to her. But he couldn't base his attraction to a woman solely on Lydia. He really didn't have time for a woman in his life, anyway. Lyddie was enough to handle. And Allie was someone who happened to fall into their lives at a moment when she was needed. The fact he had kissed her once as a teenager was irrelevant. They were adults now, with their own pursuits and problems, grown far from the hormonal recklessness of adolescence.

"Where are we going, Dad?" Lydia called out.

"You'll see."

He had a plan, a plan that embarrassed him a little when it had come to him, but he was determined to see it through. Allie's reminder about the incident at his dad's pond had shaken loose other memories from that night. In particular, something she had said about the smell of balsam, how balsam and cinnamon were the scents of Christmas. Well, he couldn't do anything about cinnamon right now, but a balsam tree in her window might be just the thing for inspiration. For some reason, balsam trees didn't do as well on the farm as other varieties, but he pampered a continual planting up on the ridge, for his own personal use. He didn't mind giving one up for Allie. She deserved it. He hadn't seen Lydia so talkative in ages.

Urging them on up the hillside with a wave of his flashlight, he smiled. In all honesty, he hadn't felt this good in a while either.

The scent drifted down on a breeze, reaching his flaring nostrils at the same instant it reached Allie's. He heard her gasp, a long, slow intake of breath, followed by a cry of delight. "Come on," he called over his shoulder. "We're almost there."

Lydia's boots pounded on the muddy pathway. She appeared beside him. He switched the flashlight to his other hand, the one holding the saw, and slipped his fingers around hers.

"Dad, are you sure?"

"Isn't it okay for Allie to have one of our special trees?"

"It's a great idea."

Luke smiled again. Allie scurried to catch up. For some reason, she hadn't fastened the boots and he could hear the rubber flapping around her calves as she neared and then passed him and Lydia, shuffling uphill with her arms wide.

"Fabulous!" she cried, spinning to face them. She stopped abruptly, arms dropping to her sides.

Her eyes met his.

"Yes. I remembered," he confessed with a brief jerk of his shoulders. She bit her lip. "No big deal," he added, trying to stave off an emotion he couldn't handle. "It'll be nice in the window. Your store will smell like Christmas."

She fell in beside them in silence. They made their way up into the balsam grove. Lydia reached to take Allie's hand with her right one, but Allie had already shoved both of hers into her pockets and didn't see. Or if she did, she pretended not to. Walking hand in hand, all three of them, would have been strange. The fact Lydia wanted to created an ache in Luke's chest.

"I think there are some trees over this way that aren't too wide," Luke said, shining the light off to the left. In unison, they turned in that direction. Once there, Luke and Lydia stopped, although Allie plodded on in her unfastened boots for several seconds.

"Let's turn the flashlights off," said Lydia. "Just for a bit."

"Okay." Luke set the saw on the ground. "Ready? You, too, Allie. One. Two. Three."

He and Allie switched off their flashlights.

"Now look up," said Lydia.

Lydia stared up at the sky, her hair caught in her hood. Allie did the same, neck arched. Smiling, Luke turned his gaze skyward to a clear, velvet blackness filled with stars, some milky white, some yellow as topaz, others with the crystal brilliance of diamonds.

"Such a beautiful night."

Luke heard a catch in Allie's voice and cut his gaze sideways. In the star-filled darkness, he saw a glimmer of moisture in her eyes.

"Allie?"

"I'm fine."

He wanted to go to her, put his arms around her, but he understood she'd been moved to tears by natural beauty, not sadness. Besides, it wasn't his place to comfort her…was it? No, of course it wasn't. They were no more than strangers. Even on that long-ago night, he'd only known her by sight, not even her name, although she'd told him after she fell. They didn't travel in the same circles. She'd been at the party because she had friends who crossed those boundaries and she'd come with them. After watching her skate, he'd realized she hadn't cared about the party. She only wanted to fly across the ice beneath the night sky.

"Temperature's dropping. It's getting a little chilly out here." He bent and picked up the saw, flicking the flashlight back on. "Pick a tree, Allie. Lydia, you can help her."

"And we can have hot chocolate after?" Lydia asked.

"Sure," said Luke. "If Allie has the time."

With the array of unexpected emotions battering at him, he hoped she wouldn't.

Chapter Four

Allie walked into the store and threw her purse and a shopping bag behind the counter. She turned on all the lights, unlocked the cash register, and performed a quick check of the displays to assure everything had been left in order at closing the night before. Satisfied, Allie jotted a quick note on a post-it to order Rory Hollis' book for the local author section, and then went to the display window. She climbed inside.

Standing in the center of the barren floor, she turned in a slow circle. Her thoughts kept drifting to the evening before with Luke and Lydia. Although she tried not to let it affect her, she had been moved by the hike into the balsam copse. The fact he'd remembered a passing remark after all these years seemed significant, and yet she knew there was no way it could be. He happened to remember. Nothing more. The mind did funny things. The smell of a cup of tea could suddenly make you recall breakfast when you were four, for crying out loud. Luke's remembering meant nothing. However, the fact he'd brought her up to the copse once the memory had returned to him couldn't be so easily disregarded.

Even so, what did it mean? Only that he was kind, which she'd already deduced from his interaction with Lydia. Entertaining any other notion was a waste of time. She had to put this sort of nonsense out of her mind and focus on the project plaguing her. In about fifteen minutes Luke and Lydia would be here with the tree, and she didn't need to be mooning around. She needed to focus. She had a bag full of cinnamon sticks and red ribbon and her plan—her half-formulated plan—was to have Lydia tie ribbons to the cinnamon sticks. After, they would hang them on the tree. While Lydia did the tying, Allie hoped to finalize some masterful idea for the rest of the window, because really, she had none. Nada. Zip.

Catching sight through the glass of a wrapped tree balanced on a broad shoulder, Allie hurried to the edge of the display area and leaped to the carpeted floor below. She ran to the door and opened it as Luke appeared, stepping aside to let him in with the balsam fir. The scent of the tree filled her nostrils. He carried the tree to the window and laid it down, depositing a metal stand beside it. Allie looked outside for some sign of Lydia trailing behind.

"Where's Lyd—"

"She won't be coming," Luke said.

Allie made a face. "Is this her punishment for yesterday?"

"She doesn't know you. I don't think she would view not being able to come here as a punishment."

Ouch. "I was joking. And she was looking forward to coming here. I was looking forward to having her. But of course the decision about what she does with her day is yours."

"It is."

Allie's lifted her brows in disconcert. "Have I committed some mortal sin I don't know about? You seem mighty miffed about something."

He turned from her and began to adjust the legs on the stand. She could gauge the depth of the breath he took in the expansion of his coat. After a moment, she heard the air release through his nose. He stared down at the stand, his hands at his sides.

"It's not you, Allie. I'm sorry. It's just…things are plenty screwed up right now. And Lydia is my problem, not yours."

"She's not your problem," Allie said quietly. "She's your daughter."

His head jerked as if he would make some sharp retort, but instead his shoulders slumped. "I know that. I can't have her pinning hopes on somebody who's going to be out of her life as quickly as she's come into it."

That sounded like a rejection to Allie. The little fantasies she'd been trying to quell all morning flittered away like birds escaped from a cage. "She's not pinning hopes. I liked her. She liked me. And she wanted to give me a hand. But I understand what you're saying, Luke. I do. If this is how you need to handle what's going on with Lydia, okay."

Whipping the tree to vertical, Luke lowered the

stump into the stand and wordlessly tightened the bolts. He removed a small knife from his jeans and made short work of the wrapping. The freed branches descended gracefully into place. He still hadn't looked at her. "Once you set that where you want it, you need to get some water in the stand."

"Okay." Allie frowned at his profile.

"And you can just drop the stand outside the barn after the holidays."

"Okay." Allie tried to maintain a neutral tone. He had every right to keep his distance. There was no history between them. He wanted his life simple. She understood how that worked. And yet she felt a little like she'd been punched in the gut.

Luke pulled a couple of browned, curled maple leaves from impalement among the needles. He shoved them into his coat pocket along with the severed wrap, running his other hand through his hair. Allie crossed her arms over her chest. If he really wanted nothing to do with her—an impression she hadn't received last night—then why wasn't he leaving?

He pivoted on his rubber heel to face her. "Actually, Lydia isn't feeling well. I think all that time in the cold yesterday, all that unreasonable, scare-the-crap-out-of-me-to-even-think-about walking, must have run her down. She's in bed this morning. Frank—the guy you met out front last night?—called his wife over to sit with her until I get home, because my folks are out of town. I wanted to make sure you got your tree. And I know you're disappointed, because I can tell you really like Lydia—"

"Luke."

He took another deep breath, a shorter one this time, and waited.

"Luke." Ridiculously, tears pricked at her eyelids, clinging to the corners of her lashes. She blinked them back.

"Allie, don't—"

"Shh." She held up her hand. "It's fine. I'm fine. Ignore these," she said, waving her pointer finger at her eyes. "Makes no sense at all. A preposterous response. Compassion is my downfall. You carry enough responsibility. Don't feel responsible for my disappointment, too. You go on home to Lydia. And if you need anything, let me know. No strings, no expectations, no whatever the heck else you're worried about. Okay? Now that I've got a tree, I have a window to decorate."

He'd taken a step nearer. She hadn't seen him do it, hadn't noticed through her moist vision or her flurry of words. He wasn't the cute boy she remembered anymore. Not one bit. Instead he was older and careworn and marked by life to the point of impossible magnificence, and she wanted nothing more than for him to get out of her store right then, before she did or said another stupid thing.

"Did you find your marvelous inspiration?" he asked.

"Not yet."

"You will. I'll come by and check out the window with Lydia, when she's feeling better."

"Not necessary, Luke."

Pretending a nonchalance she knew didn't fool

him, and which she certainly didn't feel, Allie clambered up into the window and started lugging the tree to a central position. She had to start somewhere, had to force herself to move in the right direction. More than that, she had to not look at Luke as he turned and left. She felt more than saw him pause at the glass, gazing in at her, and then he was gone. She stole a glance toward the street to be sure.

"You're an awful fool, Allison Roberts," she said, words echoing in the hollow space around her.

*   *   *

Luke gathered branches trimmed from the day's trees and carried them to the bin. Some places charged for greens, but Luke gave the fragrant castoffs to customers who asked for them, for wreaths or centerpieces or whatever they wanted. What they did with the castoffs wasn't up to him. He was glad to be rid of them without waste.

Frank had left early, so Luke pulled the chain across the driveway before heading up to the house. Lydia had been unusually quiet all day. Luke couldn't be sure if she still didn't feel well, was mad at him, disappointed, worried about the punishment for yesterday's antics that hadn't come, or what the deal was. After Beth had gone home, every time Luke checked on his daughter—and since Lydia had taken off the day before without him noticing, he made sure he did so with frequency—he found her sitting in her bed, reading or drawing. Their conversations went politely enough, but their interaction felt off.

Entering the house through the back door, Luke yanked off his boots and set them in the tray beneath the bench. The weather had definitely taken a turn, the temperature barely above freezing and the ground hard. His boots had been filthy last night after carrying the tree down from the hill with Lydia and Allie. Still bent over his knees, he looked at the two pairs of boots next to his, Lydia's bright pink ones and Zoe's old galoshes, left behind when she headed for her new life in sunny California. He pictured them on Allie's feet, flopping unfastened about her legs as she trudged along beside him and his daughter into the fragrant grove of balsam fir.

A guilty twinge unsettled him as he thought about his rudeness that morning. He didn't want to feel guilt, damn it. His fault, though. If he hadn't behaved like an ass, deliberately trying to put her off, he'd have no reason for self-reproach. She hadn't deserved that type of treatment. And when he'd tried to explain himself, she'd cried. Not because of hurt feelings, but because she felt *sorry* for him. He didn't want anyone feeling sorry for him, either, but especially not a kind, funny, and, yes, appealing woman. A woman he'd spent the day trying very hard to put out of his mind.

"Damn it," he said out loud, pushing up off the bench.

"Dad!"

Luke spun on the heel of his sock. "Lydia, what are you doing out of bed?"

Her eyes widened. "Aren't I allowed to be now? You didn't say. Was I supposed to stay there until school tomorrow because I ran away?"

Reaching out, he pulled her close, ruffling her hair. "Of course not. That's not why you didn't come out, is it? I thought you weren't feeling well. Or were mad at me."

Lydia ducked her head away. "Do you think Allie did her window without me?"

Luke flinched as if he'd been hit by a flying dart. "I know she missed you being there, but she also needed to get the job finished, so I hope she did. Don't you?"

"I guess so."

Luke took her hand and led her into the kitchen. She sat on a stool at the island. Luke yanked open the refrigerator, searching for something to fix for their dinner. "Did you finish your homework?"

"I did that on Friday, Dad," Lydia answered behind him.

Luke sighed, lowering his head against the back of the arm hooked over the open refrigerator door. Of course she had. Lydia was a remarkable child…with the exception of the whole running away thing. But Luke understood that urge, too.

"Dad?"

"Yes, pumpkin?"

"Why don't we have Chinese? You've been working all day, and—"

"—and we can drive by Allie's store? Is that what you're trying for?" He lifted his head, looking back. Lydia sat with her hands clasped together on the counter, a beautiful, dark-haired angel. Not altogether innocent though. Her expression was anything but.

"Yep," she said. "I thought maybe we could take a look at the window."

"Get your shoes and your coat and my wallet off the dresser. You call, I'll buy."

Lydia giggled. "Of course you will. I don't have any money!" As she ran from the room, she shouted over her shoulder. "You want the usual?"

"The usual," he said and straightened. Before returning to the mud room for his shoes, he glanced in the small, ceramic-framed mirror on the wall, ducking from side to side in order to check his face for smudges of dirt. He smoothed his windblown hair with both hands.

"You're pathetic," he said. But the face looking back at him was smiling.

Fifteen minutes later, snuggled in a pink coat that exactly matched the shade of her boots, a feat she had managed on her own the day he'd brought her shopping, Lydia watched him in the dimly lit interior of the truck as he steered the vehicle onto the narrow highway leading into town.

"You're not mad, are you, Dad?"

"Heck, no. I'm an adult and the word 'no' is in my vocabulary."

Lydia giggled, swiveling in her seat belt to face front. She had a fairly clear view of the road ahead. Luke could see her arching her neck for a better look. As soon as she spied the twenty miles per hour sign, she sat back, grinning.

"How long did they say before our order is done?" he asked.

"Just about now," she said. Disappointment

tapped him on the shoulder. Despite his best intentions, he had found himself hoping Lydia's plans had included a stop by the bookstore, and not just a drive-by. "But don't worry," she added. "I ordered a large veggie rice for me, instead of the small one. I figured Allie might need something for her dinner."

Luke laughed and gave his daughter's tiny knee a squeeze. "You're probably right at that. Do you think she likes vegetable fried rice?"

"Who doesn't?"

It wasn't one of his personal favorites, but he had no intention of arguing the point with Lyddie. A short time later, he pulled the truck up in front of the restaurant.

"Can I come in with you, Dad?"

He nodded and they both got out. Inside, Lydia ran up to the box of fortune cookies and asked the fellow behind the counter if she could pick her own. She spent an inordinate amount of time in the process, her gloved hand hovering over the container, her eyes wide and intent as she concentrated on the wrapped cookies, hoping, Luke supposed, to choose the best fortunes.

"Come on, Lyddie."

"It's all right," said the man packing up their order. "Slow night."

Suddenly she pounced, plucking out three. She handed them up to be deposited into the bag with their food. Luke paid and they headed back outside and climbed into the truck. "So," he asked Lydia as he hooked her seatbelt, "did you pick out good ones, do you think?"

"The best," she said with a grin.

"No, I picked the best."

"What do you mean?"

"I picked you."

She gave a very grownup snort through her nose. "You didn't pick me, Dad. I was born. That means I picked you."

Luke's heart swelled. "Good to know, sweetheart." He steered the truck in the direction of Allie's store. Within five minutes, he spotted a space big enough for the pickup and eased into it, giving his hair another quick glance in the mirror as he put the truck in park. One day soon, he should get it trimmed. He hadn't been giving his appearance much thought lately.

"Allie's not going to care about your hair, Dad."

He jumped, looking across the truck at his daughter. "What?"

"Trust me, she doesn't care about stuff like that."

"Really? What does she care about?"

"Who you are."

"Who I am?"

"Who all of us are."

Sometimes, the workings of his daughter's eight-year-old mind boggled him. She gathered information out of thin air and expressed very firm opinions about it. She couldn't really know something as profound as Allie's view of the people in her world. Could she? Could someone her age possess that type of intuition?

He thought of the rare occasions Lydia spoke

about Zoe. His wife—ex-wife, he reminded himself—had left Pennsylvania over a year ago, making Lydia much younger at the time than her current, tender age of eight. Yet, the things that came out of Lyddie's mouth and out of the blue staggered him and made him bleed. A child shouldn't recognize such deep-seated truths about her parents. Not the ones that hurt so badly.

"Hand me the bag," Luke said, pointing. "We'll see if Allie finished the window or not."

The scents from the bag of Chinese food made his stomach growl as he stood on the sidewalk waiting for Lydia to climb out of the truck. As soon as her feet hit the ground, she placed her hand in his. A day would come, impossibly soon, when she wouldn't reach for his hand like that anymore. Swallowing hard, he forced a smile to his lips.

Nearing Connor Falls Book Emporium, Luke spotted a handful of people standing in front of the display window, pointing and talking. Lydia noticed as well, tugging him forward.

"Oh, Daddy," she whispered as they came to a halt before the window.

Luke stared, too, feeling his face go numb and then hot. He shook his head once, very slowly.

How Allie had managed all of this in one day, he couldn't imagine. The tree and about a dozen books provided the only color in a display that had been made to resemble a black and white photograph. The light from a multitude of tiny white bulbs behind gauze draped along the ceiling illuminated the scene with a gentle glow, revealing a landscape recreated in varying shades of off-white and gray. A pond in the center—made from foil sprayed with a mist of white paint—reflected the light from above softly. Logs had been coated white with a dry brush to tone down their natural hue, and against one lying vertically in the fake snow beside the pond leaned a pair of old, white ice skates, the cracked leather highlighted by a skillful application of some type of dark gray glaze. At the nearest edge of the pond was positioned a large silhouette of two figures skating cautiously onto the ice, the hand of the taller hovering just above the shoulder of the child.

"Is that us?" Lydia asked, still whispering.

"I think it's meant to be every parent and child," Luke said. His gaze shifted to a sign made to resemble a scroll, affixed to a small post in the snow just to the right of the figures. Written on the parchment-like paper with a calligraphy pen, were the words:

"The radiance of winter comes from within, seeping out from our hearts to illuminate each day and light our way back to precious memories."

Below it in neat block letters was a request for people to bring in gray-scale copies of photographs of their favorite winter memories, to be hung on the tree. No photos hung on the branches, but the sign couldn't have been up more than a few hours.

"Isn't it lovely?" said a woman standing next to him.

He nodded, once again speechless. The woman moved away and someone else took her place.

"Hey, Lydia. Feeling better?"

Luke spun on his heel. A dusting of glitter

sparkled in Allie's short, cinnamon hair. She raised her gaze from Lydia's face to his. Had he ever really forgotten how luminous her chocolate-brown eyes could be?

Pulling her close and crushing the bag of food between them, he kissed her in a way he never would have done all those years ago.

Chapter Five

Allie pulled away first, breathless, the pounding of her heart momentarily drowning out the sounds in the street.

"Uh, hi," she finally managed.

Luke stared at her, apparently horrified by what he'd done. Beside him, Lydia looked up at her father with annoyance.

"Dad, I think you broke the fortune cookies." She yanked a bag from her father's fist. "Come on, Allie," she then said to her. "We brought Chinese!"

Taking her hand, Lydia led her into the store and up to the counter. "Hi, Todd," the girl said as she marched around behind. "There's enough for you, too, I think."

Todd winked at her. "Don't worry about it. I just had a hoagie." His head lifted, looking over Allie's shoulder. With a hasty nod, he excused himself. Allie turned around.

"I'm sorry," Luke said. "I don't—I'm sorry."

Allie could hear the crinkling of brown paper as Lydia rummaged through the bag out of sight behind the L-shaped counter. Allie kept her eyes fixed on Luke's as she fought the curling of her lips and the churning of her stomach.

"Those were the exact words you used sixteen years ago. Right down to the little hesitation between 'I don't' and the second 'I'm sorry'. What were you going to say? Then and now, I guess. 'I don't know what came over me'?"

"No," he said, "I know exactly what came over me. Then and now. And I am sorry."

Allie cocked her head to the side, pondering Luke's expression. She couldn't get a clear picture of the workings of his mind right then. It didn't appear to be regret. Not entirely. She suspected an inclination to run lurking there somewhere. She tossed her head. "For what? A momentary urge? Forget about it. I'm more intrigued by why you brought me Chinese."

She turned away, suppressing her own impulse to grab him by the front of his coat and kiss him again. Too late, anyway. Lydia had popped up from behind the counter to deposit food containers on the surface.

"Dad, what's wrong with you? So you kissed Allie. Big people do that all the time. I've seen it on TV."

Unable to stop the giggle bubbling over her lips, Allie headed to the back office for a couple of paper plates and napkins. When she returned, she found Lydia had doffed her coat and climbed up onto the tall stool, but Luke hadn't moved. "Luke, it's all right," she said, looking at him as she handed Lydia the plates. "I swear you haven't scarred me for life or anything."

He said nothing.

"Come. Eat. I can hear your stomach rumbling from here."

"Allie…"

At his tone, she set the napkins down and turned. "Luke. Seriously. It's okay."

The troubled expression in his blue eyes said otherwise. "Allie, can I talk to you a moment? In private."

Allie hesitated. She took a deep breath, releasing it in increments. Her stomach flipped nervously. "Lydia, man the store. We'll be right back."

"What if someone wants to buy a book?" Lydia asked, straightening on the stool.

"Call Todd. He's good at that. We're only stepping out front. We'll be back in before the food gets cold." Allie signaled to Todd before she headed for the door. And on the off chance she had underestimated the time it would take for Luke's discussion about why there would never be anything between the two of them, Allie grabbed her coat.

Outside, Allie strode away from the display window to a patch of sidewalk not as well lit. She wasn't certain she wanted him to see her face with any clarity during this conversation. When she ascertained they'd reached a point where he couldn't, she stopped, shoving her hands into the pockets of her coat.

"Allie, I…look, I don't know that Lydia's ready to handle something like this."

Allie turned her head slightly, looking at him from the corner of her eye. "Like what, exactly?"

"Like me…dating."

"Dating? We're not. I mean, you haven't said a word to me about it. No, how'd you like to go to the movies, or…well, you get the gist."

"Well no, but—"

"Were you considering asking me on a date? Frankly, I figured you kissed me to see if it felt the same now that we're both grown up, relatively speaking."

He laughed and shook his head. Some of the color came back into his face. She hadn't realized how pale he'd become until then. She knew, though, that she'd never had that affect on anyone else in her life.

"I like you, Allie. I don't know you that well, but that's usually how it works. You feel a liking for someone, or an attraction, or whatever it is that moves you, and then you do your best to get to know that person. Right?"

Allie bit her lip. This wasn't going at all in the direction she'd expected.

"That kiss should have come later. This one, not the one years ago. I don't remember exactly how I felt about that one. I'm betting I liked it just as much, though."

Allie's mouth dropped open. She sucked in a small amount of cold air.

"But what I'm saying is anything I choose to do must be done with consideration for Lydia. She's my daughter, and she's already hurting."

"Understood." Allie could barely get the word out.

"Because Lydia likes you, too. If things don't work out between two people, kids get caught in the middle."

"Stop," said Allie. "You don't—"

"Yes, I do. I want to get to know you better, Allie, but I want to take things slowly. Oh, God, I'm not even giving you a chance to say what you think. Have I just stuck my foot in my mouth?"

Allie released a breath through her nose. "I have a permanent toe print on my tongue from doing that. And no, you haven't. If you want to ask me out, go ahead and do it. My answer will be yes."

His lips lifted in a slow smile. He leaned forward and pressed his mouth to her forehead, whispering against the curve of her brow. "Perfect."

*　　*　　*

Luke scrubbed his hand across his eyes, blinking them tiredly. Remnants of his leftover sweet and sour chicken spotted the plate at his elbow, the fork on a crumpled napkin nearby. He glanced at the clock. After midnight. He and Lydia had spent more time at the bookstore than he'd intended, leaving him to start his paperwork for the day far later than usual. But he'd finished and he had the memory of a pleasant evening to ease him into sleep.

Capping the pen and closing the record book, Luke then rose and scraped his plate into the trash can. He'd been working in the light thrown from the stove hood so as not to disturb Lyddie, who'd fallen asleep on the sofa, and it pooled around him, leaving the rest of the area in near darkness. Even so, the light glittered in the glass of the picture frames above the fireplace mantel. Careful not to disturb Lydia, he moved to the photo of the two of them on the ice and stood staring at the image, his arms crossed over his chest. The silhouette Allie had made was not, of course, an exact duplicate of him and Lydia, but she'd definitely managed to recreate the mood. Although she had spoken enthusiastically about Rory's talent, she possessed an artistic ability of her own.

Taking a step back, Luke viewed the other photographs on the wall. Each of them contained at least one family member, and yet none of them were portraits. Rory used people in his photos as another element of his art, yet distinctly personal. Luke didn't quite get how Rory managed to make that happen. Luke didn't possess a creative bone in his body, but he recognized the attribute when he saw it.

At a sound from the sofa behind him, Luke turned. Lydia had rolled in her sleep, the blanket he'd covered her with slipping to the floor. He went to pick it up, pausing at the sight of a slim piece of paper sticking out between Lydia's fingers. Crouching down, he slid the paper out of her hand

and held it up to the light filtering in from the kitchen, recognizing a fortune from one of the broken cookies in the bag. Lydia's fortune, he figured, since both he and Allie had laughed over theirs but Lydia had never read hers out loud, interrupted by a bookstore customer coming to the counter.

He looked closely at it now, experiencing a small dread as he realized the words were important to her, something she wanted to believe in, or she never would have held onto the fortune through the entirety of the night. He'd done the same thing himself as a kid, and even, he had to admit, as an adult, but Lydia's wants and wishes were so often wrapped up in the bigger drama of their lives.

Your dreams really can come true.

Harmless enough, but he remembered the way she'd agonized over the picking of the cookies. She counted on this fortune. And he knew what she dreamed about, heard her talking often enough in her sleep.

Luke inserted the fortune back into her hand, closing her fingers around it. He picked her up and carried her to her bed, lowering Lyddie onto the mussed mattress and pulling the covers over her. He kissed her softly on the brow and straightened, staring down a moment at his sleeping, troubled daughter. With an expulsion of breath from his nose, he returned to the kitchen, grabbed his phone and dialed.

Standing in the yellow light from the stove hood, Luke listened to the ring, preparing in his head the message he would leave. Instead, she picked up, throwing him, causing him to hesitate.

"Hello?"

Luke cleared his throat. "Zoe, it's me."

Chapter Six

Keys in hand, Allie paused by the display window, studying it with a critical eye. Customers had been telling her the past few days how much they liked it, and yet not one of them had come forward with a photo for the tree. For that matter, neither had she. Perhaps they felt as underwhelmed with the season this year as she did. She only wanted it to be over. And why was that, precisely?

"Allie, hi!"

Allie turned, spotting Gina waving from across the street. Figuring it wouldn't kill anyone if she opened a couple of minutes late, Allie waved back and, after a quick check for non-existent traffic at that hour, hurried over to talk to her.

"Are you just getting in?" Allie asked, eying the bakery door. Nope, the sign was already flipped to *OPEN*.

"I stepped out for some air. Beautiful morning." The dark-haired woman smiled. "How are you doing? Love the window."

Allie shrugged. "Thanks. I'm surprised I managed to come up with any idea at all, because I'm not feeling it this year."

"Some years are like that. You don't quite manage the ho-ho-ho bit."

"You, too?"

"No, surprisingly, I'm good. I hired a baker to help me, which has made a world of difference to the stress I experience as the holidays approach."

Nodding, Allie checked the sidewalk in front of the Book Emporium to make sure no one was looking to get in.

"So what's this rumor I hear about you and the hot Luke Hollis?"

Allie jerked back around. "As opposed to the not-hot Luke Hollis? Does that man exist?"

Gina snorted a quick laugh.

"Where did you hear this rumor? Because that's all it is."

"Todd," Gina said. "And what do you mean that's all it is?"

"He expressed an interest and I haven't heard from him since." Allie shoved her hands into her jacket pockets, jiggling the shop keys around. "And that's fine. He has his daughter to think of, the tree farm. We're all busy now."

"Apparently, he's managed a bit of time for you."

"He—what?" Allie followed Gina's gaze and spotted Luke's pickup pulling the wrong way into a vacant space near the entrance to the bookstore. With a rushed goodbye, Allie hurried across the street. Luke lowered the passenger side window. Allie draped her arms across the opening, leaning her weight against the door. "Hi."

"Good morning." He grinned. Somehow, it didn't reach his eyes.

"Whatcha doing?"

"I came to buy a book."

"I'm not open yet."

"I can see that."

"What kind of book?"

"Something for Lyddie," he said. "She's had a rough couple of days."

Allie backed away, fishing the keys from her pocket. She jerked her head in invitation and went to unlock the knob. The solid slam of the truck door sounded behind her. "Let me get the lights on," she said.

He followed her inside, waiting in the middle of the floor as she hurried to the bank of switches.

"What's happened? Has Lydia been sick, or…?"

"I called Zoe after we left here the other night. Actually got her on the phone." He shoved his hands into his pockets, rocking back on his heels. "I wanted to know…to know how she could do this to our daughter. I've asked before and her answers have always been, well, crap. This time I kind of lost it. I got loud. Lydia woke up. She heard…me. The things I was saying. She asked to talk to her mother and I put her on the phone. How could I not? She rarely gets to speak with Zoe and I thought, okay, I've said my piece, you're her mother, Zoe, you explain it to her."

"And did she?"

"Yeah, unfortunately I think she did."

Allie flicked the last switch, lighting the area over the register. "Not good?"

"I don't even know what she said. I tried to listen, but she'd gotten quiet on the other end and Lydia's responses soon became monosyllabic. Until the end. She asked Zoe if she'd come home for Christmas to see her. To see…to see us."

Allie observed the play of pain crossing Luke's face with a wrench to her gut.

"Zoe didn't answer the phone when I called back. And Lyddie wouldn't say a word. She cried herself to sleep. She didn't want me to touch her. I let her sleep in and brought her to school late." He sighed. "She's not good, and I don't know what to do to help her now."

"Does she have—"

"A therapist? Yes. I took her. Don't know if it helped."

"And your wife—"

"Ex-wife."

"Zoe," Allie amended. "What exactly is she doing in California?"

"Following her dream." His sarcasm was obvious.

Allie remembered the stunning good looks of the woman in the photographs on Luke's living room wall. "Acting?"

"I suppose."

Luke had been right. This wasn't the time to

start a relationship. He had too much on his plate, too much upheaval and anguish and unresolved issues for that. Even so, Allie wanted to put her arms around him, hold him close. He would always be there to comfort his daughter, but who comforted him?

"What kind of book were you thinking? Something to entertain, distract, console, commiserate? What's her reading level?"

She headed for the children's section, Luke on her heels.

"The school advisor says she's well ahead of her grade level in reading."

Allie nodded. "That doesn't surprise me. Let's look around and you tell me if you recognize any of the books as something she's read recently, and that'll give me something to go on."

She crouched on the floor, pulling a few middle grade readers from the shelf and holding them up to Luke.

He knelt beside her. "This one. And this one. She read that twice, she told me."

With a smile, Allie yanked several more down, spreading them out on the floor by her knees. She placed her fingers flat on the nearest. "I'd try this."

His hand lowered onto hers. "Thank you, Allie."

She nodded in mute acknowledgment, afraid to speak. His tone moved her to the verge of tears. After a moment, she eased her hand from beneath his and rose, clearing her throat. He picked the books up from the floor and returned them to the shelf, then took the one she'd suggested from her grasp.

"You're right. I think she'll like this one."

His eyes had such beautiful form, almond shaped and long-lashed. The color reminded her of the sky in the last light of day. She gazed into them for longer than she intended. He didn't look away.

"Allie."

"Don't kiss me again."

"Ever?"

"Right now I don't want you confusing gratitude with affection."

"Give me a little credit, Allison Roberts."

She growled at him and marched to the front of the store, where she reached under the counter and grabbed a bag. She deposited the book into it when he gave it to her. "Here you go, Luke. If you don't think it'll upset her, please tell Lydia I said hello."

"I'm paying you for this book."

"Nope. It takes ten minutes for this old register to warm up, and I don't think you feel like waiting."

"Liar."

"Maybe."

"Look, Allie, you can tell her hello yourself. She'd probably like to hear from you. I don't think it would harm her to have a conversation. In fact, she talked about you before she got on the school bus this morning."

Allie placed her elbows on the counter, leaning toward him. "What did she say?"

"She said…" He swallowed. "She said, 'you like Allie and Mommy's never coming back, so you should ask her out.' What eight-year-old says things like that, let alone thinks them? What have Zoe and

I done to this wonderful child of ours?"

His heart suddenly lay in her hands. She closed her eyes. She hadn't been looking for this either, not something so complicated and heartbreaking. Still, she couldn't back away. He needed…something. A friend, a willing ear, someone to tell him he'd been doing his best. She lifted her lids and gave him a long, weighty look.

"Lydia hurts, Luke, but she's not broken. You haven't broken her. She's sweet and super-smart and, yes, extremely introspective for an eight-year-old—heck, I don't think I'm that introspective—but you love her, and she knows that. And that's important. I hate to play devil's advocate, but I think Zoe loves her, too. How could she abruptly stop? Maybe she avoids contact because it's painful to her and painful to Lydia and she doesn't know what else to do. She could be just as confused as you, having made a decision to follow her dreams, as you said, and knowing Lydia would be better here with her dad, in a stable environment." Allie straightened, turned the register key. She shrugged. "I don't know. I'm just a bookseller with no kids of my own. I see a lot of them, though, and Lydia is a special little girl."

Luke stared. After a moment, he backed away from the counter. "If Zoe had expressed even half of her motivation, it would have helped. I don't know what she's thinking. Once I thought I understood her." He shook the bag in his hand. "Thanks, Allie, for the book and…everything."

He left. No promising goodbye. Just gone. The door opened thirty seconds later. Todd walked in.

"Hey, isn't that your old crush pulling away?"

Allie blew a breath out her nose. "Yeah."

Todd shirked out of his coat and hung it on the rack. "So, you guys got plans, or what?"

"More like 'what'."

"Oh, jeez, I'm sorry." He headed into the back room to put his lunch in the refrigerator. Allie opened the register and slipped a ten from her pocket into the proper bin. Connor Falls Book Emporium was still her parents' establishment and she had no business handing out merchandise without payment. She'd get the bar code later, ring up the book and settle the till.

"I brought you a picture for the tree."

Allie turned to see what Todd was holding out. Frowning, she took the photo from his hand. "What is this?"

"You wanted a favorite winter memory. This is me and my buddies playing paintball a few winters back. Those balls were *frozen*. They hurt. I had bruises after. But we had fun. It was one of the best, last days I had with Cyril." He tapped the picture above the head of a boy standing beside him, tall and lanky and dark. "He was killed a week later in a car accident."

Allie's fingers shook. "Oh God, Todd."

"Hey, Allie, don't be crying. It's all right. He was my best friend for years. We had that time. Some people, they don't find a friend like that. How much worse would my life have been if I never had him?" He reached past her for the hole punch and ribbon she'd brought in with the expectation of photos to be hung, then removed the picture from her grasp. "I'll hang it myself, if that's okay?"

"Yes," Allie managed to croak. "Hang it up high. That's something to be proud of."

"And maybe it'll get other people thinking. You haven't asked them for the impossible. Just to share something of themselves."

Perspective. Everything was a matter of perspective. Todd's raw, honest sentiments burned into her heart. If only she had managed to say something so profound to Luke, she could have helped him.

The front door opened again, this time admitting a customer. Allie put her game face on, smiling at Jeanette Nolan as she walked up to the counter. If the woman noticed her still-wet lashes, she made no comment. "Hi, Allie. I've come for my package. How are your folks doing?"

"Enjoying Florida. Your family? Are they coming for Christmas?" Allie retrieved Jeanette's package from beneath the counter and scanned the codes from the three books into the register.

"All except Eve. You know."

Allie did know. She recognized the disappointment in Jeanette's voice each year. Allie swiped the woman's credit card and returned the books to the bag. "My parents are staying in Florida for the holidays and my brother is with his wife's family this year. I guess you have to get used to that sort of thing."

Jeanette eyebrows wiggled in dubious agreement as she reached for the bag Allie extended across the counter. "What's this I hear about you and Luke Hollis?"

Good Lord, this town wasn't *that* small. Catching the wink Jeanette sent in Todd's direction, Allie understood exactly where the woman had received her information. "There's nothing going on between me and Luke, Mrs. Nolan. We haven't even had a date."

As she spoke those words, Allie felt a little like she wanted to run and hide. After she fired Todd Wilkins.

Chapter Seven

Luke's strides took him swiftly to the bottom of the driveway to meet Lydia's bus. Since Lydia's conversation with her mother, he'd been careful not to be late. Part of him only wanted to show Lydia he was there for her, always. The other part feared she'd disappear somewhere between the road and home and this time she wouldn't be found.

The squash-colored bus pulled to a stop, lights flashing. The door opened. For a heart-thudding instant, no child appeared. And then there she was, her coat open, the plaid dress and striped tights she'd insisted on wearing this morning endearingly quirky. He'd learned not to argue with her about her attire, except as it related to weather. She was a third-grader with her own style.

She waved to someone inside and then leaped down the steps, throwing her arms out once her booted feet landed on the ground. Luke stepped forward and scooped her up onto his hip. "How was school, pumpkin?"

"We made stuff."

"What kind of stuff?"

"Secret stuff. Presents. I made one for you, and one for Allie."

Luke's stomach fluttered. "Allie?"

"Yep. And Grandma and Grandpa."

Luke waited. When she didn't go on, he asked, "And Mom? Did you make something for her?"

Lydia's expression turned solemn. "I did. I made her a special card. When everything is dry and I bring it home, we'll put it in the mail." She wriggled down to stand beside him. She slipped her hand into his. "It's cold out today."

"That's why you should have your coat zipped up."

"It was warm in the bus. Do you think it will snow?"

"Not yet, sweetie."

"How about the pond? Is it frozen yet?"

"Nope. Why?"

"I thought we could go skating again. Like in the picture."

Like in the picture. Lydia had skated a lot since Rory took the photograph, had learned to do so quite well. But Luke knew what she meant. There'd been something extra special about that day. Maybe because it was her first time and everything was new, to both of them. He hadn't taken his daughter skating before that moment. She'd always watched him from her perch on a pond-side log, sitting beside her mother, or she'd scoot around on the soles of her boots at the frozen water's edge. Zoe didn't skate. Claimed to be a klutz on the ice. And, in all honesty, she was. Her legs went in all directions like a newborn foal. She probably would have killed herself if he'd forced her out there. And he never had.

"Dad? You okay?"

"Yep. Just thinking about things. You might get your wish about the pond. An arctic front is supposed to be dipping down low by next week. You think you're cold now? You wait. You're going to need your hat and mittens and everything."

Lydia let out a whoop. "Cool!"

"Cool?"

"Yeah. My friend Edgie says that all the time."

Luke smiled. Must be a new girl. "Edgie? What kind of name is Edgie?"

Lydia shrugged. "I dunno. Hers?"

Laughing, Luke whipped the backpack off his daughter's shoulders. He tucked her football style beneath his arm and took off at a trot up the driveway with Lydia's high-pitched screams of joy warning customers out of their way.

* * *

"What's wrong, boss?"

Allie glanced up from the catalogue of spring releases to meet Todd's eye. "Besides the fact you've been blabbing tidbits of my personal life around town?"

"Yeah. Besides that."

Closing the catalogue, Allie inhaled, trying not to crack a smile. She failed, snorting through her nose before breaking into laughter. "You're an idiot, Todd. Why, why, why would you think it was okay to talk about me to people?"

"It came up. People asked how you were doing. They couldn't fail to notice how long it took you to do that window, after all, so they figured something was up."

"Right. And the reason you brought up Luke?"

He arched his brows with an 'are you kidding' kind of look. "They were all female. Naturally, they assumed your problem was the lack of a guy in your life."

"Oh, for crying out loud." Allie stormed out from behind the counter and grabbed her jacket. "I'm going to take a walk. It's slow right now. Want me to bring you something back?"

"From where?"

"I have no idea."

She exited the store into temperatures far cooler than they'd been a couple of hours earlier. The sun was nearly down, the street dark with winter shadow and streetlights glowing against the dimming sky. Windows up and down the block twinkled merrily. Allie breathed the crisp air, trying to clear her head as she made a right on the sidewalk, walking past the window without looking at it. She didn't want a reminder how she had failed to inspire the townspeople with her bid for Christmas memories. Maybe no one was in the mood this year. Except for Todd, with his jingle bell earring—knowing what the photo he'd hung on the tree meant to him touched her deeply.

Turning her collar up, Allie continued along the block, gaze glued to the place in front of her moving feet. She thrust her hands into her pockets, shoulders hunched against the chill of her thoughts as much as the dropping temperature of evening. People spoke to her and she nodded and smiled in automatic greeting, not lingering to chat. She had no destination in mind, except perhaps a rapid walk around the block and back inside again. Instead, she found herself crossing the intersection and striding up to Hannah's department store. She paused on the busy sidewalk, her eyes on the name carved long ago into the stone block of the building in old-fashioned lettering. She'd been coming to this store all her life, with her brother and parents as a child and later as an adult. Even though a shopping mall existed less than a half an hour away, it was to Hannah's she came first. Same with the bookstore. People patronized Connor Falls Book Emporium to purchase a physical book, rather than traveling to the huge conglomerate store or ordering online, and she was grateful to them for that. For the most part, Connor Falls' residents were long-term inhabitants who prided themselves on shopping locally. If not for their dedication, many of the icons of the community might have succumbed to the flagging economy.

Allie laughed out loud, causing a couple of folks to turn her way with uncertain smiles. She was beginning to sound exactly like her father—at least in her inner thoughts. Scary.

Wending her way closer to the nearest window,

Allie came to a halt in front of it. She studied the display with the same critical eye she used on her own, considering the yards and yards of fake snow, the huge, fake tree hung with brilliant balls, the oversized alphabet blocks, the wrapped gift boxes and, of course, particular items of interest displayed in the open ones. After a moment she took a single step back to view it as a whole, and not with the goal of comparison or judgment. Recalling how she used to look forward to the display every year as a child, running up to the glass and smudging it with her fingers in the same manner Lydia had smeared the plate glass of her undecorated window almost a week ago. In that instant, the old, remembered magic whipped through her like a flame and even though it only lasted an instant—that nostalgic joy of anticipation and wonder—the aftereffect remained warm in her heart.

"Looking for more inspiration?"

Allie refocused her gaze onto the reflection in the glass beside her where a tall, handsome man held the hand of a small, dark-haired girl beside him. "Nah," she said. "Just looking. It's lovely, isn't it?"

"It's magical," Lydia said. Allie smiled.

"Not that yours isn't," Luke hastened to add.

Allie winked at Lydia in the glass. "It's like being a kid again."

"I am a kid."

"I know," Allie said, "but I'm not. At least, I'm not supposed to be. But I think a big part of me still is."

"There's nothing wrong with being a kid. Is

there, Dad?"

"Nope," said Luke, smiling at Allie in the glass. "Not at all."

Allie met his gaze with a smile of her own before turning around to face them both. "What are you two doing? Something fun?"

Luke raised his hand and shook the bag clasped in his fingers. "Lights. To replace those I had. They're about ten years old anyway—before they started making strands that don't go out if only one bulb has blown. We'll save figuring out which one went for a summer project."

"That could be entertaining," Allie said. "Plugging in the Christmas lights in July."

Lydia tugged on her father's hand, pulling him away from the window. "Will you help us, Allie?"

Allie cocked her head at Lydia. "What? In July?"

"No, tonight, silly."

"I—" Allie glanced at Luke, then back down at Lydia. "I have to go back to the bookstore. Todd only lets me out for five minutes at a time."

"Todd's not your boss," Lydia announced in a long, slow drawl.

"I know. I'm teasing. But not about having to get back to work. I really do."

"Long days. You open and close?" Luke asked.

"During the holidays, yeah. Usually."

"How about after? It's Friday, so Lyddie gets to stay up late. We could watch a movie."

"With popcorn?" Lydia piped.

"With popcorn," Luke agreed. "Allie? What do you say?"

Allie searched Luke's eyes. "Are you sure?"

"We all have to live our lives. Yes, I'm sure."

*　　*　　*

Allie cut out early, leaving Todd to close the store once again. She really did need to give him a raise. He deserved one. Possibly the position of assistant manager, too. Not that there was an actual manager. She didn't have a title, but it would mean a lot to him to be officially called something and she could successfully argue the increase in salary when it came time to explain her decision to her parents.

She stopped at the bakery and bought half a dozen cookies. Seemed reasonable. Two each. Not an exorbitant amount of sugar at this hour. Besides, Gina's pumpkin-spice cookies were to die for.

When Allie arrived at Luke's home, the strands of white lights had been placed around the door and windows, as well as a set of what she presumed were battery-operated twinkle lights wrapped around the wreath. Gray wisps rose from the chimney against the night sky, seasoning the air with the scent of burning logs. Centered in the living room window a decorated tree sparkled behind glass. All the gaiety reminded her she hadn't gotten a single decoration in place at home. She didn't usually do a lot, but she liked a tree. It almost seemed a waste to get one this late.

Allie approached the door, the box of cookies tucked under her arm. She'd flossed, brushed and gargled with mouthwash in the bathroom at the store. Couldn't do anything about her clothes, though, short of going home, which would have taken way too much time. Besides, this wasn't a date. Not a romantic-type date. This was—this was what? A friendly evening, the three of them. She wouldn't think of it as anything more.

Lydia yanked the door open before Allie had the opportunity to knock. The varied scents of their earlier dinner wafted out along with the evergreen's fragrance. "Come on in! We're watching Sleeping Beauty!" With a squeal, Lydia rushed back toward the couch and leaped onto a cushion. She yanked a blanket off the arm and wrapped it around her body.

Allie stepped inside and closed the door. Luke appeared beside her.

"It's her favorite."

"Works for me," Allie said, handing him the box of cookies.

Although the couch would have held the three of them with room to spare, Allie shirked out of her coat and took the deep, soft chair next to the sofa. "Do you need help with anything?"

"Just grabbing the popcorn and we'll be set. Something to drink?"

"Do you have any type of cola? Although I don't usually indulge in caffeine at this hour, I don't want to fall asleep before the prince gets his girl."

Luke's deep, rich chuckle brought an irrational blush to her cheeks. Fortunately, he handed her the glass of soda without looking at her, then took his seat beside his daughter. He placed a heaping bowl of popcorn on the coffee table. "Lyddie, slide over closer to me so Allie can sit on the sofa with us. It'll be easier for her to reach the popcorn."

Self-consciously, Allie moved to the last cushion and sat, crossing her legs. A few seconds later she uncrossed them and reached for a handful of popcorn. The dvd had already been positioned in the player and after Allie reclined against the chair back, Luke hit *play*. She could sense his eyes on her. She tried to ignore him, but before long cut her eyes in his direction.

"Relax," he said. "And try to stay awake. I like when the prince gets the girl, too."

He tossed a purple throw in her direction. She snatched it from the air and spread it over her legs. The flames on the hearth made the room cozy, but the blanket seemed to be part of the ritual. Luke had one, too, which he balanced still folded on his knees once he stretched his long legs out, feet on the table. Lydia glanced up at her father, finger on her lips, before laying her head on a pillow on Luke's thigh. In a breathless falsetto, she hummed the brief opening refrain of "When You Wish Upon A Star" and settled down as the movie began.

Allie wondered what Todd would think if he could see her now, what he would impart to the ladies when they asked again after her emotional state. Not that it mattered. But she might give him a little fuel for his discussions. She might tell him she was happy.

Chapter Eight

Luke waited until the credits had rolled to their conclusion before moving his leg. Lyddie didn't make a sound, not even a mumble of protest. He stood and gathered her into his arms together with blanket, pillow and the stuffed rabbit she'd insisted they stop the movie in order for her to find. On the opposite end of the couch Allie slept draped across the arm, the blanket he'd given her tumbled around her feet on the floor. Up until a couple of minutes ago she'd been snoring like a puppy. He'd never tell her. At least not anytime soon.

Luke carried his daughter into her bedroom and tucked her into bed, waiting to be certain she wouldn't waken prior to his return to the living room. Lately, he'd been leaving the nightlight on. He'd heard mixed comments on that one, but he didn't care. She slept better with it on and the pennies in electricity weren't going to break him.

Allie didn't waken upon his approach. He eyed the couch, considering whether he could scoot her up onto the cushions, cover her up and leave her there, but decided things could get very weird very quickly if he did that. Besides the fact they hardly knew each other, he understood how disoriented she would be if she woke up here.

Crouching on his left knee near the couch, he looked at her. He really did like her short hair, so different from the long mass of curls of her teenaged years. Those had been attractive, too, but the flyaway, pixie strands framing her face these days had a definite appeal. He studied the shape of her eyes behind their closed lids, her long, reddish brown lashes, the freckles bridging her nose. He could kiss her awake like the prince in Sleeping Beauty, but she'd have every right to smack him if he did.

"Allie."

She didn't stir.

"Allison Roberts." He touched a strand of hair on her cheek, pushing it back.

Her eyes flew open, staring blankly ahead before focusing on him. With a gasp, she sat up and wiped her mouth with the back of her hand, blinking several times. "I'm sorry, Luke," she mumbled. "Some guest I am."

"It's all right. I expect you were tired." In fact, it was more than all right. Falling asleep like that meant she'd finally relaxed. And he wanted her to be comfortable around him, around the two of them, him and Lyddie, because he wanted Allie to come back again and again.

"What time is it?" She glanced aside at the empty couch. "Lydia's gone to bed?"

"She was sound asleep, too. I just carried her in."

She nodded, yawning. "So what time is it?"

"I don't know. Around ten-thirty, I think."

"So my secret is out. This is how I spend my Friday nights this time of year, passed out cold before ten."

He didn't want to tell her he'd had two late cups of coffee to make sure he didn't do the same. He stood, extending his hand. "Here, let me help you up. The bathroom's through there. You might want to splash your face, wake yourself up a bit. And you're perfectly welcome to stay here, if you're too tired to drive. As you've discovered, this couch is pretty comfy."

Standing beside him, she yawned again with a shake of her head. "I don't think I should."

"Your call. There are two cookies left. I'll heat up some water for tea and we'll eat them before you go."

She smiled, sleepy and amused. He imagined she might look like that most mornings and then dismissed the vision in his head, going to the kitchen to fill the teapot as she headed for the bathroom.

Five minutes later she returned, looking more awake, the hair around her face slightly damp. The kettle was coming to a boil and Luke quickly cut the flame beneath before the pot whistled and woke up Lydia. "Better?"

Allie took a seat at the island. "Better."

He poured steaming water into two mugs and gave her one, taking the seat next to her. "Some date, huh?"

She giggled. "Was that what it was?"

"Well, until the holidays are over, I think that's going to be the extent."

Allie lifted her mug and inhaled. Steam wafted toward her nostrils, no doubt fragrant with the tea bag floating in the water. "So, you still want to do this, then?"

"I still want to do this."

Her lips turned up, eyes crinkling at the corners. She took a sip of tea. He leaned in, planting a kiss on her temple.

"I like you, Allie. Lydia likes you. Which is, of course, my major concern, if things don't, well…you know."

"I know." Allie picked up one of the cookies and bit into it, chewing with an expression of mild euphoria. "Gina makes the best bakery cookies."

"It might have been better if Lydia hadn't met you, didn't know you, because I could keep this part of my life separate from family life."

Allie took another bite, talking around it. "But if she hadn't met me, it's not likely you and I would have run into each other again, is it?"

"And you wouldn't have confessed to kissing me."

"You kissed me, Luke Hollis."

"That I did." He kissed her again, on the corner of her mouth, catching a cookie crumb on his tongue from her lip. "I tried to talk to you after, but you avoided me."

"I was embarrassed."

"So was I. I couldn't believe I'd been such a jerk and you'd broken your wrist because of it."

She waved the hand clutching the half-eaten cookie. "Still works, so no harm done."

"And do you still skate, Allie-better-than-Allison?"

Setting her mug down, she turned to look at him, her wide eyes reflecting the overhead light. "No."

The muscles in his abdomen tightened in response to that single word. He couldn't help remembering again the way she moved on the ice, graceful and at ease, arms fluid, legs engaged in effortless maneuvering, as if she didn't have to give a single thought to what her body needed to do to propel itself across the slick frozen surface. "Not because of—"

"No. Goodness, no. I…I just ran out of time for that." She appeared bewildered by the admission. Luke removed the cookie from her left hand and slipped his fingers around her own.

"Let's do it together then. Lyddie wants to go out on the pond, too, but I think the first time it should be just you and me. Like a real date."

She frowned. "Tonight?"

Luke laughed, swiftly stifling the loud noise and lowering his voice. "The pond's not frozen yet, but with the trough of arctic air moving in, it should be soon enough. Once the pond is solid, that'll be our first, real date. Deal?"

She grinned and nodded. "Deal."

Luke pushed back the stool and stood. "I'm

thinking before another long day, you might want to head home and get some sleep. Are you okay to drive?"

"Perfectly."

He retrieved her coat and held it out for her to put on. She clamped the remains of the cookie between her teeth and slipped her arms into the sleeves of the garment. He zipped it up for her, fingers lingering at her chin. "I'll walk you out."

Outside, their breath mingled in a clouded dance. He'd come out without a jacket and hunched into himself against the frigid temperatures as they kissed goodnight. Overhead the stars stood out in brilliant clarity.

"Sunday is early closing, isn't it?" he called after her as she headed for her car.

She turned, walking backwards. "It is, but I have extra people on the weekends anyway, so I could leave a little early. Why?"

"Come back and have dinner. I'll make something special."

She stopped walking. "You cook? Well, of course you do." Her laughter filled the silence of the night. "I'll see you Sunday then."

Luke watched Allie's car until it was out of sight. He stood a moment longer, listening to the fading sound of the engine until that, too, was gone. As he headed inside, he told himself everything would be all right.

*　　*　　*

"Thank you, Mrs. Brennan." Allie waved at the woman as she left the shop, and then took the photo she had supplied and climbed into the window to attach it with a ribbon to the tree.

"How many is that now?" Todd asked. "Counting mine."

Allie looked the tree over. "Counting yours? Nine."

"Nine? Are you kidding me?"

"Nope. Maybe people don't have as many fond memories as I'd hoped."

"Or they're just too busy to hunt them up. Like somebody else I know."

Allie jumped from the window to the floor, hastening to grab the nearest display to stop it from wobbling. "I need to go over to my parents and look through the old photo albums. And yes, I haven't had the time."

"Right. What about tonight? You're leaving early."

"Did I tell you I was making you assistant manager? I think I've had a change of heart."

"You can't do that. I'm sure there are laws against such a thing."

"I'm sure there aren't." Allie returned to her place behind the counter. "But I wouldn't dream of taking back your promotion. You've done a good job for me."

Todd said nothing, staring at her with his hands on his hips.

"What?"

"Are you in love with your old crush?"

Allie frowned, blindly rearranging a stack of

brochures on the counter. "Are you saying you think my business decisions have been based on my love life, such as it is?"

"No. I'm just wondering if you're happy." Sticking his hands in his pockets, Todd sauntered toward the back of the store, calling over his shoulder. "Don't forget the pie in the fridge before you leave."

Right. The pie. She'd "made" a pie instead of buying one, a tasty treat she'd loved as a kid and figured Lydia would enjoy as well—chocolate pudding in a graham cracker crust. Not very grown up, but what the heck. After talking with Luke twice, he still hadn't told her what he was making, so she couldn't show up with something that might complement dinner. Apparently, he wanted to surprise her. As soon as Bridget returned from her evening meal to man the store with Todd, Allie would head over to Luke's. If she got there early enough, she could lend a hand with the preparations.

*　*　*

"Set the table, Lyddie."

When he didn't receive an answer, Luke turned from stirring the simmering contents of the pot on the burner to see where she'd gone. She stood exactly where he'd seen her last, staring at him.

"We're eating at the table?"

"Of course we're eating at the table. Allie's company. When Nana and Poppy come to eat, don't we sit at the table? Can't use the counter all the time, sweetie."

He saw her eyes shift a little and knew she was trying not to look at the framed photo by the fireplace of the three of them—him, Lydia, Zoe—at the table. He'd seen her looking at it before, many times. Always her gaze drifted to her mother. He wondered if she saw what he did in that picture, or if her young mind sought and found something entirely different. Something she wanted. Something she needed to see.

But no, Lydia saw the truth like no other. It was her gift and the core of her heartache.

"Do you think she'll come for Christmas, Dad?"

He knew she didn't mean Allie. Letting a breath out, he crossed the floor and crouched down in front of his daughter. "I don't know."

"We'll call though, right?"

"If you'd like." So seldom did Lydia receive an answer when she called her mother's number, though, it wasn't likely she'd reach Zoe on Christmas either, especially since he still didn't know what had transpired during the last mother-daughter conversation. "I'm sure she'll be waiting to hear from you on Christmas," he lied, rising, touching Lydia's hair in passing. "We'll sing her a song on the phone, how's that? Think of a good one."

"Jingle Bells. We used to sing it together, remember?"

Compressing his lips, Luke nodded and went back to the stove. "Set the table, Lydia. I'm putting the water on to boil now."

As Lydia took the dishes off the counter and distributed them around the table, Luke filled the pot at the sink, thinking about Allie. Was he making a mistake, beginning a relationship with her when so much remained unresolved in his life? In Lydia's?

"Do you like her, Dad?"

"Your mom?" he asked, wanting so much not to have to answer that question.

"No, silly. Allie."

Luke set the pot on the stove and closed his eyes. "Yes."

"I do, too. It's not wrong, is it, Dad?"

"Of course it isn't. We like many people in the course of our lives."

"But we don't love them all. What happens when they don't love us back?"

Ah, Lydia and her uncannily direct and un-childlike questions. "It hurts and we learn to live with it." At Lydia's lack of response, Luke turned from the stove, discovering his eight-year-old in silent, adult tears. He rushed to her across the floor, gathering her up against his chest. She threw her thin arms around his neck.

"Oh, pumpkin, I'm so sorry."

She hugged him tight. "Mommy hurt you, too, didn't she?"

"We're grown-ups. It's different."

"I want to be grown up, Daddy. I want to be grown up now."

Oh, no you don't, Lyddie. You stay young for as long as you can, because even though the greatest hurts are there, that's also where you'll find the deepest magic. He kissed the side of her head, the fine, dark hairs tickling his nose. At a tentative knock on the door, Luke carried his weeping daughter over to answer it. If Allie was going to be in their lives, she would have to get used to the occasional drama.

When he opened the door, though, Allie wasn't standing on the other side.

*   *   *

Allie turned up the long driveway to Luke's. He'd left the chain down and coiled to the side in anticipation of her arrival. In the passenger seat of her car, the pie sat with a wad of tissues beneath one edge to keep it level. She'd driven carefully to avoid stopping short and ending up with chocolate pudding plastered across her glove box. As she neared the front of the house she saw the Christmas lights lit once again and a vehicle next to Luke's truck. Maybe his parents had stopped by. After she parked and climbed out, pie balanced across her palm and a quick hip-check to shut the driver's side door, she realized by the plates on the other car that it was a rental. She glanced up at the house. The front door stood wide open.

She climbed with hesitant steps to the porch, pausing at the door to knock on the jamb. The overhead lights in the kitchen illuminated a meal in the making, steam rising from a huge pot, plates on the table, a variety of dishes and utensils on the counter. At a noise like the sniffling of a contained sob, Allie leaned forward to peer into a living room lit only by the lights on the Christmas tree and the glow of the kitchen fixture. Near the fireless hearth Luke stood with Lydia in his arms, both of them embraced by the stunning woman from the photographs, and all of them crying.

Zoe had come home.

Chapter Nine

Dazed, Allie slapped her hand across the coffee table's surface, seeking her phone. She'd had the foresight to set the alarm, but not to put the damned thing where she could reach it. Figuring she might need extra incentive for rising, she'd also chosen the most annoying tone. And now, of course, it wouldn't stop.

Allie swung her legs from the sofa cushions and sat up, squinting in the early light. Locating the phone, she grabbed the device and turned the alarm off. Her gaze strayed to the empty pie plate and soiled fork lying in a gob of chocolate pudding beside it on the coffee table. Vaguely, she remembered finishing off the remains of the two-day old pie last night. No wonder she felt sick.

She closed her eyes at the memory of sneaking away from Luke's open front door to her car like a thief in the night. When she'd pulled from the parking space and looked forward again, she'd found Luke standing in the driveway inches from the car's hood.

Allie, I'll call you.

It was all right. She understood. At least, she told anyone who asked her—since apparently everyone within her circle of friends, acquaintances and customers had somehow gotten wind of Zoe's return, as well as Allie's tentative involvement with Luke—that she understood. The logical, mature portion of her brain did recognize without doubt the importance of a child reunited with her mother. The other part, the part that was perhaps still fourteen years old, couldn't help but dwell on the image of Luke weeping in the arms of his ex-wife and the fact his words *I'll call you* were the last she'd heard from him.

"Oh stop being an idiot. You're going to be late for work."

Late, she couldn't be. Today what she called her 'last hurrah shipment' was due and she wanted to make sure the books received were displayed to the best advantage. After that, she had plenty of other things to take care of. Really, this time of the year wasn't the most opportune for starting a relationship anyway. She had more things to do than she had hours in the day. Look at her house. Not a single decoration in place. Tonight when she got home, that would be exactly the task for her— yanking out boxes and placing the contents in all the traditional places around the cottage. It would look like Christmas in here whether she liked it or not.

With a sigh, Allie gathered up the mess from the coffee table and dropped it in the kitchen sink, then went upstairs to dress for her day.

*   *   *

Luke hoisted the wrapped tree into Sheila Jefferson's open trunk. He watched her pull down the driveway and waved as she reached the bottom. Fortunately, the woman didn't have far to drive with the tree sticking out like that.

"It's cold out here."

Luke glanced aside at his ex-wife. "Yep. It tends to do that in December. In Pennsylvania, anyway. What's it like in California?" He shoved his hands into his pockets. A strange sort of day, weather-wise. Damp and chilly, but he couldn't tell if snow was in the offing or rain. Zoe touched his arm. His whole body went stiff.

"What time does Lydia get home?"

"Same time as yesterday. Same time as last year. Three-forty-five."

"Are you angry with me, Luke?"

Luke turned to look at her. She tossed her head, long, shiny brown hair drifting over the shoulder of a rather insubstantial jacket. "I am, Zoe. How can I not be? I don't need you any more in my life, but Lyddie does. And you…you haven't been there."

She slipped her hand into his pocket, burrowing her curled fingers into his palm. "I could stay. I could stay if you want me to."

"Don't make this about us, Zoe. Don't waste

your time and mine." Luke stepped away. Zoe's hand dropped to her thigh. Zoe was one of the few women he knew who stood nearly eye to eye with him. He couldn't imagine where Lydia's diminutive height came from. His mother's side probably. Strange thing, genetics.

"What are you thinking about?"

Luke hunched his shoulders beneath his coat. "Nothing."

"I'd like us to try. Why couldn't we try?"

"I have an extra coat hanging in the mudroom. Why don't you put it on, so you don't freeze while you're waiting for Lydia's bus?"

"See?" She backed away from him with her hands in the rear pockets of her dark jeans. "You do still care."

Luke blew a long breath over his lips and headed toward the barn. There, he picked up the cast off greens and threw them in the bin. Frank observed him from a short distance. Luke deliberately ignored the man's expression.

"You all right, boss?"

"Fine."

"You don't look fine."

"I said—"

"In fact, you look mighty troubled. It's that wife of yours, isn't it?"

"Ex-wife, Frank." At the sound of the bus pulling up, Luke turned his attention to the road. Zoe stood at the end of the driveway, a faraway, narrow figure swimming in his coat, arms wrapped around the waist to cinch it in as she waited for the doors to open. When they did, Lydia bounded out and straight into her mother's embrace. Luke's heart contracted. For so long, even before Zoe headed west to California, it had been him and Lyddie, day in and day out. He didn't know what to do with the strange, sudden emptiness in him.

"Lydia's happy to have her mom back," Frank said beside him.

"Zoe wants to work things out."

"Between the two of you?"

"That's the gist."

"And?"

"I don't want any part of that." This time, though, Luke would be the bad guy if Zoe left again. Lydia would blame him for not taking Zoe back into their lives. Because his gut told him that would be the way it would play out. All or nothing.

Turning on his heel, he snatched up a log from the ground, tossing it as he spun. The wood landed in the bin with a shuddering bang. Apologizing to Frank, Luke stormed off up the hill into the evergreens.

Lydia found him hours later, once he'd returned to the barn. He'd been doing a good deal of nothing in order not to return to the house. While he'd been expending energy on useless tasks, it had occurred to him his mistake had been letting Zoe think she had a right to stay with them during her visit. He should have packed her off that first night to a hotel.

"Daddy?"

"Hey, pumpkin."

Lydia hopped up onto a sawhorse and sat, swinging her legs. "Dinner will be ready soon.

Mommy ran out for a loaf of bread."

"Mom's making dinner?"

"Yep. And we're baking cookies after."

"That's nice."

"Are you mad at Mommy?"

Luke crouched down, eyeing the line of a board he'd been sanding. To what purpose, he had no idea. "Sort of," he said.

Lydia said nothing, her gaze glued to him, feet in pink boots swinging back and forth. Luke glanced in her direction.

"What are we having for dinner?"

"Lasagna."

With a nod, Luke straightened up and returned to sanding. "Mommy can't stay here. You understand that, right? We're not married anymore. If she's really going to stick around, she'll have to get an apartment in town and we can set up a schedule."

"A schedule?"

This was not something he should be discussing with his eight-year-old daughter. He knew that. Setting the sanding block down, he turned to face her. "I forgot my afterschool hug, didn't I?"

With a hop off the sawhorse, Lydia darted into his arms. He picked her up and snuggled her close, breathing in the cold air and shampoo fragrance of her hair. "What's the weather report say, kiddo?"

"I dunno. I didn't watch today. Do you think we'll be able to skate soon?"

"I think it's a sure bet by Christmas."

Lydia squealed right in his ear. He winced.

"Sorry, Dad. Will Allie skate with us?"

Luke didn't answer. He wasn't sure why his daughter asked the question. In all of this, he hadn't forgotten about Allie, not for a single minute, but he'd been trying not to think of her. Allie Roberts was a complication she'd never meant to be. He missed her all the more because of that.

*   *   *

Allie fidgeted with the three photos on the counter. She'd tied ribbon through the holes punched in each but hadn't yet taken the time to climb into the window and hang them on the tree. This trio brought the total to twenty-two. Not exactly what she'd envisioned when she first put up the sign. Better than zero, she supposed. She could fill in the rest of the branches with the cinnamon sticks she'd originally brought in when Lydia was supposed to help her.

At the thought of Lydia, and subsequently Luke, Allie sighed. Todd looked up from his perusal of the hoagie he was deciding whether to eat. "Are you going to hang those up or what?"

"In a minute."

"Where's yours? You still haven't brought one in."

"I know," Allie said. "I will."

"When? Fourth of July?"

"Maybe." She jerked her chin at Todd's sandwich. "Eat that, will you? You know the lull doesn't usually last long."

Marching out from behind the counter, she

headed for the window. Once there, she clutched the three photos against her chest and watched the people passing by outside. She had half-expected Lydia would insist on bringing her mother in to the store, but Allie had seen neither hide nor hair of the ex Mrs. Luke and her daughter, or of Luke either. Several times Allie had been tempted to call him, but that seemed ridiculously needy and meddlesome. He needed this time. They all did.

Allie pulled over the stepstool and climbed into the window, taking care not to trample the artificial snow. She hung the photographs, making sure they faced outward, and paused before exiting to eye the skates leaning against the painted log. She hadn't put on those skates for several years. She suddenly hankered for the feeling of the blades beneath her feet as she sped across the ice. Luke had talked about that being their first real date, a night of skating. She had no idea if it would happen now. It might do her a world of good to make that date with herself.

A tap sounded on the window. Allie jerked around, her mind immediately going to Lydia Hollis. Instead she found the woman she'd been dreading, leggy and beautiful, silky hair long, eyes the color of smoke.

Zoe raised her hand in a hesitant wave, yelling through the glass. "Are you Allie?"

Heart pounding, Allie nodded.

"May I talk with you for a minute?"

"Sure. I'll be right out."

Allie didn't even bother with her jacket. She stood on the sidewalk with her arms wrapped around a sweater too thin for the weather, trying hard to keep her teeth from chattering.

"We weren't introduced the other night. I'm Zoe Hollis."

So, she still went by her married name. Allie grimaced, turning it into a smile before the woman noticed. "Allie Roberts." She shook Zoe's hand, withdrawing her fingers as soon as possible in order to tuck them back under her arm pit. Goodness, it was turning into a frigid evening.

"Don't you want to go inside?"

"I'm good."

"I wanted to thank you for helping out with Lydia these past few days."

Allie nodded. She hadn't really been helping out, but whatever.

"I…I realize I've failed Lydia the last couple of years. And Luke. But I'm back now."

Allie nodded again, more slowly, stomach churning in anticipation of where the conversation was headed.

"Lydia seems fond of you. She's talked about you quite a bit. And yet…I don't…I want us to heal. I appreciate all you've done, but I think that healing would best take place without any distractions. You understand me, don't you?"

"I'm not sure that I do." Allie's teeth clacked together and she tightened her jaw. At this rate, she was going to come down with pneumonia.

"I think you should leave Luke and Lydia to me now. You should, well, go back to your own life."

"Huh." Allie arched her brows. "All right."

Without saying goodbye, Allie started back into

the store, but paused at the door. She faced Zoe, who watched her with a peculiar expression. "That's all well and good," Allie said, "but no matter what else you may decide to do with your life, you have to stop treating your daughter as if she's disposable. She loves you, you know."

Allie spun and yanked open the door. She walked past Todd and Emma, barely sparing them a glance, and slipped inside the bathroom, closing the door quietly. Two seconds later there was a knock.

"Go away."

"Are you okay?" Todd. Good old Todd.

"Yeah. Just give me a minute. I'm trying not to throw up."

* * *

Zoe had shouted from the front door five minutes ago that dinner was ready. Reluctant to leave the barn and Lydia's animated, one-sided conversation, Luke took his time. But he couldn't be rude. After securing the barn door, he grasped Lydia's hand in his and walked slowly across the hard-packed ground beneath the last light of evening, a blue like Lydia's eyes. Like his own. Zoe's were pale and striking, definitely the stuff of movie stars. And Allie's? Melted chocolate in candle light.

"What's so funny, Dad?"

"Just something I was thinking."

"Do you know how long Mommy is staying?"

"I don't, honey." As usual, Zoe hadn't made clear her plans. Perhaps she had none. Her spontaneity, her one-day-at-a-time attitude had endeared him when they first met. Not so much after Lydia's birth, and definitely not in the stretch of time leading up to their divorce.

"I hope she stays until Christmas."

If Zoe returned to California, free-spirited and neglectful of her daughter's needs, it would be a massive setback for Lydia. And yet he couldn't let Zoe blackmail him with that into taking her back. Sure, he wanted her in Lydia's life. Just not in his.

As he entered through the mudroom so he could remove his dirty coat and boots, the smell of homemade sauce hit him. He inhaled, deeply. Zoe was doing her best to make it hard for him to turn her out. He wondered how badly things had gone for her in California. There had to be a reason she'd come back, something more than his conversation with her or hers with Lydia. Or was he being too harsh?

Lyddie preceded him into the kitchen. When Luke followed, he almost tripped over his stationary daughter. Lydia appeared transfixed by her mother, who stood in front of the stove slowly returning her phone to her pocket, her face shining with moisture from the heat of the oven, her silver-gray eyes alight. Zoe stared for a long moment at Lydia before raising her gaze to meet his.

"Luke, we have to talk."

"Yeah," he said. "We do."

Chapter Ten

Allie spun the papier-mâché reindeer one way and then the other on the table top. She'd made it oh-so-many-years ago when she'd been in an artsy phase, painting the lop-sided body a lovely shade of lavender, hooves and antlers a deep teal, with wires through the ears dangling silver jingle bells. A silly thing, but this had always signified Christmas to her. When she put the reindeer out, the season had begun. Why she'd hadn't displayed it sooner she wasn't certain, but Todd's words as she left the store had galvanized her.

"Get off your ass, woman, and start celebrating Christmas. You don't need a man for that."

She laughed again in an attempt to lift her mood still further, and released the deer, taking a step back for a better view. The reindeer tumbled sideways and fell from the table. With a frown, she picked it up. Some damned critter had chewed the back hoof off.

Allie released a breath through her nose, reaching for a coaster. After positioning not one, but two coasters beneath the leg to make the reindeer level, she dropped onto the cushion of the couch, studying the boxes spread across the living room floor, all of them open and revealing fake greenery, glittery balls, snow globes, figurines. She looked at the glass of sparkling wine she'd poured herself, light reflecting in the tiny bubbles. With a decisive movement she stood, turned off the overhead fixture and climbed the stairs to bed.

In less than ten minutes, Allie was burrowed beneath the mounded quilt, lights off. The illuminated numbers on the alarm clock sent a green glow into the night. Quarter to eleven. She wouldn't have the energy to stay up for the eleven o'clock news again until the middle of January.

Awakening at what felt like the small hours of the night, Allie listened for the sound that had roused her from slumber. She didn't hear anything. The cottage was silent. Absolutely silent. Not even the hum of the refrigerator or the tick of hot water through the baseboard. Allie glanced at the clock, finding the face blank. She sat up and turned the light switch on the bedside lamp. Nothing. The chill of a cooling house danced along her arm.

Well, another blanket would keep her until morning. In a minute, she'd get up and retrieve a second comforter from the closet. For now, she could snuggle back into the leftover warmth trapped beneath the covers and enjoy the silence. She gave a brief thought to her parents in their home at the far side of the property—funny, how many families did that around Connor Falls, generations building on the same piece of land, staying close—until she recalled they'd gone to Florida. Back in time for New Year's, they'd promised cheerily. In the meantime, she was responsible for their house as well.

Allie pushed her arm back out into the cold and snatched her cell phone from the nightstand. Due to the frequency of outages, she had the electric company in her contacts and brought up their number, the whirring ring the only sound in the night. After five of them, the automated message came on. Allie dutifully pushed the proper digits, first to report the outage and then to listen to the status. The outage, the voice told her, was due to weather conditions in her area. Weather conditions?

Allie leaped out of bed and ran to the window, where she pushed aside the curtains. Hard to see, but the tree nearest to the house appeared to be gleaming. Ice. Crap. Not one person who had come into the store had mentioned an ice storm on its way. Discovering the cell phone still in her hand, Allie turned it over to view the time. Three forty-five. No point in trying to go back to sleep. She'd normally be up for the day in little more than an hour anyway.

Dressing in her warmest clothes, Allie ticked off in her mind the things she needed to do. First, set all the faucets in the house to drip, just in case the outage and the frigid temperatures persisted long enough to freeze the pipes. Unplug most of the appliances to avoid a surge when the electricity came back on. Then she would head over to her folks' to do the same thing there. She'd start their generator to make sure it worked after two seasons of inactivity. Hopefully she wouldn't have to use it.

Having accomplished what she needed to in her own home, she put fresh batteries in the flashlight and slipped it into the pocket of her ancient parka, followed by the keys to both houses and her cell. At the door, she pushed her feet into heavy-soled, waterproof boots for the trek across the fields. Until the sun came up and the roads were treated, she wouldn't be taking her car anywhere.

After locking the door behind her, she yanked on her gloves and reached out with one foot to test the surface of the porch steps. They were slick as a rink, the ice too thick to break up by stomping on it. She added another thing to her list: Ice Melt from her parents' garage. Traversing the steps and the slippery concrete pad at the base, Allie made it to the grass. Crunchy underfoot, the vegetation provided more stability for walking than any smoother surface. With a quick re-check of her pockets, she headed out into the night, freezing rain pelting her covered head and shoulders like thrown pebbles.

*　*　*

"Dad! Daddy! It's freezing in here!"

With a grumble, Luke rolled over. "Climb in, pumpkin." He flipped back the covers. Lydia dove into the bed beside him, preceded by a blast of chill air. "Wow," he said, "it is cold. Did the heater stop working?"

"Dunno." Lydia burrowed against his side, pressing her face into the fabric of his T-shirt. Luke glanced toward the clock as he slid his arm around her.

"Did you knock the clock on the floor?"

"Nope. Where's Mommy? She's not on the couch."

"She went to a hotel. Don't you remember?"

"Right." Lydia became silent, digging her ice cube toes into his thigh through his pajama bottoms.

"It'll be all right, Lyddie. Didn't we talk about this?"

Lydia nodded against his ribs. The discussion with Zoe had been a tough one, but everything had to be said. Afterward, he'd spoken with Lydia about Zoe's move to a hotel room until she'd figured out what she was doing. The phone call Lydia had walked in on had been from Zoe's agent in California. He had expected her to race out the door for the very next flight, but she hadn't. Maybe she really had changed.

Luke squinted at the nightstand. He caught the vague, boxy shadow of the clock, but no numbers. The electric was off. Once upon a time, he'd kept a windup clock on the nightstand, too, but Lydia had laid claim to it one morning and he hadn't seen it since. He did, however, still have a watch and he pulled it close to check the time. He groaned.

"I've got to get up. I'll start a fire in the fireplace and you can sit in front of it when it's toasty."

"What's going on, Dad? Why is it so cold in here? And dark? Is the electric off again?"

"Yep," said Luke. "Afraid so." He pulled his jeans on over his sleep pants and shoved his bare feet into a pair of sneakers, then slipped into the sweatshirt jacket he yanked from the open closet. Heading through the house to the back door, he paused a moment to peer at the patio through the glass. Rain and sleet pummeled the frozen pavers, forming a vast, treacherous sheet of water-covered ice. On the far side, a tarp covered the split logs stacked against the garage wall. With a muttered expletive, he retraced his steps to the living room and grabbed the flashlight from the mantel. The supply of wood in the basket beside the hearth was minimal but would have to do for now. Rather than risk breaking his neck, he laid the small stack across the andirons and lit the kindling beneath. As soon as he had the flames leaping high, he rose from his knees and went in search of the radio.

Lydia appeared in the hallway, trailing the blanket from his bed around her shoulders and to the floor. She walked past him and went straight to the raised hearth where she sat, the blanket wrapped around her legs. "I looked out your window. It's pretty yucky out there. Do you think I'll have school?"

"As soon as I find the blasted radio, I'll let you know."

"Try the pantry. That's where you put it last time."

"The pantry. Right."

The cell phone rang. Luke snatched it off the dead charger and tucked it against his ear as he shined the flashlight inside the disorganized pantry. "Hello?"

"Luke, it's Frank. Where the hell did this crap come from?"

"I don't know. Last I heard was rain. You have electric?"

"It's flickered a few times, but its holding. Apparently the roads are hazardous. Beth's been called in early to work due to the accidents of the insane. I'm heading out to put the chains on now so I can get her there. I just wanted to let you know I'm not sure what time I'll make it to your place."

"Don't worry about it. I appreciate the call. Hey, did you happen to hear what they're doing about school?"

"Two-hour delay, but it wouldn't surprise me if they call it for the day, soon."

"Thanks, Frank. Be safe, okay?"

"Yep, you too," said Frank, and hung up.

Luke set the phone on the counter and turned to face his daughter. She stared back at him, knees jumping in anticipation beneath the blanket. "Two hours, as of now. You can either curl up in front of the fire to sleep for a bit longer, or I can make us some oatmeal on the stove."

"Oatmeal!"

Strange kid, Luke thought with a smile. He removed a box of wooden matches from the drawer and lit the burner on the gas stove, preparing to make them both breakfast.

*   *   *

It had taken Allie a lot longer than she'd hoped to cross the fields to her parents' house, and the frozen precipitation hadn't let up. She felt chilled to the bone, her parka was saturated, and her feet had gone numb inside her boots. Once she got to the house, she couldn't hope for any respite, and she still had to go back to her own place after. She began to think she should have risked the car out on the road. At this rate, she'd end up with hypothermia.

Spotting a long, darkly shining strip in the landscape, she realized she'd reached the driveway. She walked in the grass alongside the glazed blacktop all the way to the garage, then went behind and chipped the ice from the doorknob in order to insert the key. Once inside, she crossed the garage to the interior door and unlocked that one as well. She shirked out of her parka as she stepped into the house where she and her brother had grown up. Compared to the outside, the temperature inside the kitchen felt downright balmy. She knew it wouldn't for long, though. Her best bet was to borrow a dry sweatshirt and socks from her mother's drawer before she did anything else.

Once she'd changed—adding a pair of sweatpants to the ensemble before throwing all her wet clothes over the shower curtain rod—Allie went to the living room. She hadn't planned to stay any longer than necessary, but wood had been laid in the hearth of the fireplace prior to her parents' departure for Florida. She couldn't find any kindling, so rolled up a couple of pages of newspaper and shoved them under the logs and lit them. Huddling close to what was, at best, a meager conflagration, Allie warmed her hands.

Maybe if she stuck around a while, the electricity would be restored and she wouldn't have to spend the day worrying about the water spigots she'd left open in the bathrooms and kitchen. Either that or the temperature would rise enough that freezing would no longer be a consideration. Then, the roads would merely be wet and she could drive her car into town without being white-knuckled or, worse, finding herself in a ditch somewhere.

Allie rose from the hearth as the logs caught. She put the screen in place and sat on the couch after pulling the afghan from the back of it. She spread the crocheted length over her legs and up to her shoulders, breathing in the scent of her mother's perfume trapped in the yarn. In the silence, she heard nothing but the crackling of the flames and the intermittent drip of water from the kitchen faucet. Soon that, too, would cease, as the pipes emptied.

Allie leaned her head back against the cushions of the couch and closed her eyes, spending a few self-pitying moments thinking about Luke. She would have enjoyed getting to know him. For a little extra torture, she pictured running her fingers through his soft, dark hair. He'd worn it shorter back in high school. She liked the way he wore it now. Lydia resembled him in coloration more than she did Zoe. Allie thought about that, too—the circumstances of Luke's breakup with his wife. Though the fault was likely the result of the sticky threads of two lives entwined and pulling apart, what Allie found bewildering was the fact Luke's ex-wife had left not only him, but their daughter. Not that it mattered now. Zoe was back and apparently planned to stay.

Well, there was no use crying over spilled milk, or whatever the stupid saying was. While she was biding time in her parents' house, she ought to look through some of the photo albums and choose a memory of her own for the tree in the display window. She'd let it go long enough. Todd was starting to lose patience.

Smiling at the thought of Todd at his wit's end,

Allie pulled the albums from the shelf under the coffee table and set them on top. By flashlight and firelight, she started with the oldest, which began prior to her earliest memories here in this house. Soon, she came to baby pictures of herself and Jimmy, and birthday parties, and flipped through to find a photo of her first time on ice skates. Picking out one photo representative of a cherished memory was going to prove difficult and time-consuming. She should wrap the albums in a garbage bag as protection against the weather and take them home. Lugging them across the fields didn't seem prudent either, however. Perhaps after the store closed she could drive back and grab them.

Undecided and unwilling to venture back into the sleet and cold, Allie continued to peruse the old photos. She had to wait for the fire to die down, anyway. She certainly wouldn't leave the house until she was assured of that.

Outside, the weather seemed to be undergoing a change. Ice pellets rapped against window glass with increasing intensity. A rising wind howled across the chimney and echoed down the stones. Allie glanced aside at the flames and saw them shiver in the updraft. Last time she'd watched the weather report had been three days ago. How could something like this come up so unexpectedly?

Allie gathered up the albums and carried them to the kitchen counter, where she inserted them one by one into a plastic bag for retrieval later that night. Wind whistled through a gap in the kitchen window frame. She'd have to talk to Mom and Dad about that. If not mistaken, the wind had been making a shrill calling through that same breach since she was a kid.

With her thoughts on repairs and one hand on the bag of albums, Allie reached for her parka. It was her very last thought before the world exploded.

Chapter Eleven

"Are you worried, Dad?"

"About what, Lyddie?" Luke peered through the smear left by ice-crusted wiper blades across the windshield. He turned off the truck radio to aid in his concentration. The sound of tire chains crunching along the slick roadway distracted him enough.

"About Allie not answering her phone."

"No. Like I said, she probably forgot to charge it. She'll be happy to see us, though. How will she get to work in this mess without a ride, right?"

"Right," Lydia agreed quietly.

Odd, how both he and Lydia had spoken Allie's name at the same time while sitting at the island eating their oatmeal. He couldn't even remember what he'd been about to say. He only knew that after her name had died in the air between them, leaving them staring at each other with spoons of congealing oatmeal gripped in their fingers, he had set his down and gone straight for his phone.

Receiving no answer from Allie, he'd calmly banked the fire and shut and secured the glass doors across the fire well, then told Lydia to get dressed, to bundle up. He blew out the candles, took Lydia's hand, headed out to the truck, stopping for the first aid kit on the way. Now why the hell had he done that?

His stomach churned, thinking of time lost as he'd put the chains on the pickup's tires. No choice, though, as he couldn't get anywhere on these roads without them.

Clutching his phone in her hand, Lydia looked down at the screen and directed him to take the next right. He cut off the expletive that flew to his tongue when he saw the incline. Downshifting, he felt the chains grind in. The truck crept up the hill, maintaining a slow but steady speed.

"According to this, Dad, there should be a driveway on the left soon."

"Okay, sweetie." Somewhere around ten minutes ago, he'd bitten down hard on the inside of his cheek. He could still taste blood.

Spotting the driveway, he steered onto gravel, making slow progress toward the front of a small cottage. Liberally coated in ice, Allie's car sat parked beside it. Luke stopped the truck, pulled up the parking brake.

"Stay here, Lyddie. I mean it. Stay right here and wait for me."

He climbed out and made his way to the front

door. Shielding his eyes from the headlights of his pickup, he looked through the oval glass window. Nothing moved inside. Of course, she could be sound asleep, unaware of the weather. The house sounded too quiet for her to have electric. She'd be happy they hadn't let her oversleep. Yes, she'd be happy about that.

Lifting his fist, he pounded on the door. He couldn't rid himself of the overwhelming sense of urgency. Please Allie, he begged silently, just come down and answer the door.

Suddenly he felt a hand on his sleeve, tugging at his arm. Unclenching his fingers, he stared down at his daughter. "Lydia, didn't I tell you—"

"Daddy, look over there."

Luke turned his head to follow the direction of Lydia's pointing. He sucked in a sharp breath. Over the rise the clouds were being lit from below by a vicious orange glow.

"That isn't the sun, is it Dad."

*　　*　　*

"Hold on tight, Lyddie."

Forgoing a return to the road, Luke gripped the wheel tightly with both hands as he drove the truck straight across the fields, feeling the chains rip through frozen grass to the turf beneath. Directing Lydia to dial 9-1-1, he had her hold the phone up to his ear while he gave an approximate location to the dispatcher and told her something was on fire. The woman informed him they'd received a call from a neighbor, as well, and that fire trucks were on route, if not there already.

He didn't let up on the gas pedal. 'If not there already' wasn't good enough for him.

"What'd they say?"

"It's the Roberts' place. Allie's parents' house. It's on fire."

Lydia made a little squeak. Luke risked a glance at her. Moisture stood out along her lashes.

"Don't worry," he said. "Everything will be all right."

He didn't believe that for one minute.

*   *   *

Allie felt herself floating. She knew the sensation. It was familiar to her. Her arms stretched out to either side for balance. A beginner's trick. Her legs moved smoothly, though, her ankles not wobbling at all as she pushed off on one foot, then the other, on her brand new skates. After a moment she opened her eyes. Pristine and white, ice stretched as far as she could see beneath the pearly sky. The wind seared her face, making it sting. The sound of the wind, her blades, was muffled. Of course. She wore her new earmuffs over her ears, red plaid and lined with sheep's wool. She'd gotten them for Christmas. Before long, she felt as if she'd been skating forever, and leaped and spun, then tipped her head back, forming a deep arch in her spine as she circled, her arms like wings, her hands moving gracefully through the air. From above, winter light fell upon her, soft and luminous.

The air, the whispering breeze, began to call

her name. She almost fell. Somehow, she managed to stay upright.

I don't want to go home yet.

She wanted to skate on and on forever. Alone and free. But she wasn't alone. She caught sight of two people, a man and a little girl, moving away from her. She called out to them, thinking she might know who they were, or they might know her, but they kept right on going, away across the ice.

"Stop! Stop!"

Her skate caught in an old track and she fell, hard. The winter light darkened around her.

*   *   *

Luke held Lydia's fingers tightly in his own. Silent and brave, she watched the medics load Allie into the ambulance. One of the EMT's came back over to them. He pointed at Luke's hand.

"You should get that checked out," he said. "Burns can be nasty."

Luke grunted. Lydia lifted her head to the medic. "Is Allie going to be okay?" she asked.

"She might have a concussion. She's still only semi-conscious. Her burns are minimal, all things considered. Don't think any bones are broken either, but they'll check your friend over at the hospital. Your dad did a good job, honey. Don't let any of the firefighters hear me say that, though. They don't like it when someone rushes into a burning building."

Luke closed his eyes, recalling the terror of the moment when he'd seen boot prints trailing up to the back door of a house from which flames were shooting into the sky, unimpeded by the spray of water from the fire hose. When he'd located her, Allie had been ice cold in his arms despite the searing heat of the fire. Dead. He'd been sure she was dead.

In his right arm, the one with the burned hand, he clutched a ragged, half-melted bag of photo albums. Allie had been holding them. From the look of the situation, these photos might be all her parents would have left of the contents of their home. The neighbor who'd called had told the dispatcher the Roberts were in Florida, thinking to be helpful, to protect the firemen from undue risk. No one had seen the prints shuffling across the icy grass.

Luke shifted the weight of the albums against his chest as he turned toward the truck parked at an angle in a patch of churned up mud. A single photo fluttered to the ground. Lydia bent and picked it up, holding it out to him. He took the photo, squinting at the image through the pelting rain.

In the fluffy white hat and thick cable sweater he remembered, a fourteen-year-old Allie performed a pirouette on the ice of his father's pond, right before nightfall. The sky behind her beautifully postured body glowed soft and gray. Luke turned the photo over, studying the familiar handwriting.

"Thought you might like this. R."

Rory had taken this photo. Luke had never known.

* * *

Once again, Allie thought she heard her name. This time, however, the calling possessed substance, strong, distinctly male and persistent. The voice sounded like it might be at her ear. Annoying, like a baritone mosquito. She considered swatting it away and started to lift her hand, but she remembered her wrist had broken. Right there on the ice. After Luke had kissed her.

No. That was wrong. That was years ago.

"Allie."

She lifted the eyelid of one eye. The light was bright.

"Allie."

She let the lid drift downward again. Easier to take the darkness than the light. After a moment she felt a hand on hers. "Don't. It's broken."

"What?"

Right. Not broken. Where on earth was she? "Who is that?" she managed.

"Oh, hell, Allie. Don't you remember me?"

She forced her eyes open again, squinting through her lashes. A shadow moved, blocking the light of an overhead fixture, revealing a careworn, handsome face. Allie released her breath in a sigh.

"Of course I remember you," she said. "Luke Hollis, the man who's kissed me twice without a by-your-leave."

"Without a what?"

"A by-your—never mind. I'm in the hospital, aren't I? Can you help me sit up?"

She felt his arm snake beneath her back, lifting her. She reached behind and propped the pillow into place.

"Better?"

"Yes." She could see him now. He looked haggard and gray as he raised a bandaged hand and lowered it onto hers. "What happened to you?" she asked, gaze fixed on the white wrapping.

"Nothing major. A little burn, that's all."

"A little burn? How did you—oh."

Luke lowered himself onto the edge of the hospital bed, ducking his head to look her in the eye. He held his gaze on hers. Waiting.

Allie ground her teeth together, fighting back tears. "The house is gone, isn't it?"

"Yes, I think so."

She thought of that and all such devastation entailed. She needed to call her parents and Jimmy and let them know. She needed to get out of the hospital and back over there to see what could be salvaged, for Mom and Dad's sake. As she considered everything, her head began to ache. She looked up at Luke, who had straightened. Her brow twisted.

"Why were you there? I don't remember you coming with me. No, you didn't. I walked over in the storm alone. But you…you were there. You called me back. You and Lydia. Oh, God, where's Lydia?" She started to push off from the bed, but he took her hands and held her back.

"She's fine," he said quietly. "She's with her

mother."

"But Lydia was there, too, right?"

"She was there, too. Yes."

"In the house?"

"No."

"You were in the house."

"Yes."

"Luke…"

"I came to see if you needed a ride to work and saw your parents' house on fire."

Allie frowned. She could tell he was leaving something out. "But how did you know? What would make you think to even go there? Luke, I don't understand."

Dropping his head forward, he shook it from side to side. After a moment, he looked back up at her, blue eyes bright. "It doesn't matter, Allie. Please. I pulled you out. You're alive. That's all that matters, because I thought you weren't."

"But—"

"Enough," he said, a rumbling break in his tone. He cleared his throat. "No more talking."

She found herself in his arms in the time it took her to blink. His mouth lowered over hers in a careful, lengthy communion, and then he drew away.

"There," he whispered. "Without a by-your…what did you call it?"

"A by-your-leave. Permission, basically," she

explained.

"Permission?"

She laughed, a weak sound even to her own ears. "But I was joking. You certainly don't need permission." Grabbing his collar, she pulled him close. "And neither do I."

Chapter Twelve

Allie poured the last bit of water from a former juice bottle into the dirt of the nearest poinsettia. That made fourteen floral get-wells—twelve poinsettia plants and two Christmas lilies. She hadn't realized she knew that many people well enough to receive a gift of good wishes from them, but here they were, with even more cards, filling her cottage with seasonal cheer. In the corner stood a small balsam with white lights affixed, courtesy of Luke and Lydia. Yesterday Allie had hung the contents of a box of multi-colored candy canes from the branches and a few glass balls, along with short lengths of bright red yarn tied into bows. Yep, she was getting mighty tired of staying home. Thank goodness the doctor had given her the go-ahead to return to work today. Christmas was right around the corner. Although Todd had stepped in quite efficiently, Allie was anxious to get back.

As Allie pulled on her boots, the phone rang.

"Mom, hi."

"Allison, sweetie, are you really going into work today? Your father and I—"

"Mom, I'm good. Really. You just relax at Aunt June's, okay? It's bad enough you had to cut short your time in Florida because I blew up your house." The words caught in her throat as she spoke them. She'd been told repeatedly it hadn't been her fault, how she'd been lucky the gas leak hadn't ignited sooner, catching her inside the house rather than standing by the garage. How fortunate no one else had been there. But her Mom and Dad's home, all their cherished possessions, were gone. Unable to shake the guilt, Allie had resorted to joking about it so she'd be permitted to take the blame.

"Allison Roberts, what is that tone I hear?"

"Nothing, Mom. I'm good. I just—"

"You are not good. You do realize if your father and I had been home, we would have done the same thing, lit a fire in the fireplace? But we probably would have been cuddled up on the couch staying warm when the fumes ignited. So we *all* have a lot to be grateful for. It's only things that are gone, not people."

Allie blinked back tears. "But your house, all those memories…"

"The house can be rebuilt. And the memories we still have. All of us."

Closing her eyes, Allie leaned her head against the cushioned sofa back. "Do we, Mom? Sometimes I feel like we don't."

For nearly a half minute, her mother remained mute. Allie peered out between her lashes at the contents of her living room. At one time, everything she'd placed about the room had held some meaning for her. Right now, despite the wonderful sentiment of the newest additions, the things she saw felt meaningless.

"Allie…"

The use of the diminutive she preferred brought more moisture to dot her lashes. "I'm okay, Mom. I really am. I've got to get going, though, before I decide to play hooky again."

"Stay home, then. From what I hear, Todd's doing a great job."

"I want to go." Allie pushed up off the couch. She walked nearer to the mirror, leaning toward it, frowning at the multitude of tiny, healing cuts on her face from flying glass. Her hair had been singed a bit on the right side of her head, but with some careful clipping the damage was barely noticeable.

"Allison, you don't sound…yourself. And I'm not surprised, all things considered. Just worried."

Allie frowned at her reflection. "I am alive."

"Of course you are!"

"No, I mean that's a really wonderful thing."

"It is…"

Glancing at the room behind her, mirrored in the glass, Allie made a decision. "I want to have Christmas here. In my own place. I can start a tradition. New memories."

"Can we all fit in there, dear?"

"We can damn well try."

"Allie!"

"I mean it. If we have to take some of the furniture out of the living room, we will. Tell Aunt June to come and whichever of her kids and their kids are free."

"Honey, that's a lot of work."

Allie laughed, moved by the first bubbling of amusement since before the accident. "Tell everyone to bring a dish. How's that? Less work for everyone."

"I…okay."

"I've gotta go, though. I love you, Mom."

"I love you, too, sweetie."

Allie hung up the phone and grabbed her coat. She shoved her arms into the sleeves and pushed the zipper up to her chin, thinking her mother probably thought she'd lost her mind. And maybe she had. Maybe an experience like the one she'd had brought on small bouts of insanity. Fine. She'd take it and hope for the best.

Driving into town, Allie observed people hustling along the sidewalks, chins scrunched down into the collars of coats, scarves around faces, bright mittens on hands, woolen caps in place. Clouding breath filled the air beneath the dove gray sky. Her car had barely heated in the short trip and she shivered in her down jacket. Allie thought longingly of a frozen pond, any pond, but pictured in her mind that long ago night on the solid body of water where Luke had kissed her. She hadn't seen him since the day he'd picked her up from the hospital and the conversations she'd had with him on the phone had been brief. Fun. Lively. But brief. Several times she'd heard Zoe in the background talking to Lydia before Luke stepped into another room to speak to Allie.

Despite his fervent kisses in the hospital, she still wasn't sure where she stood with him. She wasn't ready to ask, either.

Finding a space around the corner from the bookstore, Allie steered her car up to the curb, parked, and climbed out. Each meter along the sidewalk had been covered with a candy-cane striped bag. No fee during the last week before Christmas. She and the other shop owners had pushed for that, and won. At least for this year. Allie stood a few moments with her own chin tucked into her jacket's upturned collar, taking deep, protected breaths as she contemplated the walk to the store. She'd felt a little more energetic when she started out.

Avoiding the curious stares of passersby as she made her way toward Connor Falls Book Emporium, Allie considered her crazy offer of having Christmas at her tiny cottage this year. But really, wasn't it time to step up? She could do this. Hopefully her energy returned before the big day.

Nearing the storefront, she spied a handful of people talking and pointing at the display window. Well, crap, had Todd forgotten to water the tree? She pictured browned needles littering the floor. Or had it fallen down?

"Hi," said Gina as Allie drew closer. "How are you feeling? Your Mom called to tell Todd you were on your way. What do you think?"

Allie followed Gina's extended finger and swallowed, hard, then attempted to speak. No voice came out. Someone had set a tiny, book-reader spotlight on the floor below the balsam, pointing up at branches sparkling with a lightly sprayed coating of artificial snow. From each branch tip hung a black and white photograph. More than Allie could believe. "How—"

"A couple of us got together and made some calls, and pushed the townspeople with signs in our own stores. It was all Luke's idea, really." Gina winked at her. "He wanted you to be surprised."

Biting her lip, Allie stepped nearer to the glass. Surprised was not the word. Several hundred photos shifted from side to side in a current of air, some appearing to have been recently taken, others depicting moments in time from years past, made obvious by the mode of dress, the furnishings glimpsed in the background. The townspeople's favorite memories of the season, displayed to share with the little corner of the world known as Connor Falls. And at the top, in a place of prominence…

Allie raised her gloved fingertips to her mouth. "Where…where did he…"

She stared up at the photo of her on the pond, poised in an instant of grace she'd forgotten she possessed. Luke's brother Rory had taken the photograph, an eighteen-year-old man in possession of a sophisticated artistic eye. Taken it the same night Luke had kissed her, probably only minutes before.

"This is why," a deep voice said at her ear.

Allie turned to gape at Luke at her side, finding his handsome, serious face bent near to hers. "Why what?"

"Why I kissed you." His countenance creased into a smile. "And Gina lied. It wasn't all my idea. It was Lydia's. She wanted to surprise you. And there's more. Come inside."

Luke took her hand to lead her into the store. Gina gave her another wink as they passed by. "What are you doing here, Luke?" Allie asked. "How did you know I was coming in?"

"Your mom gave me a call to let me know you were on your way."

"*Mom* called you? I don't—"

"Yes, we've become quite friendly since your accident." Luke laughed as he reached for the door and held it wide for her to enter. Allie stepped inside and stopped dead.

More photos hung from paperclips slipped into the crossbeams of the dropped ceiling. Enlargements from a copy machine these looked like, and all of them of Allie, her brother, their parents in years gone by: Christmases, summer picnics, carving Halloween pumpkins, swimming in the lake…

"Allison."

"Mom. Dad!" Allie rushed into their arms, holding them close.

"Really, Allie," her father said gruffly, "if you'd wanted us home for Christmas, you could have left the house intact and just asked."

Yeah, this was where she got her whacked sense of humor in times of trouble. Allie grinned at her dad through her tears. He jerked his head to the side. "Your friends are here, too. They want to welcome you back."

For the first time Allie noticed the store wasn't filled with customers, but with people she knew. Friends, shopkeepers, and yes, customers she recognized, all staring at her with wide smiles. A banner hung over the counter reading *Welcome Back, Boss*, Todd standing beneath it with a somewhat smug expression on his tearful face. Although enlarged, Allie recognized his handwriting on the paper above his head. He pointed at it and at himself, on the chance she hadn't.

"Allie!"

Lydia pushed her way through the crowd, Zoe making a grasp for her hand and then letting her go. Allie crouched down, opening her arms. Lydia ran into them.

"So your daddy says this was all your idea."

Lydia nodded, face alight with joy. "It was."

No hedging, no demure denial. Allie laughed and hugged her. "Thank you. Where did you get all these pictures?"

Lydia glanced up at her father, who'd come to stand beside them. Allie rose, Lydia clutching her hand.

"You had a death grip on a melted garbage bag when I found you," Luke said. "It was filled with photo albums." He nodded toward a box wrapped in Christmas paper on the counter. "They're all in there, cleaned up a bit, as a gift for you and your family."

Allie released her grip on Lydia's hand and placed both of her own over her face, engaging in a bit of a meltdown behind her fingers. Words of sympathy and encouragement ran in tiny whispers among the people gathered. Allie smelled the evergreen scent lodged in Luke's coat as he came close and slipped an arm around her shoulder.

"And there's cake," he whispered.

"From Gina's bakery!" Lydia chimed in.

"There's no doubt," Allie said as she lowered her hands, "that this will be the best Christmas ever."

*   *   *

An hour later, following the departure of the crowd of people who'd come to wish Allie well, Zoe paused in front of her, Lydia's hat in her hand. "Thank you."

"For what?" Allie said, glancing aside at Lydia's animated conversation with Luke.

"For not pulling any punches with that 'disposable daughter' comment the night I came to talk to you. I've taken a job in New York. It's only a couple of hours away. We've worked out a custody schedule, Luke and I. I won't abandon Lydia again. I won't abandon either one of them. No." This, as Allie opened her mouth to speak. "Not what you think. Luke's a good father. There's no reason he has to do it alone though. Our daughter has two parents. We need to act like it, even if we're not together as a unit."

Zoe turned her head and called Lydia's name. She held the hat out to her daughter as Lydia skipped over. "Put this on, peanut. It's cold outside." She turned back to Allie. "Lydia's going with me to my hotel. We're going to have dinner and watch movies and eat popcorn in bed. I believe Luke has plans. With you."

*   *   *

The sun moved toward setting, a pale lozenge nearly invisible behind the cover of soft, gray clouds. The world was without shadow, silver and brown and green, the ice on the pond as smooth as opaque glass. Crouched on his knees, Luke helped Allie to put on the painted skates he'd removed from the window display. He tied the new laces, touched the blades' edges, freshly sharpened. He rose and held out his hand. Allie slipped her fingers into his.

"You get tired, you just let me know."

She smiled at him, lips closed, her chocolate-syrup eyes luminous. "I'll be fine."

He clutched her hand until he was sure she'd gotten her legs under her properly, and then he let go, watching her skate across the ice, sure and strong despite her recent trauma. Must be like riding a bike. Something you never forgot.

After a moment he followed, keeping his distance, his gaze glued to the elegance of her form, the confidence of her movements, the beauty that had so thrilled him all those years ago. He would kiss her again because of it, but not right now. Right now, he wanted only to watch her fly.

"Allie."

She turned, grinning at him, skating backward, her cinnamon hair blowing in wisps around her face. "Luke Hollis, I think I'm falling for you."

He skated a little nearer, so she could hear him better. "Ditto, Allie Roberts. But please don't mean that literally. No broken wrist this time around."

"No broken anything," she said, and with a laugh that rang across the ice she performed a perfect pirouette beneath the winter sky.

LIGHT *the* Heart Home

Chapter One

Emma flipped the car visor down, squinting into the sun. Driving due west on a winter's afternoon presented its problems. It didn't help that the defroster had decided to malfunction several hours into the trip's second leg. Every ten minutes or so while warm air chugged feebly on full blast through all vents, she'd been wiping the windshield with an old towel she'd found in the trunk. Thank goodness for gloves and a heated seat.

For the first time in more years than she cared to count, Emma was going home for Christmas. She'd had no particular reason to return before. Connor Falls had stopped being her home when the last Parsons sibling left it. What was there to go home to, if all the family had gone? Most Connor Falls' families had some member, or even multiple members, living in or near the small town their whole lives, but after Mom and Dad decided to retire and move south, Emma, her two sisters and her brother had headed elsewhere, one by one.

Emma couldn't imagine what whim had drawn her little sister to return to Connor Falls. Not only to live, but to start a business, making and selling candles and soaps and lotions, of all things. Sophie had rented a little storefront on a side street and set up shop, a move Emma would not have expected from the girl who'd gone to school for business and graphic design. Despite Sophie's free spirit tendencies, she'd always been sensible. She'd been the one who'd led the parade to get the heck out of Dodge, finding a job right after school that had made their parents proud. Emma had been sure Sophie would never look back.

A sigh escaped Emma's lips, fogging glass. Snapping up the towel, she wiped the condensation away. When she threw the rag back onto the seat, it struck her sister's postcard, the one Sophie had sent following their phone call two weeks ago. Emma picked it up, glancing from the glossy card to the traffic ahead and back again.

Sophie's Chandlery: Light the Heart Home.

The photo was nice—a single crimson pillar candle off-center in a frosted windowpane—but the store's name, the sentiment, seemed a bit pretentious. Emma tossed the card into the cubbyhole beneath the radio. She would need it for the address once she got into town.

Of all her siblings, Emma had possessed the strongest reason to leave Connor Falls, and that reason still existed. She didn't talk about what had happened much, even with her friends. She was supposed to be over it, given time's passage. She did speak to Sophie about old feelings on occasion, a fact which made it all the more strange to find her sister using the one carrot to lure Emma's return to

Connor Falls that Sophie knew she wouldn't be able to resist.

Sophie had a secret.

Despite all Emma's speculation and prodding, Sophie refused to spill on the phone. She didn't want anyone else to know either. Not yet. She had made Emma promise not to even mention the possibility of news. As if. Emma didn't go calling family members to gossip, or even to check up on them. Not often, anyway. They usually ended up calling her when sufficient time had passed to warrant a conversation. They all joked about how much Emma hated the phone.

And yet she kept her cell glued to her side at all times. Work, she always told herself. Only she didn't have that excuse anymore.

Emma reached into the car door pocket and pulled out the water bottle she'd been swigging from for the past three hours. She drank sparingly, chill liquid running down her throat. With a glance in the mirror before changing lanes, Emma spotted the cardboard boxes filling her back seat. More crammed the trunk. Her printer and laptop were belted in on the passenger seat beside her. Winter boots, in case she needed them in a hurry, lay on the floor beneath the glove box alongside a backpack filled with her immediate needs.

Emma had her own secret, one that would never have led her back to Connor Falls if she could have helped it. But then Sophie had called.

This was going to be some Christmas.

*　*　*

Sophie flicked the forest-green linen napkin down over a wooden crate centered in the shop window. She admired the contrast between aged wood and crisp fabric. She wondered if this was what the designers called 'shabby-chic'. Didn't matter what it was called, really. She liked the appearance. That was good enough for her.

Two holly sprigs were angled at the crate's outer edges. A cranberry-red pillar candle stood between them slightly off center in a faux, glassless window pane, mimicking the postcard she had designed for use with the promotional holiday giveaway. Fake snow had been sprinkled over the display. Beside the candle a small placard read: NEWLY SPRUNG FROM THE MOLDS TO GRACE YOUR TABLE – NINE-INCH TALL SOY AND BEESWAX PILLARS.

Emma had called an hour ago explaining some ongoing malfunction with her car, a need for gas and a pit stop, but that she'd be arriving soon. Sophie had a major secret she planned to share with Emma. She might have considered doing it over the phone, if Emma hadn't sounded so down in the dumps. Emma needed to be with family, even if only her sister.

Glancing up, Sophie noticed a dark-haired woman at the window, partially silhouetted by the streetlamp behind. She appeared to be studying the elements in the display with a perplexed wrinkle on her brow. Sophie's heart gave a jolt. She ran to the door and threw it open.

"Emma!"

Hunched against the cold in a gray woolen knee-length coat, Emma turned and hesitated, her perpetually bitten lower lip tight in a toothy grasp. Nothing ever changed. Emma, the never-impetuous, couldn't even work up the spontaneity to hug Sophie first. Sophie had no such issues. Charging along the sidewalk, arms outstretched, she tossed herself at her sister, forcing Emma to wrap her arms around Sophie or risk them toppling together onto the ground.

After a few breathless exclamations, Emma pulled away first. "You look…remarkable," she said, eyeing Sophie up and down. Sophie noted her gaze lingered on certain salient points, such as what Emma no doubt viewed her rather plain dress and the hair she'd let grow out. Sophie wore it now in a manner that couldn't help but inspire Emma's disapproval, but it hadn't been intentional. Lastly, Emma's gaze stuck on the necklace at Sophie's throat. Emma nodded at the jewelry. "Not one of my designs."

"Sis," said Sophie with a laugh, "I can't afford one of your designs."

Emma snorted. "At this point in time, I can't afford one of mine, either."

Sophie laughed again, ending it a little uncertainly. Since when had Emma gone so deadpan? Or wasn't it a joke? In a moment, however, Emma's mouth curved in her crooked, signature smile. Emma was a beauty and always had been. Mismatched brows, a slight bump on her nose from a fly ball, the irregular smile, didn't detract but added up to something truly special. All the boys in high school had been quite aware of Emma. Sophie by comparison was the pixie sister.

They said so charmingly, but Sophie read between the lines. In time, she'd made her own way among them, but for a long while the difference had been quite irksome.

"How was the ride?" Sophie asked her.

"Long," said Emma, mouth still curved, yet the smile didn't reach her eyes.

"Ems, are you okay?"

"I'm fine. Just a bit tired."

Sophie tipped her head and looked around her sister's arm to the street. "Where'd you park?"

Emma jerked her thumb over her shoulder. "Around the block. It was the only spot."

"There's one right there," Sophie pointed out.

"There wasn't when I drove past the first time."

Sophie flinched at her sister's tone. Definitely not fine.

Tucking her hand into Emma's elbow, Sophie steered her toward the shop door. "Love your coat. And your boots. You're still Elegant Emma."

Emma shrugged. "Thanks…I guess. You'd think I'd have changed a bit in a year and a half."

"It hasn't been that long!"

"Oh yes," said Emma, "it has."

"Yikes," Sophie muttered, yanking open the door and releasing the scents from within. Beside her, Emma jerked to a halt, brown eyes widening. Her nose wrinkled a little as she sniffed. Another smile played about her lips, more relaxed, maybe more authentic.

"Soph," Emma whispered, "I…I never would have pictured you doing this. What on earth has happened to you?"

Funny, Sophie had been about to ask Emma the same thing.

*   *   *

Inside the shop, Emma shirked her coat grudgingly from her shoulders. She didn't want to give the garment up. The last hour in the car had chilled her to the bone. She wondered if Billy Stiles was still around. He'd always been good with a car. He'd probably taken over his father's shop like his dad always wanted.

Emma cut her thoughts short, amazed at how quickly they had reverted to people and memories from the past. What was the point? Her life wasn't here.

She would have to get her car fixed, though. She'd look for someone on-line in the next couple days.

"What?" she said, noticing Sophie had come to stand at her side, hand out.

"Your coat," Sophie said, as if she'd said it already, which she probably had. "I'll hang it up. Unless you'd rather go straight upstairs? I have to finish a few things down here."

Emma stuffed her gloves into her pocket before handing her sister the coat. "Upstairs? Is that where you're living?"

"Yep, didn't I say? I'm sure I must have. I live in the apartment above. Quite convenient, really. The commute is all of about thirty seconds." Sophie hung Emma's garment on an old coat rack painted over in black enamel, the spiral elements on the wood embellished in lavender, pink and turquoise. Emma spied a cardstock tag hanging from an arm by a silver ribbon. The store logo was recognizable on the tag and what would probably prove upon closer inspection to be the price.

"Your handiwork?" Emma asked.

Sophie took a step back, grinning. "It is," she said. "You like it?"

"Sure," Emma said. "It's different." Emma tucked her hands beneath her arms to warm them.

"Want your gloves back?"

Emma grimaced. "Is it that obvious?"

"A bit. If you'd take a couple of extra steps into the store, you'd find it's quite cozy in here."

Was she hovering by the door? She'd been doing that lately, finding a spot near an exit wherever she went, as if the need might arise for a hasty departure. Well, maybe not the need. More like the desire.

"Sorry," she said.

Sophie waved away her apology, checking her watch. "I put a sign on the door that I was closing early today. Bad form, I know, during the holiday buying season, but I figured you and I could grab a late dinner."

"You don't have to close. I can—"

"The sign's been up all week. Plenty of time for word to get around."

"Okay," said Emma quietly.

"Sit down, Ems. Seriously. You're making me nervous. I have a few things to do and then we can head out. Or will that be too much after your drive?"

"It's fine. It'll be nice." Emma moved to a ladder back chair that had been painted to match the coat rack. The chair, too, held a price tag. Emma avoided looking at the amount as she pointed toward the seat with a questioning glance.

"It's made for sitting," Sophie said. "So sit."

Emma eased herself onto the rattan seat. She clutched her fingers between her knees, gazing around at the store's fragrant contents. There were other furnishings, too, and a rack containing what looked like charmingly illustrated note cards. Emma's gaze finally came to rest on her sister, who appeared to be checking the shelves and making notations on a small pad in her hand. Her outfit, from her dress to her brushed suede boots, looked like something from the nineteen-sixties. Emma supposed that sort of thing was back in style again. Sophie's hair had grown out since the last time Emma had seen her, from shoulder length to long and golden and curly, tamed only by the braids at the front pulled back and fastened behind her head in a hair tie. Perhaps it was some sort of counterculture persona her sister wanted to project, for the sake of the store. On Sophie, however, it looked genuine.

"When did you get all artsy on us, Soph?" she asked.

"I didn't 'get' all artsy," Sophie said, glancing over her shoulder. "I always was."

Emma stood, doing a slow turn to take in the shop again. "Well, you look the part for sure, but I don't remember you being into—" she waved her hands "—this sort of thing."

She hadn't meant the words to sound so dismissive, but the long silence behind her made it clear they'd been exactly that and had wounded Sophie in the process. Shoulders dropping, Emma turned around. "Soph, I'm sorry."

"No," said Sophie. "Don't apologize. I get it. I know where you're coming from. But seriously, this is who I've always been."

"You had a high-paying job in the city," Emma reminded her. "Doing…I don't know exactly what, but something far from this, I'm sure."

Sophie walked behind the counter, brushing her sleeve across three-inch square midnight blue tiles. She smiled down at them. "I made this counter, too, with my own two hands."

"Sophie…"

Her sister looked up. Emma saw it then, in her eyes. A knee-jerk disappointment quickly shuttered.

"What I did at my job in the city, Ems, was design. Artsy stuff, as you call it. And as a kid, I was constantly creating things, painting things, planning things, even experimenting with my old friend Pam making candles. You remember her?"

Sophie didn't wait for Emma to answer, although Emma did, indeed, remember Pam. The two of them, Sophie and Pam, had been quite annoying, really, but now that Sophie mentioned it, they had possessed a certain creativity that seemed to flourish when they were together. Emma had a quick flashback of watching them paint stones one day. Round, flattish stones gathered from the creek bank near the house, later covered in floral designs. Mom and Dad had one on display for the longest time.

"So, yeah, this is who I am," Sophie said. "This is me following my heart totally. Do you think this is beneath me somehow, or is it just that you don't understand it? I know you've always hated when you don't understand something. There isn't much you don't get, Emma, but maybe this is one of those things."

Emma stared at her sister wordlessly.

"There were elements in that job of mine which would have eventually killed the part of me I love," Sophie went on, apparently unable to stop now she'd gotten started. "You have to understand that, surely? You have the creative bug, too. You design the most beautiful jewelry I've ever seen. You know how it feels."

Emma drew short, staggered breaths in through her nose. She didn't want to talk about the jewelry. Not now. She nodded. "I didn't come here to get you all worked up, Sophie. I'm sorry."

"Again," Sophie said with a lift of her fingers, "don't apologize. Take a breath. A deep breath. What do you think?"

Emma did so, filling her lungs. "Well," she admitted, "I must say, it does smell incredibly lovely in here."

Sophie grinned. Emma's heart pinched.

"But what made you choose candles?" she asked, keeping a careful watch on her sister's eyes.

"Scent, color. I make matching soaps and lotions, too. I know I can't compete with the big stores, but that's why I came back. People here like local. They support local. Did you notice the furniture?"

Emma glanced around at the various pieces decorated in floral patterns, checks, and plaids—sometimes all on the same piece—as well as deliberately primitive animals and landscapes. "It's really something," Emma said. "You have a definite style that comes through."

"As you've probably noticed, all of it's for sale, even the coat rack. So if someone comes in and wants to buy it, you'd better snatch down that expensive coat of yours, pronto."

"I will," said Emma, "unless they want the coat, too. I wouldn't be disinclined to let it go for the right price."

Sophie laughed rather too hard, like a child. Emma observed her in silence, unable to manage an answering amusement.

Chapter Two

Emma attempted to hurry along Main Street. The chill bit at her cheeks and nipped her toes through her soles. She should have changed into the lined snow boots she'd brought. She didn't often need them in her southern existence but had convinced herself that she hadn't gotten so acclimated to the warmer temperatures in Georgia that a little cold would be her undoing. She'd been wrong.

Unfortunately, arm linked through Emma's, Sophie strolled at her side at a snail's pace. Seemed Sophie had decided it was her duty to point out every decorated window from the pub all the way back to Sophie's Chandlery. She had stories to go with most, frequently asking Emma if she remembered this person or that. Emma had stopped answering. She didn't want to remember, didn't want to be drawn into nostalgic reminiscence.

"I don't usually eat this late," Emma said at

last, trying for another hint. "I hope I can sleep."

"If I don't grab something while I'm working, I always eat this late," countered her sister drowsily, leaning her head against Emma's shoulder. "And it makes me sleep like a log."

Emma compressed her lips, sucking brittle air in through her nose.

Although the walk back to Sophie's place was becoming increasingly painful, dinner had, at least, been quite pleasant after a delay in leaving the shop. A last minute customer had arrived, rushing through the door five minutes before the altered closing time. Sophie had dealt with the man with more patience than Emma would have displayed. As a result, they'd left for dinner nearly a half hour later than originally intended.

Emma couldn't fault the place they'd eaten—a small tavern that hadn't been there before her departure from Connor Falls—or the conversation during the meal. They'd skirted around any underlying annoyance, as well as the secrets they both held. In Emma's case, she hadn't yet hinted at one. Sophie, for some reason, had decided to make Emma wait on hers. Emma hadn't bothered to try to bring the subject up. Sophie was Sophie. She'd get around to it and probably in a most unexpected manner.

Sophie's head shot upright. "I never actually asked you," she cried.

Given her train of thought, Emma started uncomfortably. "Asked what?"

"If you were staying with me? You are, aren't you? I'd planned it that way, but since I didn't mention, maybe you decided otherwise. You've seen the apartment now. It has plenty of room, even if it's not as big as yours. You'll like it, it's cozy. Please, Ems, stay with me."

Emma patted her sister's hand. "Relax, Sophie. I figured I was." More than figured, Emma had counted on it. She wouldn't say so to Sophie, though. Emma wasn't ready for questions.

"I've got an extra key. Just come and go as you please. You'll probably want to look up old friends while you're here?"

If Sophie had couched that last as a statement rather than a question, Emma likely wouldn't have caught on. Added to the names from their past Sophie had been throwing at her during their walk, Emma suddenly understood. She ceased patting Sophie's fingers and instead removed them from her elbow.

"Sophie, no. I won't be visiting anyone while I'm here but you. There's nothing in my past I want to relive. This isn't old home week for me. Understood?"

Sophie gave a disgruntled nod.

"Honestly, Soph, I don't care about anything I left behind."

"Okay," Sophie said.

"I mean it."

"Okay," Sophie repeated.

"Promise me you won't hound me."

"Okay," Sophie said one more time.

"And don't sulk," added Emma.

Sophie shoved both hands into her coat pockets. "Okay."

Sophie increased her pace. Emma, taller by seven inches, had to hurry to catch up. "You wanted to come back," Emma said breathlessly. "You've pointed out it was right for your business. Great. Maybe you have some fond memories I'm unaware of, but at one point you were as keen as anyone to move on. Yours was the rallying call for exodus, unless I'm mistaken."

Sophie stopped short at the corner. "You're not mistaken, Ems," she said. "But I was."

She turned right and started walking again before Emma could muster a response. "Soph, Soph, slow down," Emma called. At least the faster pace had started to warm her a bit, although her toes remained frozen. Outside the store Sophie halted once more, pivoting to face her, expression not quite readable, eyes glittering. Sophie might have been angry, she might have been hurt, or she might have been just plain cold.

"I was welcomed back," Sophie said, "as a business owner and as someone who had grown up here. And it's not all sentimentality. The side street and smaller store? Cheaper to rent, heat, cool, light than anything I checked into in this area. My tiny apartment—love it, by the way—more affordable by far than the place I had before I came back. The Chandlery inventory? Nothing like it in Connor Falls or anywhere nearby. The changes I made were well thought out, with a good business plan and a good life plan. I wanted roots again, Ems. I have them. I found what I had lost."

Emma released a long breath, frosting the air. Her fingers, unconsciously tightened into fisted knots, uncurled. She pressed her hands against her thighs. "That's good, Soph. I'm so glad for you."

Oddly, Emma wasn't making nice, not merely using words to placate her sister. She meant what she said. A subtle joy on her sister's behalf had sparked in her heart, surprising her like a match in the dark.

"I really am," Emma said.

Sophie's gaze lifted to hers, holding there. A slow smile curled her lips.

"Good. Let's go upstairs and have some hot chocolate."

"Hot chocolate!" Emma gasped, clutching at her middle. "I'm going to barf. How can you still fit anything into that stomach of yours?"

"Easy," said Sophie. "I'm eating for two."

*   *   *

That had been rather blunt. Sophie had planned to lead up to it, or at the very least not blurt her news out on the sidewalk. She could almost see the thoughts churning in Emma's head as she sat silently watching Sophie from the kitchen table. Sophie scooped hot chocolate mix into both her mug and Emma's before pouring steaming water from the kettle into each. She held up a bag of marshmallows, shaking it over Emma's mug. Emma shook her head fiercely. "Your loss," said Sophie, dropping two into hers.

No time could be a good time, really. Not for this conversation. But Sophie wanted Emma to be the first in her family to know. There had been a period in their lives when they'd told each other everything.

Sophie carried the hot chocolate to the table, sliding Emma's across to her before sitting down.

"Pregnant," Emma whispered, not as though she'd meant to say the word out loud. She frowned at the steam rising from her cup.

"Yes," Sophie answered, breathing in the sweet scent from her mug. Emma's head jerked up.

"How, Soph? How did this happen?"

Sophie sipped the chocolate, scalding her lip. She quickly put the mug down and pressed her tongue to stinging flesh, wrinkling her nose. "In the usual way," she said, "how else?"

Emma ignored the bright red mug Sophie had placed before her, hands moving like she wanted to shove it away. "This isn't funny."

Sophie had to agree. Not funny at all. Yet all the tears she'd expended in response to the discovery had ended the very next day. Yes, being a single mother wasn't funny, but it also wasn't the end of her world. Not by a long shot.

"Do you…do you have health insurance?"

When had Emma become the one who went straight to practicalities? She hadn't even asked the questions Sophie assumed would be uppermost in her mind, like: Whose is it?

Or: Where is he?

Or: Are you insane?

"I do." When she deemed it safe enough, Sophie took another, tentative sip from her mug. She set the mug down precisely on the damp circle from the chocolate that had dribbled over the edge when she'd burned herself. On the wall behind her head, the kitchen clock she normally never noticed ticked quite loudly in the silence.

"Emma, where's your suitcase?" Sophie asked abruptly. "You're going to need it."

"Not now," said Emma.

Sophie poked a finger at the smeared chocolate on the table. "Are you leaving then? I really didn't think sharing this—this issue with my sister would be a leave-able offense. Now Judy, well, that's a different matter…" Sophie came close to trembling thinking about what would be their older sister Judy's reaction. "It will be difficult to get Judy to understand, but I thought you might. Or at the very least, afford me the comfort of discussing my situation with someone I presumed cared enough about me to want to know."

Goodness, she hadn't meant to say that last bit. It sounded like an attack.

Yep, that was the way Emma had taken it, too. She'd gone very still.

"Emma…"

Emma shook her head in a rapid, barely discernible movement. "I need to think about this."

Sophie reached up and scratched her forehead. With the other hand, she stuck a finger into the mug and lifted out a marshmallow, stuffing it into her mouth whole. "Really?" she mumbled around the warm, melting confection, contorting her face as she tried to subdue and swallow it. "Really?" she repeated when she'd done so. "What is it you need to think about? You're not the one who's pregnant, Ems. I am."

Sophie longed to jump up and yank the battery from the kitchen clock. Picturing the conversation over the past two weeks had never been like this, with the tick-tock of a cheap timepiece punctuating heavy silences.

Emma pushed back her chair and stood. She carried the mug to the sink, poured the cooling chocolate down the drain, rinsed and set the receptacle in the drain board. Turning on her heel she headed for the door, pausing when she reached it, hand on the knob.

"I'll be back," she said in a subdued voice.

Sophie dug once again into her chocolate, searching for the second marshmallow. "Next week? Next year? In a few minutes? I'd like to know if I should be locking the door."

"In a few minutes," Emma said sharply. "I just need to get my stuff from the car."

But she didn't move. Instead, coatless, she stared at the floor. Sophie waited. When Emma didn't speak Sophie stood, too, and went to her.

"Ems?"

Slowly, Emma's head lifted. She looked straight into Sophie's eyes. Sophie recognized the uncertainty, the vague grasping for balance, for hope, in her sister's gaze. It was like looking in a mirror at the woman she, herself, had been.

*　*　*

Emma wasn't a crier. She'd never been a crier. But suddenly she was. A loud one. Through tear-blurred eyes, she watched Sophie scurry across the

160

small apartment and return with a half-empty box of tissues.

"Been using a lot of these lately, have you?" Emma said, snatching out two in order to mop her face and thoroughly blow her nose.

"Shut up, sis," Sophie shot back, eyes glistening, a wavering smile trembling on her lips. "Shut up and sit down."

This time they sat in the living room, which Emma realized belatedly was both cozy and fantastically, eccentrically, artfully decorated. Why hadn't she seen that the moment they walked in? She opened her mouth to compliment her sister now, but Sophie reached out and patted her knee in such a maternal gesture Emma's words stopped dead in her mouth.

Little Sophie was going to be a mom, a single mom, and here Emma sat, bemused and distraught and nigh on hysterical about transformations in her life that were minor by comparison.

Except they weren't. Not really. It was, after all, her life, and she needed to deal with what had happened and what was to come as surely as Sophie.

"Are you going to tell me now?" Sophie asked, leaning forward from the ottoman.

Emma took a deep breath, followed by another. Sophie held out the tissue box again. Emma waved it away with a thank you.

Emma knew Sophie possessed more sense than to believe Emma's hysterics were due to her announcement. Emma wasn't ready to talk, though. Outlining her fall from grace on her first night here hadn't been her plan.

"Emma."

Emma shook her head. "Who's the father?"

Sophie blinked, pulled back. "We're talking about you, now."

"Not yet, Soph. Who is he, if you don't mind telling me?"

Sophie bit her lip. Her eyes rounded. Emma knew that look, remembered that look. Sophie might as well have been ten years old again, and she eleven. The old I-don't-know-if-you're-going-to-like-this face usually rang true.

"Ben," Sophie said.

"Your fiancé?" Shock forced the question from Emma in a harsh croak. "I mean ex-fiancé?"

Sophie nodded. "He called out of the blue three and a half months ago and wanted to try to work things out. He came up for a long weekend. That was all it lasted, but enough time for this." She fluttered a hand over her belly and dropped spread fingers gently onto her abdomen. Her expression softened.

The simple gesture spoke of acceptance, determination, a tender devotion. Seeing it caused the apprehension inside Emma to settle and smooth out, like water when the wind has died down. "Does he know? Ben?"

"Yes," said Sophie. She shook her head.

Emma didn't need to ask anything else. She stood up, pulling Sophie with her.

"Well, let's make this a long story short," Emma said. "I lost my job. Destroyed my job, actually. There's no going back. I wallowed long enough that I could no longer afford my stupidly expensive apartment, so I broke the lease, moved whatever furnishings I couldn't sell together with a few odds and ends into storage, and packed everything else into my car, which is parked around the corner. I really don't know what I'm going to do, but if you don't mind, and you can spare the space, I'd like to bring some of that stuff inside until I figure it out."

*   *   *

Emma snored. Sophie wondered if anyone had ever told her that. Even from the kitchen Sophie could hear the sound, mellow, soft, like an exhausted, sacked-out puppy.

Sophie glanced at the clock that had annoyed her so much earlier in the night. She barely heard it ticking now, but the time displayed by the hands couldn't be ignored. It was after one in the morning.

Yawning, Sophie crossed the living room rug to the street-facing windows. She sat on the window seat, shoving her feet beneath the folded crocheted blanket. A small wind had arisen after midnight, rattling the panes. In each halo formed by the streetlamps outside snowflakes flew, sparse and delicate, settling on chilled windshields but nowhere else. Emma's car was out there, moved to a space about halfway down the block. Together Sophie and Emma had emptied the front and back seats, piling everything into the tiny bedroom where Emma had curled up on the futon shortly thereafter and fallen asleep.

Sophie's hand strayed as it frequently did to her abdomen. She smiled at the indistinguishable roundness beneath her fingers. "Hey, you," she whispered, breath fogging the glass in front of her face.

Somewhere in there, beneath the slight rolls of easy living and too many fries, a child grew. *Her* child—continuing blood lines, expanding family, bearing traits both familiar and unexpected, throwbacks to a different generation or to ten tiny fingers and toes exactly like her own…or like Ben's.

Her sigh bloomed on the chilled pane. She scrubbed the moisture away with her sleeve, staring out at the swirling flakes sparkling in the lamplight. The flame on the single candle burning in a hurricane container centered on the sill danced over the glass, reminding Sophie what she'd written long ago when she first contemplated creating Sophie's Chandlery.

Burn one candle in the window, just one flame in the night, and you will light the heart home.

Across the small apartment behind the half-closed door Emma mumbled unintelligibly in her sleep. Sophie smiled.

Life could be strange. Life could be so very strange.

Chapter Three

"I'm not staying past New Year's, Soph. I'm not. I really can't. I have to get my life in order."

For all her effort, Emma's insistence had exited her mouth a bit like a whine. Apparently even Sophie thought so. She clearly struggled against laughing while she flipped Emma's egg in the frying pan.

"And I don't eat eggs," Emma added.

"You could have told me that before I fried it up," Sophie growled. "Anyway," she said, sliding the egg onto a plate next to two buttered slices of toast, "beggars can't be choosers. This is all I've got right now. I didn't make it to the grocery store yesterday."

"Beggars?" Emma retorted as Sophie set the plate before her. "You invited me here."

"I did. And if I give you a list and some cash, will you run to the store for me? Or you could watch the shop for an hour and I'll go."

Emma's hand froze halfway to her mouth. The toast in her fingers wobbled. She dropped it back onto her plate. "I can't do that."

"Which?" Sophie returned to the stove and cracked another egg into the pan. "Go to the grocery store or watch the shop? If you mean the latter, well, people will have questions, but you can always ask them to stop in again when I'm there. Or you could just go to the grocery store. Surely you've managed to do that on a few occasions." She grinned at Emma.

Emma straightened her spine against the wooden chair back. She couldn't believe Sophie was asking her this. She couldn't believe her sister didn't even think beyond the request. "What if I run into…someone?"

"What, with the shopping cart?" Sophie tucked up to the table with her own breakfast.

"Of course not with the shopping cart," Emma snapped, immediately regretting her temper. "Sorry."

Sophie shrugged off Emma's apology, swallowing the food in her mouth. "I know you didn't mean that, Ems. I know exactly what you meant. And he doesn't live here anymore. He moved away shortly after you did."

Emma's mouth dropped open. Naturally Sophie would have that information. Sophie kept in touch with old friends, whereas Emma…Emma had abandoned them all. Why, however, had Sophie chosen to keep the information to herself?

"You never told me," Emma stated.

Sophie picked up a butter knife and slathered her toast with strawberry jam. "You never asked."

Emma narrowed her eyes. "Did I have to?"

"Yes," said Sophie in a quiet, firm voice, "because, quite frankly, I didn't think you'd want to know right after everything and later I didn't think you'd care."

Emma shoveled her egg into her mouth in silence, mind racing. This was what coming home meant. Rushing memory, old pain, curiosity, unanswered questions, admitting to your little sister you'd failed at your life's work. It wasn't like in the movies, all that sweet nostalgia and hope. It was filled with revelations like this one. Well, at least she'd be able to pick up groceries without worry.

Plowing through her toast, too, Emma chewed noisily and aggressively. At some point Sophie got up and disappeared into the bedroom. When she returned, she was dressed. She had a handwritten list in her hand and several twenty dollar bills. She pushed them toward Emma across the tabletop.

"We can start with this," Sophie said, "and then maybe we can go shopping together later this week. I need to figure out Christmas dinner anyway."

"Right, Christmas dinner," Emma echoed absently. Despite all the decorations in town and the fact Sophie's shop smelled like the holidays incarnate, Christmas seemed as far away as if it had already come and gone. Before Sophie's invite, Emma hadn't even bothered to make plans. She still hadn't bought a single gift for her niece and nephews nor had she ordered the wreath she usually sent to her parents for their front door. She hadn't given any thought whatsoever to the pending celebrations. Except for the cold, the week coming up might as well have been leading to a green midsummer for all the seasonal expectancy she felt.

"Ems, you okay?"

"Absolutely," said Emma, picking up her plate and utensils and heading for the dishwasher. She paused at the sink. There was no window here like you'd see in a house, only a solid wall that someone—probably Sophie—had cleverly disguised with a stenciled depiction of curtains and a window box filled with bright red geraniums.

Emma turned on the water. She ran her plate back and forth beneath the spray, intent on the bouncing droplets.

"Did Jack really marry her, that girl he met in college?" she asked. At her sister's long silence, Emma turned around. The light through the living room windows cast Sophie's face into shadow, but Emma could see her hands, fingers tightly intertwined, knuckles strained and white.

"Yes," Sophie whispered. "Yes, I heard he did."

*   *   *

Sophie had more than heard. She'd gone to Jack's wedding.

Closing her eyes, Sophie clutched the candle she called Christmas Snowdrift beneath her nose. She breathed in, seeking calm in the combination of lavender and fir essential oils, vanilla and the lovely, underlying cranberry and citrus hints. Sophie had hoped the subject would never come up. She hadn't known what to say then, she didn't know what to say now.

"That's why we all like your candles, dear," said a voice near the counter. "They smell so wonderful. You look enraptured."

Sophie's lids popped open. Enraptured? Filled with remorse and desperate for forgiveness was more like it—if she could ever let Emma know the truth.

"Thank you, Mrs. Rood. That's very kind," Sophie squeaked.

"I'll take the scent you have there," Mrs. Rood said, pointing at the twenty-ounce jar Sophie held. "Your expression is the best recommendation. Could you gift wrap it for me, please?"

"Happy to." Sophie hurried to the table behind the counter where she kept the gift boxes, wrapping paper and other supplies. With automatic precision she removed the hanging price tag, folded tissue paper around the candle, slipped it into the box and began wrapping, all while visualizing the day she'd bumped into Jack in the post office where he'd been changing his address.

Sophie had always been fond of Jack, always thought him a good guy, kind and honest, despite the breakup with her sister. Sophie's heart had broken almost as much as Emma's to see them split. But saying yes to his hesitant invitation? What had she been thinking? Oddly, keeping the invite to the nuptials and her acceptance hidden from Emma had been the easiest part. Harder had been not telling Emma about Jack's roundabout inquiries regarding Emma's life, how obvious it had been to Sophie that Jack still cared about her sister.

Sophie should have said something to Jack,

though, about what she'd recognized. She regretted that most of all. Instead, she'd asked an old high school friend to go to the wedding with her as her 'plus one' and never said a word.

"Sophie, dear, would you mind putting a different bow on the package? The one you're holding clashes horribly."

Sophie glanced down and gulped. "No problem," she murmured and changed the bow out. Afterward, she rang the candle up for Mrs. Rood, slipped the purchase into a bag and wished her a Merry Christmas.

The woman paused on her way out the door. "Love what you did with the window," she said. "The furnishings are charming and the one candle in the center makes a nice statement."

"Thanks," Sophie said. "Not a lot of room in there and I can't really fill the window with candles considering how hard the afternoon sun beats in. Most of them are soy and the jars would end up filled with fragrant wax soup."

Mrs. Rood laughed in understanding. "I'm going to tell a friend of mine about the painted desk and chair set. She has a young daughter I think would absolutely love it."

"Much appreciated," Sophie responded with a wave. "Again, have a wonderful Christmas."

As soon as the woman disappeared along the sidewalk, Sophie dropped her elbows onto the tiled counter and lowered her head into her hands.

She couldn't think about this. What had happened six years ago was inconsequential compared to Emma's current predicament and

Sophie's own needs. What did it matter now?

It mattered, she told herself. It did. She'd basically betrayed Emma back then. Something like that didn't go away—it got pushed into a dark and dusty corner waiting for a metaphorical broom to sweep it back out again at the most undesirable time.

Straightening, Sophie brushed her hair from her face. The morning rush had ended and the usual break had arrived before afternoon holiday customers started swarming in. She needed to eat. The baby demanded it.

Sophie crouched and opened the small refrigerator beneath the counter. Rummaging through the contents, she picked a yogurt and yanked it out. She ripped back the lid, swirled the contents with a nearby plastic spoon, and stuck the overfull spoon in her mouth right as the tiny bells over the door jangled.

Bolting to her feet, spoon clamped between her teeth, Sophie mumbled a garbled greeting at the customer silhouetted inside the door.

Only it wasn't just any customer.

It was Jack.

*　　*　　*

Sixty dollars hadn't gone as far as Emma would have hoped. Emma had two small bags in each hand and a minimal amount of change for Sophie in her jeans pocket. Nevertheless, Emma found herself in remarkably good spirits. Her mood could turn out to be fleeting, but for now she strode down the sidewalk with her head up, breathing in the crisp, cool air like she owned it and admiring the homegrown flare of Connor Falls' holiday décor. Separate from Sophie's list and funds, she'd purchased a roasting chicken and vegetables for side dishes, and planned to make dinner for her sister tonight, at a reasonable hour. It was the least she could do. Sophie had welcomed Emma into her home and into her life without demur. During the next week or two they'd help each other work things out. What were sisters for, if not that?

They might even enjoy a nice, quiet Christmas together.

So far, she hadn't bumped into anyone who'd recognized her. There had been no awkward attempts at playing catch-up. No need to prevaricate or misconstrue. She could have been in Anywhere, USA, rather than the town where she'd grown up under the scrutiny of a community filled with people who had, through the years, witnessed her triumphs and heartbreaks and shame.

Her stomach gave a sudden growl. Emma lifted her arm, bags and all, and tried to shake back her coat sleeve to check the time on her watch. She didn't notice someone had paused on the sidewalk until she plowed right into him.

Exclamations, apologies and extrication ensued. Emma managed to step away from the man who'd dropped to the sidewalk to snatch at a tin escaped from her grocery bag. Her breath caught at the curve of his ears peeking out from unkempt dark hair. When he stood, her guts rolled down into her toes and back up again to slam hard into her diaphragm.

Leaning toward her, Jack Winters slipped the fallen can back into her bag and straightened.

"Hello, Emma," he said.

His smile revealed not the slightest discomfort at seeing her again. Neither did his eyes, brown and long-lashed and friendly as ever. Had he dismissed everything between them? Maybe he had. Maybe she was the only one plagued by memories like pop-up ads.

"Jack," she said. "How are you?" Her lips had turned to lead, her voice to a breathless sigh. She wanted to kick herself.

"Good," he said. "And you? You look great."

She wanted to say something trivial and light and oh, so unaffected by his presence. What came out was a simple and barely perceptible thank you.

Jack shifted his stance, cocking his hip to one side. Emma recognized the posture. He planned on settling in for conversation. Emma opened her mouth to tell him she had an appointment.

He spoke first. "Sophie said you were in town for the holidays."

"You—you've been talking with Sophie?

When?" Emma's cheeks heated in the chill air. How much had Sophie kept from her?

Jack lifted his hand, displaying a striped paper tote with Sophie's store logo on it. "I just bought a candle called Christmas Snowdrift in her store. Sophie said it's the fifth one she's sold today. Popular scent, apparently."

Emma sucked a long breath in through her nose, releasing it slowly. "Present for your wife?"

"My mom, actually," he said, peering into the bag before lowering his hand back to his side. "She's brought up the store so many times I started to figure it was a hint."

"So, first time in there?"

"Yep."

Around his shoulder, Emma spotted her sister standing outside the shop door speaking with an older woman clasping a large bag. Emma narrowed her eyes briefly in Sophie's direction before returning her attention to Jack. "Are you here for Christmas, too? Sophie didn't mention you'd come to spend the holidays with your family."

"I don't think she knew," said Jack, "unless my parents said something to her. She seemed quite surprised to see me, though. Honestly, I haven't seen your sister since—"

"Jack!"

Both Jack and Emma whipped around at Sophie's voice. Sophie hurried toward them, waving something in her hand. When she reached them, she held a postcard-sized object toward Jack. Emma tipped her head to view it and saw it was a postcard like the one Sophie had sent to her. Sophie turned it over, revealing outlined squares framing the edge, one which had been stamped with a tiny inked candle.

"I meant to give this to you," Sophie stated breathlessly. "I keep forgetting to give them out. You get a stamp for every purchase, and when the card is filled you get a free 5 oz. candle." Her eyes darted in Emma's direction and away again.

"Thanks, Soph," said Jack, tucking the card into his bag. He made a slight, sliding movement to his right, bringing him closer to Emma. She smelled his aftershave, a scent like summertime and warmth, and so very familiar. She bit her lip.

"I have to run," Jack said, taking another step, this one putting him further away. "But I hope…well, I hope to see you both again while I'm here." He nodded at Sophie and turned toward Emma, planting a quick, light kiss on her forehead before he strode off.

Clutching the groceries, Emma stared after him. He walked in the same manner she remembered, loose, lanky, unhurried. She supposed she expected him to be changed, somehow, rather than so plainly recognizable as the man she'd known. Time had altered him a bit, small transformations in appearance such as the way he wore his hair, the lines around his eyes from squinting into the sun, laughing, living his life. These changes didn't make him different. They made him absolutely Jack in every way.

Not until Sophie had grabbed the two bags from her left hand did Emma realize her eyes had foolishly filled with tears.

Chapter Four

Later that evening, Sophie pulled a box from the guest room closet and handed it to Emma. She'd been keeping an eye on Emma all day, expecting a meltdown. To her surprise, Emma had remained calm, although quiet, and had even helped out in the shop until she'd retreated upstairs to make dinner. Sophie had come up after closing the store to delicious aromas wafting through the kitchen and a carefully set table. Sophie had always been a bit haphazard when it came to the niceties, like napkins. Emma had apparently purchased a pack at the store, rather than resorting to Sophie's use of paper towels. Sophie hadn't let it annoy her. Emma needed the things that made her comfortable right now.

"That one's yours," Sophie said, nodding at the carton in her sister's arms.

Emma dipped her head to study the folded top, brow furrowed. "This is my what?"

"Christmas decorations," Sophie said. "The ones Mom and Dad split up between the four of us kids before they moved."

Emma continued to frown down at the taped-up carton with her name scrawled across the flap in marker. "Okay. I see my name. So what are you doing with them?"

Sophie's lips twisted. "No need to get testy." She pulled out another, larger box, filled not only with the tree ornaments from her parents but the others she'd collected over the years. "You didn't take them, so Judy claimed custody of the box. I asked for it earlier this year."

"Why?"

"So I could make you take them home with you at some point." Balancing the cumbersome box on her hip, Sophie pushed the closet door shut and headed out to the living room, Emma trailing after.

"Do you even decorate for Christmas?" Sophie asked her as they passed through the kitchen. Dishes were still piled in the sink from dinner, driving Emma crazy, Sophie knew.

"I decorate for Christmas," said Emma testily behind her. "You've seen it."

"I haven't, Ems. Think about it. You've never had any of us for Christmas at your place."

Emma's footsteps stopped. Sophie continued into the living room and lowered her box onto the rug. A six-foot tall evergreen stood to one side before the window, delivered that afternoon from a boy from Luke's Tree Farm. Together, she and Emma had wrestled the tree into the stand before dinner, and wrapped it in twinkling, white bulbs.

Right now, fresh balsam competed with the lingering aroma of roast chicken in the air. Sophie was glad the all-day morning sickness had stopped several weeks prior, because even without it she was having trouble dealing with the mix.

"Never?" Emma eventually echoed in frank disbelief.

"Never," Sophie assured her.

On her knees, Sophie tore the tape from the box and folded back the flaps. From the corner of her eye she saw Emma lower herself slowly into a nearby chair, the box with Emma's name on it still in her arms. In spite of the numerous memories to be found in the box nestled in her lap, Emma's gaze remained fixed, wide-eyed, on the floor.

"Ems?"

Emma glanced up. "I'm okay."

"I don't think you are." Sophie didn't believe her sister. In the past, Emma had always been the planner, mapping out her life from the time she was fourteen. Now she'd lost her job, her home, her focus and, as an added bonus, she'd run into Jack Winters today. Okay wasn't on the agenda. In fact, it wasn't allowed. She needed to let it out.

"Really, I'm fine," Emma insisted.

Sophie shook her head and reached into the box by her knees. She pulled out a newspaper-wrapped ornament and held it a moment in her hands. Sophie's attendance at Jack's wedding was bound to come out if Emma ran into him again. Despite the much-needed release of emotion that would likely follow for Emma, Sophie didn't want her to hear it from the man who'd broken her heart.

Sophie had considered confession a vague goal for this evening, but visualization had always turned somewhat cartoonish, involving shattered ornaments and a tree toppled onto the floor.

In all honesty, what she wanted most was to avoid adding to Emma's hurt. But Jack had come home for the holidays and expressed a desire to see them both again. The truth couldn't wait much longer.

"I need to tell you about something," said Sophie.

"No," said Emma, "I need to say something first."

At Emma's tone, Sophie flinched a little. Had Jack already mentioned the wedding to Emma? No, how stupid. For one thing, Emma wouldn't have stewed on a revelation like that all day. For another, Emma and Jack couldn't possibly have been talking more than two minutes based on when he'd left the store. They'd probably not gotten past the usual courtesies before Sophie had hustled over to them in a diversionary tactic, waving Jack's postcard.

"Go ahead," Sophie said. "What's up?"

"Did you know Jack was in Connor Falls for Christmas? You said I wouldn't run into him, but maybe you didn't want me to worry—"

Sophie answered without hesitation. "No, I didn't know. Why?"

"I thought…I thought maybe you'd kept in touch with him."

Time to fess up, Sophie Parsons.

"I haven't, Ems, but—"

"I still love him."

Sophie sighed. She'd suspected as much. "That's a long time to—"

"Love a man who doesn't love me? Tell me about it."

Sophie hadn't planned to say quite those words. What had almost slipped from her mouth had Emma not interrupted was that it was a long time to yearn after what could have been. Despite what Sophie had noted in Jack's behavior the day he asked her to the wedding, he looked happy when he'd come into her store earlier, contented. He'd made the right choice for himself. She and Jack hadn't had a chance to talk about things like his marriage, whether he had kids, all the usual you asked people you haven't seen in a while, but wherever his life had taken him, it seemed the right path.

"Look, Ems, I—"

"I haven't had a bona fide relationship since Jack," Emma continued as if Sophie hadn't spoken.

"I know."

"Then seeing him today…" Emma hung her head. "I'm hopeless. Absolutely hopeless. What does that say about me as a person that I can't move on? How can I be this way? Argh," she cried out dramatically, trying to force a laugh.

Sophie shuffled across the rug on her knees and took the box from her sister's grasp, setting it on the floor beside the chair. "Aw, Ems, don't be so tough on yourself. Look at me and Ben, if you want an example of not moving on. This ain't no watermelon seed growing in my belly."

With a loud snort, Emma threw a hand up to cover her nose and mouth. Dark hair flying, she threw herself back against the chair cushion in a giggling fit. Sophie followed suit helplessly until she was on the floor clutching her belly.

"It's…not…funny," she gasped.

"So not funny," Emma choked out and went off into another bout of laughter.

At last, breathless and spent and wiping her eyes, Sophie pushed herself up off the floor. "Feel better now?" she asked.

"Better than crying," Emma answered, sucking in air tremulously in an attempt to control the laughter still lurking.

"Good, let's get back to decorating." Sophie reached for the ornament she'd dropped.

"Ben's not married, though."

Pausing with her hand above the wrapped bauble, Sophie frowned. "What's that got to do with anything?"

Emma leaned forward, pressing her fingers into her knees. "You might yet make it work, Soph. Have you thought about that?"

Sophie ripped the newspaper from the ornament, balled it up and tossed it aside. "No, we won't, and yes, I have. Ben and I have discussed it, actually, and I can assure you there's no way. We'll reach some sort of arrangement, because the baby ought to know his or her father. Otherwise, that's it. Nada. Zip."

Sobering, Emma pulled the tape from her box and began rummaging through it. "But he sure is beautiful, isn't he?"

"I assume you don't mean Ben."

"Well, he's not bad either. No, I mean Jack,

naturally."

"He'll do," said Sophie. Emma had always raved about how beautiful Jack was. A handsome man, he also possessed certain qualities, like Emma, that made him special, qualities that went beyond physical attributes. This was what Emma meant when she called Jack Winters beautiful. Sophie wondered if Emma would ever see him any other way.

"What's that you got there?" Sophie asked, nodding at a smaller carton Emma had removed from the main one.

Emma rolled back the crinkled newsprint. With an astonished exclamation, she pulled out an ornament made to resemble a snow globe, the wooden base coated in gold-flecked paint and the globe fashioned from clear, thin, crystal glass. An exquisite porcelain nativity graced the interior.

"I remember this," Emma whispered. "Weren't there four, each with something different inside?"

Sophie smiled at Emma's reaction. "Yep," she said. "They came from Germany. We all ended up with one. Aren't you glad we've kept your box safe all this time?"

Emma leaned down and hugged Sophie hard, holding the ornament at a cautious distance above their colliding bodies. "I love you, Soph."

"I love you, too," Sophie answered. "You know that."

Sophie felt her sister stiffen momentarily in her arms. Emma pulled back to look Sophie in the eye.

"You know I love you," Sophie said again, dropping her arms.

Emma's lids lowered. When she lifted them again, wariness had replaced her misty-eyed sentimentality. "What is it? What did you want to talk to me about?"

Sophie hesitated, picking at the metal hook on the ornament she still held in her hand. She didn't really want to ruin their special evening, but she should have told Emma long ago. If she held back now it would only be worse, what with Emma's disclosure about Jack. Sophie couldn't put off telling Emma another minute.

"You know when I said I'd heard Jack got married? I didn't just hear. I was there."

*   *   *

With extraordinary care, Emma lowered the snow globe ornament to the side table and released her hold on it. The glass was delicate and her grip at that moment perilous.

"I ran into him at the post office a few weeks before the date," Sophie explained, rushing, it seemed, to get the words out. "He invited me out of politeness and I said yes."

Emma gave this full thought for about five seconds. She didn't require more time to understand her sister's rationalization held an obvious flaw. "You could have said no. He would have understood. As you said, he was only being polite."

Sophie rocked back a little over her heels. After a moment, she got to her feet and hung the glass bauble she'd been holding on the tree. Folding her arms across her chest, she took a single step back to study it, as if the thing's position deserved all her attention. Emma waited, but what she really wanted was to throw something at her sister. She eyed Sophie's discarded newspaper and decided it wouldn't have the desired effect.

"I know I could have," Sophie said without looking at her. "I know I could have said no. Out of loyalty to you, I should have. But I've always liked Jack and no matter how hard I tried to muster dislike on your behalf, I've never been able to do it. You were over and done with at that point and it wasn't like he'd been some horrible monster. It killed me the two of you had broken up. I always thought he'd make the perfect brother-in-law and I was quite aware how much you loved him. But honestly, you'd drifted apart when you went away to school. I don't think he ever fully realized how much he hurt you. And I don't think he ever stopped caring, either."

Well, ouch.

Emma shifted in her seat. "But you didn't think to tell me," she said.

Sophie bent and pulled out another ornament, studying it in her hands. "I thought about it quite often, to be honest. I decided it was best if I didn't say anything. I figured Jack wasn't going to enter either of our lives again and in the end it wouldn't matter. Naturally, he would walk into my shop today and meet you on the sidewalk right after."

Sophie hung the blown glass Santa to the right and below the first ornament. "Almost like fate," she added in a mutter, reaching for the next.

"Pretty cruel stroke of fate, then, considering

how I'm feeling," Emma said.

"Fate's not always kind."

Emma pushed up from the chair and began emptying her box, setting ornaments on the cushion side by side.

"How are you feeling?" Sophie asked, having hung a dozen more decorations while Emma unpacked.

"Feeling?"

"Exactly. How are you feeling right now?"

Emma moved to stand beside her sister, contemplating Sophie's arrangement on the tree. It had looked haphazard from where Emma had been sitting, but she recognized a deliberate pattern now. Rather than spoil what had been begun, she handed Sophie the frosted glass pear dangling from her finger.

Emma gave the question thought, handing Sophie ornament after ornament from both boxes. Each decoration hung brought back memories. Christmas as a child had been filled with enchantment, recollection making each one perfect rather than what they probably really had been— hectic, emotional, exhausting and fraught with childish bickering. Yet the more she remembered, the more Emma understood what brought families back together. Moments like this, for example, as she worked side by side with her sister to create a new memory. And as with youthful Christmases, Emma might remember only that and forget the pain of this day as the years went by.

Emma took another ornament from the box. She peeled off the newsprint. Her mouth widened into a smile. Crouching, she hung the angel she'd made in school near the bottom. She couldn't believe her parents had held onto it or that they'd packed it up for her. Giving the paper mache creation a knock with her pointer finger, she watched the glitter sparkle in the light before she straightened to stand beside Sophie again.

"When I first bumped into Jack today I was shocked and a bit angry," Emma said, "but it was really good to see him."

Sophie reached into the small space between them and squeezed Emma's hand. "Wouldn't it be nice if everybody stayed? If no one ever went away?"

*   *   *

Yes, thought Sophie, tracking car lights across the bedroom ceiling. Wouldn't it be nice if everybody stayed? Life didn't work that way. Families grew, evolved, individual members moved into their own spheres.

She remembered the day she'd decided she wouldn't come back. She'd met Ben by then, had been flying full steam ahead with school, her future, her love. Mom and Dad were already talking about moving to North Carolina. Sophie's siblings were waffling about whether one of them should buy their parents' home, keep the roots going. It had been Sophie who'd encouraged them all to take flight.

Why had she done that?

Connor Falls didn't always fit into the

inevitability the world had fashioned. Many folks stuck around. Generations stayed within its boundaries. The fledgling young often returned. She had. She'd returned with a purpose, to regain the sense of home she'd lost.

Christmas was supposed to be a time when families gathered, friends stopped by and all were welcome. Five Christmases had come and gone without every Parsons member, by blood or marriage, roosting somewhere together. Someone was always missing. Most recently, it had been Sophie and Emma.

Lying in the dark, waiting for the next roaming headlight to shine through the wooden shutters, Sophie pondered the path her life had taken. Many acquaintances viewed her as quite insane, leaving a good job for the dicey territory of the self-employed. Sophie had no regrets on that level. She was happy, happier than she'd been in a very long time. Her ability to look after a child was assured within the shop's confines, as well. Many neighboring stores were in similar circumstance, family-run, children underfoot. She would make it work.

No, it was Emma who worried her.

Self-assured Emma, elegant Emma… Heartbroken Emma.

Sophie might not be able to do anything about the emotional issues related to Jack or whatever had happened at work, but she sure as heck had a market for Emma's talents, if she could only convince her to stick around.

Turning over in bed, shutting her eyes against car lights, Sophie heard a noise beyond the creaking of her bed frame. She sat up, shoved her legs over the mattress edge, feet searching for slippers before she even discerned the nature.

"Ems?" she called, but not loudly. The noise hadn't come from the apartment. It had come from downstairs.

Oh hell.

Sophie slapped around on the nightstand, feeling for her cell phone. She dropped to her knees and rummaged beneath the bed. Nothing. Where had she left it?

The only landline she possessed was in the store, and that wouldn't do her any good now.

Kitchen. Her cell phone had to be in the kitchen. She scurried toward the nightlight's soft glow beside the sink, listening hard for another sound from below. Hearing a bump, she swore softly. Why would someone break into her store? No one could possibly believe they'd be seizing a fortune from her register and candles weren't exactly a hot ticket item on whatever market burglars traded their wares.

Unable to locate her phone, she pivoted abruptly, heading for the guest room. Emma always kept her cell phone glued to her side. No need to waste time.

Without knocking, Sophie threw open the door. Emma's bed was empty.

Chapter Five

Sophie's shop was *magic*. Emma couldn't explain it. Quiet as she could she'd crept around peering at the merchandise, lifting candle lids to smell the fragrances, examining labeled lotion ingredients by the streetlight, admiring the packaging in which the soaps were wrapped, studying the enchanting scenes on furnishings. She'd peeked in at a roomy, well-organized workspace where all these things were created and prepared. Finally, she'd taken a decorated child's chair and, after ascertaining she'd do no damage, set it a few feet beyond where the light through the window cast myriad shadows. For the past half hour she'd been sitting on it in the darkness.

Sophie had done this all herself. Emma couldn't imagine the drive, the determination, the ability to take a dream and make it reality like this. It had to be tough, being both creative and business-minded. For Emma, the undertaking would be darned near impossible.

A couple passed outside, making their way from some late night assignation. Their voices vibrated against the glass like music and drifted away into the snowfall—a mere flurry—dancing through the glow from the curbside streetlamp. A few moments later church bells rang softly in the air. Emma listened as they finished their gentle melody and chimed the hour.

"Midnight."

Emma jumped. Head snapping around, she spotted her sister in the opening to the workroom, where the stairs to the apartment were located.

"Lucky I checked your room first," Sophie said, "or I would have been coming down here with a baseball bat."

Emma snorted, lips curving. "No you wouldn't have. You'd have been on the phone to the police. At least, that better be your first course of action. I don't ever want to learn you've charged down into this shop when you thought an intruder was inside."

"I hear you, sis," Sophie said, coming closer. She shuffled to a stop beside Emma with her feet clad in fuzzy red-nosed reindeer slippers.

"Or," said Emma, "just let the burglar spot you in those. You'd be picking him up off the floor."

"Ha. Ha." Sophie lowered herself next to Emma's borrowed chair. She stretched her legs out, waggling her feet from side to side. "I think they're cute. What are you doing down here?"

"Sitting."

"I see that," said Sophie. "Why?"

"Thinking."

A loud and undisguised sigh escaped Sophie's lips. She drew up one knee and plopped her chin on it, wrapping her arms around her bent leg. "About what?"

"Everything."

Sophie didn't bother to respond. Several more people passed the window, one singing a lively Christmas carol while another told him to shut up. In a moment their boisterous conversation had vanished into the night's singular quiet. Emma could hear her sister's steady, soft breathing.

"It's a whole world out there," Emma said.

"Well…yeah," said Sophie.

"And it's almost like a sanctuary in here."

Sophie rolled her head on her knee, turning to look at her. Reflected light gleamed in Sophie's eyes. "That's an odd thing to say."

Emma looked at her sister and away. "Not really. You've created this haven for yourself, Soph. Not to hide away, but to work and live and thrive in the way you want. You've taken a dream and made it reality. You should be proud of what you've done. I am."

Wriggling her bottom across the floor, Sophie pressed close to Emma's legs. She encircled Emma's bare ankle with her fingers and squeezed. "Thank you."

"Not a problem," said Emma. "Just calling it like I see it."

"And what about you?"

"Me?"

"Yup."

An anticipatory thrum, almost fear, vibrated

through Emma's temporary peace. Emma's problems couldn't be easily catalogued, repaired, solved. Her life had tumbled into a disastrous mess. She hadn't left her job on good terms, would probably never get a reference worth a damn. All her recent designs were company property and both anger and sorrow had muddied her creative vision into non-existence. Add Jack Winters' current arrival into that mix and you had one, huge cocktail of hopelessness.

Sitting up, Sophie cupped a hand around her ear and leaned sideways. "What was that, Ems?"

Emma eyed her sister askance. "You're not five anymore. Spit it out."

"You need a place, too. A place to breathe for a bit, to get your life in order. You'd like to stick around."

"Oh, is that what you think I'm saying?"

"No," answered Sophie, "that's what I say you're thinking."

Emma stood. She grabbed the chair and returned it to its place. "Lovely piece," she said, to change the subject. "Nice and sturdy. Judy would like that for Alice. You should talk her into buying it."

Biting her lip, Emma watched the light snowfall through the window. Sophie thought she could read people so well. She always had. What made her assume she knew what Emma was thinking, about anything? Sure, Emma needed to come up with a plan to bring her life back under control, but here, in Connor Falls? No. After the holidays, she'd be on her way…to where, she had no idea, but she was determined to have a strategy in place by New Year's.

Her gaze slid once more around the shop. Could she do something like this? Was she capable? Not here, of course. Not in Connor Falls. But somewhere…

Sophie suddenly scrambled upright, beckoning her across the store with a waving hand. "I want to show you something."

Reluctantly, Emma followed Sophie to a cabinet Emma hadn't noticed in her perusal. "When'd this get here? Did you have it delivered today?"

The small curio cabinet stood about four feet tall and had clearly been made many years ago, sometime, perhaps, in the early twentieth century. The wood was dark, the short legs narrow and fluted, the glass on both sides curved. An ornate metal knob on the glass at the front showed where the door opened. The shelves inside were empty.

"I bought it when I moved here, at a flea market." Sophie ran her hand over the top. "It's been in the workroom. I've always had big plans for it."

"Plans? Like painting it?"

"No, not painting it. Unless you think I should?"

"Me?" Emma studied the curio again, confused. "Why would it be up to me?"

Reaching past her, Sophie grabbed the little knob between her thumb and middle finger and tugged the door open. She reached inside. Emma had been wrong. The cabinet wasn't empty. Sophie pulled a folded cardstock sign from the center shelf and held it out to her.

"What's this?" Emma asked.

"Look at it," said Sophie.

Emma brought the card over to the window, turning the cream-colored paper toward the light. Blurred snowflake shadows swirled across four words inscribed by hand using a thick calligraphy pen.

Jewelry by Emma Parsons.

*   *   *

Perhaps the middle of the night hadn't been the best time to bring her idea up to Emma. To be honest, she hadn't been able to tell from Emma's reaction whether any other time would have been better. Their conversation beforehand had made it seem like the right moment, though. However, Sophie's perception had probably been skewed due to a lack of sleep two nights running.

Emma, on the other hand, had decided to sleep in this morning, right through breakfast. She was up now, though. Sophie could hear her moving about in the apartment. Footsteps, a chair sliding, water running through the pipes into the shower. Across the shop the curio cabinet Sophie had moved out from the workshop the day before looked stark and forlorn rather than the way she'd imagined it many times since purchase.

Believing Emma would be content working from Sophie's store had been foolish. Foolish and impractical. Emma couldn't make a living from whatever she'd sold through the Chandlery, especially considering what she'd been earning. But they would have been doing something together.

Sophie frowned at the cabinet, recognizing her own selfishness in her wishes. She would sand and paint the stupid thing. An antiqued, crackled finish in ivory with a lavender floral motif could work. But she'd been envisioning the cabinet filled with Emma's perfect designs all these months. Something made just for the store. It was tough to consider the piece used for anything else.

A clunk on the counter recalled Sophie to the customers moving about her shop.

"These gift baskets are a splendid idea. I'll take both, one for each of my daughters-in-law. Don't need them wrapped, but could you put on a nice bow?"

Sophie chose two from the box and rang up the customer. She remembered to stamp the free candle card and put everything in a bag. Wishing the woman a merry Christmas, Sophie spotted Emma making her way from the back room with a knit hat shoved down on her damp hair. She slowed by the curio cabinet, bent and peered inside, and moved on, straight for the door.

"Emma—" Sophie began. Her sister left without looking back.

"Sophie, was that your sister?"

"Oh, Mrs. Nolan, hi," Sophie said, belatedly recognizing the woman who had come to wait at the register. "Yes, that was Emma. She…she had to run out somewhere."

"I haven't seen her in years. Does she still

make that exquisite jewelry? If she's got anything for sale, I'd love to take a look. You'll let her know I asked after her, won't you? And yes, I want both of those, and this one, too," Jeanette Nolan said as Sophie lifted two candles questioningly. Sophie rang them all up, wrapped them in tissue paper for safety, and slipped them in a bag.

Once Mrs. Nolan walked away, Sophie's focus moved again to the empty curio cabinet.

She'd told Emma last night there would be a market in this town for her jewelry. She'd told her, too, there were other outlets, including the website she was paying Todd from the bookstore to help her build. Emma hadn't wanted to hear it. She said her interest in that industry was finished. The harder Sophie tried to convince Emma what she did wasn't industry, but art, the more Emma displayed no inclination to listen.

"Like a two-year-old," Sophie muttered, reaching to take another bite from the apple she'd brought down with her when she'd opened the store.

"Excuse me?"

"Sorry," Sophie apologized to the man who popped up from behind a display. He stood about her height and looked vaguely familiar. "Talking to myself."

"No worries," he said. "I'm sorry as well. I was blatantly eavesdropping on your conversation with the woman who just left. I heard you say your sister makes jewelry."

Sophie straightened, putting the apple back down onto its soggy napkin. "She di—does.

Outstanding jewelry. She worked for a company based in Atlanta but has decided to take a break from the manufacturing angle to focus again on the artistic side of her craft."

Heck, if she was going for public relations on her sister's behalf, she might as well make it good. It would have been better if Emma had been here to speak for herself, but Sophie held a suspicion she would have blown this guy off rather than discuss what she'd been doing.

The man approached the counter. Beneath a thatch of sandy hair, he possessed a pleasant face, friendly and open. He had an affable manner, too, with a comfortable, calming smile as he extended his hand to her. "The name's Will. Will English." He shook her hand and released it so he could reach into his pocket. He placed a business card on the counter a few inches from her apple. "Don't let me stop you. I can talk while you eat."

"Will English, Sophie Parsons at your service," Sophie said, making new grooves in the fruit with her front teeth. "And I'm starving," she added around a mouthful, "so thank you."

"Nice shop. I assume you're the Sophie in Sophie's Chandlery?"

She nodded her assent, still chewing.

"New?"

"Second holiday season," Sophie said, covering her mouth while she spoke. "Opened a year ago September."

Will seemed undeterred by the fact she was answering him in bits around masticated apple. He smiled. "You're doing well."

"Trying," she said, lowering her fruit.

"Eat," said Will. "I'll just look around a bit more."

Sophie kept an eye on him as she quickly finished off the apple. He bent to peer at a small, painted jewelry box and straightened with his profile in view for the first time. Tossing core and napkin into the trash, Sophie hastened around the counter. "Are you any relation to the woman who runs the bookstore?"

He turned with a start. "I'm her cousin. I didn't think there was that much family resemblance."

"Your profile," said Sophie. "Allie and I went to school together."

"I'll mention I stopped in your store when she and I have dinner tonight."

"Great. Tell her I said hi." Sophie stood a moment in awkward indecision, wondering how to bring up Emma and her jewelry again.

"Do you have any photos of your sister's work?" Will asked, as if reading her mind.

"As a matter of fact," said Sophie, "I do. Hold on."

Sophie returned to the counter and grabbed her cell phone. She flipped through the photos to find the most recent. Emma hadn't exactly shared them with her. Sophie had happened upon an article about Emma's company in a magazine at the dentist's office and excitedly taken pictures with her phone. She held up the cell and showed them to Will, one at a time.

"You're very proud of your sister, aren't you?" Will said, taking the phone from her to study one in particular more closely.

"I am," Sophie stated, lifting her chin.

He handed the cell back. "With good reason. These are fabulous. Each piece seems to possess a stark but lovely contrast of fragility and strength."

"Just like Emma," Sophie said, before she had a chance to edit the words escaping her mouth. She sucked in a breath and made a face.

"Don't worry," Will said with a chuckle. "I won't tell. Have her call me, will you?"

"Sure," said Sophie. "I'll do my best."

He cocked an eyebrow at her, confused by her words.

"What I mean is that she's a little busy with the holidays, but I'll give her your card and hound her."

"Thanks." He started to turn away but spun back with a sheepish grin. "I almost forgot my reason for coming here. I need a gift for my sister. She's in love with your beeswax lotion. I think the scent is called something and ivy?"

"Right over here," Sophie said, stepping out from behind the counter. By the time he left, Will had purchased not only the lotion but matching soap and a square votive candle. Sophie boxed and wrapped them for him. In the meantime, several more patrons entered the store, all waiting with questions. Forty-five minutes passed before Sophie realized she hadn't yet looked at Will's business card, nor had Emma returned.

Sophie held the card under the desk lamp beside the register. Her breath stilled in her lungs. She picked up her phone to call Emma, set it on the counter again. Not a phone call kind of conversation. This could change everything.

*   *   *

Emma had had to drive quite a distance away to find what she needed. The small town where she'd grown up had somehow avoided the sprawl of new construction all around, while still remaining viable. Upon leaving the town limits, one found smaller neighborhoods, or two- to nearly three-hundred-year-old homes nestled in the valley bordered by hills and open fields, or large working farms with woodlands in between. In order to reach anything resembling the shopping she'd gotten used to in her adult life, Emma took to the main road and followed it for twenty-five minutes. Now, laden with several bags and a slightly guilty conscience due to the money she'd spent, Emma headed back to Connor Falls.

The investment could be worth it in the end, if only for the happiness she might bring her sister. Even though she'd rejected Sophie's suggestion, a sleepless night to reconsider had revealed its merit. Emma hadn't planned on returning to what Sophie termed her "art"—at least not yet—and if Sophie was hoping for holiday sales it was a little late, but Emma had never seen her sister so earnest, so centered, so in control. Anything she could do to help with that made sense.

Emma took her time returning, enjoying the landscape. Even mostly leafless, the hills had a lovely, rounded appearance. In the summer, they would be green and lush. She'd worked one early

202

autumn after school in an apple orchard. She'd nearly forgotten. Hard work, it had been, but there had been something special about being outside enjoying the seasonal change as she and a few other kids labored among the regulars in the orchard. If she recalled correctly, her biceps had become rather impressive that year as well.

Spotting the sign for Luke's Tree Farm, Emma impulsively took the right. Turning at the entrance to the huge evergreen farm, Emma maneuvered with care past people lined up at the wrapping machine waiting for their trees to be secured for transport. Many put off tree-buying until the last minute. To ensure their trees remained fresh through the holidays, Emma supposed, or was it their particular tradition? The Parsons had always gotten their tree early, the longer to enjoy it even if the evergreen was shedding its needles all over the floor by January. Emma, however, hadn't had a Christmas tree in her apartment, ever. It had seemed like too much trouble in a space already cramped. She'd been surprised when Sophie had one brought into her small place, and yet when they'd finished decorating the tree it had been more than beautiful. It had made Emma feel like she'd come home.

Home. Connor Falls was not her home. Not anymore.

Emma snorted through her nose, pulling into a parking spot on the graveled lot. What a ridiculous sentiment from the woman who was essentially homeless.

Wreaths decorated and undecorated lined the exterior barn wall. Emma climbed from the car and went over to examine them. She tugged on the needles, checking for freshness as she studied the pine cones, dried flowers and holly branches adorning a select group. Other greens had been added, giving the wreaths additional texture and interest. As she mentally calculated whether there would be enough time to package one and ship it to her parents, she felt a light pressure on her arm.

"Emma?"

Emma gasped and spun around. "Jack!"

"I'm sorry," he said. "Did I scare you?"

"No, no, just startled me," Emma stammered. "What are you doing here?" What a dim-witted question, almost accusatory. "Are you shopping for a tree?" she added, hoping to sound more reasonable.

Jack reached past her with a smile to flip over the price tag on the wreath next to the one she'd been studying. He looked windblown and fit and she wanted to smack herself for noticing. "Nope," he said, "just a wreath for my old neighbor. I noticed his door is still barren and he doesn't get around much these days. I thought I'd surprise him with it this afternoon."

Jack Winters, always unfailingly thoughtful. Even when they'd broken up there had been no unkind words, no finger pointing, only quietly stated fact. Emma remembered trying to provoke him. Why? Perhaps because then she could have justified it all.

"That's very nice of you," Emma said. She glanced past him to the lot, where several children were running between the people chatting as they waited to get their trees bound. Jack had wanted children. They'd talked about it on and off. She wondered if his wife and any offspring might be among the tree shoppers. Somehow, she couldn't bring herself to ask.

"I'm late with gifts this year," she said instead. "I'm hoping I can get this wreath to my parents in time."

He shrugged, tilting his head with a small shake.

"What?" she said. "You don't think I can?"

"You're probably better off ordering one from a florist, to be on the safe side."

He was right, of course. She usually did just that. What on earth had made her stop to buy a fresh one from Luke's?

Because, a little voice inside her head whispered annoyingly, a purchase from Connor Falls would have been special—for her parents and for her. Connor Falls had been their home as a family.

Emma let out a breath in a sigh.

"You okay, Emma?"

"Yeah…"

"I don't think you are." Jack lifted his wreath off the nail and held it at his side. The wintery scent filled Emma's nostrils, prompting a strange, sad longing. "Want to get a cup of coffee?" he said. "I'm happy to be whatever ear you need."

Her head jerked up, eyes meeting his. Compassion and concern marked his expression. She wanted so very badly to say yes, to sit across from him at some small table sipping hot coffee, communing in a bubble like they used to, telling him about her life. But her life wasn't part of his anymore, and his wasn't hers. She couldn't pretend any differently. She had to stop looking back.

"Another time," she said, sidling toward her car.

"Emma."

She lifted a hand, waved and moved a little more quickly. She didn't want to be rude. She only wanted to get away from there before he said something that might make her stay.

"Emma, please."

Emma stopped. She looked at him, at a countenance no longer displaying concern so much as regret. "Jack, I—"

"I'm not married anymore, Emma. You don't need to run away."

Everything in Emma went still, as if time had stopped. She didn't need to ask him to repeat what he'd said. She'd heard him quite plainly. His words had rushed into her skin, her molecules, like quick-drying cement. She stood rooted to the spot. She couldn't even breathe.

Had this been some romantic movie, they would have rushed into each other's arms while sappy music rose to a heartbreaking crescendo. But this was no movie. This was real life. He stood with his wreath in his hand, looking unsure why he'd spoken. She worked to wriggle free from shock and managed a step back. Her mouth moved. Speech came out.

"That doesn't make a difference, Jack," she said. "It can't."

Turning her back on him, Emma hurried across the lot and into her car. Numbly, she backed out, eyes on Jack in her rear view mirror. He hadn't moved from the spot where she'd left him, but he was watching her. She looked away, pulling out onto the road.

I'm not married anymore, Emma.

The phrase circled inside her head, a wispy, clicking insect in a glass jar. She wanted to release it, let it go, but instead it remained trapped and battering against its boundaries. She needed to study it, she supposed. To figure out what the change meant.

But it meant nothing. Like she'd said, his marital status couldn't make a difference. Not after all this time. Not after all she'd put herself through. The latter was her fault, of course. No one had made her feel the way she did. No one had forced her into the mental and emotional gyrations. Certainly Jack hadn't.

Not that she'd spent all the intervening years longing for the man she'd lost. That would have been scary, in retrospect. But whenever she'd thought about Jack it had been with fondness, regret and a kind of bereavement she'd never quite shaken.

"Focus on the road, loser," Emma chastised herself when she nearly ran a stop sign. The distance from Luke's Tree Farm to Connor Falls couldn't have been more than two miles and yet it had turned into the longest two miles of Emma's life—or at least the one requiring the most concentration.

I'm not married anymore, Emma. You don't need to run away.

Those two sentences from Jack's mouth had been quite revealing, truth be told. He seemed to have recognized the emotional baggage she'd been carrying around. Or was it uttered in reaction to the moment, when he realized she couldn't even manage something as simple as having coffee with him?

Banging on the steering wheel with her open palm, Emma made her way through town to the narrow street where Sophie had her store. She pulled the car into a parking space and, with the engine still running, sat behind the wheel gazing blankly through the windshield at her past.

There'd been a time, perhaps prematurely considering their ages, when she and Jack had talked in a rather permanent way about their future. They'd even found a house—not for sale—they both would joke about as if it would someday be their own, teasing each other about white picket fences and gardens and sandboxes. Right here in Connor Falls. Emma supposed she should thank Jack for that, being the deciding factor in her exodus. If not for him, she probably would never have left at all. Of all her siblings, she alone had been the one who might have stayed. The irony wasn't lost on her.

Chapter Six

Around midday, Sophie started to wonder if her sister was coming back. She hadn't left with any of her things, though, Sophie reminded herself. And she wouldn't do that. She wouldn't just walk out without a word. Besides, where would she go?

When the store quieted down, Sophie put the be-right-back sign on the door and ran upstairs to use the bathroom and to make a quick cheese sandwich. She made two, in case her sister showed in time to eat one. If not, well, she certainly wouldn't complain about eating the second sandwich, as well.

When she returned to the shop balancing two plates, she discovered Emma's face peering into the interior from beneath a curved hand pressed against the door glass. Emma lifted a fist to knock as Sophie rushed over to unlock the door. Snatching up several shopping bags and a cardboard box, Emma struggled inside and hurried past her.

Without speaking, she deposited everything on the counter.

Sophie followed her over, holding a plate out. "Hungry?"

Emma glanced at her and away with a subdued head shake. Her eyes were red-rimmed, her nose pink.

"Ems, you've been crying."

"I don't want to talk about it."

"Fine," said Sophie, placing the plate on the counter among the bags. "Eat a sandwich then."

After several seconds, Emma poked a finger at the bread, lifting the top slice. "What is it?"

"American cheese and mustard. Nothing fancy, but it won't kill you."

Emma snorted, took a bite and set the sandwich back on the plate. "Thank you," she mumbled.

"No problem," Sophie responded, starting in on her own. She indicated the bags with a chin jerk. "What's all this?"

"Stuff."

Sophie rolled her eyes at her sister's back. "What kind of stuff?"

Emma didn't answer. One by one she pulled out the bags' contents and placed everything on the counter. Eventually Sophie understood as she recognized with some surprise the artist's hand mannequins and facial models, together with more typical jewelry displays being arrayed across the tile countertop. Emma opened the cardboard box and removed various pieces of jewelry. Sophie remembered Emma had decided not to bother bringing that particular box in from the trunk.

As if reading her thoughts, Emma spoke. "The company didn't want these designs. They're mine to do with as I please."

"More fool they, for turning those down. They're beautiful."

Emma thanked her, voice quiet.

"So you've decided to set up something in your cabinet?" Sophie tried to keep her tone light. Emma seemed quite fragile at the moment. She looked as though she might burst into tears at the slightest provocation. "I'm really glad."

"Me, too," said Emma, still avoiding her eye. "But I won't…it's only…even after I leave I can send you pieces, if you want."

"Of course, I want. That would be great." She didn't say anything else, finishing her sandwich in silence while Emma arranged the jewelry for display. At one point, her sister's hands shook. What on earth had happened while she'd been out?

"Ems."

"Help me carry these, will you?" Emma picked up a hand mannequin upon which three bracelets had been draped over the palm and one slouched around the wrist. "Do you have hang tags? I'll price them all. I'll need your guidance on that."

Sophie grabbed what she could and preceded Emma to the cabinet, where she piled everything from her arms on top before opening the door. "I'll get you the tags and a pen. You set it up how you think best. I have some lights for inside. Just run the cords through the holes in the back."

Emma squatted on the floor, studying the interior. She stuck her head inside, possibly looking for the holes Sophie had mentioned. "How can you be so nice to me after my asinine response to your offer last night?" Emma asked, voice muffled by her position.

"I'm not nice," Sophie responded. "I just know a good thing when I see it."

Emma said nothing. Her shoulders drooped. After a moment they began to tremble. Yanking her head from the cabinet, Emma slumped over her knees, her face in her hands. With an exclamation Sophie dropped to the floor beside her. She pushed the hair back from her sister's face.

"Ems, what is it? What's happened?"

"I—" Emma sniffed and gulped, struggling for control. "I'm sorry," she said, looking up, her eyes and cheeks awash with tears. She wiped the moisture away with spread fingers. "I hope no customers come in. This would make one pretty picture."

"Talk to me, Ems. Please," Sophie begged. It killed her seeing Emma like this. Emma had always been strong—or had Sophie been mistaken? Sometimes overwhelmed people put on the bravest face. From what Emma had mentioned regarding recent events, she was dealing with a lot. Something today appeared to have pushed her to the breaking point.

"It's nothing," Emma said, shaking her head. She started placing items in the display cabinet without much notice as to order.

"You can stay with me as long as you like," said Sophie. "For as long as you need. I'm not chasing you out. I—I like having you around."

"That would wear thin before long, I'm sure."

Emma reached up for another piece. Sophie yanked the necklace and display form from her reach and held them against her chest. "Why would you say that?"

Dropping her empty hands onto her thighs, Emma frowned. "I'm not good company right now. There's a lot I need to sort out. I should have been doing that for a long while, but I got caught up in life, you know?"

She met Sophie's gaze, brown eyes dark and wounded. An ache settled into Sophie's heart. "You'll find your way again, sis," she whispered.

"I don't have a job. I don't have a home. My friends, well, let's just say they're not very happy with me at the moment. I've taken such huge steps away from my family I'm not sure I can close the gap. And today, today I felt as if I got dumped down a rabbit hole. I'm still sitting in the dark at the bottom wanting very much to climb back out to daylight, but I'm not sure how."

Sophie's mouth opened. Breath came out but nothing else. Emma returned to arranging the cabinet. Sophie watched her, recognized the determination to slough off her troubles. That wasn't going to work. Not this time. "Am I…am I allowed to argue with you?" Sophie asked.

Emma grunted. "Feel free," she said. Her lips twisted.

"You have a home, if you want it," said Sophie. "I don't know why your friends aren't happy with you, but they'll get over it, if they're really friends. Your family will always be your family. There's not much you can do about that. As far as a job, hold on a second, I'll be right back."

Sophie hurried to the counter, grabbed the jewelry remaining on the tiles together with the business card from Will English. She dropped the bangles and bracelets and exquisite necklaces beside the rest on the cabinet top and shoved the business card at Emma.

Emma took the card slowly, as if it might burn. "What is this?"

Sophie sighed in exasperation. "Look at the card, Ems, will you? Will English is the buyer for Hannah's and I'm pretty sure he wants your jewelry."

*　　*　　*

Hannah's was Connor Falls' one and only department store. The store had been around for more than eighty years. Emma knew it probably never would have survived on its own in this small town, except that long ago Hannah's had been the place where all the neighboring communities came to shop as well. People in this area possessed loyalty to reputation and quality and both had assured longevity for Hannah's even through times when it could be said not to matter.

Emma turned the card over several times in her fingers, as if something might appear on the back side to explain why this guy had left it with Sophie, how he knew about Emma's work. Well, perhaps that was obvious. Sophie had told him. But how had the subject come up?

Above her, Sophie continued to stare. Emma could feel it as surely as if Sophie stood there tapping on her head. She supposed Sophie expected this turn of events to change everything, but it hadn't. It couldn't. Everything had gotten so complicated, like a knot in a thread. One thing wouldn't unravel it. In fact, one more thing might break it.

The bell rang over the door. Sophie had no choice but to attend to the customer. As soon as her sister walked away, Emma released a held breath. With deliberation, she continued to arrange jewelry in the open cabinet. The exchange between Sophie and the customer drifted into hearing, but she didn't let the content into her thoughts. She'd lost it twice now in the past half hour in sniveling weakness. She needed to hold herself together, finish what she'd set out to do when she left Sophie's apartment this morning. It had made sense to her then. Nothing much made sense to her now.

Jack wasn't married anymore. Divorced, she'd assumed, but she hadn't—she wouldn't—ask.

Suddenly she stopped dead, clutching a necklace in her hand. What if it had been something more terrible, a more enduring loss? She hadn't even stuck around long enough to find out. What was *wrong* with her?

She closed her eyes, remembering Jack's face in the rearview at Luke's. She'd professed to still love him and yet had not taken five minutes to discover the pain he might be in. He'd offered to listen to her over coffee. She'd walked away without a similar courtesy. They didn't have to be friends. They didn't have to be anything. But they had been once. That should count for something, because, thanks to Jack's generous nature, they'd never been enemies.

A bracelet had gotten tangled with another. Emma gently extricated the two pieces, taking a moment to listen now to the conversation between Sophie and her customer. Every time Emma witnessed an interaction between Sophie and a patron, she recognized her sister's easy rapport with everyone who walked through the door, friendly and kind and welcoming. She seemed happy, truly happy, and at home in her environment. Emma envied her the comfort she'd found.

She couldn't decide, however, if this was something Sophie had always possessed, perpetually carried it around inside. Perhaps it had been enhanced by her return to Connor Falls. Emma figured her sister would like her to believe the latter. She seemed determined to make Emma feel some reconnection to the place where they'd all grown up. Even this cabinet filled with Emma's jewelry appeared designed to that purpose.

Pulling the business card from the shelf where she'd laid it down, Emma studied it with her teeth in her lip. Had Sophie somehow arranged this? That would explain a lot. Like how this guy had even heard of Emma. Emma didn't like being manipulated. Who did?

Glancing over her shoulder at her sister, Emma tried to visualize Sophie engaging in such tactics. Maybe it hadn't been for any self-centered reason. Maybe it had only been because she wanted Emma to be happy, too.

Emma shook her head. Emma didn't know what would make her happy. What could make Sophie believe she knew?

Palms outstretched, Emma closed the cabinet door with a quiet click. Pushing up from the floor, she gave Sophie and the customer a wide berth while making her way to the counter to look for the price tags. She glanced at her sister as she passed by her, noting the way she stood with arms down but crossed at the wrist, fingers interlocked, body leaning slightly forward. She looked politely but sincerely interested in whatever the customer was saying. She'd always possessed that demeanor. It served her well, but it wasn't false. This was Sophie, through and through. Perhaps Emma needed to pay closer attention and learn something. According to human resources at her exit interview, Emma rubbed people the wrong way.

She hadn't always though. She knew she hadn't. At what point in her life had she changed?

As if sensing Emma's gaze, Sophie turned her head and smiled, a brief, gentle smile that nevertheless shot like an arrow straight and rather painfully into Emma's heart. "I...hang tags?" Emma whispered, pointing toward the blue-tiled countertop.

"Bottom drawer left," Sophie told her before returning to her conversation with the man standing nearby.

"Bottom drawer left, bottom drawer left," Emma chanted under her breath. At the counter she squatted and yanked the indicated drawer open.

Although not tidy, the drawer did hold a tag-filled sandwich bag as well as multiple ballpoint pens. Emma decided on the purple one. Having freed the two items from the jumble, she started to rise. A photograph fluttered to the ground. With a gasp, Emma seized it.

Jack. Jack and Emma and Sophie as teenagers, sprawled out on the Adirondack chairs on the porch, grinning at the camera. Eyes narrowed, she studied Jack's easy posture, his broad smile, the unkempt condition of his clothes and hair—it looked like he had just returned from a foray into the fields. He often did that, searching the field boundaries for interesting oddments turned up by the plow, unearthing old glass bottles and fragments of who-knew-what. Sure, there stood a bottle balanced on Jack's knee, a lovely sea green color with the added bonus of a half-rotted cork still in place.

While Sophie remained distracted, Emma rummaged further through the drawer, discovering tucked up against the edge an envelope filled with photographs. She flicked through them. They were all centered in and about their old home and contained not only Sophie and Emma, but all family members. The photos naturally included friends as well. Most conspicuously, Jack. She and Jack had been inseparable for so very long, friends first, and much more than that later.

A weight dropped into Emma's stomach. She shoved the loose photo in with the others and pushed the drawer shut. Unable to imagine why Sophie had all those family photographs stuffed into the drawer, Emma rose. Knowing Sophie, she'd been reliving old memories now that she'd returned home, but it seemed odd to be doing it in the store. Whatever the reason, Emma had no plans to ask. She wouldn't open up that floodgate. She wanted no strolls down memory lane, as the saying went. No revival of days gone by. Emma especially didn't want to talk about Jack. Talking about Jack would lead to Emma confessing what she'd learned, which would in turn encourage Sophie and her belief in fate. After all, both Emma and Jack had returned to Connor Falls at the same time, blah, blah, blah.

Sophie had finished with her customer, who was leaving the store with a promise to return. Sophie watched him until he'd disappeared through the door, and then she spun to face Emma. Starting guiltily, Emma clutched the sandwich bag filled with tags to her chest.

"What's going on, Ems?" Sophie asked.

"What do you mean?" In Emma's whirling thoughts, the question could pertain to many things. Emma dumped the tags onto the counter, beginning to untangle the thin threads, avoiding her sister's eye.

When Sophie didn't answer, Emma said, "If you're asking why I've changed my mind about selling some of my stuff in your store, well, why not? That jewelry isn't doing me any good lying in a box in my trunk. And I...I was touched that you thought of me, Soph. It took me a sleepless night to get my head around all of that. Sorry for my usual delay."

"And?"

Emma shot a glance at Sophie's earnest

expression before returning to struggling with the fine threads. "And what?"

"Do you think you'll give Will English a call?"

Emma shrugged. "Probably. Not right this second, though. I'm in the middle of something." Goodness, she sounded like a petulant child. All she wanted, though, was not to be hounded, not to be the subject of implied fantasies about her returning to Connor Falls, not to be expected to make decisions about her life immediately. She'd given herself a timeframe. She'd stick to it. She'd promised herself she would. "Let's get through Christmas, first, shall we?"

"Sure," said Sophie in a flat tone. "Let's get through Christmas." She grabbed some knotted tags from the counter and began to assist in pulling them apart, keeping her gaze firmly glued to the task.

Emma studied her sister from the corner of her eye. Sophie's fingers moved listlessly in an attempt to detangle the tag threads and eventually stopped. She dropped her hands to her sides, pushed her palms along her thighs. Her head lifted, looking past Emma to the display shelves behind, although Emma suspected she wasn't looking at a single thing on them. Sophie's feelings were hurt, Emma knew. Emma regretted being the perpetrator, but she wasn't sure which had offended Sophie more, the fact she hadn't jumped on the phone to Hannah's buyer or her abrupt, verbal dismissal of Christmas as a calendar date to be gotten through rather than what Sophie viewed as a season.

Sophie had always loved Christmas. That Sophie had invited Emma to spend it with her meant something special to Sophie. It wasn't casual to her. It was joyful and spiritual and nostalgic and magic. Kind of like Sophie's shop, Emma realized, straightening from the hopelessly tangled tags for a look around.

Why hadn't she noticed straightaway? This shop reflected Sophie more deeply than Emma had understood. It celebrated what her sister believed in, the wonder she held in her heart. No surprise people loved it. No surprise people loved her.

"I'm a river, Soph," Emma stated quietly, "with no calm place. You, you're a small and shimmering lake."

*   *   *

A *lake?* Sophie stood a moment, struck speechless by her sister's statement. Where the heck had that come from? A bland and boring lake, while Emma imagined herself as something roaring and powerful and never-ceasing. Huh. Maybe not quite that, but essentially the comparison was there.

"Well thanks," Sophie said, returning to her struggle with the hang tags.

"I think you misunderstood me," said Emma. "What I mean is you have depth and you're serene and comforting to be around. I run fast and shallow, can end up all over the place and give no one comfort, I'm afraid."

Sophie's cheek twitched. After a moment, she laughed and tossed the tags down onto the tile counter. "In that case, those were two rather amazing metaphors. Maybe you should take up writing in your spare time. However, you're none of those things, Ems. What would make you say so?"

"Because that's the way I feel."

"Oh, goodness," said Sophie. "I'm so sorry. I don't...I don't know what to say, except it isn't true. You're not a river. I don't think of rivers like that, anyway."

Emma jerked her head in a short nod. She wanted to drop it, Sophie could tell. The bell jangled at the front door. Glancing back, Sophie spotted a woman moving straight to the desk and chair set Mrs. Rood had pointed out. "I—I'll be right back."

"Okay," said Emma, giving the tags a tug. Several broke free, the threads still remarkably intact. Sophie headed across the store.

"Hi, I'm Sophie," she said to the woman standing with her chin in her hand, studying the desk. "If you have any questions, I'll be at the counter and happy to answer them."

"Thank you," the woman responded absently, taking a turn around the set. She lifted the price tag and released it as Sophie walked away. This was a customer who didn't want to be bothered. If the woman needed to know more, she'd come looking.

In the thirty seconds Sophie was gone, Emma had disappeared. Sophie snapped her head from side to side. "Ems?" she called softly.

"Over here," Emma answered from somewhere near the floor. Sophie found her on her knees before the cabinet, tags and pen in her hand, listless focus on the objects inside. With an eye on the customer, Sophie bent close so only her sister could hear.

"What happened today, Emma? Something momentous, I'd say."

Emma breathed in and out, her sweater rising and falling. "I…" One syllable, nothing more, and her voice trailed off.

"Don't make me drag it out of you, sis," Sophie threatened with a gentle smile.

"I ran into Jack," Emma said.

"Where?" Sophie realized how loudly she'd asked the question when the customer turned around with raised eyebrows. Sophie lowered her voice again. "Seriously, Ems, where?"

"At Luke's Tree Farm. I stopped for a wreath for Mom and Dad but, as Jack pointed out, it wasn't likely to get there on time."

"Right," Sophie drawled. "So it wasn't a quick how-do-you-do."

"It wasn't a particularly long conversation either," said Emma quietly, "but it was significant."

Sophie was dying to know, but the woman up front lifted a hand to wave her over. "I'll be just a minute," Sophie said. "Don't go clamming up on me when I get back. I want to know what's got you so off balance."

It happened that Sophie spent longer than a minute with the customer, who now had many questions and finally ended up putting a deposit down on the set, promising to come back for it before week's end. Sophie pulled the desk and chair from the floor and placed them in the storeroom. By the time she returned, Emma was full bore into pricing and barely looked up when she approached.

Sophie stood over her, hands on her hips.

"How's it going?"

"Fine," said Emma, although she sounded anything but. "I'm guessing on these prices. You'll let me know if I'm off-base, won't you?"

"Sure."

At her short response, Emma glanced up at her and away.

"So, you bumped into Jack," Sophie prompted again, "and…?"

"And he wanted to have coffee."

Sophie knew that couldn't be all. No matter how emotional her state these past couple days, Emma wouldn't lose composure over an invite to a hot beverage. Even with Jack. "That was friendly," Sophie said, almost like a question.

"Yeah," said Emma, abruptly giving Sophie her full attention, her brown eyes wide. "And I ran away."

Sophie had a sudden, vivid image of her sister hightailing it like a rabbit. "Surely not…not literally?"

"Just about."

"No," said Sophie on a breath.

"Right after he told me he wasn't married anymore."

Stunned, Sophie's mouth dropped open. She covered her parted lips with her hand. "When did that happen?" she asked through her fingers.

"I told you. When I stopped at Luke's. Forty-five minutes ago, maybe?"

"I don't mean the conversation," Sophie said. "I mean Jack's marriage."

"Oh, right," said Emma. Turning away again,

she picked up several tags she hadn't used and twirled them between her fingertips, watching them spin. "I don't know. I didn't ask. I just took off."

Sophie almost blurted out that Jack still cared for Emma, but she held it back. The last thing Emma needed was to go searching for whatever strength she required right now in a man she'd once loved. Emma had to find that strength inside her, now more than ever.

"Maybe coffee wouldn't have been the best idea, then," Sophie said.

"He was offering as a friend, so we could talk. I'm thinking he needed a friend, too. I didn't even ask what had happened. For all I know, she might have died or something."

Sophie sighed, dismayed by Emma's quick assumptions, her easy guilt. "What were his exact words?"

"I'm not married anymore."

"Divorced, then," Sophie said. "A widower would have expressed it differently."

"Do you think I should have had coffee with him?"

Lifting a shoulder, Sophie backed away. "Not my call, Ems. The only thing I'm thinking is that you can't straighten out your life by complicating it further, but you might find some peace of mind if you talk things through with him. That's your decision, though. But remember, I'm here for you, okay?"

"That sounds ominous," Emma said.

"Not meant to be. Only trying to be supportive."

Emma rose from the floor. She dusted off her knees, her expression suddenly determined. "You're right," she said.

Sophie raised both hands. "Whoa, I'm not taking responsibility for any decisions you make. They're yours. But I'll have your back, Ems, you know I will."

"No, seriously, you are right," Emma went on, ignoring her. "I gave myself a timeframe for getting my life back on track. I don't need complications, I need forward momentum. Even if I wanted to reach out to Jack, clear the air, I don't have his phone number, so I don't—what?"

Sophie could have cursed her oh-so-readable face. She closed her eyes, opened them again. From beneath a creased brow, Emma's attention was suddenly focused, intent, suspicious.

"Sophie. What?"

"I have his number," Sophie admitted reluctantly. "He gave it to me for you yesterday, when he was here."

Chapter Seven

Emma stood outside in the cold waiting for Jack to show up. She held the note with his phone number crumpled against her chest in her hand, like a talisman.

Time to face your past, Emma Parsons.

Time to stop being a coward.

Had she always been this way? Not that she could recall. She'd once considered herself a fierce presence in the human race, someone with smarts, someone to be reckoned with, who planned to take on the world. Not a coward. Never a coward.

Once more she opened the note between her fingertips, studying the well-remembered slant that had marked Jack's handwriting. He'd written down both his first and last name, as if she'd relegated him to the annals of ancient history, a distant profile without connection.

Had it been a natural inclination to do so, because he'd been thinking about her in that fashion? Or, perhaps he hadn't been thinking of her at all. He'd had a whole other life. And she'd needed one.

The door to the coffee shop opened. Emma stepped aside for a couple exiting into the chill air. Breath rose in wisps from their mouths, meeting the steam rising from covers on delicious-smelling brew. The afternoon sun had quickly moved toward the horizon and two days in northern climes hadn't gone very far in getting Emma used to the freezing temperatures. She eyed the patrons through the window, at least half with their coats draped across chair backs. Clearly, *they* were warm.

"Why on earth are you waiting outside?"

Emma spun on her heel toward Jack's voice. "I—um…" She didn't want to speak the truth, which was that she stayed outside so she could make a hasty retreat if she changed her mind. She didn't want to say anything at all once she got a good look at him. Her heart rolled over.

"Hi," she said. Like an idiot.

Smiling crookedly, he leaned to the side and peered through the plate glass window. "Any tables left?" he asked.

"There might be one in the corner," Emma answered slowly.

"Nope, someone just sat down there."

Emma experienced a twinge of disappointment. "Oh. Well, why don't we—"

"Get a nice big one to go? That sounds good."

"You need a coffee that bad, do you?" Emma

teased. She wanted to kick herself for falling into that kind of lighthearted repartee. "We can do that and reschedule, if you'd like."

He turned from his table assessment to give her the onceover. "Actually what I was thinking was that we'd both get a nice hot cup of coffee to hang onto and take a walk. Or have those Georgia winters thinned your blood to water? You are shivering a bit."

"It's cold," she said defensively, before she had a chance to register what he'd said. How did he know she'd been living in Georgia? Oh, right, Sophie had likely blurted it out when he'd stopped in the store.

Jack tapped on the window frame, where a thermometer hung. Incentive, Emma figured, for customers to flock inside. "It's forty-two degrees."

Emma narrowed her eyes at him.

After a moment he laughed and shrugged. "Just saying, Georgia-blood."

With his easy way, he acted like they hadn't spent years apart. Enough. Stepping past him, Emma grabbed the handle and yanked the door open. Jack followed her inside.

"My treat," he said.

"I'll have a plain old coffee, then, two sugars, two creams."

"Hasn't changed, eh?"

He remembered. Why? Why would he remember something so mundane? Jack Winters, she thought, you're scaring me.

Beside her in line at the counter, he chuckled. "Am I?"

Oh, crap, had she said that out loud? "I—" She stopped. She wasn't about to explain herself. It would only get worse if she did. Instead, she bit her lip and picked up a nearby glossy sheet from a shelf, turning it over in her hand. The slick paper announced something called The Garland Ball.

"Wow," said Jack, "they've reinstated that, have they?"

Grunting, Emma returned the paper to its place. She didn't want to discuss the quirky events Connor Falls might be planning. "I don't even remember it."

"You're really not happy to be home, are you?"

Emma bit her lip again. She released a long breath through her nose. "I don't know what I am," she said.

Jack studied her in silence before stepping forward to give their order. Emma backed away from the counter, allowing room for several more people who had entered after they had, and also to obtain some breathing space. She hadn't meant her meeting with Jack to go this way, off-balance and revealing and uncomfortable. In her head it had been more like a quasi-interview, skirting around personal feelings and dealing instead with facts.

"Here you go."

With a jerk back to the moment, Emma reached out for the to-go cup Jack held out. She circled her fingers around it, bringing the cup to her nose and breathing in the scented steam drifting through the slit on top.

"A table's opened up by the window, if you'd rather?" Jack said, tipping his head toward the huge expanse of glass.

"No," said Emma, surprising herself, "let's walk. What's a little frostbite, when the coffee's good, right?"

"It's forty-two degrees," Jack reminded her. "Frost bite isn't even in the forecast."

"If you say so," said Emma, pulling open the door and stepping out onto the sidewalk. She looked left and right. "Which way?"

"To the park?"

Emma glanced down at her feet. At least she'd had the sense to put on her winter boots. "To the park," she said, steeling herself to remain unemotional, to discuss specifics and not sentiment. She started off toward the park without the slightest need to think about direction, aghast that she recalled so clearly. She'd been determined for so long to put Connor Falls behind her and yet it had remained somewhere inside, like a virus.

Jack walked beside her, not speaking. She cut her gaze sideways several times, catching the look of him, the way he walked, the forward tilt of his head, dark hair brushing across his brow, and bit her lip again. She could do this, she could.

"So," Jack said after slurping still-too-hot coffee from his cup, face contorting in a quick flinch, "tell me what's wrong."

It took no more than that, a simple request from the well-remembered Jack, to destroy her determination. The words flowed from her mouth as if they'd been released from a faucet: the artistic stagnation in her job, the self-doubt, the withdrawal from her friends, the increased tension at work, the final blow-up, the destruction of the life she'd fashioned, the defeated return to Connor Falls.

When she finally stopped babbling, Emma realized they were deep in the park, which had been decorated for the holidays. Quaint and somewhat cheesy, the holiday figures lining the path, the stars hanging from the branches and the light-wrapped trees glimmering in the twilight, made her break into tears.

Jack didn't make a move to touch her. If he had, she would surely have run away and never, ever looked back. Instead, he stood an arm's length from her studying a caroler made from plywood and paint. He rocked a little on his heels, coffee in one hand, the other tucked into his coat pocket. Eventually he pulled the hand out, holding up a tissue in his gloved fingers.

"Don't worry," he said, "it's clean."

Lips quivering on the verge of either more tears or laughter, Emma took the tissue and blew her nose.

"You came back to Connor Falls," Jack said once she'd completed the noisy process, "because you needed to be home."

"Connor Falls isn't—"

"It is, Ems," said Jack.

Emma opened her mouth to argue further, but closed it without speech. In the near distance, church bells sounded the hour. Five o'clock. No wonder it was very nearly dark, the lights glowing ever more brightly on the trees. Tipping her head back, Emma listened to the voices on the sidewalk and unseen on the park's pathways. She thought of

Sophie, steady, maternal Sophie and her wonderful little shop. She considered the photos she'd found in the counter drawer. Memories came rushing back at her. And she didn't cringe from them. Not one little bit.

"It is," Jack said again.

Maybe he was right.

*   *   *

Sophie lowered the wrapped box into the bag's flat bottom and gave the bag handles a little shake to make sure it had settled properly. She slipped the already marked promotional postcard in next to the box. Now that she'd put the postcards on the counter, she actually remembered them every time.

"All set," Sophie said.

The woman who'd been hovering near the greeting card rack strolled back to the counter. "Your store was recommended to me by someone earlier today. Out at the tree farm," the woman said, scooping up the paper satchel. "I don't live around here, but I'm glad I came."

"I'm glad you did, too," said Sophie with a smile. "Was it Luke, the owner? I'll have to thank him."

"No, though I did meet him. It was someone else. He didn't work there, but he helped me tie the tree to my roof. Will…something." The woman shrugged. "He mentioned you by name. Maybe you'll figure out who it is."

"English?" Sophie asked. The name simply popped out. He was the only Will she knew.

"That's it," said the woman. "Nice man. Thank you for the gift wrap, it's lovely. And have a wonderful Christmas."

"You do the same," Sophie responded, pleased that Will English had mentioned her store. She was even more tickled he had remembered her name. He must really want Emma's jewelry for Hannah's.

Frigid air blasted through the store as the customer exited. Outside the crisp night had settled in. Sophie tilted her arm to read the watch face resting against her wrist. Her stomach growled. Emma had offered to make dinner and bring it down to the store for them to eat, but she hadn't yet returned from her coffee meet-up with Jack.

Ignoring the time and her grumbling digestive system, Sophie wondered how the meeting was going. Given Emma's recent state of mind, Sophie had a tough time imagining. The fact Emma hadn't yet returned could mean just about anything.

When her stomach growled again, Sophie dove toward the mini-refrigerator. Her leftover yogurt from earlier in the day would have to do for now. She and little bump couldn't wait any longer.

The door opened. Sophie sighed, snagging the yogurt from the fridge. Every time she put something in her mouth lately, someone was catching her at it—probably because she was always eating. Hoping to find Emma with something like take-out in her arms, she scrambled upright.

Will English stood hunched in his coat about a half dozen feet from the closing door, his eyebrows arching. "Did I catch you at a bad time? That's not your dinner, is it?"

Sophie waved the yogurt cup. "No, I'm waiting on Emma for that, but it's getting late and I'm starving. Sorry if she hasn't called you yet. She's been running around a bit today."

"No rush," said Will, strolling further into the store. He picked up a candle, lifted the lid, sniffed, and then absently replaced it, returning the candle to the shelf. Shoveling in yogurt, Sophie waited. It appeared Will had something on his mind. Sophie really hoped he wasn't about to tell her Hannah's now carried candles.

"Oh," she said in sudden recollection, "thank you for sending a customer my way." When he looked confused, she added, "From the tree lot? She said you helped her tie her tree onto her car."

"Sorry, right. I remember." He picked up another candle but didn't open this one, rolling it instead between his hands.

Sophie set the yogurt container down and jabbed the spoon into what little remained at the bottom. "Um, did you...did you need help finding something or..."

Blowing a breath out his nose, Will turned to put the candle back where he'd found it. Unfortunately, he jostled it into two more and the three candles clanked together. With an exclamation, he hastened to amend the situation and knocked one right over. Trying not to laugh, Sophie hurried around the counter to his aid.

"I know they're glass, but the containers are made to withstand heat so they're not as fragile as one might think." She returned everything to its proper place. "No harm done."

"Thanks," he said.

"You're welcome. What's up? Are you all right?"

"Is it that obvious?"

"Well, yeah," said Sophie, jerking her head toward the candles with a smile.

He drew a deep breath, one she heard him suck right in, and released it. His lips twisted into a crooked grin. "Silly, that I should be so nervous about this. Makes a good impression, doesn't it?"

Sophie's brow creased. "No worse than throwing the merchandise around," she joked in uncertain tones. Maybe she'd been totally wrong. Was he going to withdraw his offer to purchase Emma's designs?

"Well, I guess I should get right to it. It's just been a while and… What?"

A vague suspicion began to circle in Sophie's brain as he spoke. She had no idea what he could see in her face, but she managed to compose her expression. "Nothing," she said. "Go on."

"Okay. Good. Would you like to have dinner sometime?" he asked, running the words together. "With me," he added unnecessarily.

"I—I figured you meant with you," Sophie said, fighting the urge to giggle at the ridiculously endearing way he had asked. However, laughing right then, even something as tiny as a giggle, would probably chase him straight out the door.

"I guess this is unexpected."

"Yes," Sophie agreed, "it is unexpected. And rather complicated." She bit her lip.

"Ah, the store. Busy time for you. Not much time for dinner. How about something quick like a drink?"

"It's not that. It's—"

"Oh, you're involved. I asked, but I guess I was misinformed." He backed two steps away and paused, one eyebrow arched. "*Are* you involved with someone?"

Goodness, he was charmingly inept at this. He hadn't seemed that sort at all when he'd been in the store the first time. "I...no, it's—"

"Got it. I understand," he said, and took one more step.

"No," Sophie said, "you don't. I assure you, you don't. I'm pregnant, Will. Just pregnant."

*   *   *

Emma strode along the sidewalk, head bent against the cold, chin tucked into the bright red scarf tied around her neck. Every time she breathed, she smelled him in it, his aftershave's scent or his soap. Before they'd parted ways, Jack had wrapped his scarf around her neck. He called it a loaner, saying she could return it to him when she got her own. As if he expected to see her again. As if the absurdly intimate kindness wouldn't send her skittering away.

And it hadn't. She'd merely thanked him and told him she'd get the scarf back to him soon. As if she expected to see him again, too.

Hunching her shoulders, Emma burrowed her face a little deeper into the knit protection. She really didn't know that she would see him again. Making such a choice seemed like the rabbit hole she ought to avoid. But the spiral of her recent life appeared suddenly to have slowed. Maybe the spewing out to Jack regarding recent events had contained some catharsis in a way saying those same things to her sister hadn't. To be honest, she'd left out quite a bit in her breakdown to Sophie. Jack had heard it all.

Compared to most men she knew, Jack showed no inclination to fix it, to tell her what she should or shouldn't do. He was like Sophie that way. A good ear.

A good man.

In which case, not like Sophie. Emma snorted into the scarf.

Spotting the Chandlery sign, Emma tightened her grip on the bag in her hand and quickened her pace. Despite her promise to make dinner, the sub sandwiches she'd picked up were going to have to do. Sophie had to be starving by now.

Only slightly touched by remorse at having been gone so long, Emma yanked open the shop door. Sophie stood about three feet from the counter staring at the floor. She didn't even look up when Emma entered.

"Soph?" Emma hurried forward. "You okay?"

With a start, Sophie looked around. "Hey, Ems."

"What's wrong?"

"I..."

Emma clutched Sophie's arm, giving it a little shake. "Are you feeling all right? Is the baby—"

"Baby's fine." Turning on her heel, Sophie's lips twisted up into a crooked, sheepish smile. "Sorry, didn't mean to scare you. I just…well…I have a date."

Emma's mouth dropped. "A date? Like, a *date* date?"

"Yes," Sophie said in a slow drawl, eyebrows arching, "like a date date."

"I don't—"

"I know."

"But I—"

"Yep."

"With who?" Emma finally managed.

Sophie's lip quirked up again. "Well, aye, there's the rub. With Will English. Your possible new employer or whatever he would be called. And before you ask, no, I didn't agree to go out with him to make sure he takes your jewelry."

"That last part was a pretty lousy attempt at a joke, Soph. But does he—" Emma's eyes flicked toward Sophie's stomach and back up. "Does he know?"

"Of course," Sophie said, turning and walking behind the counter. "I told him straight out. How could I not, especially if we sat down to dinner and he found himself paying for three? I eat like a horse these days. Seriously though," she added, searching across the tiled countertop for something she didn't seem focused enough to find, "whatever he expects from a date or two, I certainly didn't want to find myself in a position of telling him later. He'd think I'd been holding back some deep, dark secret. And there's nothing secret about the fact I'm having a baby and certainly nothing dark."

"I agree," Emma said, although a small part of her had been wondering what Sophie planned to do about letting people know. Obviously, this was what she would do. Straight and open Sophie Parsons all the way. "How'd he react?"

Sophie shrugged. "Okay. I think. He still wants to go out. Hot chocolate and fresh baked goods from Gina's, then a stroll to listen to the carolers in the park."

"Good Lord," said Emma, "he sounds perfect for you."

A little burst of air slipped from Sophie's nose as she smiled. "Would you mind watching the store for me tonight? Only for a little while near closing. You can call me if you have any problems."

"I'd love to."

"Liar."

"Well, I'll do it, no matter how great my fear of the cash register. And customers. And questions," Emma said with a laugh.

"Thank you, Ems."

"You're welcome, Sophie." They stared at each other for longer than usual. A tiny chill danced down Emma's spine, followed by rushing warmth. Emma wanted to run across the store and take her sister into her arms in a great, big hug. Instead, she reached up to slip Jack's scarf from around her coat collar.

"You broke down and bought yourself a scarf?" Sophie nodded at the garment now in Emma's grip.

Emma's fingers tightened around the weave, squeezing out cold air. "It's Jack's. He loaned it to me."

Sophie's hand hovered above the small tray where she kept paper clips beside the register. With a quick movement she snatched out a purple clip and fastened together two sheets of paper from the counter. "Jack's, huh?"

"Yes," said Emma. "Jack's."

"And he loaned it to you."

"Yes."

"So he expects to see you again to get it back."

"I—yes."

Sophie's lips curved. She started humming "It's Beginning to Look a Lot like Christmas" as she gathered up several more papers and clipped them together, too.

"What?" demanded Emma, starting to feel like she was being judged.

"I didn't say anything. Are there sandwiches in that bag? I'm starving."

Emma marched to the counter and dumped the bag's contents across it. "The turkey is yours. I'm assuming you're still okay with turkey? No odd non-cravings?"

Bringing the wrapped sandwich to her nose, Sophie breathed the contents in deeply. "Turkey's not one of them." She ripped off the paper and took a huge bite from the end, talking around it. "Your time with Jack went well, then?"

"You could say that." Emma carefully pulled the tape from the wrapping on her own sandwich.

"Well I sort of just did." Sophie paused eating long enough to twist the cap from a water bottle and take a swig. "I'm asking what you thought of it."

Emma considered for a long time. She ate half her sandwich while Sophie quietly consumed hers, waiting, remaining more patient than Emma could believe. Sophie had started in on a dark chocolate bar stuffed with caramel Emma had hoped they'd share later before Emma opened her mouth and answered.

"He's still Jack," she said.

Sophie bit her lip.

"He's still *my* Jack," Emma amended.

Sophie gathered her trash, crumpled it and dropped it into the can beneath the counter. "Literally or figuratively?"

Emma thought about that. While she and Jack talked, the years apart had been glaringly evident, but she'd realized they'd only been so because in an organic and natural way they had disappeared, vanishing not as if they'd never existed, but as if they didn't really matter. She'd relaxed into herself for the first time in ever so long. As for Jack, the expression in his eyes when he looked at her had torn her heart to shreds in a lovely, delicious and frightening way. Jack, her Jack…still.

She bowed her head, fingering the red scarf stuffed into her pocket. "It could be both," she whispered, "and I don't know what to do."

"Well, you'd best figure it out, sis," Sophie said, coming around the counter to do exactly what Emma had decided to forgo, wrapping her arms around Emma and squeezing her tight. "Time marches on whether we keep up with the beat or not."

Chapter Eight

Sophie, as usual, was absolutely right. Not that Emma could figure out her whole life in the next few days, but she ought to be able to figure out a part of it, if only a tiny little part of it.

Like what to do what all her mixed-up emotions regarding Jack, emotions that had been hanging on since…well, since the day they broke up. Not really a tiny part at all.

In frustration, Emma banged the side of her head lightly against the door's edge. She returned her focus to Sophie and Will English strolling side by side along the sidewalk, heading for the bakery and then the park on their simple, but perfect, first date. When they reached the corner Emma stepped back inside, pulling the door shut. She wrapped her arms around herself against the cold she'd let in, thoughts shooting guiltily to Sophie's heating bill.

Will appeared to be a nice man. His interest in

Sophie was obvious, in his smile, his quiet solicitation, the corny jokes he made three times in ten minutes to make her feel at ease. He needn't have bothered with the latter. Sophie seemed quite comfortable in his company—maybe too comfortable. Did she not have the same interest in him?

Emma dismissed that idea as quickly as it came to her. Sophie had always been confident, calm, something that had intimidated the boys back in high school who expected someone giddy and flustered and perhaps a little in awe of them. Emma had envied Sophie's self-assurance.

Going over in her mind the steps Sophie had shown her for using the register—why was she so nervous about this?—Emma returned to the counter and took up a place behind it. She ran her fingers over the smooth, lovely blue surface Sophie had created before sticking her hands in her back pockets. Only an hour or so and Sophie would be back to close up the store.

When some time passed without a customer, Emma figured they must all be at the park observing the caroling. Her shoulders relaxed. Remembering the photos by her feet, Emma bent and opened the drawer. She had a sudden, stupidly sentimental desire to view the old photographs again. Except for the pens, the tag-filled bag and two or three post-it notes, the drawer was empty.

"Crap," Emma muttered. She pushed the drawer shut, holding her hand flat against it. Really, she didn't need to get caught up in reminiscence. All she needed was to get her head on straight.

Even as she tried to dismiss her curiosity, Emma pulled open the other drawers. Rummaging through each one, she didn't find a single photo. Wondering what Sophie had done with them all, Emma searched several baskets on the shelf. One held the promotional postcards and another held a stack of invoices. The last contained only a pad filled with handwritten notes. She glanced at the top page, which resembled an informal holiday inventory.

As the store remained empty, Emma decided to take a quick peek in the storage room. On the long worktable, evidence of Sophie's craft was everywhere. Emma located more notes pinned to a huge corkboard, these scribbled with new scent ingredients and sketched designs for a painting on a child's desk. At the bulletin board's far end a single photo hung, too large to be what Emma had been searching for. She sidled over for a look anyway.

Sophie had blown up a photo she'd taken of herself holding a sonogram picture angled beside her cheek. Across the bottom she had written the words, "This is us."

This is us.

Emma's breath rushed out in unexpected response to the scrawled sentiment. She pressed her fingers to her mouth. Tears ran down her cheeks. She missed Sophie, missed the rest of the family, she even missed this town, for crying out loud. What on earth was wrong with her, getting all emotional? Besides the wreck of her life, of course—that could explain something, but not quite all. Christmas blues? Maybe. Jack? Definitely.

Emma hurried from the storeroom, scrubbing her damp eyes with fists clenched like a child's. "Get a grip," she muttered fiercely.

"Are you all right?"

Emma's hands dropped. Her eyes flew wide. "Jack! I didn't even hear the door open!" In her shock, she sounded as though she were accusing him of sneaking in. "I'm sorry. I—"

"The door wasn't quite closed. The bell didn't ring," Jack said, jerking a thumb over his shoulder toward the offending entryway. His brown eyes studied her in frowning concern. "What's happened, Ems? Are you okay?"

"It's nothing. Everything is fine."

His expression changed in a way she couldn't quite read.

"Really," she insisted, even though she had to give her right cheek another swipe. "It is."

Jack let loose a long, deep sigh and shook his head. "Emma, you haven't changed. You fight the fight alone, even though there are people who care about you, who are willing to help or even just to listen. There always were."

"I know," Emma said quietly.

"Do you?"

"Of course I do."

Jack's lip twitched at the corner. He nodded toward the counter. "Where's your sister?"

"Sophie's out. On a date."

"A date?"

It did seem a bit absurd, when Emma thought about it. The last weekday evening prior to Christmas and Sophie goes out on a date, leaving her business in Emma's dubious control. Generally, though, Sophie wasn't irresponsible. She must possess some belief in Emma to do all the necessary things. Emma glanced quickly around the store before returning her attention to Jack. "What…what are you doing here, anyway?"

"Me?" said Jack. "I brought you something."

"You did?"

"I did."

"Coffee?"

"Not coffee." Jack reached into his jacket pocket and pulled out a small bundle wrapped in white tissue paper, tied around with a thin silver ribbon. He held the package out to her.

Emma raised her brows at the gift and hesitated. "What is it?"

Snatching her hand from her side, he dropped the package into her palm. "You're supposed to open it," he said. "That's how you find out."

Biting her lip, Emma tugged at the ribbon, releasing the bow. No tape had been used and the tissue paper fell away. Nestled inside lay a scarf in the loveliest green color Emma had ever seen, a color like springtime layered in fog. She lifted the scarf from the paper and held the soft weave to her cheek. "It's beautiful," she whispered.

Jack leaned forward on his toes, shoving both hands into his jeans pockets. "I figured if you're going to stick around a bit, you'll need your own."

"What makes you think I'm going to—" Emma began, and stopped. Jack's expression had softened, becoming almost amused and with something else lurking in his eyes, something that made Emma's heart leap in her chest.

"You might," he said. "It wouldn't hurt."

"Jack, I…" She couldn't say it, couldn't put into words all the turmoil, the longing, the confusion and indecision circling in her heart.

The hope.

"I know," he said. "Me, too."

*   *   *

Sophie sipped the hot chocolate in her hand. The past hour had been fun, so much fun, but now Will stood beside her in silence. The carolers were in rare form, yet she knew it wasn't only their talent suddenly tying his tongue.

They had been getting on, as her grandmother used to say, like a house a-fire. Sophie wasn't exactly sure what that meant, although it likely had something to do with the conflagration aspect. Yep, a house-afire, until…

Until.

Sophie lifted her head, shaking away the hair pressed into her eyes by her hat. She drank a little more hot chocolate.

He'd said her being pregnant didn't matter. They were going on a date, nothing else, just something fun to do together. But after a particularly long bout of laughter, or perhaps a smile held too long, she had witnessed the realization bloom in his eyes.

She was a package deal. If it came to that, anything he might hope for in the future included another little person.

Her gloved hand strayed to her coat front and rested there. Fa-la-las filled the air, nearly overpowering the church bells in the distance. Two teenage girls, twins from their nearly identical features and hair and bright pink hats, paused on the pathway, blocking Sophie and Will's view. Will stepped right, Sophie left, increasing the distance between what had been their bumping elbows. Sophie drank again, swallowing hot cocoa gone lukewarm.

Dating while pregnant had been the last thing on her mind. Dating during the busy Christmas season should have been. When she envisioned such a thing as a date—which came to her only in vulnerable moments few and far between—it had been as some vague consideration in the very distant future. She couldn't imagine what it would be like for Will or any man to embark on a path, however casual, with a woman carrying another man's child. Pending changes in enormous proportion had to float between them like a growing balloon they both knew would pop.

Still, Will had insisted even after she told him. Probably hadn't had enough time to process the facts. Or he was merely too nice to do an abrupt about-face.

Spotting a trash can, Sophie walked over and tossed the almost empty cup inside. She took off her gloves and stood a moment readjusting her scarf before pulling them back on. Her breath frosted in the air.

"Hey."

Sophie spun slowly on her heel. "Is for horses,

my grandmother used to say."

"Mine, too," Will admitted. "I looked around and you were gone."

"Sorry about that. I was throwing away the dregs of my chocolate."

Will reached past her, tossing his coffee cup in after hers. "The carolers are wonderful."

"Amazing," agreed Sophie.

"And so are you."

Sophie's shoulders jerked. "What?"

Will locked his gaze on hers, speaking quickly. "You've done a lot in the past couple of years. You were certain what you wanted and focused on getting there. You successfully accomplished many changes in your life. I'm sure having a baby wasn't in the plans, and yet, well, you've made adjustments and you're happy with them. I admire you."

"Um, thank you." Though pleased by his praise, Sophie sensed the "but" coming like a breath that could only be held for so long.

He turned toward the carolers as they began their next tune. "I just had to get that off my chest."

Sophie moved up next to him. She pressed both hands deep into her coat pockets. "Because?"

He glanced at her and back to the singers. "I wanted you to know."

"Because?" Sophie prompted again.

"Because," he said without looking at her, "I like you and—"

"And this is weird," Sophie finished for him.

He sighed in a swirl of white. "Not the word I would have used, but yes. This is weird."

There, out in the open now. Sophie lifted her

chin, her gaze on the group performing before them. "I get it," she said. "I understand."

"Is it weird for you, too?"

Sophie thought for a second. "As an in-the-moment sort of thing, it was fine."

"Until you realized how well we were getting along," he said. "I'm asking myself, when has that ever been a bad thing?"

Sophie flinched, even though she knew he hadn't meant what he'd said in the way it sounded. "Getting along with another person is never a bad thing, Will. Sometimes, though, it can be complicated." Look at Emma and Jack, she thought, or even she and Emma, for crying out loud. Drawing a deep breath, she faced Will. "But I think we're getting ahead of ourselves."

He had raised his hands to clap along with everyone else at the song's conclusion, but slowly lowered them back to his sides. "Right," he said. "First date."

"First date," she echoed. She forced a crooked smile to her lips. She didn't feel much like smiling. Odd. She'd been told she always had a smile for everything and everyone. "I really did have a wonderful time. This was pretty perfect for me, hot chocolate, a warm pastry, carols in the park, but I'm thinking I should get back to the store. Emma's not very experienced when it comes to handling customers."

Will's shoulders slumped inside his jacket, whether in relief or disappointment Sophie couldn't be sure. It might have been both. "Tell her I'll be giving her a call to schedule an appointment to meet," he said.

"I will." Sophie took a step back. She waited a second to see if he planned to offer to walk her to the store. His remark regarding a call to Emma seemed to indicate he wouldn't. "Enjoy the music," she said, to completely let him off the hook.

"Oh, no, I can—"

"I'm good," Sophie said. "You shouldn't miss the rest of the program." With another hard-won smile, she took a few more steps away from him and waved. Pivoting on her boot heel, she strode to the park entrance. She didn't trouble herself with listening for footsteps following after her. She knew there wouldn't be any.

*   *   *

Emma plugged in her phone and set it down quietly on the bedside table. She'd put it on silent an hour ago so as not to disturb Sophie. When the screen lit up yet again, Emma quickly read the text and typed a response before snuggling down into her pillow with a smile. She pulled the quilted blanket up to her chin, turning her gaze to the streetlight's glow outside the window.

Passing voices drifted like whispers through the glass and from the television in Sophie's bedroom. Sophie had claimed to be tired, exhausted from her day. Even so, Emma had begged for particulars about her date with Will English. Sophie had been non-communicative except to say it had been nice. Nice. What did that mean? When Emma briefly showed her sister the gorgeous scarf from Jack,

Sophie hadn't had much to say about that either. She'd smiled, genuinely pleased, without asking any questions. None.

Something was off with her.

Emma picked up the phone to check the time. Nine-fifty-five: way too early for bed, especially considering all the thoughts zipping through her skull. Emma listened for a few more minutes to the television. It had been on the same nearly non-existent volume since Sophie had said good night and slipped inside, quietly shutting the door behind. Trying to make as little noise as possible, Emma sat up, untangled her legs from beneath the covers and planted her feet on the floor. She hastened back into the clothes she'd removed a short time ago, pressing her feet into her winter boots. After wrapping the scarf from Jack around her throat, she snatched up her coat, her phone, her gloves and the key Sophie had given her to the back door, the one that led to the fire escape.

Stepping into the hallway, she heard nothing but the droning television from her sister's room. Emma crept closer and tipped her head toward the door. Slowly she turned the knob and peeked inside. "Oh," she said in surprise, "hi. I thought you were asleep."

The flickering light from the television screen danced over Sophie's face. "Just thinking. Where are you off to?"

"I'm not very tired. I thought I'd go for a walk."

Sophie whipped the covers back. "Want some company?"

"I—now? Sure. Okay."

Leaning against the doorjamb, Emma waited while Sophie hastily pulled clothes on over her sleep pants and tee shirt. At one point Sophie glanced in Emma's direction. "Lovely scarf," she said. "In case I forgot to say that earlier. From Jack?"

Emma grunted acknowledgement. Boy, Sophie's mind really must have been elsewhere. "He said I would need it if I decided to stick around a while."

"Nice man, our Jack."

Emma's lips curled.

"And are you?" Sophie asked, tugging on her boots. "Sticking around a while, I mean."

"Maybe."

Sophie paused in tying her bootlaces and then resumed the action, forming the bow with a quick snap. She straightened, fluffing her hair free from her sweatshirt collar. "Let's go to the pub. I'm not drinking, of course, but I could eat a horse."

"You're still hungry?"

With a smirk, Sophie aimed the pointer finger on both hands toward her stomach. Emma laughed and tossed Sophie's coat to her. She nodded toward Sophie's haphazard attire. "You don't want to put on something different?"

"Nope."

Together they clambered, giggling, down the metal stairs outside. Low clouds overhead diffused light from the town's streetlamps. Snowflakes began to fall before she and Sophie had exited the alley.

Sophie lifted her face to the sky. "You okay with this?"

Emma pulled her scarf tighter around her throat and yanked up her hood. "Perfectly."

Snowflakes drifted onto their faces, shoulders, caught in their hair as Emma kept pace with her sister's stride. On the rare occasion they had snow in Georgia Emma stayed home. The feather-light sensation against her skin was something she hadn't realized she missed before this moment.

Abruptly, she halted to peer into a shop window.

"What?" Sophie returned to look around her outstretched arm.

"Those dresses are gorgeous," Emma whispered.

"You're smudging Cindy's window," teased Sophie. "Come on."

"Cindy? Not Cindy Michaels?" Emma and Cindy's younger sister had been in the same class. Cindy had made a marvelous blouse Emma had bought from her when she was a high school freshman.

Sophie nodded. "Yep."

"What a lovely store." Emma's brow wrinkled. "Maybe Cindy would be interested in a line of jewelry specifically designed to go with her dresses?"

"So," said Sophie quietly, "are you staying around a while, then?"

Emma backed from the window. She looked up and down the street, hard edges gentling in the snow. Sure, Connor Falls presented an enticing picture in all its Christmas finery, especially with a timely snowfall, but was it home?

It had been, once. Being here, now, with Sophie, made her remember that. She'd spent her adult years without roots. Standing in this town, on this sidewalk where she'd walked more times than she could possibly remember, she felt them stretching down below her feet and outward in every direction.

"Maybe," she said, wavering, because there was Jack. There would always be Jack.

Sophie studied her a long minute before tugging her sleeve. "Hungry. Me. Can you *not* hear my stomach growling?"

"Loud and clear, sis." Emma linked her arm through Sophie's and started once more toward the pub. At the corner, she stopped again. Her breath swirled through the snow. The tavern was close enough for voices and music to drift out through the opening door and become muffled when it shut. Emma met Sophie's gaze and held it.

"Does it ever feel like defeat?" she asked. "Coming back?"

Sophie smiled. "Not to me, Ems. Not ever."

Chapter Nine

Sophie stretched, squinting at sunlight glistening off the snow outside onto the ceiling above her bed. What a strange, exhilarating night she and Emma had wandered into at the pub, filled with noise and laughter and an exuberant, contagious cheerfulness. It wasn't the drink—well, for some perhaps it was the drink—it was more the atmosphere, the knowledge that these were the people she knew, and if she didn't know them, they still shared this town with her, and they were together celebrating the holiday season. Even Jack had been there, dining with some friends at a corner table. As soon as he spotted Emma he'd called out, "Georgia-blood!" and came to her side as if he'd never been away from it. They'd resolved something between them, those two. Sophie couldn't imagine when. There really didn't seem to have been enough time. Maybe there didn't need to be.

Exhausted from the late night, she'd wandered through yesterday bleary-eyed and stupefied, but fortunately Emma had been in attendance all day to lend a hand. Today though…today was Christmas.

Snuggling back beneath the covers, Sophie closed her eyes, palm resting flat on her abdomen. Last Christmas, the first with the Chandlery, she'd spent by herself. This Christmas she had Emma, and even if she hadn't, she still wouldn't have been alone. She could feel precious life within her like her own breath.

Suddenly, bare feet slapped along the hallway. Sophie heard the melodic beeping alerting Emma to a text on her phone. This was followed by two more. "Ems!" Sophie called lazily, "who's blowing up your phone?"

The door opened. Emma's tousled head appeared. "Nobody. Go back to sleep. You need it."

"Jack?" Sophie persisted, grinning.

Emma shut the door.

"Fine," Sophie mumbled, "don't share." She rolled over, burrowing her cheek against the pillow. Peering through one eye, she brought the numbers on the nightstand clock into focus. She could afford another half hour. She'd put all the packages under the tree last night, including those she still had to mail, with apologies, to family. Their appearance around the Christmas tree made the living room look more festive. However, if she heard one crinkle of paper she'd be out there in a flash.

Remembering how Emma hated to wait, she yelled out to her as she passed by again. "No peeking!"

"I know," said Emma from the hall.

Satisfied, Sophie curled her fingers over the growing mound of her stomach. "Merry Christmas, little one," she whispered, closing her eyes.

When she next opened them it was exactly an hour and thirty-five minutes later and the apartment smelled like coffee and cinnamon. Sophie scrambled from the bed and into her robe and reindeer slippers. She hurried to the kitchen, where she found Emma tending to scrambled eggs in the frying pan. On the counter stood a platter filled from side to side with freshly baked cinnamon buns. Emma glanced over her shoulder.

"I was just getting ready to call you," she said. "Brunch is almost ready."

Sophie shuffled over to the buns and stuck her chin out over them, breathing in. "Did you make these from scratch?"

Emma snorted. "Remember who you're talking to, Soph."

"Right." Sophie scooped a bun from the plate and bit into it, icing dribbling onto her chin. Emma deftly flipped eggs onto plates, tucked toast at the edge and a bun for good measure. Beyond her, in the living room, two tray tables had been set up with utensils, napkins and steaming mugs.

Following her gaze, Emma said, "Yours is hot chocolate. Coffee for me, though, nice and strong."

"Remind me to keep you around."

"I don't think you have a choice," Emma shot back, carrying the plates into the living room.

Grinning, Sophie trailed after her sister. "Ems!

You've been moving the gifts."

"Especially those," Emma said, pointing to four identical tubes. She sat at the table with her coffee and began eating. "I shook them a few times. Still can't figure it out."

"Well, open yours then," Sophie said, tucking into the eggs while they were still warm.

"Now?"

"Yes, now. I wish they'd been finished in time for me to mail the others out for Christmas, but at least you'll have yours."

Emma leaned sideways, stretching her whole body in order to grab the package with her name on the tag and not get up from her seat. Sophie had always removed the wrapping from her gifts with precision, saving the paper for craft projects. Emma, on the other hand, was a ripper. Paper littered the floor before Sophie had swallowed her second mouthful. Unrolling the tube's contents, Emma gasped. She tipped the printed collage toward the light streaming in through the window, exclaiming over each picture.

"I wondered what you were doing with all those photos in the drawer," she said. "You had one made for each of us?"

Sophie took another bite from the cinnamon bun in her left hand and nodded, warmed by Emma's smiles. "I reckoned the holidays we couldn't be together," she said around a mouthful, "we'd still have these reminders of ourselves as a family."

Emma's smile faded. "We'll always be a family, Soph. Always." Her phone vibrated on the table. She snatched it up for a quick read, pecked in a reply and put the phone down again before rising. "I've got something special for you, too."

"Finish eating first," Sophie said. "I have patience."

"Well I don't." Emma headed for the back door, grabbing her coat and keys from a kitchen chair. "It was too big to fit under the tree. I'll be right back."

Sophie took her plate over to the window, watching for Emma on the sidewalk below. In the next few weeks or months, they would surely get under each other's feet in this small apartment, but they'd adjust. Emma's life was going to change, as would hers yet again in short order. It would be okay, though. Everything would work out as it should.

After a few minutes, Sophie realized Emma hadn't exited the alley. She maneuvered around the tree for a better look, not finding her. At clanging footsteps on the fire escape, Sophie hurried back across the apartment in time to see a huge box with a bright red bow press against the glass in the door. Sophie swung the door open and stepped out of the way.

"Emma, what on earth have you done?" Sophie cried with a laugh. "Whatever's in that box is going to have to hang from the ceiling, because there sure as heck isn't any room on the—"

Sophie's hands flew to her mouth. On the fire escape landing behind Emma and the lowering and obviously empty box stood their brother Robbie and his wife with their two kids, while below them, waving and grinning, were Judy and her family.

"Merry Christmas, Soph," said Emma. "I knew this was what you wanted most of all."

*   *   *

Emma couldn't believe she'd pulled it off. Yet here they all were, together for Christmas, except Mom and Dad, of course. It had been impossible for them to get flights. Emma had made the calls early on Christmas Eve morning, never expecting anyone to change their plans. Well, how wonderfully nice to be so very wrong.

Her phone went off in her pocket. Emma pulled it out, smiling at the screen. This time the text was Jack, wishing her a merry Christmas. Where they were headed, she and Jack, Emma had no idea. She wouldn't count on anything, but she also wouldn't count anything out.

Leaning against the kitchen counter, Emma texted Jack back and returned the phone to her sweatshirt pocket. Robbie came into the kitchen with a load of dishes, depositing them in the sink. Everyone had brought something. There had been plenty to eat.

He kissed her on the cheek. "You've done good, sis," he said. With a grin, he shambled back into the living room.

She had, she had done good and doing good felt great.

Movement at the door caught her eye. A man stood centered in the window, looking over his shoulder. When he turned front, Emma recognized him straightaway. She hurried over to the door and opened it.

"Will?"

Stepping inside, Will glanced toward the living room. "Emma, hi. Merry Christmas. I…I actually didn't expect there to be a houseful today, from what Sophie had said. Can I…I'd like to talk to Sophie for a second."

"Sure." Catching Sophie's eye, Emma waved her sister over and then vacated the area so they could speak. She tried not to look too many times in their direction, but as she wasn't the only one filled with curiosity, every eye eventually turned their way. One of June's children, Emma wasn't sure which, asked rather loudly, "Who's that with Aunt Soph?"

Laughing at the question, Sophie brought Will into the living room and introduced him.

"Will, you can stay for a bit, can't you?" Robbie asked. "Sit down. I'll get you a plate."

"I'll get it," Sophie said. She grabbed Emma's elbow on passing, tugging her into the kitchen. Emma held the empty plate Sophie handed her while Sophie ladled food onto it.

"What gives?" Emma asked. "Everything okay?"

Sophie arched a brow. "He said he can handle weird if I can."

Confused by the reference, Emma snorted. "And is that a good thing?"

Sophie took the dish from Emma's hands and smiled. "I guess we'll see."

As Sophie carried away the heaping plate, the

phone in Emma's pocket sounded again. Emma yanked the phone out and read the message. *Would you have a little time to step outside?*

Rolling her eyes, she texted back: *Where are you? You are allowed to come up, you know.*

I'm in front of the store. Let's take a quick walk.

Emma's gaze lifted to her family crammed into the living room. Except for Mom and Dad, they were all here, all together for the first time in quite a few years. An odd sensation crept into her chest, a mixture of heartache and incredible joy. For the first time, she thought she might truly understand why Christmas meant so much to Sophie—her little sister Sophie, soon to be a mom, standing to the side in observation and wearing a quiet and happy smile. As if sensing Emma's eyes on her, Sophie's turned in her direction. Emma pointed at the cell phone she held, then the door, and then made a silly walking motion toward it with her fingers.

Sophie's smile deepened. She nodded.

Emma grabbed her winter gear and went down through the store, to avoid a fuss. She wouldn't be long. By the time anyone noticed her absence she'd be back. After shutting and locking the shop door behind her, she stepped out into the frigid sunlight where Jack stood hunched in his coat, waiting for her.

"Nice scarf," he said.

"Yeah, some guy gave it to me. Apparently, he wanted his back."

"I'm sure that's not the only reason."

"I'm sure it isn't either," she said.

The slow spread into a grin she remembered so well hadn't changed at all. She didn't think it ever would. When she'd first bumped into Jack, she had worried those little reminders would always process as painful. She'd been wrong about so many things.

Jack tipped his head. "Walk?"

Emma fell in beside him, chilled hands stuffed into her pockets, chin tucked into the scarf's whisper-soft folds. Snow had fallen again during the night, freshly coating objects in a fluffy, crystalline layer. The cold bit at Emma's cheeks, but she had no urge to complain.

"Where are we going?"

"You tell me," he said.

"What?"

"Pick one place you really want to go within walking distance, and we'll go there."

Emma stopped dead on the corner. She could tell by Jack's expression he wasn't kidding. "I don't know of any," she said.

"Give it a minute, Ems. Some place will come to you."

Compressing her lips, Emma released a loud breath from her nose. "Okay," she said, "this way." Turning left, she walked faster than she intended until she reached Connor Falls Book Emporium. Warmed by her pace, she halted before the front door. Jack strolled up slowly to a standstill beside her. Emma pressed near the glass, peering inside the closed, book-filled shop.

"I used to save up my babysitting money to come in here and buy books on jewelry-making," she said.

Jack nodded.

"You came with me once or twice," Emma added, meeting his eyes in their reflection. He'd sit beside her, patiently waiting while she viewed each page before deciding to buy. Drawing a deep breath, she headed back onto the sidewalk. "Am I only allowed one place?"

"Of course not," he said.

Checking for non-existent traffic, Emma trotted across the street, her rubber soles crunching the frozen slush piled near the curb. Outside From the Hart bakery, Emma eyed the gingerbread house front and center in the window. There'd been a bakery in this location since well before Emma's birth, most recently changing hands right before she went away to school.

"Gina still makes the best baked goods in Connor Falls and beyond," Jack said beside her.

"Are you tricking me into a walk down Memory Lane?"

"Not tricking you at all, Ems. These choices are yours."

Right, she thought. Mine.

Walking more slowly, Emma continued down the block with Jack at her side, all the way to Hannah's. The huge building took up the whole corner, the first floor lined with enormous windows filled with Christmas displays in an amazing variety. There had always been something magical about Hannah's at Christmastime.

"The buyer for Hannah's is interested in my jewelry."

Jack said nothing, rocking a bit on his heels as

he viewed their reflections in the glass. After a moment, Emma moved on, past the tavern where she and Jack and Sophie had had such fun two nights ago. When they reached the church, Emma clasped the black iron fence surrounding it in her gloved hands. The bells started up, beginning, as they always did at Christmas, with a few measures from a recognizable carol.

We talked about getting married here someday.

"We were young," Jack said, as if she'd said those words out loud. "Really young."

"I know."

"There's a lot of history, together and apart, and all of it is important, Ems. It makes us who we are now."

"I know," she said again.

He took a step sideways, closer, curling his hand over hers on the fence. "And then," he said in a quiet voice, "there's always the future."

"I know," she said, one last time. He leaned toward her, pressing his lips gently onto hers. The church bells filled the air with their old familiar song.

Home
for the
Holidays

Chapter One

Fallen leaves lay along the roadside in faded colors. At some point a light snowfall had coated the crisped brown edges with a sugar dusting, making me stupidly hungry, reminding me I'd skipped breakfast. I always told my clients, "Don't skip your morning meal, it sets the physical and mental tone for the rest of the day."

You think I'd have learned after all this time.

But no.

About a lot of things.

My phone trilled in the cup holder. I glanced down at the text from Mom and away. She could wait because a) I was driving, and b) I was almost there. Another five minutes and I'd be pulling into the driveway. A very long driveway, leading up to the expanded farmhouse she and Dad had purchased ten years earlier after selling the house nearby where we'd grown up. The house stood on about twenty acres a couple miles outside Connor Falls, bought with a dedicated plan to follow her midlife crisis dream. She'd not been wrong.

I spotted the sign for Hummingbird Farm. A

new one, it looked like. Mom had been talking about a replacement and it seemed she'd taken care of getting one over the summer. I hadn't been to see Mom and Dad since springtime. I had a silent bet with myself this would be the first thing she mentioned. Not my haircut, not my new car, not the fact my brother only lived ten miles away and he probably hadn't been there since springtime either.

Turning into the driveway, I noticed the fields to either side pocked with cornstalk stubble. She and Dad didn't grow corn. They rented the fields by the road to a local farmer. Those closer to the house were strategically planted each year with various sunflowers, zinnias, mums and other hardy flowers for cutting, as well as pumpkins and summer vegetables, the sorts Mom used in her business. What didn't get used she sold elsewhere or sometimes gave away. I caught sight of the ornamentals as I got closer to the house. Fall blooms in pots dotted the walkway together with white gourds that had somehow avoided damage from the recent freeze. At intervals between, small evergreen trees with burlap-wrapped root balls had been settled into metal buckets. Wreaths decorated the front windows on both floors as well as the front door, and a huge one had been affixed to the barn. Every year my dad climbed up on a ladder and hung the fresh greens. Every year I got pains in my chest thinking about him doing it. He wasn't getting any younger.

He'd get downright surly if he ever heard me say those words out loud, though, so I didn't. One day I'd have to. My brother darned well better make the ten-mile trck to join me for that conversation. Better still, he should come and hang the wreaths instead.

And maybe he did these days. We'd never talked about it.

Frowning, I pulled the car over into a "family" spot. Parking spots were designated for us, for customers and for those utilizing the venue. Quaint little metal signs on black posts advertised these spaces clearly, pointing out who went where and how to get there. The signs for ours read Hardwick Family Only. Someone obviously couldn't read. I parked my car next to a dusty black Jeep with Delaware plates. Whoever they were, they hadn't come half as far as I had.

I eyed my short 'do in the visor mirror, spot-checked my teeth from force of habit since I hadn't eaten, then turned off the ignition before grabbing my purse and shoving my phone back into it. I'd leave my luggage in the trunk until later. The plan was for a longer than usual visit, up to the day after Christmas, so I'd brought two bags with me. No need to walk to the door encumbered since I anticipated hugs before being chastised for having stayed away since spring.

My boots crunched on the gravel, echoing off the beautiful red barn where events were held, from family reunions to weddings. The upcoming weekend's affair happened to be a wedding, holiday-themed and all. Mom had sent pictures of the planned décor, the bride's and bridesmaid's gowns. *You always wanted a winter wedding*, she'd written in her email. Yeah, when I was twelve and thought the whole thing would be terribly romantic and beautiful.

Despite my cynicism, I still carried around the image in my head. The bridesmaids wore cranberry, the men ivory, long-tail tuxes. The flower girl I'd pictured with a delicate floral wreath on her head, skipping along the carpeted aisle in a leaf-green dress, tossing flowers here and there (what did I know? I'd been just a kid myself), while I dressed in a gown over which a forest green velvet cloak draped to the floor. The wide hood took a veil's place, my face hidden demurely within its folds. Poinsettias lined the aisle and evergreen draped each pew. I remembered there were lights, too, in my imaginings, warm white lights like on old-fashioned Christmas trees.

Egads. Really? I must have been watching too many Disney movies.

The front door opened before I'd mounted the porch steps, interrupting my thoughts. I expected my mother's face, but instead my gaze met the back of someone's head. A man, a bit tall, fumbled for the screen door handle behind him without turning. I heard my mother's voice in the shadowed hall beyond. I kept climbing, stopping at a safe distance from the swinging door and the man's anticipated exit.

"I'll see you in a few days, then," he said as he stepped backward. I reached out a hand on the off chance he'd keep coming. He did. When my hand made contact with his back, he jumped a mile and spun around.

"Sorry," I said. "I didn't mean to startle you."

He rocked to one side and straightened, staring at me. I had the uncomfortable feeling he didn't know what to say. No problem would have worked, or that's okay. Or even, hi, I'm insert name here. Instead, his gaze shifted to my feet. He mumbled something unintelligible and darted past me and down the porch steps. Mouth open, I pivoted on my heel to watch him stride with an odd hurried gait across the gravel to the parked Jeep and climb inside. The engine revved. His face turned in my direction behind the closed window, hand lifting as he ducked his head in what I supposed might be a greeting or an apology, after which he backed the vehicle up and pulled away.

I turned to the door, to Mom standing there watching him, too.

"What on earth?" I said.

"Oh, don't mind him," she answered, stepping out.

"Who is that?"

Apparently too distracted for traditional hug-type hellos, she continued to look after his car as he made his way to the driveway's end. "The new photographer I've been working with," she said. "Had you been here anytime in the past six months, you'd know."

And cha-ching. If I'd made a literal bet, I'd be rolling in the cash. Or not. Sure things didn't generally come with huge pay offs.

Mom reached out and grabbed me in a one-armed embrace. "Hello there, daughter. I like your hair. Come on inside. We're letting in the cold."

* * *

I trailed after her down the hall and into the humongous kitchen, also decorated for Christmas, including the equally humongous fireplace, big enough to roast a whole hog in if such were your fancy. Greens and holly hung from the mantel, giving off a wonderful scent.

I shirked off my coat, draped it on a chair, and headed for the coffee pot. I touched the Pyrex: still warm. Helping myself to a mug, I filled it halfway, dumped a hefty spoonful of sugar inside and headed for the fridge for some creamer. As I opened the door, I realized neither Mom nor I had yet said a word since I'd entered the house. If I lived there, this might have been considered halfway normal. But, as she'd reminded me, we hadn't physically been in each other's company in more than six months. Sticking my head inside the refrigerator, I checked the usual place for the creamer, then four more.

"So," I said, locating some half and half and sniffing the container to be certain the cream hadn't turned, "he travels an awful long way to take photos."

I heard a clank and pulled my head from the appliance. Mom had set a small metal pail on the kitchen table I hadn't even noticed she'd been carrying. Poking out from the top were the remains of what had once been fern leaves, dried on the plants to leafless but intricate design. They would make a pretty addition to the greens across the fireplace, I thought, and stopped myself. I'd never had a yearning to be crafty. I'd been trying to stifle it in my blood my whole life.

"What makes you think he's come a long way?"

"Delaware plates," I said, pouring enough half and half into my coffee to turn it a very light brown.

"Oh, I guess he hasn't taken care of it yet. He's been living in Pennsylvania for about seven or eight months now. In Connor Falls."

"Huh," I said, taking a sip from my mug and wrinkling my nose. "Someone who hasn't been born here actually moving to Connor Falls."

"What's wrong with that?" Mom asked, shooting me a glance as she bent over the few ferns she'd spread out on the table. "It's a wonderful place."

"I know it is. I'm just wondering what would draw a person here. It's not a hotbed of industry. He couldn't have made the move on some vague hope he'd be guaranteed a living."

Mom drew a deep breath. I heard it across the room. "He was seeking peace and quiet," she said, her tone meant to shut me up. How long had she known me? That never worked.

"And what's his name?" I persisted. She looked at me again. "It's not like we were introduced," I reminded her.

"Arlo. His name is Arlo."

I slugged down more coffee. What I really needed was food. "Like Guthrie?" My mind went to a finch I'd once had, when I was ten.

"Like Guthrie," she said. Shoving the ferns back into the bucket, she exited with it, stage left. I followed.

"Where are you going with that? Do you need some help?" I called after her. When she didn't answer, I pursued a different path. "Why is Arlo looking for peace and quiet?"

She stopped dead, pivoting on her heel to face me. "Because he needs it. If you want to know more, you'll have to ask him."

"I don't know him."

"You would," she said, "if you came home more than twice a year."

Ouch. Twice in fifteen minutes. "We talk all the time, you and I. That counts."

Her shoulders dropped. With her free hand she pushed hair loosened from her ponytail away from her face. The sunshine through the rear door highlighted the silver in the russet brown, the laugh lines at her eyes, the slight crease in her brow. Really, she hadn't changed much at all since I was a kid. People said I looked like her. I should be so lucky.

"You're right, Suze," she said. "I'm sorry. I'm just a bit stressed about the wedding this weekend." She shrugged, lifting her shoulder toward her ear. I stepped forward, grabbing the fern bucket.

"Well, I'm here now. What are children for, if not to be at their parents' beck and call?" I smiled at her and kissed her cheek, breathing in the fragrance of her shampoo. "What are you washing your hair with these days? Smells delicious." I pulled away and moved with her toward the enclosed back porch.

"Do you like it?" she asked, tossing her ponytail so the scent wafted my way once more. "I make it myself."

"Of course you do, Mom," I said.

Generally speaking, my mom possessed the ability to do just about anything she set her mind to. The words "no, you can't" had been eradicated from her mindset while still in the womb. If she hadn't already learned a skill through osmosis, she set out to acquire it.

I found myself painfully reminded of this fact when I stepped out onto the porch and spied row after row of beautifully arranged centerpieces on wooden trestle tables, each one fabricated with items from the garden, the woods, the fields, and local markets. I wouldn't even know where to begin. But once Mom had decided to start this business of hers, and convinced Dad it would be worth his while, too, she'd set about gathering the knowledge to perform every aspect herself. Not that she did it all. That would be too much. For one, it hadn't been long before she'd turned over feeding the attendees at barn events to caterers. However, before doing so, she'd gone from the simple meals she'd raised us on to complex gastronomy.

She often tired me out just watching her. Maybe I kept my visits to a minimum for good reason. Not true, of course. The winds of change were drifting into my sails.

"You creative types make me sick," I said.

Mom snorted.

"Seriously, though, those are gorgeous."

Hands on hips, she eyeballed her creations. "I've been tossing around the idea of teaching a course on how to make table centerpieces like these in January, when things slow down."

"Okay, now you're just showing off." I plopped the bucket on the nearest table.

With a laugh, she scooped the ferns out and carried them over to a table with a much-painted expanse of cardboard covering its length. She glanced back. "You look nice. You might want to change if you're going to help me."

Her smock hung nearby. Since she happened to be wearing a ratty sweatshirt, I took the smock down and slipped the stained, paint-spattered garment over my sixty-dollar sweater. "I'm good," I said.

Mom handed me a can. I turned it over, reading the label. "Metallic-red spray paint? Don't you usually keep these things natural?"

"The bride wants some glitz."

Alerted by her change in timbre to a lower register, I shook the can and popped off the cap without further comment. Mom pushed some latex gloves at me. I tugged them on. Side by side, we merrily transformed elements that had been a deep, lovely brown into a color resembling a soda can, hanging them to dry by clothespins on an overhead line as we went along.

"So tell me more about this friend of yours," I said while we worked.

"The bride? I hardly know her." Again, that tone.

"I mean Arlo. I can tell you're fond of him. How did you end up deciding to use him for events? How did he even find you?"

She clipped another gleaming fern to the twine before answering. "I'd been advertising, after Debbie gave notice. He had references."

She seemed to be holding something back. "Is he like my age?" I asked, trying to draw her out. "Does Dad know you have a thing for a younger man?"

"Susan!"

"Kidding, Mom. I'm only making conversation."

"You're only being nosy," she said.

"Could be," I agreed, "but after the way he practically ran from me outside, I have a right to be curious."

"No," she said, "you don't. Like I said, you have questions ask him next time he's here, which will probably be the day before the wedding. He deserves that courtesy. I won't talk about him behind his back."

I blew a long breath out over my lips and returned to shaking and spraying and hanging in silence, but I couldn't hold out for long. "Tell me about the bride then. Her, you don't like. I'm sure you'll spill about her."

Releasing a resigned chuckle, she did. In detail and warming to the subject to the point she set down her paint can and forgot about the ferns. The bride, in her mid-thirties and therefore ought to be knowing better according to Mom, had been understandably fussy in the beginning, but over the past several weeks had called with countless changes, to everything.

"Are you charging her for these alterations?" I asked.

"I wasn't, but I'm going to have to. It's in the contract that I can. The wedding and reception are this weekend and these changes may end up being costly, if they can even be accomplished." She pushed her hair away with her forearm and reached for her paint can, looking with surprise at the now empty table and the bright red desiccated ferns drying overhead. I snapped off my gloves.

"All done," I said. "I'm assuming this, too, was last minute."

"Uh-huh."

I shook my head. "I don't know how you do it."

"I don't know how you do what you do," she said. "I love my work, all of it, even with the issues."

"Are you thinking I don't?" I asked, but gently.

I only wanted to make sure I understood her meaning.

"That's not what I'm saying, no." She took off her own gloves, laid them down on the cardboard to dry and reuse, and then switched a small oscillating fan on low to move the air around. "But do you? I'm just curious. Do you? We've never really discussed your feelings for your job in detail. I only know it took you…away."

My lip quivered, like I was two. I turned my attention to the gloves I'd cast aside, trying to straighten them out for re-use as Mom had done. She focused her attention on returning the spray paint to the shelf beneath the table, giving me a moment.

"I like what I do," I said finally, abandoning the fidgety latex. "I don't love it. I never imagined I'd love it, but I'm really good at it. Like you. I just don't have the added bonus of love."

In more ways, I realized, than one. I wondered where Dad was. I asked.

"He had to run to the rental store for table linens. Apparently white no longer works."

"Ugh," I said. We both laughed.

It was good to be home.

Chapter Two

My older brother had been residing in England for work the past three years. Mom never complained about his infrequent visits. Having an ocean between them made all the difference, I suppose. However, in the morning, my younger brother Simon drove over from his whopping ten miles away. We had the same initials, Shepherd, Simon and I, including middle names. We were the SHH. Mom and Dad thought giving us those initials hilarious, like a perpetual shushing.

I met Simon outside in the driveway as I headed into the barn carrying replacement linens from the back seat of Dad's car. Simon and I kissed and hugged awkwardly around the tablecloths before dividing the load in half. He followed me into the cavernous space carrying his portion which, I have to say, I made sure was larger than my own.

He'd been a tall, gangly kid and had become a tall, gangly adult with two tall, gangly kids, ages seven and nine. They took after Dad, my Gran said last time we were all together, like lick on spit. I'd never heard the saying before, but I do remember I almost split my jeans laughing. I stood beside him now, looking up at his face, the rafters behind his head whitewashed and lined with tiny, clear LED lights.

"It's pretty amazing what they've got going here, isn't it?" I said.

His mouth twisted: Dad's mouth. "You're just noticing this now?" he drawled.

"Let's just say I'm really recognizing it now."

His ruddy eyebrows lifted and he turned on his heel, looking up at the ceiling, then the tables and chairs folded and piled against the wall. "Maybe we should set these out?"

"Not right this second," I said. "There's fresh coffee inside and I ran out earlier and picked up some baked goods from Gina's."

"What time was that?"

"About six."

"You were actually up at six?"

"Ha-ha. That's when the bakery opens. I like warm donuts. This is the only time I allow myself to eat them, when I'm home."

"You'll need a nap soon."

"Nope," I said.

"How much coffee have you had already?"

"Enough."

We looped our arms together and headed back to the house doing a fair imitation of Dorothy Gale and her lanky, straw-stuffed companion skipping along the yellow brick road. When we were halfway across the large graveled lot, I glimpsed Arlo's black Jeep parked between my car and Simon's. He still sat inside, silhouetted against the cold morning sun. I stopped, jerking my brother to a halt.

"Arlo," I said.

"You've met him, then?"

"Not yet." Releasing Simon's arm, I marched over to Arlo's vehicle and paused beside it, tapping on the driver's door window. His reaction was immediate and alarming.

"Oh, no, oh, no," I said, knees bending to bring my head closer to the glass. "I'm sorry! I didn't mean to startle you again!" I grabbed for the door handle. He beat me to it, pushing the door open. I jumped back before the door struck me, although it probably wouldn't have. I only imagined it might, based on his abrupt movements.

"You shouldn't do that," he stated.

"Shouldn't do which? Tap on the glass or try to open the door?" I felt suddenly off-kilter and defensive. I hadn't done anything wrong. I knew I hadn't, yet it seemed as though I'd been accused.

"Tap on the glass," he said. "You did startle me."

I sucked in a breath, took another step backward. He exited the Jeep and stood, tall enough I had to tip my chin way up to look him in the face. A puffing breeze tossed his very dark hair across his eyes. He shoved the strands from his forehead, his gaze on the ground.

"Is Mrs. Hardwick in? Mary?"

"My mother, you mean?"

"Yes," he said, much as if he didn't recognize the slight sarcasm I meant to convey. He met my gaze with a brief glance and quickly looked away to the front door. "I know you're her daughter. You look just like her."

"I, uh, well yes," I stammered. "She's inside."

He swung the Jeep door shut and strode past me, taking the porch steps crookedly and two at a time, like a man in a hurry. Opening the screen door, he knocked with his fist on the wooden one. Several seconds later Mom opened it, ushering him inside.

"What is up with that guy?" I asked the air in general. My brother answered.

"It's a long story and not mine to tell. You should probably ask him."

I should ask him. *I* should ask him. I didn't know him well enough to ask him any personal questions and our interactions seemed to indicate to me I never would. Simon and I trailed after Arlo into the house, where we both headed for the kitchen, the coffee and the fragrant donuts calling my name. Mom's voice and Arlo's drifted in from the enclosed back porch. I couldn't quite hear what they were saying with Simon going on about the kids and the upcoming Christmas play, I understood my opportunity for eavesdropping was nil. Not that I engaged in that sort of thing. Not usually anyway.

I jerked my head toward the hallway leading to the back door. "Maybe they'd like something? Should I go offer?"

"Suze," Simon said in response, "you're incorrigible."

"Incorrigible? Is that a word we're using nowadays?"

"If the shoe fits," he said.

"Idioms, too. You're getting old." Ignoring his smug expression, I arranged a few pastries on a plate, gathered up some napkins and made my way to the porch. I peeked through the door panes before entering. Arlo and Mom stood side by side, attention drawn to something Arlo appeared to have placed among the centerpieces on the table. Dipping my head to the side, I glimpsed a few photographs. I elbowed my way in through the partially open door and held out the platter.

Mom glanced up. "Sweetie, how thoughtful. Thank you. Arlo, would you care for a pastry?"

He did care for one, although he didn't say so. He waited until I neared and offered him a napkin, which he took, as well as an éclair.

"Thank you," he said, not quite looking at me.

"I don't think you've been introduced to my daughter," Mom said. "Arlo, this is Susan. Suze, this is Arlo Woods."

"In the driveway," he said. "We sort of met in the driveway when she knocked on the glass." He turned to me and held out his éclair-free hand. I took it, slipping my fingers into his grasp. He shook my hand, a nice warm shake, the kind I liked. I hated it when men barely gripped your hand as though they feared they might break you.

"I'm sorry," I started, but he interrupted me, too.

"Don't be. Don't be sorry. It's not your fault I'm like this."

When his gaze met mine, my breath hitched. I dropped his hand and almost dropped the plate. He caught it as it slipped, settling the dish gently back onto my palm, all pastries still intact. I hooked my thumb over the edge.

"It's nice to meet you, Arlo," I said.

"Likewise, Susan," he answered with an odd formality belied by his twisting lips.

Confounded and actually blushing, I hastened back to the kitchen.

*　　*　　*

In my other life, my real life, I coached and supported people with eating disorders, and here I stood, stuffing in a third donut. Thank goodness my clients couldn't see me. Even so, I felt as though I betrayed their trust by my actions somehow. To make matters worse, Mom caught me at it. She didn't say anything, though, didn't even give me one of her looks. She probably had no idea I was on my third. Either that or she understood chastising someone for their eating habits never did anyone any good.

"Whatcha got there?" I asked, jutting my chin at the photos in her hand. Arlo had left. I had seen him walking by, heard the front door open and close. I'd almost gone after him, to try once more to engage him in something resembling conversation.

"Arlo brought these over. The bride—"

"Does she not have a name, or did her parents christen her 'bride' in anticipation of her future calling?"

Mom's lips curved in a tired attempt at a smile. "She has a name. I just don't want to use it right now."

I wiped a crumb from the corner of my mouth and nodded in understanding.

"Anyway," Mom went on, "she wanted to see more sample poses. More than the other hundred she's already seen. I have a thumb drive with digital copies on it. I'll email them over to her in a little bit. Any coffee left?"

I took her washed cup from the drain board and poured her some, no sugar, creamer a miniscule splash. "When did the bride advise you of this new demand?"

Mom took the mug from my hand and held it to her nose, breathing deeply. "Last night," she said. "Texted me around ten-thirty."

"Ten-thirty?" I echoed. "Are you kidding? Whose spoiled child is she? Do I know her?"

Mom shook her head, possibly disinclined to tell me in fear she'd further prejudice me against the poor darling.

"If she calls again, let me handle her," I said.

"That would be something to witness, certainly, but the day is nearly here. There's not much more she can alter at this point."

"Okay," I said, "but you know, if you need me, I've got your back."

She laughed out loud, reaching past me for a sweet concoction. "You better wrap these and put them away for Simon to take home to the kids," she mumbled around a mouthful. "Where's he gotten to, by the way?"

"The barn, maybe? He was eyeballing those tables when we were out there."

With a sticky noise halfway between a moan and a garbled cry, Mom led the charge from the kitchen, I figured to stop Simon in his tracks. I trotted to keep up with her. Simon might look like Dad, but unlike our father he loved to take control. Even I knew the tables did not come down for dressing until the morning of the event. Other things needed to be cleaned, moved, shoved, placed and perfected before crowding the floor with seating.

I skidded to a halt behind Mom in the open barn doorway. Inside, Simon and Arlo conversed with interspersed grunts. Table legs thumped the floor. We peered through into the interior. Nearly all the tables had been set in place. I fully expected Mom to lose it, what with the bride's harassment already fraying her nerves. Instead, her lips curved, slowly, her expression holding a mixture of sad and happy.

"It doesn't matter," she whispered.

I had a suspicion she didn't mean for me to hear her words.

My brother spied her in the shadows. Arlo turned at his expression, following his gaze. Both saw Mom, but not me yet. I stayed in the shadows when she went forward. Arlo looked at her briefly before he slid his eyes away. So it wasn't only me. A little slower than with me, but he did it with her, too. Habit, maybe? It seemed an odd type of habit to develop.

Yet he turned back a few seconds later, the smile he now offered bright and astoundingly engaging. "I hope you don't mind I gave Simon a hand. He looked like he could use one."

Simon laughed, clapped him on the shoulder. I saw him flinch, recover himself, smile again, a bit more cautiously this time. Mom took his hand in both of hers and held on a moment.

"Thanks," she said.

He shrugged. "Anything else I can do let me know."

"I'll keep you to that."

"Please," he said, quite solemnly, "do."

Mom dropped her hands and stepped aside as he started to circle around her. He gave both Simon and Mom a nod before heading toward the door where I still stood being nosy, discovering too late I couldn't duck into hiding. I'd already learned sudden movements and abrupt noises around Arlo weren't good, so I stood my ground and waited.

He paused next to me, head up, squinting toward the chilly sunshine outside. His dark hair curled at the ends, right over his coat collar. His left hand he'd stuck in his pocket. The other he held out a little from his side, palm parallel to the ground.

"How long are you staying?" he asked.

"Until the day after Christmas," I whispered. Why was I whispering?

"Good," he said and left, walking over to his Jeep, climbing inside. He drove away without another glance in my direction. I let out a breath, not realizing until that moment I'd been holding it. Behind me, Mom and Simon had entered into a discussion about leaving the chairs go until she'd had a chance to do some other things in there. He agreed, said he'd be back on Saturday morning to get them set up. She thanked him then for helping Dad with the wreaths again this year. Again. I turned around and caught my brother's eye, smiling at him from across the room.

"So what's next on the agenda?" I asked, striding over to them, trying to dismiss the fact Arlo thought it a good thing I'd be sticking around for a while. Perhaps he didn't. Perhaps the odd exchange was only his way of making a stab at conversation. I couldn't help but wonder if he'd always been this way.

Simon rolled his eyes. "Oh, you're going to be sorry you asked her that. Mom probably has a list a mile long."

Mom reached into her coat pocket. She pulled out a list, a literal list, creased and folded and a little grimy. Her fingerprints marred one edge, made bright by the red paint we'd used yesterday. If she murdered anyone with that list she'd be sunk. Whipping a pencil from her other pocket, she snapped the paper semi-flat and used the point to tap each item.

I met Simon's no-longer-rolling eyes. "This is your fault."

"I know," he said, "but you encouraged her."

Mom ignored us. She reached the list's end, flipped the paper over and back again. "I think we're good." She looked from my face to my brother's. "For now."

"Hallelujah," said Simon. "I've got to get home anyway. Kids have early dismissal."

Simon worked from the house most days now. Lucy commuted an hour each way to her job. They'd been lucky enough to find a way for Simon to be there when their sons returned from school. I admired their relationship, Simon's and Lucy's, the practical way they worked together toward solutions to benefit their family. It wasn't always easy, and it wasn't always possible. Mom and Dad were like that, too. Shepherd and I, well, not so much. Not that we had families. Shepherd had a wife, though, Malory, a woman he'd met and recently married in London. No one had been able to travel to England for the event on such short notice. I'd been hoping they'd make it back here for Christmas. No such luck. Not this year. I knew Mom was disappointed. So was I.

"I'm going to head into town for a bit then," I said. "I've got some Christmas shopping to finish." They both gaped at me as if I'd sprouted a gross and unnatural rash. "What? I'm not like you guys. I'm ill-prepared, remember? The last minute thing is my fun."

They waved me off in dismissal. I scurried to the house to retrieve my purse and keys and to check if I remembered to comb my hair this morning. I didn't always.

By the time I came out, Simon's car had disappeared and Mom stood on the walkway frowning at a text on her phone. She glanced up at me.

"I'm not even answering this one."

"Good for you," I said. "Do you need anything while I'm out?"

"Coffee creamer. I know that half and half isn't your thing."

"I don't need it," I argued. She really didn't have to cater to me. She had enough going on.

"Your brother likes it, too."

"Well alright, then, that's settled. Creamer it

is." I patted her arm and continued down the walkway, stopping after another few feet when she called me. I pivoted on my heel, eyebrows arched.

"I love you, Suze."

I melted inside. "I love you, too, Mom."

"Try to be home for dinner. I'm making your Dad's favorite."

"Will do," I said, vowing to be back early enough to lend a hand. With a little wave, Mom turned and made her way up the steps and into the house. She didn't look back or she'd have found me still standing there. I couldn't imagine what she would have seen on my face. Biting my lip, I headed to my car and town.

*   *   *

I made my first stop the bookstore. I had little time if I wanted to make it back to the house to help with dinner preparations. Like Mom, I also possessed a list. One I'd made yesterday morning on a torn envelope before getting in the car.

To accompany what I'd already bought and wrapped, I wanted a book each for Sammy and Stuart. My brother had continued the Hardwick tradition naming his sons. I asked myself why, constantly. What I hadn't asked was what the boys were into these days, reading-wise. I ended up taking longer than anticipated trying to come to a decision regarding proper material. Despite my eleventh-hour tendencies, I didn't like to grab without thought. I enjoyed buying Christmas gifts. I enjoyed making them special. After seeking assistance from some guy named Todd stacking books, a most helpful individual, I exited the store with my purchases and moved on, checking my list again.

I had Mom, I had Dad. I had also previously mailed two lovely art journals to Shepherd and Malory at their new address. I still needed Simon and Lucy and one more for Mom, a little gift, something special. Lucy loved candles, raved about a store that had opened in town fairly recently. I went there next, walking straight up to the woman behind the counter.

"Do you know Lucy Hardwick?" I asked.

The woman looked taken aback. Recovering, she smiled. "She's a customer."

"Good. I'm her sister-in-law, and I want to get her a candle, but I don't want to get her one she's already bought. I know she shops here. She talks about it all the time."

"That's wonderful," she said. "Tell her I said thank you."

"I will. You're the owner?"

"That's me. The Sophie in Sophie's Chandlery." She grinned. "And I think I have the exact candle for you. It's not a Christmas scent. Were you looking for a holiday fragrance?"

I told her I was not. She guided me over to a display on a side wall, lifted a candle from its place, popped off the glass lid and held the container out. I took it, leaning in close, but not too close, and breathed. Instantly I found myself transported to someplace warm, tropical and embracing.

"Perfect," I said. Lucy loved southern beaches.

"There's a matching soap."

"I'll take that, too."

"Gift wrapped?"

"Sure. Thank you." While she packaged and wrapped the soap and candle, I wandered around the store looking at the various hand-painted furnishings. I only knew they were painted by hand because the little card on each told me so. The pieces were impeccably executed. "These are lovely," I said. "Do you—"

I stopped, backtracked, snatched up a small wooden box from the tabletop where it had been nearly lost. Exquisite flowers had been painted on a green-stained background, a ruby-throated hummingbird fluttering delicately over one. Not for nothing had my mother named the place she and Dad bought Hummingbird Farm. Every year she cleaned and placed dozens of hummingbird feeders in her gardens and they came in droves, so many that sometimes the air filled with a sound nearly beyond hearing from their tiny wings. When she managed a good long break in her day, Mom would watch them for hours. She'd captured them in photos small and large, framed and hung around the house.

"I'll take this, too," I said. This was more perfect than Lucy's candle. More perfect than anything. Mom would love it.

Satisfied and with only one more gift to pick up, I headed back to Main Street. In the world of gift-giving, Simon remained a conundrum. I really had no idea what to get him. Lucy hadn't been able to help when I asked. She was finding herself in the same position. We all did, every year. So, I peered for inspiration into every window I passed, moving little by little toward Hannah's. The department store had been founded long before my parents were born, surviving through periods of economic upheaval and still strong. Its endurance remained a point of pride among the older Connor Falls' residents, as if they had singlehandedly managed to keep it going. Still, I didn't want to shop in there. Not today. I didn't want to buy Simon a nice shirt or a tie—especially since he rarely wore either these days—but something more personal.

I slowed to a halt at the corner, my thoughts clicking away on ideas. Pulling out my phone, I checked the time. My gaze snapped to the sidewalk in front of Hannah's decorated windows. Several people gasped at the same time I noted Arlo bent double like he'd been pole-axed at the waist, his right arm extended and hand spread flat on the sidewalk. Slowly he righted himself. He stood a moment, settling himself into place, murmuring to those who offered to help him as he waved them away. His eye briefly caught mine.

I couldn't have felt worse. I recognized his fervent wish to be anyplace else but there. Hoisting my packages, I darted across the street and up to him.

"Are you okay?"

"Yeah," he said, "thanks." He turned on his heel, checked with his arms out slightly from his side, and a moment later started walking in the opposite direction he'd appeared to have been headed. I fell in beside him, not caring whether he wanted me there or not.

"Where are you going?" I asked.

"Home."

"I'll walk with you, if that's okay."

"You're already walking with me," he said. "You don't have to. I'm fine now. Even if I wasn't…" He let the sentence hang, walking with his head up and his brown eyes holding steady on a distant point.

"What happened?"

"Just now?"

"Yes," I said, thinking *as opposed to when?*

"I gave up my cane a few months ago. This hardly happens anymore. I'm good at catching myself."

Not an answer, Arlo. Not a direct one, anyway. "Is that why you walk with your hand out a bit? Because your hand is used to a cane?"

"Everything takes a lot of concentration some days," he said. "Even now. Even talking."

I took the hint and shut up, moving with him in silence. After a few minutes his stride steadied, his pace increasing. Not outstripping mine, by any means. He didn't seem inclined to race away. His gaze still held tight to that isolated point somewhere ahead.

"The most insidious injuries are those others can't see."

I shot a sideways glance at him, unsure if he wanted me to question that, or if he'd only uttered those words as a general complaint to the universe. Suddenly, though, I got it. I understood.

"How did it happen?" I asked.

"Car accident. Nothing broken, except my brain."

"I'm sorry," I said quietly.

"Don't be. I'm getting better."

I nodded, not speaking, mulling over how sorry I felt, not for him, but about what had happened to bring him to this…whatever it was exactly. We'd walked another block on the quiet side street when he halted on the sidewalk, resting his hand on a white wooden fence. I stopped beside him.

"This is it," he said. "My house. You've walked me home."

I looked up, startled. I hadn't been spending any time picturing Arlo's home, but if I had been, it wouldn't have been this. I studied the house's façade, a quaint bungalow similar to many others inhabiting the back streets as you got away from the lovely and simple Folk Victorians on either side of Main. White siding, black shutters, a paver walkway curved to the front door surrounded by carefully tended grass and a few strategically placed evergreen bushes. In summertime, flowers probably filled the pots on the little porch. Right now, they stood empty, one to each side.

"Well, okay then," I said awkwardly. Should I make sure he got inside okay? I doubted it. Whatever had nearly taken him down fifteen minutes earlier seemed to have relaxed its grip. I had no idea if he'd accept the offer, or if it might outright offend him. Pretending to shuffle my bags, I eyed him from beneath my lashes. I found him staring at the sidewalk near my boot tips. He glanced up, met my gaze and moved on.

Time enough, though, to recognize what I'd witnessed earlier when Mom introduced us. Arlo Wood possessed profound determination in the most beautiful eyes I'd ever seen.

Chapter Three

Some people unnerved you with their constant staring. What was the opposite of that? Arlo. He didn't stare at all. His gaze constantly went elsewhere, like to my feet, or past my head, or sometimes, I'd noticed, his eyes closed when he spoke, as if in concentration. Probably was in concentration, given the brief reference to a brain injury. I had no idea what he saw behind his lids. I wanted to. I wanted to understand his thoughts, his life. With further consideration—what I mustered up between climbing into my car and reaching the halfway point to Mom and Dad's—I decided my interest made sense. Arlo held an important place in my mother's life. My family knew him well. The color and shape and deep conviction in his eyes were and should be secondary to such plausible analysis.

Yes, this was what I told myself. By the time I pulled into a family parking spot, however, I'd begun to question my ability to reason.

I found Mom sitting on the front porch steps, her face to the sun. The day's temperature was far from warm, but the sun did feel good. I joined her.

"What's up?" I asked, setting my bags onto the step beside me. "Bride-alert?"

"Nope," Mom said without lowering her head,

her lids shuttering her eyes. "Nothing since the earlier text. Which, I'll have you know, I did not answer."

"So, what are you doing, getting a dose of vitamin D?"

She grunted in a not-quite-committed way.

I fitted my hands together around my knee, studying the empty fields through narrowed lids. "I ran into Arlo while I was out."

Another grunt. Maybe she didn't want to know. Maybe she only wanted to sit in the sun in silence, undisturbed. I started to get up.

"Go on," she said.

I sat back down. "He told me about the accident. Well, that he'd had one. No details, but that's okay. I don't really need them."

"Good."

"He's getting better though, right?" I persisted, despite her closed eyes and limited responses. "That's the impression I got anyway."

"Yes."

Okay. I got up again.

"It's been a long road," she added, rising to an abrupt upright position beside me. She brushed the loosened strands from her ponytail away from her face. "He's a good man, Arlo is. Come on, let's get dinner started. Your dad will be home soon."

I gathered my packages, hopped up the last step and opened the door for her. She paused before going in, eyeing my bags.

"Did you get all your shopping done?"

"All except Simon," I said.

"Good luck."

"Did he tell you what he might like?"

She gave me an 'are you kidding' look and marched inside.

Dinner preparation required music blaring and lots of singing. It had always been this way. I still turned on my old cd player when I made my own dinner. It seemed too quiet otherwise. I wondered as Mom and I danced around with vegetables in our hands how Arlo would fare in this environment. He seemed ill-equipped in his present condition for loud noise. To me, his condition also seemed to isolate him. I might have been wrong. Even so, I thought about asking him to Christmas dinner.

Dumb idea, I decided a minute later. He had a family somewhere, and friends. Besides, he'd think we were all crazy. Heck, we were all crazy. I realized that every time we got together. And I loved it.

Why *did* I stay away so long between visits?

Because I had a life, another whole life, and it wasn't situated in Connor Falls, Pennsylvania.

With a sigh, I stopped dancing and started peeling. The peeler whispered over each potato, skins curling from the utensil to plop into the sink. I realized with a start I could hear them slithering over each other onto the stainless steel. Mom had turned the music off. I glanced aside at her.

"Honey," she said, clutching a half a dozen carrots in each hand, "what's wrong?"

"What? Nothing, Mom. What makes you think something is wrong?"

"Your face," she said. "Do you not realize how transparent you are?"

I turned back to my task, blinking desperately and rapidly.

"And the tears," she added. "That's a pretty big clue, too."

Stupid face, stupid tears, stupid whatever this was making me cry like a baby. I dropped the peeler into the sink and dashed first one hand, then the other, across my eyes, filling my nostrils with the scent from raw potatoes. I heard the carrots clunk on the tabletop. A second later Mom's arms went around me, making me cry harder still.

"What's going on here?"

Beyond Mom's shoulder, Dad stood in the doorway, his brows arching up toward his hairline, which was a feat. He'd really gotten quite bald in the front.

"Nothing," I said, stepping from Mom's embrace, pulling my sleeve over my fingers to scrub at my eyes again. "I don't know."

"Oh. Well maybe I should just step outside, give you a minute."

Mom snorted. "I think our daughter's feeling a bit homesick, that's all," she said, sneaking past me to take over the peeling. "What are you doing home so early?"

He shot me a crooked grin, whipping two small floral bouquets from behind him, each one wrapped in holiday-patterned paper and likely picked up from the grocery store on his way home. "I just figured I'd spend a little extra time with my homesick daughter before dinner, and to give you both these."

* * *

Later, when the house went quiet, I snuck out.

Bundled in my coat and boots and scarf, I crept across the porch, crossed the driveway and walked slowly into the fields beyond. My breath frosted in the air. Overhead, stars glittered hard and bright in the dark night sky. Far across the open field white-yellow eyes glowed as several deer watched me, gauging my intent, my direction. I kept walking, not toward them, but in a wide arc around the house, heading toward the area where Mom planted all her flowers and vegetables. A few pumpkins had withered on the vines, but I managed to spot their humped signatures in the shadows before I fell over them.

I shoved my hands down into my pockets, reassured by the hard edge from my cell phone burrowed deep in the right. I didn't anticipate any need for it, and once upon a time no one had little phones constantly on their person, but if I happened to miss a pumpkin or just a furrow in the ground, I could find myself glad to be so indoctrinated. Stuff happened. Stuff like slipping on the ice and fracturing an elbow (a long time ago, thank goodness). Stuff like car accidents which left a person in a condition I couldn't quite fathom. One day I might acquire a fuller understanding, but probably not. Christmas was a-coming. The day after that I'd be driving home.

However, he did perform freelance work for Mom on a pretty regular basis, I'd been told. When I came to visit we'd meet again, and maybe sooner rather than later, because Mom was right. Her daughter was feeling a little homesick. More than a little. How odd. At least I told myself it was odd. Maybe it wasn't. Maybe it really, really wasn't.

I kept walking, past the raised beds that would in warmer weather house all the cutting flowers, along the pathways where vegetable plants would grow to either side, around the gleaming hulk of the greenhouse erected over the summer. Mom had pointed it out to me through the window, thrilled with the practical addition. She would start her seedlings in it, rather than filling the back porch with them. She also intended to force paper white and narcissus bulbs and grow poinsettias for sale next fall. Always planning was Mom.

Always.

After the wedding and reception on Saturday, I figured she'd get down to Christmas preparation in earnest. Not everything could be performed months in advance, no matter how carefully a body planned. Some things had to be last minute. Like baking dozens and dozens of cookies, packing them into tins for family members, friends, gifts and donations. The Christmas after they'd moved into Hummingbird Farm Mom and Dad started purchasing balled trees for inside the house, planting them in another field out back after the holidays. Mom liked to have three of them, one in the huge kitchen, one in the living room, one on the front porch. The trees were already in place, but one hadn't been decorated yet. I liked that part, breaking out the old boxes, looking through the ornaments, hanging each one and the lights. As for dinner, Dad always made the turkey. Roasting the turkey was his specialty. Simon made bread, usually delicious bread. Occasionally I'd make a pie. My success in the pie-baking arena had been so sporadic I often pretended I forgot and would run out for a store-bought one.

Every year I looked forward to these last-minute things. They, and family, were what made the holidays special.

I started shuffling my rubber soles through the fallen leaves while I walked, the crisp sounds trailing after me, echoing off the greenhouse. An owl hooted nearby, answered by another in the distant woods. I did miss Connor Falls. I truly did, but it wasn't my home anymore, no matter how much it felt like it when I came back. What was I supposed to do with those feelings? What good did they serve? In a practical world, home was where your job took you. In an emotional one, home was where your heart resided. Very rarely did the two meet. In my parent's world they had.

Some nocturnal creature darted through the leaves. Once my heart rhythm returned to normal, I headed around to the front porch and quietly let myself back inside. I made my way to the kitchen, turned on the light over the stove. Shirking my coat off, I draped it over a chair back along with my scarf and set about warming up milk in a pan. People, people like me, always dismissed simple remedies and opted for staring at the television all night hoping to drop off again. Or took a walk in the cold and the dark with the very thoughts keeping them awake coming to full light in their heads, blood pumping furiously through a chilled body, because yeah, that would knock a person out. Mom believed in the whole drink your warm milk thing. It worked when we were kids, back when we trusted everything as truth. It might work now.

"Can't sleep?"

The spoon in my hand flew through the air and clattered on the floor.

"Mom! Jeez, get a bell."

She came in, eyed my coat, sat in the chair next to it. "Been out rambling, have you?"

We wore nearly identical sleep attire, Mom and I. Ratty old sweat pants and a heavy, seen-better-days tee shirt. Maybe I'd become her one day, morph right into my mother. I could do worse, I knew.

I scooped up the spoon, rinsed it and gave the pot's contents a stir. "Want some?" I offered, reaching for the container I hadn't yet put away.

"Sure."

After tipping more milk into the pot, I took two mugs from the cabinet and set them side by side on the counter, fidgeting in a compulsive way with the handles until they were lined up.

"Want to tell me what's on your mind?" Mom asked.

Not really, I thought.

"You don't have to, you know," she added, as if I'd spoken.

"I'm just working through some stuff, Mom." Stir, stir, stir. I lifted the spoon to the light, checking for steam. Satisfied the milk had heated through I filled the mugs and carried them to the table, setting Mom's before her. I picked mine back up, went to the small alcove where the counter and cabinets ended, and shimmied myself into the deep window sill. If I'd grown up here, this would have been my favorite place, a cozy, not-quite hideaway near enough to the fireplace to see the flames, feel its heat. Even now, the embers glowing in the ashes from the earlier fire emitted warmth.

"What kind of stuff?" she asked, taking a tentative sip from the cup held in both hands.

"Life stuff. The kind of stuff life throws at you. Things you have to work your way through, make up your mind about, maybe even change."

"That never stops."

"I know."

Mom set her mug down, fingers clasped and interlocked around it. "What would you change?"

I sighed, leaning my head back against the cold window glass. "Maybe everything."

Wow. I couldn't believe I'd said that out loud. I swallowed a quick hit of milk, followed by another. Mom watched me from across the room. The stove light highlighted the lovely silver in her hair.

"You can't change everything," she said, stating what I knew to be the obvious. "What's most important to you? That's what you work on first." She lifted the mug to her mouth again.

"Aren't I too young for a mid-life crisis?"

And clunked it back onto the table, choking on the milk she'd been swallowing. I started to get up from the window sill. She waved me back.

"I'm fine," she said, wiping her chin with the back of her hand. "It's not a crisis, Suze. It's recognition. I say it's never too early for that. Or too late."

She finished her calcium sedative and went back to bed shortly after, leaving me with the washing up, as was fitting. I'd made the mess.

*   *   *

I woke up with the winter sun beating through the parted curtains onto my face. That, and someone pounding on the door. I thought I might have imagined the second part, but when it repeated along with a young voice calling my name, I tossed back the covers and leapt from the bed in a race to the door.

"What?" I shouted as I yanked it open.

Seven-year-old Stuart stood on the other side, totally unperturbed by the fact his aunt had just yelled at him. He grinned at me and gave me a saucy little salute, right hand to brow.

"Don't you have school?" I asked.

"Not today."

I stared at him, waiting.

"Gran needs you. She says get up."

"Is she hurt, leg broken, anything like that?"

"No."

"Good," I said. "I'll be down as soon as I get dressed."

"Better hurry. There's a lady in the living room and she's crying an awful lot."

Fully clothed in two minutes flat, I hurried toward the living room, combing my hair with my fingers. I could hear the snuffling and stuttering words my entire trek down the stairs. I heard them still as I rounded the corner, punctuated by Mom patiently trying to soothe. When I entered the room,

I saw a stranger who looked to be younger than me perched on the ottoman's edge, head in her hands, shaking it as she continued her nearly unintelligible communication. Mom sat on the couch, patting the woman's back distractedly. She looked up as I crossed the floor, staring with some unknown intent at me over the woman's head.

The bride? I mouthed. She nodded.

I went straight up to them both, fitted my hand against Mom's back and pulled her up from the sofa. I propelled her lightly away and took her place.

"Wait," said the bride, her reddened eyes following my mother's movements. "Where are you going?"

"My mom's going to make us some tea," I said. "We'll pretend we're in England where tea soothes all wounds."

"Y-your mom?" she stammered, gaze on me now, searching my face as Mom made a hasty exit.

"Yes. I'm Susan. What's your name?"

"C-Carla. She's making us tea, you said?"

"Yep. In the meantime, why don't you tell me what's wrong? Why are you upset?" This woman's wedding reception was supposed to be taking place here tomorrow. Only one reason for being so distressed came to mind.

She scrubbed her eyes with the heel of her palm, smearing mascara. High color splotched her cheeks. "I only want it to be perfect. That's what I've always dreamed I'd have—a perfect wedding."

I took a deep breath, recalling my silly childhood dreams for a winter wedding. Eventually you outgrew such nonsense, or at least came to realize perfection wouldn't be found in the wedding, but in the reasons for it.

"Why do you think it won't be exactly what you wanted?" I asked. Please, I begged silently, don't say it's because he dumped you. There'd be no coming back from that.

She didn't. She shifted on the ottoman, smoothed the skirt she wore. "I don't know. I keep second-guessing myself. I'm sure I've been driving your mother crazy. I'm just afraid that…that when the time comes, he'll be so disappointed."

"He? Your fiancé, you mean?"

She nodded.

"Disappointed in what? The reception?"

Again, the nod, her lavender bangs falling into her eyes, catching in her damp lashes.

"Did he have any input in the planning?"

"Yes," she whispered.

"Has he made any complaints?"

She shook her head.

"Does he love you?"

Her eyes flew wide. "Yes, he does. We love each other very much."

I straightened, pulled away slightly, adopting a no-nonsense manner. "Then I don't quite understand all the stress about perfection. You love each other. That's all that matters, right? Nothing in this life is ever going to be perfect. You're marrying a man you love and who loves you back, so I think the plan would be to always face those imperfections together, yes? Make the best of them."

She stared at me for a few moments in silence. I caught a glimpse of Mom in the hall. She stepped back from view.

"Okay," Carla said. "Okay."

"Come on, let's go outside and walk through this, so you can see it in your head without all the worrying. I'll tell Mom to skip the tea. She'll have to come with us because, really, I don't know the first thing about event planning and what you guys have cooked up. Sound good?"

"Yes, please," said Carla, rising with a watery smile from the cushioned ottoman. She snatched her coat off the couch and put it back on, shoving her arms in the sleeves. "Will you be there? Tomorrow, I mean. I know your mom will be. She said she always is, to make sure things run smoothly. But will you be there, too?"

"Of course, she will," Mom said from the doorway. She waved a hand for us to follow. "Carla, you're going to have a great day."

Together, we went through the converted barn and the details of Carla's reception, from décor to music, seating to menu, and all the mini-events to take place within. I had seen Mom's brochures, which explained her dream and the humble beginnings of Hummingbird Farm before outlining everything available on the property and in the fabulous, eclectic venue. I had a feeling Carla hadn't read the brochure, because when Mom launched into her heart's journey, Carla listened with utter fascination. Afterward, she threw her arms around my mother and hugged her.

"Thank you so much. I'm sorry for being such

a pain," she said.

Mom dismissed the apology as unnecessary. "We all get jitters over something. I'll see you tomorrow, Carla. I'm looking forward to it."

"Me, too." Carla giggled, tears long gone. She fluttered to her car like a butterfly, relieved and happy. Mom pulled the barn doors closed, locked them. She turned to me.

"Thank you," she said.

"Ah, it was nothing…short of a miracle." I laughed. She didn't.

"I'm serious, Suze. This is what you do. Talk to people. It's a gift."

We started walking back toward the house. "Well, I did go to school for it. Let's not dismiss all the money spent."

"No degree gives you what comes to you naturally. You've always had it, even when you were little. You talked, people listened. It's your tone, your demeanor, the things you say."

Inside, I experienced a quiet, fizzing joy. Outside, I shrugged. Mom touched my hand, squeezed, let go.

"There's something I'd like to do, Mom," I said.

"What's that?"

We mounted the porch steps, crossed to the door. I stood for the briefest moment staring at the screen, at a delicate milkweed seed trapped in the mesh. I let out my breath. "I want to invite Arlo to Christmas dinner."

"I already did," said Mom. She smiled at me in an odd, gentle way and went inside.

Chapter Four

"You'll do what?"

I gazed at Mom across the breakfast table. Dad sat opposite her and opposite me sat young Stuart, his head turning from me to Mom and back again. I had no idea why he'd spent the night without his brother. Maybe so he could beat me at checkers nine out of twelve games, or maybe because he knew his grandmother would prepare his favorite pancakes for breakfast. Before bed, he'd also cajoled me into agreeing to a walk in the fields with him first thing. We'd already accomplished our trek, watching the sun rise. I'd pay for that later, I knew. It was going to be a long day.

"I'll tend the bar," I repeated, "with whoever you've hired." I'd helped pay my expenses in college by bartending. I didn't want to be at Carla's wedding as a guest, or even on the sidelines in a semi-managerial position. I wanted something I could concentrate on, to keep me busy and diverted from the crowd. I'd never been good at parties, always the one who opted to hover near the door or do the washing up, repeatedly, throughout the night.

Mom blew a breath from her nose. "Fine.

You'll have to wear the uniform, then."

"White shirt, black pants? Not a problem."

Recognizing the crisis had been averted, Stuart returned his attention to his pancakes. Dad winked at me over his coffee mug. He'd never been one for crowds either. Dad understood.

"Arthur," Mom addressed him, "would you mind clearing away the breakfast mess? Lots to do, little time."

He smiled at her and then set his wink on Stuart, who broke out into giggles.

"Suze?" she said to me. "Coming?"

I hadn't exactly volunteered for the morning setup, but I could see Mom wanted me to join her. I didn't mind. Simon was out there already, as well as two guys in their early twenties she kept "on-call" for the job.

"I brought the wagon around last night," she told me as I followed her out to the porch. "We'll load the centerpieces into it and bring them over, get the tablecloths on, make sure those boys have gotten the chairs where they belong, and, well, you know the drill."

I did. Whenever I was around and an event had been scheduled, I lent a hand. Why not? It helped Mom and Dad and allowed us all to have more time together. If I went my own way instead, I'd never see Mom on those weekends.

Once the tables were topped with cloth and tableware, tiny lights in hurricane jars were lowered into the middle of each centerpiece and extra lights hung above to add to the fairytale Christmas atmosphere. More plants were brought in, the bar wiped and cleaned and stocked. Wreaths adorned the walls. The caterers arrived in the midst of the minor chaos, setting themselves up in the kitchen at the barn's back end. Locating the vacuum, I engaged in constant battle with the leaves being tracked in. Finally, only the caterers were left, chattering away at a distance, confined for now to their work in the kitchen. They supplied the wait staff, too, which would be arriving about a half hour before the guests. Simon had retrieved his youngest and gone home. Mom and I stood in the middle of the floor alone.

"What's next?" I asked.

"Grab the seating chart. We'll put out name tags and the favors. The DJ will be here about two hours before the reception starts and he'll get the sound system set. I have no idea how to do that and no desire to learn."

"There's something in this world you don't want to conquer? I'm ashamed to be your daughter."

She shot me a withering glance before pivoting full circle on her heel for another look around.

"Everything is beautiful," I assured her. "Carla and her new hubby will be thrilled."

Mom nodded, lips compressed. She opened them to speak, closed them again.

"What?" I said.

"Are you sure you want to bartend? When Carla asked you to be here, I pictured us together, somehow, working the room."

"Working the room? Mom, you make us sound like comedians."

She sighed, closed her eyes, opened them.

"Obviously you don't find me as amusing as you once did," I added, "so no standup routine for me, I guess."

"Susan."

The diminutive of my name had fallen by the wayside. Manipulation hovered in the offing. Oh, to be a child again and not resent being stage-managed by my mother. Oh, wait, I did then, too. Probably more so. Now, for the most part I merely shrugged it off and moved on.

"Mom, if you want something, please just ask me, okay? I'm assuming us doing this together today means a lot to you. Mom? Say yes or no."

Her mouth quivered, seeming to struggle to hold back a smile. "Yes."

"Okay, then. I'll see if I brought something halfway decent to wear."

"Thank you."

"You owe me."

"I birthed and raised you," she said. "I think I win this round."

"Yeah," I agreed, "you do."

I had a nice dress in my suitcase I hadn't gotten around to hanging up yet. Leaving Mom to speak with the caterers about some issue, I hurried to the house to yank the garment out and hang it in the bathroom for a little steam therapy while I showered. Passing the upstairs den, I spotted my dad watching television, slouched into the heavily cushioned sofa with his legs crossed at the ankle and propped up on the coffee table.

I skidded to a halt, leaning into the room. "Not

that you don't deserve it, but how can you be so relaxed with everything going on?"

"Your mom tells me I have to be," he said. "And far be it from me to disobey her orders." He grinned.

Dad had retired the year before from the job he'd held for twenty-five years, but still worked two to three days a week as a consultant. Mom liked to see him relax, and I certainly didn't begrudge him the opportunity. It surprised me he could, though, with Mom going full-bore.

"What are you watching?"

He glanced at the flat screen hanging on the wall opposite. "I have no idea."

I nodded. "Best way to relax. Don't get invested."

I started again down the hallway. He called me back. Sticking my head around the doorframe, I smiled at him.

"Yeah, Dad?"

He rose from the couch, walked over and placed his hand on my shoulder, a large hand lying gently. "It's good to have you home."

"It's good to be here," I said.

"You mean that, don't you?"

"Of course I do."

"We miss you when you're not here."

I blinked back tears, unable to respond. I took his hand from my shoulder, squeezed it.

"Honey," he said, "are you sure you're okay?"

I nodded. "I will be. I have some stuff I have to work through, and I'm avoiding it."

"Can I help?"

I looked up into his face, the face Simon's would surely become in later years. "You already have."

I left him standing there gazing after me, the way he used to if he happened to be around when I headed out on a date or an evening with my friends. At the bedroom door I glanced back, caught a glimpse of him watching me still. I recognized his concern, his love, and then he turned away.

I didn't want him to waste his whole day worrying about me. I would work things out. I always did.

Digging through my suitcase, I found the dress rumpled at the bottom. Not exactly wedding material, but a sleek-fitting little black dress always served its purpose. I'd brought two sweaters with me to wear with it, having been unable to make up my mind. The one was definitely in the running for our annual ugly Christmas sweater competition, but the other, lightweight, gray and mid-thigh length, would provide a much more sophisticated effect. I located a hanger and slipped the dress onto it. The material was such that most wrinkles fell right out from gravity. I figured I'd leave it hanging by the window for a bit instead of the bathroom and let the sun through the glass warm up the fabric. Perhaps I wouldn't need to do anything with the garment except put it on.

I hadn't accounted for how tall these old farmhouse windows were. In order to reach the curtain rod, I climbed onto a chair and then stepped onto the deep sill. I still had to stretch to hook the hanger onto the rod above the frame. Was I that short? Really?

Balanced in the window, I took several minutes to enjoy the view. Beyond the fields gray woods dotted with evergreen marched up the nearest hill. At night the pinprick lights from a house perched at the top would glow. By day the house remained hidden, no matter the season. The road out front continued past the hill into Connor Falls proper. To the left, more hills lay like plumped muted pillows. In spring and summer they would be greener than green and in autumn filled with color. I'd grown up in this beautiful area. I missed it.

Through the glass I heard gravel crunching and leaned close to peer to my right, toward the visible family parking spaces. I watched Arlo's black Jeep pull in and park, spied him behind the wheel by squashing my cheek flat against the glass. He sat a moment, head bowed, his fingertips pressed to his brow. After a few seconds he lifted his head, stared out across the fields. He got out, pushed the door closed, and with his hand touching the vehicle every few inches, made his way to the grassy area in front of it.

I saw him clearly now, hunched against the cold in his suit jacket. He had his head up, his eyes steady on a horizon, his dark hair blowing crazily around his face in a sudden breeze that whipped his jacket back, too. The expression on his profiled features remained impassive in the manner I now recognized as intense concentration. He'd told me about the need for it, in the ten minutes we'd remained on the sidewalk outside his house before he'd said goodbye and gone in. He said he was better, so much better than he had been, but he still had to spend some time orienting himself whenever he exited a moving vehicle, waiting for the sensation like his brain rolling away to end. He had to focus hard, too, when walking from point A to point B. He still searched for words that used to come to him without any conscious thought, but it was better, he said, than not being able to remember them at all.

Watching him from the window, I understood what he meant about the injuries a person couldn't see. Not being able to focus on a cast, a limp, a physical scar, made it extremely difficult for a person to understand the injury's extent from the outside. He'd done a lot of talking in those ten minutes, Arlo had, haltingly, weighing vocabulary to construct into sentences, me in silence, just listening. I couldn't imagine how I would feel, no longer possessing an ease of function in my everyday environment. I'd said as much to him. He hadn't answered. He thought I felt sorry for him, I could tell. I didn't feel sorry for him. I felt humbled to know a person fighting so hard to get their life back. We all did it. We all fought for something. That didn't make his journey any less important or any less impressive, and it sure as heck impressed me.

Down in the yard, Arlo turned his head. Not quickly. He couldn't do quickly. Even so, I reacted as if he could, as if he might catch me spying on him, and I took a hasty step back. Right off the sill. I landed with a crash, but unharmed, on the carpeted floor. I'd barely caught my breath before a fist pounded on the door.

"Suze! Are you all right?"

"I'm fine, Dad," I called out. "Dropped my suitcase off the bed. Sorry if I scared you."

"That sounded pretty darned heavy for a suitcase," he said. "You're sure you're okay?"

I righted myself and scurried to the door, cracking it open, smiling out at him and hoping my embarrassment wouldn't show. "I'm good, Dad. See? All in one piece."

"Well, if you say so."

"I do," I said. "Go back to relaxing. And thanks for checking."

With a grunted reply, he returned to the den. I shut the door, went back to the window. The lawn was empty. Arlo had gone.

*   *   *

Mom gave my attire, my entire person, an approving nod. "Those earrings are cute. Didn't you give me a pair like them?"

I fingered the tiny, festive wreaths on my lobes. "I did. Maybe you could wear them today. We'd at least fit it with Carla's wedding theme."

"Good idea," she agreed. Turning on her heel, she hurried up the stairs, presumably to get them. The wedding party would be arriving shortly for photos. The DJ had set up, the wait staff was receiving last minute instructions from the caterers, and Arlo had temporarily joined Dad in the den. We'd crossed paths in the upstairs hallway. Arlo had given me a swift hello, his eyes not on my feet, but on the dress I wore. I supposed that was progress.

Mom returned, affixing the earrings into her ears. She looked gorgeous in a fabulously understated, sophisticated way. The earrings might have detracted a bit from the effect, but I knew Mom wouldn't care.

"So, what do I have to do?" I asked her. "What are my duties as your sidekick?" This was another reason I had wanted to bartend. I preferred a specific function in a situation where strangers abounded, rather than being responsible for making small talk beyond what-are-you-having. Mom didn't know that, or if she did, she probably considered my introverted nature something I needed to get over. The ability to talk to people and have them listen to me didn't mean I had a talent for conversing with everyone willy-nilly.

She and I started out the door, but not before Mom called up to Arlo, letting him know she'd spotted the limo with the bridal party maneuvering into the drive. The first photos were to be taken around and inside the gazebo, a lovely white-washed structure that had been planted beside the barn and surrounded by a small garden pretty much solely with event photography in mind. For this occasion, it had been decorated yesterday with greens and poinsettias and twinkling lights, per the bride's request. I hesitated on the porch, watching the limo pull up across several event parking spaces. Mom went on ahead, somehow managing to appear both friendly and business-like. I took a deep breath. The door opened behind me. A step on the floorboards vibrated beneath my comfortable yet dressy flats.

Not Dad. He stomped as if warning all the earth's little critters out of his way. Stomped like a giant, even though he didn't possess a giant's girth. Tall, yes, but like Simon, a good wind might topple him.

"Steady on," said Arlo. "They won't bite."

I turned to make certain he spoke to me and not himself, because I figured those words could work for me or him. "I hope not," I said. "I'm probably past due for a tetanus booster."

He laughed out loud. I liked his laugh, liked the charming, contagious sound of it. I fought to keep a straight face, but in the end I gave in.

"Stupid joke," I said. "Thanks for laughing."

His eyes met mine, slipped away. Suddenly he looked down, reaching into his pocket. He pulled out two small objects, separated them and fitted one into each ear. I tipped my head for a better look. They appeared to be soft, flesh-colored earplugs.

"Those help?" I asked.

He nodded. "Too many conversations. Plus loud noise." He shrugged, lifted his finger and wiggled the plug in his left ear.

"Got any extras?"

"Afraid not," he said, "but I'll bring some next time."

He didn't ask why I wanted them. Quite honestly, I didn't know either, except I envisioned dampening down the noise could be quite soothing. I didn't need a head injury to find a wedding reception's bombardment overwhelming.

I also didn't ask about the *next time*, about the two words thrown out there, hinting at a promise or a hope—or merely uttered without thought. After all, he would be here at the next event requiring a photographer, whereas I had apparently fallen into the habit of staying away for six months at a time. A habit I wanted to break. A habit I wanted to more than break.

We descended the stairs side by side and crossed the lot. I asked him if he needed any assistance setting up equipment or lighting, but he assured me he had it under control. I asked him if he'd always done photography for a living, or if he'd done something different before. I didn't have to say before what. The accident had been a defining moment in his life.

He shook his head. "It used to be a hobby. Even—eventually I found I could still do that. My old job? I didn't go back."

He said nothing else. I kept my curiosity to myself. Inside the barn we went our separate ways, he to my mother's side to address the pending photos, and me to a corner, standing in the shadow of a tall, realistic fake evergreen decked out in clear lights. I rearranged the ones nearest to me. Mom caught my eye, made a face and a quick hand movement. I ceased toying with the bulbs and went over to where she stood.

Carla, who had been conferring with her bridesmaids, turned her head and spotted me. She hustled over with crisp, sliding satin noises. A man I presumed to be her husband stood on the sidelines next to another tuxedoed guy. He appeared patiently amused by the proceedings.

"Susan!" Carla hugged me as best she could accomplish, given the gown's massive volume. She stepped back. "I love your earrings! Your mom has the same ones on."

"Festive, right?" I touched the jewelry at my lobes. "You look beautiful."

Grinning, she twirled on the spot. Behind her, the bridesmaids in their silver-sashed, celery-green gowns eyed us with a mere half second of curiosity before turning a collective gaze on Arlo. Speculation showed itself in each unguarded expression. Naturally, being a wedding, they would check him out that way. Weddings were notorious for hookups or for the conjecture about hopeful eventualities. Something interesting existed about the person of Arlo Woods, for sure. I'd been trying hard not to notice it.

He looked up from wherever his concentration had taken him, straight into my eyes. He smiled. My breath rushed out. Before I could smile back, he returned his attention to my mother. I noted how still my mother stood when speaking to him and how he managed to keep his focus on her face. I, on the other hand, was always quite animated around him, what with random head movements and the constant repositioning of body parts. Therein, I realized, might lie the problem. I reminded myself to be more tranquil next time we spoke.

"The photographer," began Carla, turning to me. "What's his name again?"

"Arlo," I said.

"Yes, right, Arlo. He's really good. Your mom

said he was, but I didn't quite believe her until I saw samples. I'm afraid I still gave her a hard time. I just…well, you know."

"I know."

"Is there something wrong with him?"

I straightened my spine. "What do you mean?"

"Is he slow or something?"

I knew what she implied. And like my mother and brother before me, I knew his story wasn't mine to tell. Instead, I said, "He's deliberate in his actions. He has to be. Does that matter?"

"Oh, no," she said, "not at all. I only asked because I didn't know if I had to be careful in any way, so I wouldn't unintentionally upset him."

I cocked my head to the side, studying her profile. She'd asked out of kindness, not condemnation or ridicule. "He had an accident," I said. "He's getting better every day. Please don't tell him I told you. Please don't mention it at all."

She nodded. "I won't."

Mom called them all over. Dresses were lifted from the ground, hands clutched bouquets, tux sleeves were smoothed. They all followed Arlo and Mom outside. The gazebo's positioning was such that the sturdy red barn protected it and its occupants from the wind's usual direction. Left to my own devices, I strolled around double-checking place settings, smoothing tablecloths, chatted a bit with the DJ when he came out from the men's room, made sure he had the opening music list, spoke with the wait staff hovering near the kitchen door. Finally, I went out to witness Arlo and my mom in action.

They worked well together. He asked her opinion and she respected his. Mom shuffled the party around at his direction like pieces on a chessboard and the camera clicked away. Arlo staged faux candid as well as dramatic and formal poses. He moved in for close ups and even used a macro lens for what would undoubtedly prove to be a striking photo of the rings on the bride and groom's interlocked fingers. Afterward, Mom escorted the party to a lounge area to await the guests' arrival. Arlo and I were left by the gazebo alone.

"You should go inside," he said without looking at me. "You're cold."

"What makes you think that?"

"You're shivering."

I watched him gather up the equipment he'd brought outside with him, systematically packing up what he'd only have to unpack again inside. His actions revealed a careful routine designed to prevent, I realized, his forgetting.

I didn't speak again until he'd finished. "Why did you move to Connor Falls, Arlo?"

He glanced at me and away, settling his gaze on the solid, level lines of the barn. He slung his camera bag over his shoulder. "I used to visit my grandparents here. I liked it then. I like it now."

I fell in beside him when he started moving. "I didn't realize you had a connection to the area. Do your grandparents still live here? Oh, stupid question. You said 'used to'."

"They moved to…" He paused and squeezed his eyes shut, then opened them. "Arizona. My folks, too. I don't see them all as much as I'd like."

"Me either," I surprised myself by admitting. "And I don't live anywhere near that far away."

He stopped by the door, put his hand on the wall and turned to face me. "Why did you leave Connor Falls?"

I bit my lip, sucked in a long breath through my nose. "Long story."

"You'll tell me sometime?"

"Sure," I said. "I absolutely will."

Chapter Five

I kept an eye on Arlo. Not because I thought he needed me to, or that he required any help. He wouldn't have tolerated that, I'm sure. I suspected he'd been treated as though he did, folks jumping to conclusions, thinking he was in some way weaker or lesser equipped than they, not recognizing the hidden strength he likely had to summon up to make it through the day. The impulses in our brains controlled everything we did, didn't they? What an extraordinary mess that would be, if our brains went awry.

I kept an eye on Arlo because I couldn't help myself. I observed him working his way through the crowd with the camera, pausing every now and then to get his bearings. Framing the shots, clicking away, every step made in awareness to where he placed his feet, to his surroundings. It had to be exhausting. It exhausted me to watch and yet I couldn't look away. He caught me at it, more than once. I had no idea what he thought about my unintended surveillance. Occasionally he smiled. More often than not he turned back to his job without acknowledgment.

Mom caught me doing it, too, when she had to ask me three times to fetch a corkscrew from the house because the one belonging to the caterers had broken and they'd been unable to locate another in the barn kitchen.

"What on earth are you looking at, Suze?" And then she saw. "Oh." The single syllable expanded like a bubble around us, filled with a kind of semi-silence pushing the clamor from the reception away. She stared at me, her expression unreadable until her lips formed a slow curve.

"The corkscrew in the house, Suze," she said, eyebrows lifting. "Can you get it?"

"Corkscrew. Yes. Right."

I hurried from the barn, grateful for the flat shoes on my feet. I scampered across the driveway, up the steps, across the porch, not stopping until I reached the kitchen. My cheeks burned. From the cold, I told myself. I could do that sometimes, lie outright to myself, recognize the falsehood and still insist on it silently in my head.

Scrabbling through the drawers, I searched for the implement. From upstairs I heard the television and a sound I recognized as Dad's snoring. The old farmhouse felt comfortable, welcoming, embracing somehow. I'd never wondered why Mom and Dad had bought it. I wouldn't have hesitated either. The house possessed good vibes. So much so, I stood for a few minutes longer in the kitchen, found corkscrew in hand, and attempted to absorb a little more of them into my reeling senses.

I had to admit I wasn't watching Arlo only

because I admired his determination, or because he had that certain windblown appearance to him which always caught my eye, or because I recognized and empathized with a bruised soul refusing to wither. Mom knew. Mom *knew*. She knew I liked him, liked him already, this man I hadn't even heard of three days ago, this man whose presence in my mind I couldn't allow to influence my decision-making. I'd expected to come home this Christmas, the season for hope and promise and forgiveness and love, to sort things out in a quiet space away from my own.

My first mistake had been thinking it would be quiet. There was a wedding going on sixty feet away for crying out loud.

A wedding needing the corkscrew. Focus Susan Hayley Hardwick. Focus.

By the time I returned, Mom had borrowed one from a guest who apparently carried a multi-tool in his pocket wherever he went and however he dressed. She still appeared relieved to find I'd brought a better one, or perhaps merely that I'd come back. According to the schedule I'd previously viewed, the wedding cake would soon be brought out stimulating the ensuing photo op, followed by the whole garter thing while the cake was cut up for serving. Carla wanted to hold off tossing the bouquet until she and Steve were ready to depart. They had a late plane to catch, so it couldn't be much longer, leaving the guests free to dance the evening away after they'd gone. The bar would close and coffee would be served in massive quantities to assure safe driving at the appropriate hour. With effort, I avoided checking the time on my watch every five minutes. With a stronger effort, I forced my gaze not to drift after Arlo.

Someone bumped against me. I turned to find the bride at my elbow, all her pearly whites showing in earnest.

"Carla," I said.

"Everybody's having a great time."

"Of course they are. Are you?"

She nodded.

"Steve?"

"Yep," she said. "It's just like you said."

"Don't sweat the small stuff and all that?"

"Yes." She wriggled from side to side in time to the music. She'd cast aside her veil at some point. Her short lavender hair stuck out in places it probably wasn't meant to. "This is the perfect time of year to get married. Not June."

"I used to think I'd like a winter wedding, too."

Her smile dropped. "Used to?"

"Well," I said, "when I was younger and wanted to get married someday, I thought it would be a magical season for one."

Frowning in consideration, Carla pivoted her hand back and forth, the liquid in the glass she held sloshing up at the sides. "And you don't want to now? Get married someday, I mean."

"It would be nice to love and be loved first. After all, arranged marriages are so last year."

She burst out laughing. I managed to rescue the glass from her fist before whatever it contained ended up on her gown.

"You're so funny," she gasped. "I like you."

"I like you, too, Carla," I said, sniffing at the glass I cupped in my hand.

"He does, too."

"Steve? That's nice. I try not to be totally disagreeable, if I can help it."

She snorted back a guffaw, wiping at her eyes with her fingertips. "I don't mean Steve," she said, "although I think he does. I bet he does. I'm sure he does."

I waited, struggling to keep a straight face.

"I'm talking about the photographer."

I blinked, fully aware of my dramatically sweeping lashes. "Arlo?"

"There's only the one," she said.

I wanted to ask how she knew this, and at the same time I didn't. I wasn't standing next to Betsy Gruber at junior prom, agonizing over Robby Smith's affections or lack thereof.

"Whenever you disappeared for a minute, I'd see him glancing around for you," Carla went on. "And when you left the building a little while ago? He asked your mom if you were all right."

"That doesn't mean anything," I started to argue, but she smirked and took back her glass, giving me a long, knowing, somewhat inebriated look before she suddenly waved to someone and hurried off.

Mom appeared at my side. "Carla looks happy," she said.

"Yeah," I said, "but don't put too much stock in it. She's also delusional."

*   *   *

I missed the bouquet. Deliberately, in fact. Mom had pushed me into the fray when all the single ladies were called upon to trust their future hopes to the ball-catching abilities they may or may not have garnered as children. I stood with my hands folded together at my waist. Just because I was in the crowd didn't mean I had to play. Unfortunately, the fragrant, over-sized posy landed within inches of my feet. I stared at the fallen blooms while all the women who'd missed their chance at the prize stared at me. After a momentary indecisiveness, I snatched the bouquet from the floor.

"Goodness," I said, "we've never had this happen before. Carla? Shall we give it another go?"

Carla agreed. I returned the bouquet to her and slipped from the group, almost bumping into Arlo, who stood at the ready, camera in hand.

"You didn't get a shot of that, did you?" I asked in an undertone close to his ear so he could hear me through the plug. He smelled good, like an herbal soap.

"I'll remember to delete it," he said, raising the camera to his eye. "I promise."

"I'll hold you to it."

As the night would soon be winding down, I went over to the bar and asked for a wine spritzer. The bartender handed me the twelve-ounce bottle, opened, and a glass. I slid the glass back at him with my forefinger and a smile. "I'm good," I said. A yell on the floor indicated someone's success with the bouquet. I knew her, the girl who'd caught it. I used to babysit her. I took a dainty swig from the spritzer bottle, feeling older than I had when I walked into the reception three hours earlier.

Mom strolled over. She jerked her head toward the girl still jumping up and down on her toes, the bouquet plastered to her chest. "Didn't you babysit her at some point?"

"Yeah, I did." I handed her my bottle for a sip. She took it, looking straight into my eyes with an expression I couldn't misinterpret. "We're not getting any younger," I added.

"Shut up." She laughed, a small, short sound, and drank down half the contents. Afterward, she coughed and wiped her hand across her mouth. "What is that? I thought it was some kind of fancy water."

"Sorry. A blackberry wine spritzer."

"Ah, okay." She turned her head to perform a crowd-check. "Why are you drinking?"

"I was in the mood. Besides, they're not that strong."

"Not unless you slug down half a bottle in one go, I expect."

"Yes, there's always that. You going to be okay?"

"Always," she said and walked away to see the bride and groom out the door to the returned limo.

I slowly finished the spritzer, since I really wasn't sure about the alcohol content. I'd always assumed on the occasion I'd had one that it wasn't quite the same as, say, a glass filled with bourbon, but what did I know. In the present environment and as an unofficial representative of a Hummingbird

Farm event, I needed to keep my wits about me.

Ninety minutes following the newlyweds' unconventional early departure less than a dozen couples remained on the dance floor, no longer in sweaty, disheveled gyration, but embraced and moving to slower, quieter tunes. The other guests were seated at tables enjoying coffee and conversation. The bartender had closed down the bar, but remained at his station, offering soda and water to anyone who asked. Mom had been solicited for two further events. I'd witnessed the exchange between her and the interested parties and the brochure with an attached business card she'd slipped into their hands.

I bent my elbow, pivoting my wrist to check the time on my watch. I stifled a yawn.

"Past your bedtime?"

I jerked around, forgetting my determination to move slowly around Arlo. I couldn't help it. He'd startled me. "Yes," I said, "yes, it is."

He smiled; a slow and lazy gesture that could have been from exhaustion. Whatever the cause, I liked how it looked, how it made me feel. I noted the camera bag slung from his shoulder and glanced around for the larger containers in which he transported the lights and reflectors he'd used earlier.

"All ready to go?" I asked.

"I put everything else in the Jeep a little while ago, so, yes." He stood with his feet slightly apart, an infinitesimal swaying to his body. I detected a tensing in him, muscles tightening as he regained control over his balance. He slid his finger beneath the strap to his bag, pulling the slipping case back up.

"I'll walk out with you," I said.

His lips curved again.

The temperature had dropped considerably. I hugged myself as we crossed the lot to the family side, to Arlo's dusty Jeep parked in the glow thrown by one of the many old-fashioned lantern-style lights illuminating the parking spaces from their poles. Nearing his vehicle, I saw something move inside. When we got within a couple feet the driver's side door opened. A woman stepped out bundled in a winter coat, a scarf and earmuffs. I wondered if she'd been waiting long. I wondered who she was. Not someone from the party. She wore jeans and boots, not fancy dress.

"All set, Arlo?" She turned her gaze to me. "Hi."

"Hi," I said, step slowing.

She held out her hand. "I'm Jenny."

"Susan," I said, shaking it. "Suze." I let go, my hand slapping down to my side.

With an ease from casual and frequent association, she flipped open the back to Arlo's Jeep. He lowered the camera bag inside, Jenny patted his arm, shut the hatch. He turned to face me.

"Well," he said.

"Well," I echoed and added, a few beats too late and confused by my hesitation, "have a good night. I…I look forward to seeing the photos." Dumb thing to say. Why would I be seeing them?

"Okay," he said. I breathed in, released the air, lungs deflating. Arlo turned and got into the Jeep's passenger side. With a wave, Jenny climbed behind the wheel. I backed away to give her room to pull the vehicle out. The brake lights shone red on the gravel, my shoes. Arlo's hand lifted in my direction behind the glass before he turned to say something to Jenny, this Jenny person no one had bothered to mention to me.

I went back inside the barn to finish up the night.

Chapter Six

Mom shoved a mug filled with hot cocoa across the table in my direction. It slopped a little up the sides, rocking the floating marshmallow. I pulled the mug closer, inserting my nose over the steam. "I really just wanted to go to bed," I said.

"Really?" she responded, as if shocked. Maybe the shock truly existed. Maybe she thought her daughter took after her in more ways than looks. Maybe she thought the entire world was made from sterner stuff, the same stuff that appeared to be her composition. Because yes, after a long, activity-filled day, my mother did emerge as energized and fully awake. I heaved a sigh that rolled the cocoa steam into a great, big curve. Mom sat down across from me with her own mug.

"So," I said, "what's up?" Besides you, I thought. Dad had gone to bed sometime between my retrieving the corkscrew and Mom and I stumbling in the door with arms full of things she didn't want to leave out in the barn.

"What do you mean?" She took a careful sip from the steaming liquid.

"I figure you wanted to talk or something," I mumbled, frowning down at the marshmallow slowly melting.

"About what?"

I made a noise like my lovely old Scottish neighbor, deep in my throat. "I don't know. Pick a topic. Otherwise, I'm going to fall asleep in my chocolate."

"Are you dating anyone?"

My eyebrows arched. "Excuse me?"

"I'm picking a topic."

"Don't bother with that one. It's a one-word answer: no. Next?"

"How's work?"

I sighed again, lifted my mug, tried to confiscate the marshmallow with my tongue. No luck. "It's…work," I said. "Nothing new going on. But it's more than my job, Mom, it's my business."

"I know. I'm glad you were able to reschedule everyone so you could come home."

"Me, too." I meant it. Goodness, how I meant it, despite all my inner griping. I'd never been fool enough not to recognize the value of a place, a person, a thing merely because it had the capability to annoy me. I could be plenty annoying myself and I knew some people valued me.

"Okay, then, let's talk about Christmas," Mom said.

"Christmas. All right. What's the plan of attack?"

"The what?" Her brow wrinkled.

"I don't mean it that way. I mean, how are we going to get everything accomplished in the next few days? I'm sure you have a long list you would already have been checking off if it hadn't been for the wedding."

Her shoulders dropped, her right hand coming up to rub at her eyes. She finally looked as though her energy had begun to flag. "You're right," she said.

"Can I see it?"

"See what?"

"The list, Mom. I know you have a physical list lurking around here somewhere. Let's have it."

"In the morning." She sipped at her cocoa, clutching the warm mug close to her face after. "We'll tackle it over breakfast, make our battle plan." Her lips curved. "There's something I need to tell you. I'm supposed to be keeping it a secret, but it's added a great deal to what there is to do."

"Okay," I drawled, "spill."

She sat back, closed her eyes, a drawn-out grin spreading across her face. "Shepherd's coming home, Suze, with Malory and her parents, and her younger sister. A much younger sister? I think she's fourteen or fifteen."

I let out a whoop, quickly stifled so as not to wake Dad. "I can't believe it. All of us home for the holidays this year. I—wait. Is everyone staying in your house?"

"Yep," Mom said.

"Oh, crud," I said, "you'd better break out that list now."

She did not, but we discussed briefly some items on it while we finished our hot cocoa. She freely admitted certain bedrooms hadn't seen a vacuum or a dust rag in more months than she cared to count.

"My house isn't half as big as yours nor am I half as busy, but the entirety of my place is probably in the same condition." I brought our mugs to the sink and washed them both, turning them upside down to drain and dry in the rack. "We'll get them spruced up, Mom, don't you worry."

"I'm not worried," she said.

"Good." I started toward the hallway, pausing with my hand on the switch to the light above the kitchen table. Mom pushed back her chair and stood, following me up the stairs. Outside the room where I'd been sleeping, she gave me a quick, warm embrace. "Sleep well," I whispered into her fragrant hair.

"You, too."

I watched her walk down the hallway. As she closed the bedroom door, hers and Dad's, I called out: "Who's Jenny?" but not loudly, not loud enough for her to hear me or to answer. I don't think I wanted to know.

* * *

In the morning, Mom and I made a new list. We made it from hers, but divvied up projects between us on separate paper. I stuck mine in my pocket along with a pencil and she did the same.

"Shepherd's coming home," I said, grinning at her. "And we'll finally meet Malory in person. The phone, even FaceTime, doesn't quite cut it."

We'd all been sent photos and videos from their wedding, but like the phone, it wasn't the same as physically spending time with my new sister-in-law, or my older brother for that matter. I knew Mom felt the same.

We went our separate ways, furniture polish and rags in hand. I cleaned the other three bedrooms, including changing out the sheets that had been languishing on the unused beds for who knew how long. Mom tackled downstairs. I washed the windows—something I rarely bothered with at my house unless I caught sight of some obvious smear in the sunlight—and vacuumed the curtains when I brought the vacuum up to do the floors. Confiscating three leftover poinsettias from Carla's wedding, I placed one to a dresser, hung a wreath on each mirror and lined the windows with strands of warm-white Christmas lights. Afterward, I stood back with my fists on my hips, the dust rag hanging from one, and felt extraordinary pleased with my efforts.

I checked my watch. Record time. I went to see how far Mom had gotten.

Finding her still in the living room, I whipped out my list and crossed off everything from the bedrooms with a flourish. "Ha! How far are you?"

"It's not a race, Suze." She sounded oddly subdued, perhaps a little dazed. I rushed to her side.

"Mom? Are you okay?"

"I just got off the phone—"

I grabbed her arm, thinking it could only be bad news. "Sit down."

"I…I don't need to sit down," she said. "I need

a new list."

"Why?"

"Maybe I will sit down." She plopped her rump onto a sofa cushion, hands folded together between her knees. "I might have…I think…well, I did mention to some of the family, some that weren't involved in the secret, about Shepherd and Malory coming."

"Uh-oh," I said. It slipped out the way words sometimes do when you're not intending to say them. I sat down too, right next to her.

"Your dad's sister called, said they'd all been talking. I'm not sure who the heck 'all' are, but you know your Aunt Charlotte, it could be the world. She said to expect some calls, because they thought, since no one was at the wedding, how wonderful it would be if everyone converged on my house on Christmas Eve."

"She didn't use those exact words, did she?"

"No. But close enough. So I had to quick call Shepherd, right in the middle of his work day, to see what he thought of it. He'd apparently received a few calls himself and was going to talk to me once he got home this evening." She bit her lip, blew a breath out her nose. "There's not enough room in here," she muttered.

"Hello, Mom," I circled my fingers around her wrist, testing her pulse to see if it matched the panic on her face. "You have a whole venue right there in the barn that just housed well over a hundred people. We can manage an impromptu family reunion, don't you think? This is what you do."

She eyed me askance, flicked her gaze to the

empty hallway, then up at the small, antique clock on the narrow fireplace mantel. "Don't they have anything better to do at Christmas?"

"Mom," I whispered, "this is the best thing to do at Christmas."

She released another breath, a long, slow one, and clapped her hands on her thighs, inadvertently shaking mine off. She stood, suddenly animated. "Okay, let's finish cleaning down here, make some calls. We need numbers, a real headcount. Then we can plan a menu, including what certain people could bring with them. I'll still bake cookies, can't skip that. Carla didn't want any of the décor she paid for, so we can reuse what her guests didn't take with them. I'll hold onto the table linens that weren't soiled and send them all back after Christmas We should have music, Christmas music. I have a boatload of holiday cds and that old player of yours."

She went on for another several minutes before she wound down, turning mid-pace to look at me. I still hadn't gotten up, using my list's blank side to scribble down all she was saying.

"What are you doing?"

"Taking notes," I answered, pencil poised.

"Good idea." She walked from the room. A moment later I heard her rattling around in the kitchen. I followed.

"What's up, Mom?"

"Making a fresh pot of coffee," she said. "I don't think I'm going to get through the day without more."

"Why are you stressing out? How many

hundreds of times have you done this?"

She glanced at me, the coffee pot in her hand filling with cold water beneath the running spigot. "This is different. This is family."

"Yes, this is family," I said. "Family is better, isn't it? What do you think they're going to expect on such short notice? A wedding reception to make up for the fact none of us got to go?"

Her eyes glazed over in contemplation. The water started bubbling from the pot into the sink. I hurried to her side, took it away and shut the spigot off. "Mom, stop. Stop, stop, stop. Go sit. I'll make the coffee."

She didn't move. I danced around her, gathering what I needed, filled the machine, turned it on. Leaning against the counter, I studied her face. "It'll be fun. It doesn't have to be the posh party of the season. Remember who we're talking about here."

"Right." Mom retrieved last night's mugs from the drain board. "None of us made it to your wedding either," she said, not quite out of the blue considering the conversation. My heart performed a funny thump, though.

"That was a long time ago, and I didn't have one, you know that. We got married and afterward had dinner with a couple of friends. Nothing else. Good thing. What a colossal money-waster it would have been for a marriage that didn't last out the year."

"Do you think you'll ever get married again?"

I stared at her, considered not answering. Pulling out the coffee pot, I stuck a mug underneath the flow to catch it and poured from the pot into Mom's cup, after which I performed a handy reversal with mine and waited for the coffee to finish, arms crossed.

"Suze?"

"Marriage isn't every girl's dream," I said.

Her lips scrunched up. She didn't speak.

"As I told Carla yesterday, it would probably be worthwhile to find someone I love and who loves me in return first. Don't you think?"

"Yes," she said. "Yes, I do."

"Great. Let's divvy up this new list then, shall we? Do any of these folks text? It would be a lot easier and more efficient than spending the rest of the day on the phone."

We agreed on texting. All talk of my erstwhile marriage ceased. To be honest, I'd given my brief married life very little thought over the past near-decade. We'd both been ridiculously young. Not that age always mattered, but in my case and his, it clearly had.

Texting, receiving initial responses, writing down the definite affirmatives and the volunteered foodstuffs took up the remaining morning hours and a quarter of the afternoon, especially as some relatives decided it would be simpler to call back rather than type in their answers. Both my fingers and my voice had grown a little weary with the task. I hadn't talked to this many family members since Simon and Lucy got married.

At one point I snuck off to the kitchen to dip a tablespoon into the peanut butter jar. We'd agreed not to pause for lunch until all contact had been made, but I was starving. Mom came in right as I stuck the spoon in my mouth. Wordlessly, I reached behind me into the drawer for another and held it and the open jar out to her. She dug in, twisting the spoon for a hefty scoop.

"What about Arlo?"

I frowned at her question, the spoon glued to my tongue and my thoughts jumping from place to place, speculating on her meaning.

"Should we get him for photos?"

Oh. "Everyone has phones," I managed around the stickiness.

She shot me an odd look, stuck her spoon in her mouth. I turned away to rinse my utensil, drop it into the dishwasher, ignore her weighty gaze on my back.

"I just thought—"

I pivoted on my heel. "It's not worth the unexpected expense though, is it? We'll all be taking pictures. We can share them."

"Okay," she said, "that's smart." But she didn't sound convinced. Her gaze remained on my person as though I had suddenly announced I'd be running off with the postman. Befuddled, maybe disappointed. I waited for her to say something else. When she didn't, I retrieved the scribbled list from the counter, glanced down.

"What next?"

And so it went, on through the day, Mom and I whittling down the itemized chores, her occasional mentioning of Arlo's name in conjunction with other topics, not quite obvious, but obvious enough. She'd recognized my interest, I knew. This led me to the conclusion she didn't know about Jenny, marching me to the further conclusion I wouldn't be able to get any information about the woman from her, even if I wanted to—which I didn't. Blatant curiosity could never be an excuse for mining into a near-stranger's life. This is what I told myself.

Eventually she gave up and moved onto other spaces in the house. Relieved, I drifted into a silent cleaning pattern. I ended up out on the back porch sweeping debris from the centerpieces off the tables and into a dustpan with a rag. Most of those had gone home with guests after the reception, and no wonder: they were beautiful.

A low flying red-tail hawk caught my eye out the window. I went closer to the glass, watched it sweep gracefully over the fields, hunting for rodents, I supposed, or merely enjoying the wind supporting its wings. I wanted to feel a bit more like that sometimes, ignoring the hunt for the necessities in life for the enjoyment of living it. Everyone probably experienced that longing, now and again. And I had a job, a practice, and was, as Mom had pointed out, good at it. Lately though I missed what I could only term my roots. I missed this place, I missed the way it felt, I missed my family and the friends I'd left behind. Yes, I spoke with my family fairly regularly, and the friends to catch up on occasion, but it wasn't the same.

If I came back here, though, what would I do? Therein lay the dilemma. Giving up a successful endeavor for uncertainty seemed a ridiculously idiotic thing to do. Too risky, for one. Too irresponsible. Too self-indulgent. Too much like I was giving up.

I opened the back door and stepped outside, the chill air striking my bare face and hands in a tiny slap. I headed toward the greenhouse with no particular objective. With long strides, not a slow meander, I reached the glass structure in no time. I peered through the windows to make certain I wouldn't disturb any tender plants by opening the door, and then slipped inside. It smelled like soil and moisture in there. Like mint, too, and lavender, making me look more closely at the rows of planting boxes. At the very back two boxes were green with wild spearmint, transplanted presumably from outside. Gardening gloves lay to one side and a small pair of child's scissors.

I touched a leaf, rubbed it between thumb and forefinger, brought my hand to my nose and sniffed. A smile crept onto my face, the scent comforting and familiar. Above the mint several wooden dowels hung suspended from the ceiling. From them, lavender tied with twine into bunches had been left to dry.

I had no idea what Mom intended to do with these herbals, but here, as everywhere, I found evidence of her industrious, constantly planning nature. If only I had a plan, a single plan, I might figure out what to do.

The door opened behind me. I whipped around. Mom stepped inside, latching the door against the breeze.

"I saw you from the sewing room," she said.

"You're not actually cleaning the sewing room? No one's going to go in there."

"I know they're not. That's why I figured it would be a good place to hide some things I have no idea what to do with."

"Good thinking." I sniffed my mint-scented fingers again. "Love that spearmint."

"It makes tasty mint jelly. Tea, too. You'll have to have some."

"Okay," I said, suddenly awkward, suddenly blinking back tears.

Mom eased past me, reaching up to check the lavender's condition. Several dried bits fell onto her hand. She held them out to me, fingers spread, the tiny purple flowers cupped in her palm. "Smell that."

"Oh my goodness," I cried after a deep breath, "that's wonderful."

"Isn't it?" She set the petite petals aside on the wood ledge reluctant, no doubt, to toss them away. Lifting her head, she continued studying the drying lavender. Her signature ponytail had come loose as always, the band tying it back having slipped a good three inches from her nape, liberated strands rioting about her face and neck.

"Are you ever going to tell me what's wrong?" she asked without looking at me.

"Of course I am," I whispered.

"Now seems like a good time."

"Does it? I…I'm too old to be so…unable to move forward."

"How old are you?" she asked, facing me.

"What, you don't remember?"

"Of course I do. I just want you to say it out loud."

I backed up against a potting box, planting my hips against it, arms crossed. "I'm thirty-three."

"Not old," Mom said. "Not by a long shot."

"Yeah, well, too old to be so undecided, too old to be crying my woes to my mother."

"Needing someone to talk to, someone who has known you your entire life, loved you your entire life, isn't something you outgrow. You don't think I miss my mom still for that very reason?"

I started crying in earnest, head-in-my-hands spearmint-scent-and-all type weeping. To her credit, Mom didn't rush to take me into her arms. She stood very still and quiet, her hands together in front of her, waiting. Giving me time, time to finish bawling, time to recall the strength I actually did possess, the strength I'd learned from her. I finally stopped, wiping the tears away with my sweatshirt sleeve. I looked at her through my filmy vision, sniffling.

"Let's go have some of that spearmint tea right now," she said, "shall we?"

In silent, grateful agreement, I followed her back inside.

Chapter Seven

Only three days until Christmas Eve, so only two more days to accomplish everything on Mom's constantly appended list. The nervous breakdown I'd thought she'd been heading for right after her phone call from Aunt Charlotte had clearly been avoided and forgotten. Dad remained his usual go-with-the-flow self. Simon had arrived with the kids and Lucy to lend a hand later Sunday afternoon, after my talk with Mom. A talk we hadn't discussed since. I remembered it though, nearly word for word. It hadn't been a long conversation. More time had been spent in consuming tea than in speech. The silences, the many silences, had contained no unspoken judgment, no undue concern.

"Whatever you decide," Mom had said at the end of it, removing our teacups from the table, "you know your dad and I are there for you."

I hadn't briefly spilled my soul because I wanted them to feel responsible in any manner, and I understood from Mom's face she didn't. Her sentiment had been uttered in the very literal, comforting sense.

Now, standing in the Monday morning sunshine on the sidewalk in Connor Falls proper, I pulled the most recent list from my jacket pocket and went over the baked goods bordered with a penciled box. Some folks were bringing their best holiday confections, but not enough for all who were attending. Simon still insisted he'd bake bread, but Mom, fearful he might throw up his hands in defeat if the loaves didn't turn out as planned, wanted to arrange for fresh-baked rolls and several extra pies. I hurried into From the Hart Bakery and gave my order to the young girl behind the counter. Gina was nowhere in sight, leaving me unable to exchange a quick hello. I would have liked to see her before I left. I wasn't sure if that would happen now.

Next, my Christmas gift for Simon, which had also expanded to gifts for Malory's sister, her parents, and I supposed Shepherd and Malory themselves, since I couldn't be sure their package from me would arrive before they flew out to come home. I decided to make it simple and headed to Sophie's Chandlery again. She had lotions and soaps so something like that would work for the sister, since I knew nothing about her. I'd make sure the scent wasn't too strong. Two cheery, holiday-scented candles would be nice for Shepherd and Malory as well as for the in-laws, and not a problem for the return flight. My brother and his new wife would have the journals waiting for them when they got home.

After exiting the candle shop, I headed again to the bookstore. Simon did so enjoy baking, although two years after the bug had bitten him, he remained in the learning stages. There had to be a book with exciting but not overwhelming recipes for bread-making. I didn't want to frustrate him, after all.

I approached the same young man who'd helped me the other day and asked him to point me in the right direction. Setting my package down by my feet, I started pulling out books to examine. A voice carried to me from the next aisle over. Open book in hand, I paused, listening despite myself.

"I don't know what you're so upset about," said a woman's voice.

"I'm not upset, only concerned."

I recognized the male voice. Arlo.

Now I was in a quandary. I had business in this section and didn't want to walk away until I'd concluded my search, but I didn't want to eavesdrop either. Making my way around the corner, saying a quick hello and returning to look for Simon's book might be the best course. Arlo would be warned away from saying something personal and I wouldn't look like an imbecile if he caught me within earshot, having said it. Clutching the promising book I hadn't fully perused and picking up my bag, I stepped around the shelving.

"Hi," I said, "I thought that was you."

Oh.

Well.

Jenny.

"I'm sorry, I didn't mean to interrupt." I started to turn away.

"Susan," Arlo said. "Don't go."

Against my better judgment, I didn't. I waited.

"Shopping?" he asked.

I gave the bag a shake. "Yes, last-minute gifts. My older brother and his wife and family are coming. It was supposed to be a surprise." I shrugged my shoulder in a slow lift. "Also, there's an impromptu and huge family gathering now on Christmas Eve."

He smiled, glanced at Jenny and back at me. His eye contact lasted longer than usual. I wondered if my practiced, relative immobility could be paying off.

"Might be a good idea if you didn't have extra mouths to feed on Christmas Day, then?" he said. "S—seems like you all have enough going on."

"Oh, no!" I was, perhaps, somewhat more emphatic than I should have been. Beside him, Jenny's eyes widened. "Don't be silly." I continued. "You don't want to disappoint Mom when she's putting a spread on."

"I'd never want to disappoint your mother," he said. He meant it, I could tell.

"Arlo," Jenny said, her hand on his arm, "you don't have to say yes to an invitation just because someone feels sorry for you."

My breath huffed out in shock at the nerve of her. I couldn't let the statement go undefended.

"My Mom doesn't feel sorry for Arlo. No one in my family does, as a matter of fact. My mother invited him because she views him as a friend." I slapped the cookbook up against my chest, clutched the Chandlery bag handle tight. "We will see you Christmas day?" I didn't wait for an answer, from either of them. "Good." I strode to the counter, paid for the cookbook and departed without looking back.

Still grumbling inwardly from the encounter when I arrived at Hummingbird Farm, I stomped up the porch steps and into the house, continuing straight up the stairs to deposit the two bags on my bed. I stood for several minutes without removing my coat, staring out through the window glass to the blue sky.

Was that what he thought? Was that what Arlo really thought? That we felt *sorry* for him? Or might this be only Jenny's perception? Nothing could be further from the truth. My mom especially never bothered with something as detrimental as feeling sorry for a person. Feeling sorry for someone didn't do anyone any good. Caring helped. Recognizing a person's strengths and encouraging them helped. Taking time to listen helped. Pity did nothing except make the recipient feel worse, as if their condition held some shameful connotation.

Growling, I unclenched my fists, yanked off my gloves. I tossed them on the bedspread next to the bags, followed by my coat. Remembering the list in the pocket, I snatched it out, checking to make sure I hadn't forgotten anything in my outrage. Nope, all good.

Mom called me from below. "Coming, Mom," I answered in my best Emma Watson imitation. Mom wouldn't recognize it. I didn't think she'd seen any Harry Potter movies, at least not more than once. I went downstairs. As soon as she spotted my compliance, she returned to the kitchen, slipping the damp dishtowel in her hand over the oven door handle. She smoothed the fabric out.

"Everything go well in town?" she asked, brushing back her flyaway strands.

"Hunky-dory," I said. "This list can go in the trash. How about here? No calls?"

"One."

I kept silent, anticipating Arlo's name along with a cancellation for Christmas dinner.

"Alice. She's bringing a whole turkey with stuffing. Fully cooked, since she hasn't far to come."

Having expected nothing resembling Mom's words, I found myself momentarily lacking in response. "Oh—oh good," I finally stammered. "Did you get a chance to add it to the chart?" I headed that way in case she hadn't, to the chart on copy paper hanging on the refrigerator door. Baker's twine attached to the magnet holding it in place held a pen at its nether end. I snatched the pen up, clicked out the point. "Ah, you did already."

"As soon as I hung up the phone," Mom said.

I nodded, lips twisting. No surprise there. Straightening, I released the pen, letting it swing. I felt tempted to bring up my conversation with Arlo and his girlfriend in the bookstore, but Mom was the last person I wanted to be troubled by an insensitive remark. She was used to them occasionally coming from me, unfortunately, but Jenny had made a rash judgment without proof or merit. I calmed myself before Mom picked up on the annoyance in my body language. She'd always been way too good at reading people.

"So what time are Shepherd and the rest getting

in again?" I asked, for something to say. I knew their flight landed three-thirty-ish.

She repeated the information. Simon was lending me the only vehicle among us that could accommodate four extra adults and a teenager together with their luggage. ABE wasn't that far away. I could handle a minivan for the short trip. Even so, I made Simon promise to bring it over early, telling him I was paranoid about not leaving enough time. Truthfully, I wanted to practice driving it up and down the driveway. I hadn't owned a car bigger than a compact since day one.

He would have laughed at me, had he known. He probably would also have insisted he pick them up himself rather than letting me drive his van, but he had work and I didn't, so I had no plan to reveal my anxiety until after my return from the airport.

"Ready to make some candy?" Mom interjected into my overlong silence.

"Candy?" I echoed. "What happened to cookies? Cookies are on list number three."

"I've scratched them off for this year," Mom said, tapping the list taped to the cabinet door. "Seems like everyone is making a favorite to bring. So, I thought I'd make candy instead. I bought boxes over the summer when I first had the idea. We'll fill each one with candy and wrap them up with ribbon."

"Huh."

"What?"

"I have an idea, Mom. Why don't we skip the candy, too?"

She jerked her head back, affronted. "Why?"

"Because…because there's enough to do. We have enough sweets to rot everyone's teeth from their heads. If you don't kill yourself with all of this, you're going to kill your one and only daughter. And because you and I are going to take a breather and go to lunch." I checked my watch. "Brunch. No arguments."

She stared at me in silence. To give her credit, the silence and the stare lasted no more than two seconds. She sighed.

"Okay, let me get my coat."

"You might want to brush your hair while you're at it," I called after her. I understood now where I got the blasé attitude about simple daily habits. It struck me like an epiphany, one that made me laugh and reach up to check I hadn't gone through the morning's shopping sporting bedhead. Especially, you know, in front of Jenny.

With a noise resembling a cross between a frantic bird and a distressed puppy, I rushed up the stairs to find my comb.

*　*　*

"This is very nice of you, taking your old Ma to brunch," my old ma said from across the table. "I can't remember the last time I've been out to eat during the day."

"Frankly, I can't either. I used to go out to lunch every now and then, but I've taken to eating in the office." I opened my menu. We'd decided on Shelly's, a family-friendly place known for its reasonably priced diner style offerings. Any evening you'd likely find families filling nearly every table. On a weekday just before noon, however, my mom and I were two of only a dozen or so patrons in the place. Like the other establishments in Connor Falls, the restaurant had been decorated for the holidays. Shelly's relied on the vintage for its special appeal. The decorations reminded Mom of her childhood. She had something to say about almost every one. I had to stop her by opening her menu, too, and sliding it across to her.

"Oh," she exclaimed, distracted but excited anew, "they have actual brunch specials."

I rolled my eyes and turned my attention to the selections. They had quaint names. Mom pointed out that the names had been taken from song lyrics from the nineteen-sixties and seventies.

"Cute," I said. She picked up on my tone right away, unintentional though it had been.

"Grumpy, are we?"

"No. I said 'cute', didn't I? I just don't remember some of these lyrics, I guess. Oh, this one, and this one, too. You still play this music sometimes."

"All the time," she said. "You're not around to hear it. And don't take offense. That's a statement of fact, not a criticism."

"Gotcha." I lifted my menu closer, ducked my head.

"I miss you, Suze."

The menu dropped, splat, on the table. "I miss you, too, Mom. You know I do."

"I do. What are you having?"

Glad for the changing subject, I decided on the *Back to the Garden*, a scrumptious-sounding salad with spinach and fruit both dried and fresh and candied pecans for good measure. The menu promised the salad was small, since it also came with a slice of quiche. Mom decided to have the same right as the server approached, pad in hand. We both sat back, awkwardly smiling at each other as she left with our orders.

"So how long are you giving yourself?" Mom asked, harkening back to our conversation the day before. I'd assumed she'd have more questions.

I turned my head to the window, to a woman with a child passing by on the sidewalk. "I'd say as long as it takes, but that's really too open-ended and I might never decide."

"Yep," she said, "you're probably right. That's why I mark things on the calendar, the physical calendar. Simon gets on me about it, telling me to set reminders on my phone, put things on the pretend calendar, because that's why those apps or whatever they're called are there. I say baloney sauce. The real calendar is what works for me."

I looked back at her. "I'm pretty sure they're both real calendars," I said, taking a swallow from my water glass. "But I get it. Believe me, I do."

"I see the calendar every day, multiple times a day. It's a much more efficient reminder for me. Plus, I love the picture reveal every month. This year, it's national parks. Beautiful."

"Don't let Simon try to tell you what to do. You're you. You're independent and have your own way of doing things that works for you just fine. His way is great for him. That doesn't mean it's great for everybody else in the world and even if it was, so what? You do what you do, period."

She smiled, lips closely curling. "You're so much like me."

"I know. I know I am. You're lucky you have Dad. He's happy with who you are. Any man who thinks they're attracted to me hightails it out of there when they get a whiff of how little I really need a man around the house…so to speak. They're good for some things." I rolled my eyes again. Mom guffawed, almost losing the tea she'd sipped. She covered her mouth with her hand.

"Oh, honey," she said, "you have such a way with words."

"I try."

Our meals arrived. Temporarily talked out and both hungry, we ate without intermission for a good ten minutes. The fruit combo in the salad was particularly tasty. I committed the contents to memory so I could make it myself sometime.

"Who's that?" Mom said, lowering her fork to her plate. I turned my head, following her gaze. On the corner, waiting to cross the street, stood Arlo and Jenny. Arlo looked tired, as if he'd had enough for one day. Jenny was chattering away like a bird.

"That's Jenny," I said.

"Who?"

"Jenny. I don't know her last name. She and Arlo are together apparently."

I went back to my salad, to remembering everything in it. I felt Mom's eyes on me.

"When did you meet her?" she asked. Her

nonchalant tone didn't fool me. She might even have been a little miffed at not having known before. She and Arlo did seem close. I was surprised he hadn't mentioned Jenny to her.

"She was waiting in his Jeep for him Saturday night after the wedding reception. To drive him home. I do remember him mentioning he doesn't drive at night right now. And then…and then I ran into them both in the bookstore earlier."

I refused to tell Mom what she'd said. I absolutely would not.

Mom set the napkin from her lap onto the table. "I'll get the scoop. Shall I?" She started to get up. I reached over the table and grabbed her hand.

"Mom, no. Please don't. You can interrogate him next time you see him, okay?"

She settled back down. I released her hand. She spread her napkin on her lap again, picked up her fork. "But you like him," she said.

I dipped my head a little to the side, spearing a strawberry. "I don't know him, so…"

Mom let out a long, slow, quiet breath before digging into her quiche. I appreciated her keeping any further questions to herself, because I really didn't know how I'd answer them.

Later that night, when the house was once again quiet, Mom and Dad tucked up in their bed, I went for another midnight walk. This time I bundled up more warmly so I could stay out longer. I snuck out from the back porch and headed straight into the fields. My breath frosted, the stars shone, my boots cracked the thoroughly frozen vegetation. With my hat tucked down around my ears, I only heard my footsteps on last season's corn stalks in muffled repetition.

I had decisions to make, decisions that could never include Arlo, no matter how much I'd like to get to know him if not for Jenny. They couldn't include my family either, not really. These decisions had to be solely about me, so they'd be clear, definite, well-reasoned. And so I'd have no one to blame if they didn't work out, I added with a snort in the dark.

Christmas was coming, days away. The family, a great many members, would all be together for the holiday. It would be nice if I could reach a resolution by then, come to terms with it, perhaps share my plans with others, move forward. My heart-brain wanted one thing, while my logical-brain insisted on pointing out all the arguments against. It liked to do so with particular emphasis during the night, when things like sleep yearned contrarily for the upper hand.

"Ah, who needs sleep," I muttered out loud as I trudged my way further afield. Again, I spotted deer at a distance, only two, observing me with caution. Some lone traveler scuttled away low to the ground. I heard a car on the road, a rumbling hum, coming toward Hummingbird Farm, passing it, disappearing over the crest. I paused and turned around, looking back at the house. Starlight reflected in a pale gleam off the windows that weren't lit by the clear twinkle lights. This close to Christmas Mom and Dad kept them on through the night.

Realizing I wouldn't likely come to any decisions bleary-eyed and tripping over the terrain in the darkness, I debated going back…for about thirty seconds. Instead, I tugged my hat down lower, shoved my hands in my pockets, and walked on. Before long, I found myself approaching the bordering woodland. The closely grown brush at its edge looked impassable without a machete and the shadows beyond stretched black indeed. An owl hooted nearby, very nearby. I tipped my head back and looked around, spotting its shape, its eyes glowing in the dark. I'd read somewhere that owls didn't possess eyeballs per se, but that their eyes were shaped like tubes and held in place in bone, which was why they turned their heads in all directions to see with their wonderful binocular vision. I kept myself still so as not to frighten it away. After a moment, the bird launched itself from the branch where it had been sitting and sailed off into the forest in absolute silence.

I released my breath, trying to follow the owl's path with my own comparatively ineffectual eyesight. I lost it within no more than twenty feet, but my gaze landed on something else. Not quite sure what I looked at, I moved to the side, trying to find a way into the trees. Neither Mom nor Dad had ever mentioned another building on their property. I glanced back, making sure I hadn't left their acreage. I appeared not to have done, at least relative to the boundary lines they'd pointed out in the past.

Breaking out my phone, I turned on the flashlight and held it high above my head in order to prevent the tangled shadow from nearby branches blocking my view. I glimpsed fieldstone walls and empty window casements and a slate roof which looked, in spite of the weathering, to be in halfway decent shape. At least it wasn't falling in. No more than a storey tall, I figured the structure might be a long-forgotten outbuilding. After all this time, anything might be living beneath that roof. Once again, I stood in debate about returning to Mom and Dad's, this time because the unknown building seemed to be drawing me in. I genuinely wanted to see it, its exact shape and size, whether it had become a decrepit wreck or was a well-built aging edifice doing its level best to withstand the elements and the passing years, whether or not it could be salvaged, repaired, renovated, made livable for someone.

Made livable for someone like me.

In sudden, bursting clarity, I rushed back across the fields. I would need to see the building by day, of course, and there would be oh so many considerations, but in the instant I'd pictured myself living there, living back in Connor Falls, my heart-brain had burst out in joy and told my logical-brain to stuff it. I felt better than I had in many months.

Letting myself in the back door, I tiptoed up the stairs and into my room. I shirked from my coat and hat and gloves, kicked off my boots, threw myself down onto the bed with a pen and paper pad I'd snatched off the nightstand, ready to make notes, ready to make a list. My cheeks tingled in the room's warmth. I smelled the frigid night air in my short, static-filled hair. I touched the pen's point to the ruled yellow paper, thinking, thinking hard about where to begin.

The next thing I knew morning had come, the sun burning bright once more upon my face. The pad lay beside me on the covers, five words printed and underscored at the top.

Susan Hardwick is coming home.

Chapter Eight

Dad, Mom and I hiked back across the fields before Simon's appointed time for dropping off his minivan. We brought loppers and a shovel, although why we might need the latter, I wasn't quite sure.

The forecast was calling for snow. I could smell it, see it in the pale gray cloud cover, hovering low. No one mentioned accumulation today beyond an inch or two. Christmas Day might be another matter. I hoped the snow would hold off until I'd returned from pickup at the airport, though. Simon and Lucy's van did have front-wheel drive, but I'd gotten used to the all-wheel of my car when the weather took a turn. I kept reminding myself an inch or two was nothing. The cargo, however, was priceless and drivers on the road during the first snow could be somewhat nuts.

When we neared the place in the woods where I had located the building, I put airport shuttling from my mind.

"It's a lot of acreage," Mom was saying. "We haven't explored every inch of it. We haven't had any reason to."

"There's no accusation going on here, Mom. I just happened across it last night—"

"In the dark, alone," said my dad.

"In the dark, alone, yes. I'm just really curious. You can't tell me you both aren't, too. You wouldn't be traipsing out here with me right now if you weren't." I hadn't revealed to them the whole reason for my interest. Not yet. I still had things to work through, in my head and in my life.

Upon our approach, a fox darted from the underbrush, his rich red pelt brilliant in the wintery illumination. Both my parents turned to watch the animal race across the stubbled field. I witnessed respect and awe in their eyes. My heart swelled. I couldn't help my admiration for them both. Once they pivoted to face me again, I pointed with the lopper handles. "Through there. I couldn't get in, but I could see it."

"Okay," said Dad, "let's get lopping."

While Mom stood leaning on the shovel, Dad and I pruned a path to the other side. Not a big one, only enough to pass through. We hadn't any reason for too much disturbance. I walked ahead of him toward the building looming in the still shadowed wood.

"Honey," he called back to my mother, "would you look at that?"

I heard them tramping in behind me, my mother giving a small cry like something had jabbed her, probably a barb from the multiflora rose growing everywhere. She came up next to me, sucking on her pinkie.

"You okay?" I asked.

"Fine."

Sweeping the lopper end back and forth across the groundcover, I went closer to the structure. In winter, snakes in Pennsylvania enter a state called brumation, a kind of partial dormancy. This building would be perfect habitat. I wanted to make sure not to disturb any. Dad appeared at my elbow with a large flashlight.

"Let's have a look, eh?"

The door stood wide, seemingly in decent shape, possibly because it opened inward and had been protected. Dad shone the light around. A wooden floor had suffered badly, boards missing here and there, but the entire building stood on a stone foundation, beneath which existed a cellar of some kind. The floor beams looked solid enough. Underneath, several feet down, I glimpsed a cobbled subterranean floor. All the building's windows were broken, some still retaining shards of ancient glass. The walls inside, what we could see, had no bow to them. Various timbered uprights remained solid. The flashlight didn't reveal insect damage or rot, but that could show up on closer examination. Flipping the beam up toward the roof, Dad swept the light from side to side. Several old barn swallow nests clung to the hand-hewn trusses. No daylight showed through underlayment or the slate above. My lips curved.

"It's beautiful," I said.

"Yeah, sort of," Mom agreed behind me. "I can see that."

"Be nice to resurrect it," said my dad.

"Yes," I answered him, "it would."

* * *

The snow held off. The first flakes didn't speckle the windshield until I pulled into the driveway with my passengers. None appeared worn out by their flight, chatting non-stop the whole ride. Malory's sister Nester possessed a heavy accent I couldn't understand half the time. I confessed myself charmed nevertheless. Mom and Dad must have been waiting at the window. They hurried out before I'd even put the van in park. Simon followed with Sammy and Stuart. He held his hand out for the keys from me the minute the introductions, hellos and hugs had concluded.

"Dad told me about you practicing in the driveway. If I'd known…"

"Oh for crying out loud," I said, dropping the keys onto his palm. "You're kidding, right?"

He swept around the vehicle, eyeing it for damage. Ignoring him, I set Sammy and Stuart to carrying smaller bags and I grabbed two others. The whole crowd of us piled on into Mom and Dad's, where more hasty greetings took place and then everyone was shown where they'd be sleeping by Mom. Dad took the two cases I'd been carrying. I went back outside.

"Did you see the front quarter panel?" I yelled to Simon. "I side-swiped an SUV when I exited the cell phone lot."

"Not funny," he said.

"I thought it was. If you were that worried, why didn't you go? You obviously had the time, since you're here."

"Honestly, I only finished up work about forty-five minutes ago. I wouldn't have been able to manage it."

I walked up to him and punched him in the upper arm. Lightly, I swear. "You're a dolt," I said.

Snowflakes fell with increasing volume, catching in my eyelashes, clinging to my hair, my coat sleeves. Slowing spinning, I lifted my face to them, eyes closed.

"What are you doing?" Simon asked.

"Reveling."

He snorted. We all had that habit, snorting. A fabulous tool was a snort, appropriately employed in so many exchanges, its meaning infinite. While I continued to spin, I heard the porch door open, rapid footsteps crossing the gravel. Someone snatched me from my feet, twirling me at a much faster rate than I'd been enjoying.

"Shepherd," I cried, opening my eyes, "put me down."

In appearance, Shepherd was a cross between our mom's father and Dad, but without Dad's height. When we were young, Simon and I used to insist he didn't look like anyone else and had been adopted. Hearing the taunt at one point, Mom broke out some photos of Granddad when he'd been a kid, effectively shutting us up. She'd also told us rather sternly that even if Shepherd had been adopted, he'd be as much family as if he'd been born to it. She hadn't been very happy with me and Simon that day. Funny how things came back to you. Family was family was family no matter what the configuration. Blood didn't matter. Love did.

I stepped back from Shepherd, my hands on his

arms. I looked up into his face and Granddad's dancing eyes. "You've got a secret," I said.

"What? How do you know?"

"I can see it. Plain as day. You're bursting to tell."

"Okay, but you have to stay mum. You, too, Simon. For a bit anyway. Promise?"

Simon and I both nodded.

Shepherd leaned forward to whisper. "We're pregnant. Well, Malory is doing the actual carrying, but we're pregnant."

I threw my arms around his middle and hugged him, really, really hard. Simon slapped him on the back.

"You do know the dress Malory's wearing isn't hiding that fact, don't you?" I said to Shepherd, whose grin nearly split his face. "I had my suspicions the minute she unbuttoned her coat to get in the van. You better tell Mom and Dad soon, because Mom's going to pick up on that, too."

The porch door opened again. A human squeal drew my eye around Shepherd in time to see Mom trotting down the steps toward us. Behind her, Malory shrugged palms up from the doorway. I poked Shepherd in the stomach with my forefinger.

"Secret's out, Shep," I said.

Following congratulations, we trooped inside, shaking snow from garments and shoes on the mat before entering. Voices and laughter bounced around the high ceilings, sounding as though twice as many people were housed beneath. Mom crooked her finger discreetly. I followed her into the kitchen.

She appeared downright giddy. "Great news,

eh?" she said, turning to replenish the coffee pot with fresh stock. I couldn't help thinking how far away her new grandchild would be living, but I said nothing about that and agreed with enthusiasm.

"And what about your news?" she continued, measuring hefty tablespoons of ground coffee into the filter. "Will you be sharing?"

"Not yet," I said. "That's okay, isn't it? It's not quite as fabulous as a new family member, after all."

She smiled, slapping the lid onto the coffee container. "It is to me."

I shook my head. "You're my mom. That's pretty much guaranteed."

"Ah, I wouldn't bank on that." She poured the water into the maker, turned it on and spun herself around to lean against the counter. She crossed her arms. "I possibly could have ended up not being able to stand your company. I got lucky though."

"Me, too."

We stood silently for a moment before she loosened her arms and reached back, tapping a knuckle on the nearest list hanging from the cabinet door by painters' tape. "I'm thinking we should hide these."

"Agreed," I said.

"And count them for now as done as they're going to get."

Again, I concurred, carefully peeling back tape from each paper and taking them down. We decided to tuck them away in the pantry temporarily, figuring no one would go digging there.

"And," she added, dragging out the word,

"we'll spend the remainder of the evening hanging out with everyone. I say we order something in for dinner, too, because tomorrow's going to be another busy day."

One more time I assented. Arms looped together we headed into the living room, calling out for preferences. I had no idea what Malory's parents and sister would make of our casual dinner management, but we were one family now, take us or leave us.

* * *

The parents in bed, Lucy gone home with the boys, and Malory frankly asleep in the deep chair with the ottoman, Shepherd, Simon and I sat on the floor close to the flames leaping in the living room fireplace, the twinkling lights on the evergreen by the window the only other illumination in the room. Behind us, Nester lay curled on the sofa, an empty mug on the table nearby, the hot cocoa long gone from the interior. I'd glanced back twice expecting to find her asleep, but instead caught her watching us in silence, a small smile on her lips. I gathered we were amusing her somehow. It had been a long time since the three of us had been able to get together. We were harkening back to old tales and old times, no doubt bizarre out of context and to a sixteen-year-old who hadn't lived our collective past.

"So, got a man in your life?" Shepherd asked me unexpectedly.

"Oh my gawd," Nester said from the sofa. "Seriously, Shep? I wouldn't answer him if I were you," she added to me, swinging her legs off the cushions and sitting up. "Truly, I wouldn't bother. Him, he's got the idea everyone should be tucked up in a sweet little relationship." Despite her caustic words, the tone wasn't there and the smile she sent him fond. She went to her sister, shook her gently and pulled on her hands, urging her up from the chair. "Time for bed, sleepyhead."

Malory mumbled goodnight as they headed from the room to the stairs. Shepherd watched his wife disappear from sight with emotion raw on his face.

"I'm happy for you, Shep," I whispered.

"I'm happy for me too."

"You should be." I stood, gathering up Nester's mug and the two glasses on the hearth. "Anyone want something else?"

"You're avoiding my question," Shepherd said. "And yeah, I'll take another half glass of that mead, thanks. Simon?"

Simon lifted his hands. "I'm good. I'm heading home soon."

Shepherd got up, followed me into the kitchen. He stood at my elbow as I deposited the mug and glasses into the sink and filled a fresh one with the locally brewed mead.

"Only half," he reminded me when I'd almost finished.

"Too late. You can break out a funnel, though, if you want to pour some back into the bottle."

Smirking, he reached into the cabinet for a tumbler and dumped a portion from his glass into the second one. He handed the tumbler to me.

"Thanks," I said, not really meaning it.

"Is there anyone in your life, sis? Come on, spill."

I experienced a quick leap in my head to Arlo—Arlo the man I barely knew, Arlo of the infamous Jenny/Arlo combination, Arlo with whom I'd hardly shared thirty minutes' conversation—and jumped away again. "Nope," I said. "Not a one."

"Is that why you're moving back home?"

I sputtered into the glass I held to my mouth, bubbling the honeyed contents. "Jeez, Shepherd!" I wiped my chin with my shirtsleeve. "Of course, that's not why. Who told you I was moving back anyway?"

"Dad. You are, aren't you? He said something about a house out there in the woods they didn't even know existed."

I sighed, clunking the tumbler onto the counter. "He wasn't supposed to say anything."

"To be honest, Simon mentioned it first and then I asked Dad about the house and—"

"Simon knew?"

"Well, yeah."

I closed my eyes, exasperated with the whole blabbing lot. Maybe I should reconsider my plan. However, unless I kept every aspect in my life to myself for eternity these things would always get shared. Families didn't keep secrets. At least not the one I'd grown up in.

Opening my eyes again, I shot Shepherd a look before dumping the mead from the tumbler into the sink. I started rinsing all the dishes stacked in the basin. Shepherd yanked open the dishwasher for me so I could fit them inside.

"It's not a house," I said as I worked. "Not yet. It's more like an ancient, not very large outbuilding I'm hoping to restore and renovate. A number of trees will need to be cleared back from it. It'll need a well, septic, electric, a lane for access, permits…" I stopped, the enormity of my half-baked plan hitting me. I lifted my gaze to the window, my face a ghostly reflection in the glass.

"Wow," said Shepherd quietly. "That's a project."

"Ain't it just?" I drawled.

"What made you decide to do this?"

"Roots."

"Like the PBS show?"

I huffed out a breath. "No. And that's called 'Finding Your Roots' by the way. I'm talking about my personal roots in the here and now. I've lived half a dozen places since moving away and not one ever felt quite like home to me. I still think of Connor Falls as home, whenever the word comes up. The place I live now? It's my house. That's how I hear it in my head. How I feel it. My house. Not my home. I want my home."

"You know, Suze, home is where the heart—"

"Don't say it. No, do say it, because my heart is here. Maybe if I had a significant other in my life, I might feel differently. But I don't think so. And I'm not going to base my decisions on that what-if anyway. I want to change my life. Part of that plan is coming home. I've been working through it for a while now. It was no quick decision, believe me. Seeing that building solidified my ideas somehow, yet even if I hadn't seen it, if I can't make the building work, I'll find someplace else here."

Shepherd shook his dark head. "Big changes in the offing, then."

"Big changes."

Simon came to find us, snuggling a folded blanket and a pillow against his chest. "Just texted Lucy. I'm crashing on the couch. See you at breakfast." He shuffled off back to the living room in his sock feet.

"I'm heading up, too," I said to Shepherd. "Enjoy your mead."

"Right behind you." He tossed off the remainder and deposited the glass in the dishwasher. We walked up the narrow stairs not quite side by side, parting ways in the hallway outside my door.

"I'd like to say I'll help you in whatever way you need," he said. "My arms may be long, but they're not quite long enough to reach across the ocean and wield a hammer. Still…"

"I know." I smiled at him. "You're going to have enough on your hands pretty soon anyway."

"Oh, yeah, right. I almost forgot about that."

"Baloney sauce," I said, using Mom's favorite expression. He walked down the hall and paused at the open doorway to an even narrower staircase leading to the two attic rooms above.

"It must be nice to be so brave," he called softly along to me.

"Or stupid," I said. "We'll see."

Chapter Nine

Afraid I might oversleep, I picked up my phone to set an alarm for the morning—well, for later. It was already morning, the very wee hours of it. Christmas Eve. Someone had texted me from an unknown number.

Thanks for being understanding. Jenny can be overprotective sometimes. See you Christmas Day. Enjoy your unexpected family reunion.

I sat down slowly on the mattress edge, clutching the phone in my hand. How had he gotten my number? Moreover, what was I supposed to do with his message? At an appropriate hour, I would respond in some vague way, but otherwise, I didn't quite know what to make of the text or why Arlo felt it necessary to send. I didn't need thanking. In fact, I thought my response to Jenny's statement hadn't been at all tactful or understanding. I'd been annoyed and figured I'd made that clear.

I slid the phone onto the nightstand, confused with how I felt about him contacting me at all. If not for Jenny, I would have been quietly thrilled. I did like him, despite barely knowing him. I supposed it happened like that sometimes, meeting new people and finding something in their company that pleased a part of you, made you want to know them better. But there was Jenny. No getting beyond that fact. His text hadn't implied anything other than a simple communication, and I was glad. I wouldn't have wanted him to be the guy who'd complicate or risk a relationship he already had.

Besides, with big changes coming, I didn't need a man in my life.

Yes, this was what I told myself as I shirked off my clothes and yanked on the tee shirt and sleep pants I wore for bed. I continued to tell myself the same thing while I shimmied under the covers, pulling them up to my chin. I said it aloud when I nearly jerked my arm from the socket in order to snatch up the phone and reread Arlo's message.

Nope, all innocence. No interest there. Good. Yep, good.

I snapped off the lamp and threw myself face down into my pillow.

Sunlight streamed into the room way too quickly. I knew upon greeting it, eyes wide, I had seriously overslept. Right through the alarm even. Or I'd turned it off without waking. Either way, I couldn't believe Mom hadn't come hunting for me with a vengeance.

Forgoing a shower for expediency, I hastily dressed and clomped down the stairs. I found only Mom and Dad in the kitchen. "Is everyone else still asleep?" I shot a glance to the clock, making sure I hadn't misread my phone.

"Nester is," Mom said, "but Shep took

everyone else for a run into town to grab some pastries."

I reflected for a second on the whole order I'd recently placed.

"I know," Mom said, apparently reading my face. "I told them to pick those up, too. They may as well get what they want for breakfast, though. I'm sure after tonight there'll be nothing left of any of it."

"Maybe set some aside for Christmas Day?"

Mom grunted her agreement. Dad looked up from his coffee. "So, you ladies have lists, yes? Give me one and let's get this day going."

I laughed out loud and wrapped my arms around him in a huge hug. "Yes," I said, "and let's."

With Simon's help and Shepherd's when they returned, we five made short work of the final to-do's on our lists. Nester was quite helpful once she climbed from her bed, giving Mom a hand in the venue kitchen with early meal preparation. No one had bothered to put back the tables and chairs after the wedding, saving time in setting those up, although they were being rearranged to accommodate the smaller group. I made sure all the lights were lit, the few leftover centerpieces I'd found on the bar strategically placed, and then I hurried inside to ascertain everything in the house remained in tiptop Christmas-y display. I found Malory and her parents seated in the living room, looking uncomfortable.

"Isn't there something we can do?" Mrs. Hudson asked.

"Sure," I said. "How are you with a peeler?

Mom and Nester could use a hand with the veggies. They're out in the barn kitchen."

Mr. Hudson stood up from his chair as if prodded. "And me? What can I do?"

I felt awful. They'd been left in the kitchen to enjoy breakfast and then, in all the fuss, forgotten. Naturally they wanted to be part of everything. They were family.

"Dad, Shep and Simon are out in the barn, too. They're just shoving tables and chairs around, but I think Dad has a couple things left on his list he could use help with."

Grinning, the Hudsons headed out the door, donning their coats. I could have told them the coats weren't necessary, but I let them go. The trip from front door to barn was a short one and Mom had made sure to turn on the heat to warm up the cavernous room inside. I half-expected Malory to accompany them, but she remained at my side.

I smiled at her. "If I forgot to say so in all the commotion yesterday, congratulations."

"You didn't forget but thank you again." Her hand dropped to her abdomen, settled there. She brushed her hair away from her face with the other. "This is a very nice thing you're all doing today. Not just for Shep and me, but for everyone."

"We try," I responded with a short laugh.

"I'm serious. I know how hard it sometimes is on Shepherd, not being around his family and old friends. I know how hard it would be for me, were the situation reversed. It's difficult enough I'm not seeing my brother this year. He couldn't come, you see. Has Shep spoken with you yet?"

"About what?"

"Typical." She smiled, her dark blue eyes reflecting the light in the dim room. "My brother is standing in as godfather, and we wanted to know if you would be godmother to our baby. Say you will. I know you'd have to travel to our side of the ocean for the event, but then it would be my turn to welcome you to the home I've always known."

Goodness it was a day for handing out hugs left and right. Malory seemed startled at first by my effusive reaction but quickly returned it, the early but generous baby bump pressing against me. I released her and stepped back. "Feel like helping with the lights? I want to make sure they're all on before people start arriving." I glanced at the mantel clock. "Which should start any minute now. Crap."

Malory laughed, turned away, started with the big evergreen by the window. Bending, she plugged the lights in. "I'm thinking every room has something?" she said, glancing up at me.

"Every single one," I said. "Bathrooms are no exception."

"Lovely. I adore Christmas."

I grinned. "Me, too."

"Could we…could we attend a midnight service here? Do you?"

"I haven't in a good many years," I admitted. "But yeah, let's do that if we can."

I had exaggerated the time, but family did start showing up during the next hour. I spotted two cars pulling in while I was primping the beds and plugging in the window lights in the bedrooms. The early comers, those who lived closest, those bearing food, stood in the parking area clutching containers, undecided whether they should go to the house or straight to the barn. I hurried down the stairs, grabbing Malory's hand in passing and dragging her outside with me.

So began a wondrous day, for Shep and Malory, for my nephews, for all of us. I spent precious time with people I hadn't seen in ages, people I loved and didn't say so to often enough. Before long, before dinner, talk began about making this gathering a regular, standing occasion at another time during the year. I didn't know if those desires would reach fruition, but I had great fun discussing the possibilities. Once we all slipped away again into our own lives, I figured only a certain few would remember the emotional reaction engendered by our impromptu Christmas Eve gathering. That was okay. We were here now.

In a night filled with laughter and conversation, good food and shared memories, one thing stood out for me more than any other. No matter how infrequently we thought about each other on any given day or during any given year, once together the connection binding us all remained as strong as ever. Family ties, whether blood, marriage or friendship, were exactly that. Family was more than a noun. It also held the connotations of an adjective, with its ability to enrich and enhance simpler terms, and even a verb, if I could have managed to use it as such in a sentence. To family was to be, making the word one of action, of activity, of momentum.

The last turning cogs in my plan clicked into place, relaxed into place really, as I settled finally and certainly into acceptance. Moving back to the place I'd grown up would be like coming home for the holidays for good. I didn't imagine it would all be wine and roses, or in my case the occasional spritzer and sunflowers gathered warm in the sun, but the connectedness would be there, the feeling I belonged, the deep, underlying welcome we offered everyone for the sake of the season.

I stood by the door, watching them all and drying a few stupid, happy tears from my face. No one showed any indication they wished to leave. Some lived close enough the drive wouldn't be taxing, no matter when they headed out, and the rest who had come had booked a place to stay overnight nearby before making the drive to their homes to celebrate Christmas Day. My gaze followed Mom and Dad on the dance floor, moving to music other than Christmas someone had put on. Simon and Lucy were there, too, as was Stuart, with a cousin's daughter about his age, both making silly faces as they swept dramatically around without cognizance as to the music's slow, steady beat. Shepherd and Malory sat with her parents, Nester nearby lifting her phone to snap photos.

I stood aside in observation because this was how I conducted my life. I would continue to do so even upon my return to Connor Falls, but never had it meant I wanted to be apart from living. This was just my place, my comfortable place. I remained happy with it, embracing all I saw in my heart and soul nevertheless. I felt that more here, though, than any other place I'd ever lived. I had no need to be in the middle of everything, only within contact distance.

I saw Malory glance at her watch. She turned her head. Looking for me, I realized when she made eye contact and got up from her chair. I met her halfway.

"Church?" she said, when I drew near. "Do you still want to?"

"Sure. Is anyone else interested? Should we ask?"

"Mum and Dad are a bit knackered. And Shep's okay sticking around here. I'm afraid if we start asking we'll break up the party and people will feel uncomfortable with whatever answer they give."

"That make sense," I agreed. "I'll just let Mom know. It's not a long service, if I remember correctly, so they probably won't even miss us."

Nester ended up accompanying us as well. We three climbed into my little compact and headed out into a night where the stars had begun to disappear behind gauzy clouds. I eyed the sky with a frown as I turned left from the driveway, heading toward town. "I hope the snow holds off until everyone has made it home. I thought it wasn't supposed to start until midday, but the clouds are already gathering."

"You might end up with more people than you expected for Christmas dinner," Nester stated, quite happily.

"If that happens," said Malory, "we'll all help. It'll be fine."

"I wish we had more time."

Malory and I both glanced at Nester in the back seat. "More time for what?" I asked.

"To stay. I like it here. Also, I would have made a Christmas pudding. I know how, you know. Mum taught me a while ago. How about next year?"

I grinned. "Next year sounds wonderful."

We drove along Main Street at less than the twenty mile per hour limit, because Nester wanted to exclaim over everything she saw. It didn't matter. Traffic was pretty much non-existent. Lights twinkled in windows and on the wreaths hanging from lampposts, bringing another smile to my lips. We parked down the block from the church in the middle of town, as the small parking lot was full, and walked toward the building arm in arm at Nester's insistence. Perhaps her mood was caused by the season, or her excitement at her first time in the States, but I found her exuberance at sixteen years old utterly delightful. I seemed to recall I had a rather blasé outlook on the world at her age, although time might have managed to warp my perspective in that regard.

The church had been built in 1890 and retained everything of its antiquated charm. Focal lights on the ground illuminated the brick building, painted white before I'd been born, the dual doors with their matching wreaths, the tall steeple with the bell that would shortly be ringing. The light from inside the tall, narrow windows made jewels of the stained glass. At the door, we were given battery-powered tealights to hold. It was a candlelight celebration, modernized for safety's sake. The tiny devices didn't throw much light, but real candles secured in sconces lined the walls, flames flickering, together with electrical fixtures dimmed to accommodate the atmosphere.

Due to Nester's gawking, we'd arrived a bit late and could only find a seat in a back pew. I smelled evergreen and perfume, wood and the paper in the hymnals we took into our hands. Fresh, cold air had wafted in with our entry, clung to our coats, drifted around us to mingle with the other scents.

"So," whispered Nester, leaning close, "is this, like, your church?"

"It was once. A long time ago. I don't live in Connor Falls right now. But I'm moving back."

She nodded. "Good."

The service was almost exactly what I remembered, joyful and triumphant, as the song goes, but also serene, lying gently in the soul. At its conclusion everyone turned, neighbor to neighbor, with wishes for peace and a merry Christmas. Possessing such close proximity to the doors, Malory, Nester and I were some of the first to exit. I stood a moment on the walkway, contented, studying the night sky, the gathering clouds, the stars glimmering beyond dimmed by the town's lights. The church bells rang out above our heads.

"Who's that?" said Nester. I dropped my head, looking at her. "There's a man watching you. Do you know him?"

I followed her gaze, my own lighting without surprise on Arlo. Jenny stood beside him, speaking to another woman. I drew a deep breath. He spotted me as if he'd heard it.

"Here he comes," Nester whispered.

And so he was, once again looking completely at ease in his suit. I wondered again what he'd done for a living in his prior life. "Susan," he said.

"Arlo," I answered. "This is my sister-in-law, Malory. And this—"

"I'm Nester," said Nester, stepping forward and shaking his hand. "Malory's sister. The younger and better-looking sister."

Her tone said joking, her coy look said flirting. I frowned, only half in amusement. Yet I'd seen that sort of behavior before from young girls when confronted with a charismatic man. Because in his way he was that, even if I hadn't truly noticed it before this moment. She could have been a thirty-something throwing herself at him, rather than a bantering teenager, and I don't think it would have mattered. He seemed to only have eyes for me.

For *me*. He had to stop. He couldn't do that.

"Nice to meet you both," he said, giving Nester and Malory his brief attention and a nod. He glanced toward the church behind us, focusing as I now understood on a level line, and then back down again, straight at me. Jenny hurried up to his side.

"Are you okay? You know how the dark and the street lights—"

"I'm fine," he said, turning to her with a patient smile. "I told you how much better I am. You've just got to learn to believe me when I say that."

"Hi," said Nester. "Happy Christmas."

Jenny's eyebrows arched. "Hi. Merry Christmas to you, too."

"This is…Nester, right?" Arlo said. "And Malory, and Susan you've met. This is my sister Jenny."

"Your sister," I said, not very loudly. He heard

me anyway. So did Nester, who gave me a slow, amused look.

"Sorry, didn't I say?"

I shook my head. "Nope." My lips turned up, almost as if they were a separate entity. I didn't seem able to stop them from doing so. Arlo's expression matched mine in short order, two people smiling at each other for no good reason.

Except maybe there was one. A reason. A darned good reason.

*　　*　　*

Family headed out early on Christmas Day, not coming by for breakfast, intent on avoiding the snow. It had been more than ten years since Connor Falls had seen a heavy snowfall on Christmas Day and it looked not to be holding off for the afternoon as had been the original prediction. Some hearty souls with all-wheel drive and not far to travel decided to stick around through the early dinner. We had a contingency plan in case they needed to spend the night. Three (Alice and Herb, who'd brought Gran) would bunk down at Simon and Lucy's, while the rest would take my bed, the bed Nester had slept in, and the sofa in the den. Nester and I agreed to sleeping bags on the back porch. She clearly rooted for the large sleepover.

Another vehicle possessed the equipment to plow through winter weather: Arlo's Jeep. He and Jenny showed up about an hour before mealtime, Jenny at the wheel. I could well imagine how the swirling flakes in his vision might be a problem for

Arlo. He'd phoned earlier asking Mom if it would be okay to bring his sister. Seeing the container in Jenny's hand as she climbed out, I understood she came prepared not to be a burden to feed. Not that she would have been. We had more food than needed. I stood out on the porch hugging myself in the cold, watching the two of them interact in the driveway. I don't know how I hadn't recognized the brother-sister thing immediately. Not only in a physical appearance that had, with knowledge, become obvious, but in the way they treated each other.

"Welcome!" I shouted from beneath the sheltering porch roof. Jenny waved with one hand, clutching the Rubbermaid with the other, and still managed to extend her arm toward Arlo. He rolled his eyes at her and ignored the offer, making his way across the snow-covered driveway unaided. They mounted the steps and stopped at the top, stamping snow from their boots. I jerked my head toward the front door, which I'd left cracked a little. Wonderful scents drifted out into the cold air, along with the strains of barely heard music and enough conversation I couldn't determine the content of any.

"Go on in. Nobody bites." I held the screen door open. Jenny pushed the inside door wide and stepped over the threshold. I moved back to let Arlo enter, too. Mom appeared in front of Jenny, ushering her all the way in with a hearty greeting. Before we could follow, she pushed the door closed on Arlo and me. Deliberately and with a look I couldn't mistake. A second later the door opened again and a coat flew out at me. Not mine. I don't think Mom cared whose it was.

"Well," I said, "that couldn't have been any more obvious. Shoot, did I say that out loud?"

"You did."

I took a moment to shove my arms into a coat made for someone taller and broader and carefully fastened the zipper. My cheeks heated.

"It's okay, though," he said.

I grunted.

"Do we have time for a walk?"

I spun toward him, startled. "I—sure. Anyplace in particular?"

His mouth had widened into a grin, his eyes on mine. Steadily. I stayed still so they would, too. I liked him seeing me, although I think he did more often than I realized.

"You're not nervous, are you?" he asked. "You don't seem the type."

He wasn't being coy. The question appeared quite sincere.

"Not at all," I said.

"Show me this place you're thinking of moving into."

My brows lowered. "How do you know about that? Does everyone know about that?"

"Simon," he said. "He gave me your phone number, too. Didn't you wonder where I'd gotten it?"

I laughed. "Yeah, for a hot minute, and then I forgot to ask." I moved to the porch steps, staring out toward the snowy fields and the flakes falling thicker and faster. "Will you need my arm?"

"I don't think so. If I do, I'll let you know?"

"Works for me."

We stepped down from the porch onto the walkway, feet crunching in the frozen residue left behind by his and Jenny's footprints quickly filling in. Snowflakes brushed my cheeks, caught in my hair, my lashes. We walked side by side, the humps and bumps in the field delineated by the snow.

"I like Connor Falls," he said when we were halfway to our destination. No other words had passed between us. I recognized our silence with a start, yet I didn't view it as some telling lack in communication. Things were said that needed to be said. I'd noticed that with him, and I wasn't usually much for small talk anyway. "I've decided to make it my home."

"I like it, too, more than like it, which is why I'm remaking it my home."

"I'm glad." Yes, not small talk. Saying things that he meant to be said.

We reached the place in the woods where Dad and I had cleared the path. I heard nothing but our footsteps, our breathing, the rustle of my borrowed coat and the snowfall's gentle, whispering hush. Together we entered the narrow path. He dropped behind when we could no longer walk side by side. When we reached the clearing, I swept my hand out toward the building looming like frosted gingerbread. Arlo drew a sudden breath.

He didn't mention how much work it would be, didn't point out the structure's condition, didn't question my sanity. "It's perfect for you," he said.

"I think so." My shoulders settled, dropped in

the oversized coat. My breath frosted in a long, slow release. "I had a bird once. A little finch. I named him Guthrie after Arlo Guthrie. You?"

"Same," he said.

"You had a little bird, too?" I teased.

"No. My parents had me. They were fans."

"Of you, I'm sure."

Grinning, I bumped my elbow against his. He smiled and took my hand. We watched the snow gently outline the fieldstone walls, coat the slate roof. An owl hooted nearby. Seeking its mate. A fox darted out from behind the building, auburn flashing through the white.

It was good to be home.

Thank you for taking the time to read *When the Heart Brings You Home – A Connor Falls Christmas Collection.* I hope you enjoyed it!

You might also enjoy *Hurry Home for Christmas,* the first in the series and a novel which has been updated with new content and re-released as a new edition in celebration of the collection.

Also, look for these upcoming releases ~

~ The Garland Ball ~

and

~ I Knew in a Moment ~

As always, your readership is appreciated. A book is only paper and ink without you.

Robin Maderich